The Honour of Forgiveness

Bringing together of two books
into one complete story

"The Colour of Envy & Driven by Honour"

All rights reserved.

No part of this publication may be reproduced or transmitted, in any form or by any means, without prior permission from the author.

Copyright: David Mattches, 2015

Dedicated to all the nowhere people.

He is a real nowhere man,
Living in a nowhere land,
Writing all his nowhere thoughts,
For nobody.

(John Winston Lennon)

Thanks to:

Bob Watson, for all the help he has given to me. Bob – has taught me everything I know about writing; he is simply the best. He is the only person I know who ISN'T – an expert.

Carolyn, for all her enduring support and kindness, she is truly an extraordinary person.

William Henry, for the fun we had working together.

June for all her suffering for the sake of literature.

This book is a work of fiction and should not be understood in any other sense. It is set in the context of history to give the story literary credibility. Many of the place names in this book are real, but their descriptions do not necessarily portray accurately the places mentioned. Most of the characters are fictitious. All thoughts or comments, speech and opinions are from the author's own imagination and should not be attributed to any third party, unless otherwise stated. Historical information has on occasion been adjusted to fit the story

The cover artwork is by the author.

If the reader has any comments about the book, the author would be pleased to hear from you.

sebastian.dave.swan@gmail.com

Sebastian Swan was born in the North East of England not far from Bamburgh, he lectured in Yorkshire then, as the salmon returns to the place of its birth, he returned to the North East when he retired and began writing. All his life he had struggled with the written word, being dyslexic. Where he did excel, was his artwork, he drew and painted from being a small boy.

He had cancer, which forced him to retire, while he was ill, he started to read for pleasure, he couldn't do much else for a while. He found that in reading he could be transported away from the pain to another place, a "Dream World".

One day he thought he could create his own dream world, he would do it through writing, with a little help from his friends, and draw from the vast resources of history and beauty on his doorstep. Writing, he thought, was only an extension of his childhood games. The only limitations were down to imagination.

Most of his books are played out in the beautiful North East of England, where the places in the books can be seen and touched.

Come to the North East, sit on the quiet beaches, close your eyes, and be transported into the world of Sebastian Swan.

All things begin and end with a story.

David Mattches BA

Follow Sebastian Swan on "Face Book".

BOOK ONE

The Colour Envy

CHAPTER 1

Sir Richard Maillorie leant against the gunwale to steady himself, enjoying the fresh sea air blowing on his face. It was a fine day. He narrowed his eyes and looked up into the bright blue sky mindlessly staring at the billowing sails, resplendent, he thought. Each in a perfect arc, filled with the southwesterly, which was powering them home, and held to their work by the taut creaking sheets. His face lit up with the broadest smile, he was happy.

Nothing out of the ordinary in this particular crossing, there was ever traffic back and forth across the narrow sea these days.

He paid little attention to the activity on the deck; he was more concerned with thoughts of home and setting his feet once more on English soil. It had been three years since he'd left his father, hoping to find some coin and position to restore the family's fortune.

Contrary to his unwelcome family name of Maillorie, life had taken a turn for the better. His name came from the old French adjective, maleüré (unhappy, unlucky), up until this point, it had fitted his family well. Now their luck had changed, this had been a very profitable time, and he hoped it heralded a better future. He had found plenty of opportunity for an able knight to make money and these were rich lands, *yes*, he had done well, he patted the saddle-bag laid across his shoulder and smiled.

In 1154, a young man from Anjou by the name of Henry Plantagenet was crowned King of England. He was the son of the Empress Matilda and grandson of Henry the First of England. This had changed the fortunes of Richard's family. Richard's father had stood against The Empress, all who'd chosen that course and fought for King Stephen, opposing "Henry's mother" were now made to count the cost of displeasing an Angevin.

As far as Richard was concerned, he would seek out a new life, although he thought the treatment of his family unjust, his father had said, "Any who seek revenge had better dig two graves". He would heed that advice and determined to lay aside any resentment. Instead, he would make the most of what opportunities came his way and he'd heard that there was wealth and honour to be found across the sea.

Henry was only twenty-one when he became King, but he was already an experienced ruler. At sixteen, he had become Duke of Normandy. Two years later, his father Count Geoffrey of Anjou died and Henry succeeded him.

The following year he became Duke of Aquitaine, when he married Eleanor the heiress to the duchy. A duke twice over, he now added King of England to his many titles. His vast empire stretched from the highlands of Scotland to the Pyrenees.

Compared to Normandy and Aquitaine, England was the poor relation. Henry had done well when he married the beautiful Eleanor, even if she was ten years older. It was reportedly a love match; in fact, Richard had heard that they were first attracted when she was still married to the King of France. How true that was he didn't know. Perhaps that had cooled since the early days; there were rumours, ever rumours, of divisions within the family.

England had been through a time of unprecedented disorder during the civil war between King Stephen and Henry's mother, the Empress Matilda. The Barons had ruled in the anarchy, and Henry's first task had been to establish a new order. He created a meritocracy, advancement by ability, but any system Henry favoured had only one purpose, to give him complete control. Thomas Becket was the perfect example of the new opportunities. He had risen from a humble merchant's son to be King Henry's closest friend, Chancellor of England, and now Archbishop of Canterbury. Slowly the old order had given way to the new.

There was a hotbed of discontent amongst the Barons as their power was slowly eroded, but they would not dare challenge *this* king as they had the previous one. On face value, the new system Henry had introduced was admirable, but the rumblings were not only from the Barons, there were others who had forgotten the conditions, and were made to suffer for the lapse. Any generosity by the King needed to be set against his expectations. He was the consummate politician; he was astute and knew how to play one against the other. Every generous gift, and Henry could be generous, came with a hefty price, "Complete and utter loyalty to him" and woe betides anyone who failed to meet it. Any wavering and the legendary Angevin temper would be unleashed.

From what Richard had heard Henry's best friend Becket had forgotten the rules and had been either banished or forced to escape to France, Richard wasn't sure which. The latest rumours were that there had been some restoration and that Becket had returned, but in any event, the stormy relationship was the perfect example that no one was exempt from this King's fury, best friend, Archbishop, his children or even his Queen.

For Sir Richard this world of politics was a game for others to play, he had stepped out and been blessed. He was an insignificant stipendiary knight, able, but penniless. His friend William Marshal had also been an impoverish knight, but was now wealthy, renowned for his bravery and chivalry.

In 1168, William Marshal's uncle, was killed in an ambush by Guy de Lusignan. William was injured and captured in the same skirmish. It was known that he received a wound to his thigh and that someone in his captor's household had taken pity on the young knight. He received a loaf of bread in which were concealed several lengths of clean linen bandages enabling him to dress his wounds, using the bread as a poultice. This act of kindness by an unknown person, had perhaps, saved William Marshal's life.

Richard smiled whenever he thought of the tale, thinking how such mundane events could determine one's future, but for this simple kindness, he might never have met William Marshal and his own fortunes may have been completely different.

When the news of William's capture eventually reached the Palace at Poitiers, and Eleanor of Aquitaine, Queen of England no less, she saw to it that his ransom was immediately paid, and he was taken into the safety of her favour.

It was at her court in Poitiers that Richard first encountered him. William Marshal was only three years older than Richard, but he had qualities, which years alone had not gifted him. He had charisma that flowed from him in waves. Richard had once asked a knight, who knew him, what sort of person he was. The knight said, "Picture the perfect human being and dress him in armour, put a sword in his hand and you will recognise William Marshal".

Unknown to Richard, William had watched him practising at the pell and quintain; he must have been favourably impressed for he asked him to join his band of men in the tournai.

Richard knew that tournaments offered knights like him an opportunity to hone their warlike skills, and win fame and treasure when no real wars were taking place. Where there are winners there are inevitably losers, but what young knight worth his salt made that a consideration, and Richard was no different. It was a very dangerous amusement; some lost more than fortunes, they lost their lives.

What had he to lose, he thought, and he had all to gain? Certainly, working as a mercenary knight was not going to make him rich, not in peacetime for sure.

Richard knew as the months rolled on that he'd been fortunate, he had been fighting with the best there was, and was well rewarded.

He quickly discovered that the tournaments were not only, fought in the green open spaces of the French countryside, but also inside the castle walls of the rich and powerful.

The Marshal and his men wintered at the Queen's court in Poitiers. There were ever those jealous of the privileged position that he held, and constantly tried to undermine him with scurrilous gossip, but his honour seemed like an invisible shield.

Richard was sure at that point, that it was the very first time he'd really understood what the Marshal had always been trying to tell them. Which was that, "One must set *honour* above any other consideration". He knew that William Marshal would do what was demanded by his strict code of chivalry, even if it meant losing all. He'd said, "Your honour cannot be taken from you, it is yours, and within your power – to keep – or throw away. Without honour, we are no better than the beasts of the field".

When Richard thought that it was time to return to England, he had made it known to William, and William had sent him on his way with his blessing. Richard knew his father was unwell and that was forever on his mind. The coin he had earned was considerable by any standards, and his father's need was great, he must return. When he told William, there was something about the look he had given, which made Richard wonder if perhaps William too, thought it was time to move on to pastures new.

This was now the next stage of his life, and sailing to him always felt like an adventure, even this short trip across the Channel. He relaxed and was enjoying his ruminations on what life might hold in store. He leant back on the gunwale, with his arms folded, and glanced down at five men playing dice on the deck before him. It was of little interest to him, men played dice. That was what men did in each other's company, to give some distraction from the vagaries of life, a common enough sight. Not him though, it presented no attraction for him, he had better use for his coin, and to throw it away when he'd risked life and limb to get it, seemed a fool's occupation. The Marshal had frowned on gambling, none of his men were permitted such activity, to venture to test his resolve on that issue, would have meant dismissal and a bleak future. To be rejected by the Marshal, once having been part of the elite band of brothers, would have placed you in a more dire position than if you had *never* been part of the group. You would have been hence marked as a "Failed" knight, one who'd been rejected by the Marshal.

Fools he thought, he could see they were playing for excessive coin. One was a knight by the look of him; Richard had seen him, and his wife boarding at Calais. In truth, it was not so much the husband he'd noticed, but the wife. She was a golden-haired, green-eyed beauty, and no mistake, whoever they were, and Richard's head was not the only one she had turned. She was at this moment sat with two other women, on some sacks of grain on the opposite side of the ship, her maids, he guessed, by the look of their dress. He watched her laughing and talking freely with them, she even honoured him with a glance, which he acknowledged, returning her smile and bowing his head, it was clearly not appreciated and she quickly turned away.

He had to smile again as he watched her, for though she wanted to confirm her superiority, and he of no consequence to her, while her head was bowed in conversation, she had lifted her eyes once more in his direction. She saw his smile and was clearly furious that he had caught her looking at him.

"Oh my", a haughty piece, if ever I saw one, but undoubtedly startlingly beautiful, he thought. Aye, a fine beauty, a thoroughbred by the look of her; who would trample you without a second's remorse if you approached her on her offside. Suddenly he was distracted from his pleasant diversion.

'Join us, and a chance to make your fortune, young sir,' one of the men playing dice, at his feet, offered.

'You are very generous, but I think not. More likely, I'd lose a fortune, if I had one to lose. I'm poor enough already,' Richard replied, the fellow laughed. In truth to look at this threadbare knight, it was not hard to believe, which suited Richard perfectly. The last impression he wanted to create in a watchful eye was that he might be a man worth robbing. What was contained in his saddle-bag, many would consider a fortune, but as far as he was concerned, it was not his alone, but for his family's future. Any interested observers might have given Richard's wealth a little more consideration if they noticed him with his horse; it was clearly expensive. However, for a man who made a living on horseback it was not surprising. Most knights worth their spurs would rather spend coin on their horse than on themselves. They knew that their life could well depend on the quality of their mount.

Following the *kind* invitation, he now watched the group with a little more curiosity. It did not take any great skill at dice, to see that the others were taking advantage of this knight; he was an innocent before wolves. As if to confirm Richard's suspicions, the knight suddenly swore as he lost another hand.

'Hell's teeth…' he heard the knight who was playing dice call out, thumping the deck with the side of his fist. The heads of other travellers nearby turned in his direction. 'Give me coin the worth of this,' he hesitated for a moment, and then tipped a large emerald on a gold chain from a pouch into his hand. The stone caught Richard's eye, it was beautiful, clearly valuable, but not to this young knight apparently.

The men he was playing with looked at each other, and then shrugged their shoulders. One of them took coin from the pot and offered it to the knight.

'WHAT, this is worth fifty-fold, even a hundred-fold of that meagre offering!'

'What use is that bauble to the likes of us, might be glass for all we know. Take it or leave it,' the man held out his hand with the coin they offered, waited, jingled the coin temptingly in his palm, then pulled a face as much to say "Please yourself", and tipped it back in the pot.

The young man now turned his attention to Richard, 'What about you, what will you give me for this?' Richard was startled that he was unexpectedly drawn into the heated exchange; he hesitated clearing his throat, glanced at the group, pushed himself from the gunwale then reached down and took the jewel examining it in the light.

'WELL!' The young man agitatedly demanded. Richard raised his eyes slowly considering the anxious man before him.

'Hold, less haste, if you want my advi…'

'A pox on your advice; do you want the stone or not?'

Lackwit… Richard thought, narrowing his eyes, then returned to his study of the stone. 'Mmm,' he said, and took his purse from his belt without speaking, tipped half of its contents into his hand mentally counting the coin, and showed the young man his open hand.

'Not enough!' Richard hesitated, looked again at the jewel, and drew another five gold coins from his purse.

'It's worth *far* more.'

'No doubt, but not to me, this is but what little I have saved. Make up your mind fellow, before I change mine.'

'All right, take it, but I hope you rot in Hell, and may it bring you naught but festering pox-ridden luck.' With that he slumped down into his place on the deck. Richard looked again at the emerald in his hand then slipped it into his purse, pulled the drawstrings tight, tied it to his belt, tugged it to ensure that it was secure, refastened his gambeson to cover his purse and leant once more on the gunwale.

The fellow was right; Richard knew this emerald was worth considerably more than he'd paid. He had robbed the fool, ah, what matter, it's better in my purse than being washed down the gutter by these reprobates, after a night in their cups when they reached Dover. Thank you very much Sir knight, your loss is my gain. That was a satisfactory moment of unsolicited good fortune. It seems as if the Maillorie family's luck has indeed changed, he thought, smiling to himself.

It wasn't long before he heard the young man cursing once more. He stood, viciously kicked an empty water barrel, and slunk off in the direction of his wife. The men he had been playing with laughed at him for the fool he was.

When he reached where she was sitting, he leant silently over the gunwale with his head hung down. She ceased her chatter, stood, and laid her hand on his back, clearly aware that he was troubled. Richard watched the tender scene with some interest as it unfolded. Suddenly it erupted into a violent exchange of words. She was obviously furious; she even pushed her husband, bystanders made a space around them, probably in fear for their lives from this apoplectic woman. She turned, glanced in Richard's direction and he was compelled to smile. Her eyes bulged, she gave him a look of pure contempt, such a look could turn the blood in a man's veins into molten lead; so ferocious was the heat of her gaze. He quickly changed his expression, but it was too late, she was no longer looking in his direction. She pushed her beaten husband yet again and stamped off to the stern of the ship, cursing and flailing her hands in the air as she went. The young man clung to a shroud with a face of abject misery.

Richard guessed that he'd mentioned the fate of the emerald. 'I better put some distance betwixt myself and those two once we strike land, or I may find a sudden sharp pain in my back and a hand in my purse.'

CHAPTER 2

It was evening before they docked and began to disembark. Richard stood and watched his new-found "Friends", careful to keep them at a distance. There seemed to only be five of them in their party. The knight and his wife, her two maids and a boy, fifteen or so, Richard guessed he was a squire of sorts.

Richard didn't want any unnecessary trouble; trouble was ever present without looking for it. They didn't seem to have horses, there were only five horses onboard, and one was Ares, his horse.

The horses were being winched ashore as Richard watched, which created somewhat of a dilemma for him. He would have dearly liked the knight and his group to be well clear before he disembarked, but the crew were already strapping Ares to the hoist and looking round for his owner. He would have to go to him and take his chance that the knight's party quickly disembarked and were on their way before he was ready. Ares was no sailor and did not take well to the passage. He had spent most of his time kicking and struggling with his fastenings throughout the voyage. Richard knew he would have to walk with him once he was offloaded, so he had time to recover and calm himself.

He helped the crew the best he was able by holding Ares' bridle and talking calmly to him. Once secure and lifted free of the deck, Ares displayed his fury with a violent thrashing of hooves, which he intensified as he was swung out over the side, so much so that Richard feared he would break the winch, fall and be killed.

Richard hurried to the gangplank, and almost collided with the mysterious high and mighty woman, they were both distracted, watching his frantic horse kicking wildly at fresh air. He bowed and gestured with an open hand that she must go before him. She showed her gratitude by pushing past him followed by her maids, husband, and squire. Richard almost felt sorry for the poor fellow, for it was clear to him that this woman was more than he could handle. However, his surly face overcame Richard's compassion. They had delayed him, now Richard had to hurry to get to Ares before the men working on the dock unhitched him, and left him to fend for himself.

Richard reached Ares just as they released him and took hold of his bridle gently patting his nose, which rippled and quivered with pleasure. He could see that Ares was relieved to be out of the sling and back on solid ground. He shook himself like a wet dog; Richard patted him once more, laid his cheek against Ares soft nostrils and Ares nuzzled into him. Richard knew that a knight's relationship with his horse could mean the difference between life and death, and for the last few years, Ares had been his closest friend.

Once he was confident that Ares had settled, he patted him again, and slipped the saddle-bag over his withers, where he could keep an eye on it as they rode. Not that riding was really an option with all his worldly possessions piled high on Ares' back. Ares twisted his head round clearly needing to keep Richard in view, and then he began to nudge Richard's hip with his nose. Richard laughed; he *knew*, that Ares *knew*, there was an apple in his pocket. Taking hold of the bridle, he slipped his hand into his gambeson pocket, brought out a red apple, which he had brought with him for this very purpose, and offered the treat to Ares; it was enough to distract him for the time being.

'That's better old boy, come let's get away from all this hustle and bustle, we'll walk for a while and see if we can find a place to stay this night. We're both ready for a good sleep my friend, let us hope this night affords us such a blessing before we set off on the first of the morrow's light.' Ares snorted as though to confirm his agreement, Richard smiled and patted his neck. He took a moment to cast his eye over the people milling around on the quayside.

'Mmm, no sign of our new friends Ares, thank God for small mercies. They must have had people waiting for them, and they never said goodbye, how churlish,' he smiled.

Richard wasn't sure of the direction he needed to take. He couldn't recall the route that had brought him here three years past. He pushed his fingers under the front of his coif and scratched his head. Looking at the streets leading away from the landing, his eye was drawn to the castle on its commanding chalk vantage point. He remembered the Saxon church nearby; he'd celebrated Mass there before leaving England. He decided that he couldn't go far wrong if he went up the steep hill in that general direction, away from the quay.

The street was narrow and a fair climb; he was forced to stop several times. It was getting dark so he needed to find a place to stay for the night. No doubt, he would be able to get directions for the morrow's journey from someone where he found lodgings. He was relieved to see a place up ahead that looked to have some stables. As he neared, a young fresh faced, smiling youth, stepped from the stable door with a bucket in his hand, and asked if he wanted a place this night for his horse.

'Aye, I do that, lad, and for myself too.'

'We's a stall for thee 'orse, maaster, but nay rooms int' place, they be aall teken, they's teken up every inch oft' floor in the haall tee. Thee be welcome in't here wi' thee 'orse. Best we can dee. Ye'll be well enough; it's the same price, me, I'd prefer thee 'orse's company. Thee must please thee sel'.'

'That suits me fine, lad. My horse and I have spent many a night together. What about mete?'

'Inside, but it'll cost ye extra.'

'You're not from round here.'

'Aye, ya's right there, I'm fromt' North. A were shipwrecked two years past, and stayed on. I've 'ad enough oft' sea tee last me a lifetime. Settle thee 'orse and come see what mete there be. Thee stuff'll be right enough, am aalways, in and oot, till dark any ways.'

The jolly, affable, young lad left him, Richard smiled, hoping he'd caught most of what he'd said, and he began to unload Ares. Richard set down his precious saddle-bag at the front of the stall, and pushed some straw over it with his foot, then he removed the rest of his belongings from Ares' back, and stacked them on top of his saddle-bag. He unbuckled his sword belt, stood his sword next to him, and removed his gambeson hanging it over a rail.

'I must organise the purchase of a pack animal before we travel any further, unless I want to walk home,' he said to himself smiling.

Richard had sold his packhorse in Calais, it was regular practice to buy and sell the animals in the port, cheaper than transporting them and often the ships travelling back and forth had limited room for horses, which demanded excessive space and more than a little inconvenience, loading and offloading for the short crossing.

'We've slept in worse places than this, old fellow, aye, this will do us just fine,' he said looking around the stable.

The stable was full; they were fortunate to get a place, not much room for any more horses this night. He felt as relieved as Ares to shed some clothes this warm evening, and have a good stretch, and scratch at whatever had been biting him these last days. Glancing at the water trough, he thought he would take this opportunity to have a good wash and be cleaner for his ride home. First, he must attend to his horse; he bent down, took a handful of fresh straw, and started to rub Ares' back. Ares had been saddled this whole day and more. Richard had eased his girth for the voyage, but he would have been uncomfortable so it would be a relief for him to have this massage.

Ares' muscles trembled in appreciation of the kindness, and he helped himself to the ample provision of hay; all the while Richard talked gently to him.

Richard was suddenly uneasy; he paused, slowed his breathing, and cast his eye to where his sword was. Ares skittered slightly. Richard dropped to his knees, rolled over, and sprung up with his sword in hand facing trouble. None too soon, in the split second of his movement a sword swept through the air and struck the stall where he'd but a moment since been standing. This was his world, after a short time on the tournai circuit, a knight developed a sixth sense of impending danger, or he died.

He saw that he was faced not with one assailant, but four. Not good odds, but he was in a sound defensive position between his horse, the stall, and a wall at his back, so they were limited, they could not all attack at once. They would be wise not to venture too far in Ares' direction or they were risking broken bones, or even worse from a flailing hoof. Ares had had a difficult day and he was not blessed with the sweetest disposition at the best of times. Swords, daggers, any weapons near him not held by his master were his signal for action and that meant all-out warfare. He was a killing machine, biting, kicking, stamping, or simply using brute force. Richard had known him charge a horse, and knock it to the ground, and even bigger horses than he. All this was Ares, the god of war; he was worth every penny Richard had given to buy him. Richard never talked about owning Ares; he was his friend, an extension of himself. On the battlefield, they were *one*, bringing hell and destruction to all who stood in their way.

Making a quick assessment of what he faced, it looked like only one of the attackers had a sword, two had daggers, and the fourth was brandishing a cudgel. Richard suspected he most likely had a knife of some sorts too. They eyed each other, the one with the sword regained his composure, and took another swing at Richard, but it was crude without any finesse, almost an insult to one of Richard's mastery. Richard parried the move with ease, directing his blow immediately above the cross-guard and the assailant's sword shattered. Richard knew this was the point of contact to test a sword's mettle. The further from the handgrip one made connection the flex in the steel would absorb the shock. Strike as near to where the sword was held as possible. The energy of the blow would suddenly explode into the blade and the person wielding the weapon would either drop it, or the inferior blade would shatter, which was what had happened here.

All in the one practised movement Richard drove his boot into the man's groin. He tumbled to the ground and doubled over in agony. Richard kicked him in the head as he hit the stone floor and he immediately ceased his groaning. He didn't want to kill the man; it would have been nothing short of murder, he was so inept. He hoped that the others would have seen enough and taken the opportunity to run. Unfortunately, that moment of mercy had been a mistake; the fellow with the club struck Richard a glancing blow to the thigh as his outstretched leg delivered its kick. He clenched his jaw as the numbing pain shot through his whole body, staggering, he only just managed to keep his feet. The man took a second swing intent on felling him at this moment of weakness. The difference in Richard's attitude to combat, and the approach of these untutored amateurs, was that in the fight, he wasn't merely reacting to each thrust. He didn't jerk from one action to the next, his movement continuously flowed, ever aware of the whole action. His next move was already played out in his mind, with an eye to the advantage. His muscles, footwork, and weapons, in fact, his whole being was merely the instrument of his intellect. Even if he found himself at great disadvantage, his mindset was the same. This was his trade and he was a master. William Marshal had spotted this latent ability when he saw him at Poitiers, and he had honed it, he'd said, "Great warriors are born Richard, not made".

Richard stooped as the cudgel descended towards his head; he leaned to the side, and drove his sword upwards into the man's stomach. There was a split second of utter disbelief on the assailant's face, the club fell from his hand to the floor, and he continued his forward momentum. His weight pushed onto the sword, which forced the hilt against the timbering of the stall, making it impossible for Richard to withdraw it. The blade was driven through his body and out of his back, trapping it between bone and muscle. Richard redirected the death fall with his left hand pushing the fellow to one side. The confined space was now working to Richard's disadvantage, limiting his choices of movement. He knelt trying to tug his sword free. The two with daggers came cautiously towards him. He gave up trying to retrieve his sword and drew his rondel dagger. He struggled to push himself to his feet; the lucky strike had numbed his leg to his toes, paralysing his thigh muscle. It took all his strength to keep himself upright. This was anyone's game now; he narrowed his eyes and faced them, he'd given them a chance, and that mercy had cost him dearly. There would be no second chance, if they came on at least *one* of them was bound for Hell this night.

'Fighting has been my occupation since boyhood and against the best which – you – are not, if robbery is your game you have shown singularly bad judgement in your selection of a victim. You unfortunates have choices to make, be sure you make the right ones, or they will be your last.' Richard's words were spoken in a fearfully modulated voice to intimidate them. He tried to sound as if he was in full control of the outcome of this fight, and he saw his words had the desired effect, there was suddenly a flicker of doubt in their eyes.

'We're no a-feared of the likes of thee,' the biggest of the two responded, in a voice which sounded in contradiction to his words.

'Well feast your eyes, whilst you can, on the men at your feet.' Richard had learned in the mêlée that the mind was often the weak link in an opponent's armour. William Marshal had taught him that; "They must see *their* defeat in *your* eyes. When you charge an opponent, you will always meet where you set your eye. So, make sure you fix your gaze where you want the contact to take place. You may not always look where you are going, but you will always go where you are looking" and Richard knew he was right; one ignored the Marshal's advice at one's peril. Richard's glare at this moment was enough to make them hesitate, fatal in battle. In that split second of doubt, Richard slashed across the knife hand of the one nearest, severing tendons and scoring bone, that hand would never hold a knife again. The knife fell from the mutilated hand clattering onto the stone slabs. The man stumbled back against the outer wall trying desperately to wrap the wound and stem the bleeding.

The would-be-thief, yet uninjured was, Richard sensed, about to turn tail and run. Unfortunately, the one he'd kicked in the groin and had fallen on the floor had recovered enough to grab Richard's ankle and Richard fell helplessly, but even as he fell, he managed to gain some advantage by driving his dagger into the man who held his leg.

'WHAT'S THIS, stand villain if you value your life!' The fellow with the knife swung round at the sound of the voice, paused, and made a thrust at the stranger who'd just entered the stable. He was too slow and the welcome guest scythed him a blow to his neck, the lout staggered forward, his knees buckled and he dropped to the floor clasping at the horrific wound. There was a gurgling sound from his mouth as he desperately gasped, and gulped, trying to inhale any last drops of air he could to satisfy his anxious body, but they would never reach his lungs. Instead, the air percolated in red bubbles from the grotesque purple laceration across his throat. He kicked his legs violently once more, and gradually stilled.

The blow was so well delivered it had almost severed his head. This was enough for the man with the slashed hand; he saw his opportunity and made a dash for it, pushing past the elderly knight, and out into the alley.

'Ah, he can go; though I think it would have been a mercy to dispatch him too, by the look of the blood dripping from that wicked wound. If that gash doesn't turn putrid, I'll eat hay with a donkey.'

CHAPTER 3

Richard reached for his dagger, and pulled it free, this foe was dead too. Richard's thrust had stabbed through his eye socket into his brain. Confused and unsure as to what was happening, he stared at the stranger old enough to be his father.

The man held up the palm of his hand, saying, 'Still yourself young fellow, I mean you no harm. I have not got to my years without being able to spot a warrior of superior talent, you are not a man to tackle if one values his life, even with these odds. Are you injured?'

Richard took a second to respond. 'You flatter me Lord; I have just witnessed the speed of a gentleman twice my age, that would humble many a younger knight in his prime. As for these rascals, they caught me off guard, I've no more than a dead-leg, as far as I can tell at this moment, aye, and it is thanks to your timely intervention, my future was in grave doubt until you became part of this tableau.' Richard eased himself awkwardly to his feet, favouring his good leg; his rescuer sheathed his sword and came to aid him.

'My thanks again,' Richard said offering his hand; the man took it in his firm grip and smiled.

'What were those villains after, do you have such as would warrant this outrage?'

'To be sure, I am at a loss to know,' he frowned, pursed his lips, and thought for a moment. He wondered if perhaps they knew of his treasure or perchance, they had been on the ship and seen the emerald, no, he was sure he knew not their faces, 'Alas, I cannot guess, perhaps they were simply opportunists after some easy coin. Or maybe they were for taking some of this fine horse flesh to sell.'

'Aye, that could well be the truth of it, most of these horses are mine; I came outside for some fresh air, and took the moment to see that they were settled and cared for. If that was the way of it, I might be the one who is in your debt. Let me introduce myself, I'm Sir John FitzWilliam, thankful to meet you,' now he offered Richard his hand.

'I'm Sir Richard Maillorie, and perhaps we have favoured each other this night.'

'Aye indeed we have... Maillorie, Maillorie, not a common name, I knew a Sir *William* Maillorie, we fought together with King Stephen,' he paused for a moment as he reflected. 'That was at Lincoln, in...' he crunched his face together in thought, 'it would be forty-one, aye forty-one, a grim day for us. Matilda's half-brother Robert, the Earl of Gloucester, soundly thrashed us that day. The truth of it is, Sir William Maillorie saved my life. I was unhorsed, yet he stood by and defended me – aye, and no small risk to himself, a lesser man would have made his escape, but not my friend. He risked all until it was the Blessed Virgin's will to see me remounted. We escaped the field together and spent the next weeks sharing a bed in the hedgerows, ha, happy days. You may not believe this, we were in a perilous position, we would have been most like hanged if we'd been caught, and yet we laughed together as if we had not a care in the world. I remember we'd killed a rabbit, skewered it on a stick and roasted it on a dismal, smoky wood fire, with naught but Adam's ale to wash it down, we hadn't eaten for days. Never had mete tasted finer or was there two more contented vagabonds as we.' The smile died on his face, 'Aye… youth thinks not of the morrow's cares, the next hour is a lifetime away. Life is a place for fun and adventure – *aye* – ha, good-times,' he sighed. 'A better friend a man never was blessed with. He'd a small son about seven or eight when I last saw him.'

Richard smiled, 'Do you recognise this Sir?' wiping the blood from his dagger on some straw, he passed it to Sir John.

'Ha, by the Blessed Mother of Christ, to be sure I do,' and his face lit up.

'I was the small boy, and you gave me this, it was the finest gift you could have given to a boy wishing to be seen as a man.' They both laughed and embraced each other and then Sir John looked sombre and released him.

'I was mightily sorry to hear of your father's death the year past.'

Richard's eyes widened and his face was suddenly washed in pain. 'My father's *dead!* I knew naught of this.'

'I'm sorry Son… I didn't realise – that was the news which came to me, God forgive me if I'm mistaken, but I fear it is the truth.' Richard turned and leant his head against the stall and slowly beat the side of his fist against the woodwork. Sir John placed his hand tenderly on his shoulder.

'Come inside with me, and I'll buy you a tankard of ale, I will tell you of what I know, or perchance you wish some time alone with your thoughts?'

'Thank you, Sir, it is a shock. He was ill and loaded down with worry, that much I knew fine well. These have not been blessed years for the Barons since the new King asserted his rule. Aye, and the better part of his resentment he has dispensed to those who fought against his mother.' Richard ceased his talk, and glanced down at his foot, gently tapping the toe of his boot against the side of the stall. 'I was never the best of sons. The day we parted, I was in an ill humour, and said some cruel things. Aye and I hurt him, I *meant* to, but he said naught, that silence was a fearsome blow and it stung my heart. I have prayed countless lonely nights since that day and asked that the Blessed Virgin might pray to Her Son for my forgiveness. I have had time these last years to reflect on that moment and many's the day I nearly packed my belongings and made for home, to cast myself at his feet, but I wanted to do more than just throw myself on his mercy. It was my intention to make good the deficit, by restoring his fortune, to make him proud of me, but alas, it appears it is not to be. What think he now for coin, perhaps a loving son would have been riches to him. It is but fools we young are, ever sharpening our claws on the hearts of those who love us, never imagining that life would set such distance betwixt youthful folly, and wisdom, and thus rob us of a chance to make right our foolishness. Alas there is no second chance, regret and sorrow are now my reward.'

'Aye, and we all ever live in the truth of that, Son. *Perhaps* our reward is "Understanding", a lesson learned, and we will in turn afford that to our children.'

Richard lifted his eyes from his despair, at the crust Sir John offered, 'Experience can indeed be a harsh teacher, I have learned that already. I'll think on your kind words. I *will* join you for some ale. I'm tired, hungry, and thirsty, and in some measure relieved that my father is released from the many cares he has had these past years, though it may not have been as timely as I would have wished. Keep short accounts with those whom you love and are loved by, he would often counsel me, but I understood not his meaning, until this moment. Such understanding comes too late now, I fear. I will not have to dwell on that, and instead be thankful for this gift from the Blessed Virgin that it was my father's old friend who broke this sad news to me.'

On the pretext of checking Ares before he left, he went to speak to his horse and inspect the concealment of his saddle-bag. It would be safe enough for now, he knew Ares would not tolerate any strangers near him and they would need to squeeze past him to uncover the bag.

'Come, I will be honoured to introduce you to my family. I came here with horses to meet them.'

'What of the villains Sir John?'

'I will make our plight known to the Inn Keeper, and then he must do as he wishes. I care not what that is, for all I know, he was part of this night's work.'

They walked across the yard and into the alehouse. As soon as they stepped through the door, Richard saw her, then her husband; his heart sank. He stopped in his tracks, closed his eyes and shook his head in disbelief hoping against hope, that when he opened his eyes, that it was not she and he'd been mistaken. Slowly he scanned the room through the narrow gap between his lids.

'Awe… Hell's teeth,' he said under his breath. He knew without a word being said, that they were Sir John's family, he just – knew it. This is some evil joke thought up especially for a "Maillorie" … this was Maillorie luck.

She stood as he neared, her eyes filled with venom. 'Now then, this is my son Gervase, and my daughter, Julianne,' Sir John proudly declared.

'I do not wish to be known by this, this, thief!' She was incandescent with rage.

Sir John was momentarily struck dumb, his jaw dropped and his eyes widened, he gasped then exploded, '*Julianne*, you will apologise this instant!' He was mortified at her inexplicable outburst.

'By the Blessed Virgin, and all I hold sacred, I will most certainly not,' she glared at her father.

'Then you will leave us and go to our rooms,' he said in a voice, which sounded as if he didn't really know how to deal with this outburst.

'With pleasure,' she responded, and with that, she stormed off.

'I will leave too Father,' the son said, not so much from impassioned conviction, but more personal shame.

Sir John was speechless, Richard felt for this old man's embarrassment. Sir John's eyes followed his son and daughter as they left, and he slumped down onto the bench. Sir John's knights, seated at the table, had up to that moment been laughing and idly talking, but they were now, very quiet. They visibly shrunk into their clothes and stared at their mete before them.

'Forgive me Sir, I have caused offence, and discord betwixt you and your family, I will leave you.'

'You will do no such thing,' Sir John revived slightly, 'this is unforgivable, I, I, am heartily ashamed… Can you cast any light on this disgraceful exhibition of bad manners? The like of which I have never afore been witness to, I would expect better from those accursed villains we have this minute left in the stable.'

Richard wearily sat down next to Sir John; they were alone now; their company had tactfully disappeared. All that was left of the happy band of knights were plates of half eaten mete.

'Perhaps you are too harsh Sir. I can tell you what I know, but you must be clear that this is only my account. As we crossed the Channel this day, I noticed your son losing heavily at a game of dice. I was not involved I was simply a bystander. I paid little or no heed to them; dice is not for the likes of me. From the sense I made of it, your son must have run out of coin. He withdrew a very fine emerald from his person, and presented it to his companions, demanding its exchange for more coin, the others in his company showed little interest, or at least they were not prepared to pay what your son wanted. He turned to me, and offered me the jewel. I was startled at first. I saw it was a fine stone and told him what I could afford. I knew it was worth more than I could pay. He begrudgingly took my coin and, that is all I know. I suspect he also lost the coin I gave him. He and his wife, I mean his sister, argued, I fancy because of the jewel, and it seems she now holds me responsible for the loss. At that time, until now, I assumed that they were husband and wife.'

'The fool, I can only apologise once more. The jewel belonged to my wife, and it was given to my daughter, that's why she would be so angry, it was not his to sell. I do not offer that as any excuse for her behaviour, or his you understand.'

Richard loosened his purse strings and withdrew the emerald necklace. 'I would be honoured Sir if you would accept this as a gift, I do not wish to be the cause of this family's trouble.'

Sir John stared down sadly at the necklace, which had much meaning to him.

'Thank you, Sir, for your generosity, but I cannot accept it. *However*, if you will permit me, I will purchase the stone from you.'

'There is no need.'

'I insist.' Richard told him what he had paid Gervase for the necklace. He could see that Sir John was upset that something so dear to him; had been treated with so little worth by his son.

'Thank you, Sir, for your chivalry, it would make the noble William Marshal proud.'

'Perhaps he is indeed to be thanked for I fought alongside him and learned much from him.'

'You fought with the *Marshal*, well, you are indeed a man to be reckoned with, he is no fool and a fine judge of a man, from what I hear. He is becoming famous throughout Christendom… One more boon I beg of you to assuage my shame. Will you ride home with us tomorrow and give my wanton miserable offspring a chance to redeem themselves?'

'Do you think that wise Sir?'

'I beg of you Sir, for I am ashamed.' Sir John was insistent and Richard felt for the old man. He was hurt and wanted to make amends for what he clearly felt was a shameful reflection on him as a father. Against his better judgement, Richard assured him that it would be his pleasure to travel with such an old friend of his father's.

'It will be a fine opportunity for me to learn more about my father from someone who really knew him.'

Richard and Sir John talked for some time; Richard had the feeling that Sir John had something else to say for which he was struggling to find the right words.

Sir John sighed... 'I'm saddened to be the one to deliver the news of your father's death.'

'I am glad that it was you Sir, truly.'

'Mmmm, there is more Richard... I know also that Sir Guy de Buford has been given your manor as a reward for the support he gave to the old Empress. Henry favours those who fought for her at the expense of those who did not. I suppose that's to be expected, I'm so sorry lad.' Richard showed no reaction; he sat silently flexing the muscles in his jaw.

'I faired better than your father because of my brother, whom my son and daughter have been visiting in Gascony, he was a supporter of Matilda, civil war is a wicked evil that sets brother against brother, and father against son. When Henry was crowned, Simon, my younger brother, spoke up for me. This was when your father ended our friendship; he was the noblest of men. He said I must not be known to associate with him. Saying that there was a chance for me, because of my brother, and any friendship with him would jeopardise my home and family. I asked your father how he thought that I would live with such a treachery, he said, "Do it, or you are lost to me anyway, if you sacrifice your home and family for me, you are not worthy of my friendship, family is everything". We embraced and both wept, for we were so close that when one was cut, we both bled. We only met once more, by accident, he ignored me, I knew he'd seen me and he clearly felt the pain keenly; I saw it in his eyes. I sent coin to him when I heard of his hardship, but he returned it. Never doubt him Richard, he was the finest man I ever knew. Now I have a chance to redeem my honour by helping my dearest friend's son. I again beg you to come and stay with me for as long as you will, at the very least, until you decide your way forward. It is some trifling kindness I can do in memory of my old friend, or perhaps, because I am the lesser man, I do it merely as a salve for my conscience. You see the sort of fellow I am Richard, no reflection here of your much-celebrated friend, William Marshal.'

CHAPTER 4

Richard had been reluctant to leave Sir John, and Sir John it seemed had needed to talk to him, but Richard had work to do before he slept. They wished each other well, embraced, and Richard made his way outside and across the courtyard to the stables. He liked Sir John, how could his children be so contrary in nature to him, surely, they must have some of this man's noble character within.

He did not have time now to reflect on their talk *or* this day's activities, it seemed a lifetime ago since he had left the shores of France. He would give them some thought once he'd finished his night's work.

He stood in the doorway of the stable and drew his sword, casting his eye, around peering into the shadows for anything untoward, ensuring he was alone; the first thing he noticed was that the bodies had been removed.

'I didn't fancy a night with three rotting corpses as bedfellows.' He saw too that some fresh straw had been spread around. Patting and speaking to Ares as he passed him to look where he'd hidden his saddle-bag, checking that all was just as he'd left it. There was no blood on Ares' hooves, or body parts lying around, so he guessed no one had been near him, smiling, he set about his work.

He rummaged inside one of his bundles and pulled out a smaller bag, which contained his personal washing paraphernalia.

'Humph,' he snorted as he withdrew his soap. He was down to his last bar of castile soap, which he'd purchased for no mean coin. It was made with olive oil and lavender, not the usual soap made with tallow, beef or mutton fat and wood-ash. What was good enough for the Marshal was good enough for him he'd made, as justification for the expense.

Richard had never liked being dirty, even when he was a boy, thus he thought that this soap was a luxury worth the coin. He decided to go back to the hall, beg at the kitchen and see if they would sell him some of their everyday soap to wash his clothes, and hopefully they would fill a bucket with hot water, if they had any.

Fortunately, when he went to the kitchen their fire was blazing and they quickly heated him some water, they were very obliging he thought. He was even subjected to some friendly flirting with the two maids, but he had too much on his mind to develop that possibility. It was not the perfect laundry, not quite up to the standards of the one in the palace at Poitiers, he had to confess, but he would be able to wash his undergarments and shirt, which he did and hung them over a makeshift line he'd strung between the low rafters. First, he made the most of the hot water and his precious soap to wash himself. He dried his face and felt his beard then stropped his dagger blade on his belt, whipped up some soap with his badger haired brush, spread the creamy lather on his whiskers and began to remove the last few day's growth.

'Ahh,' he said once he had finished, running his hand over his chin, 'that's better. Odd how simple soap and water and feeling clean can make the weight of one's troubles feel lighter.' He smiled; the Marshal was always insistent that his knights looked all that they claimed to be. "We are judged first on the person we present, one must always look the part, but remember that our whole being takes life from what's inside. Prayer and meditation before God, beautifies one's heart, and from such devotion, let that beauty work on one's appearance, and then chivalry will be our natural disposition. Our outward display should not be one of vanity but a manifestation of the rightness within".

Richard's night had been troubled; he'd been comfortable, and warm enough, but he was more than slightly disturbed by the bizarre day past. All he had planned and hoped for was now turned into dust at his feet. It seemed that his destiny would be linked to Sir John's for the foreseeable way ahead. The journey into his future was to commence by travelling north with this family friend, and, his son and daughter who apparently loathed him. He smiled, 'Ha!' From one tournai to another, it seems, but this mêlée might require a better man than me, to survive it in one piece.

It was ever dangerous to travel, but never more so than to journey alone, as he had originally intended. Travelling in numbers made for greater safety from villains who might have an eye to owning what was his. He would accept this offer of Sir John's, and be thankful for the safety of their number.

'Mmm,' he would proffer a prayer to the Virgin that the loathing did not venture further than black looks and sharp words. He supposed that they would keep clear of him and he would certainly endeavour to keep well clear of them. For now, he had been offered a place and he would make the best of it, as he had all his life. He was not penniless and he was able, perhaps the Blessed Virgin was watching over him and praying for him after all.

'I've never had much, so I have not lost much, perhaps this is all a blessing in disguise.'

He'd slept the best he was able, with his hand on his sword, naked, but for his gambeson and boots. He was concerned about the journey, yes, but he'd thought much about his home and all that had passed. He wondered sadly, if he would ever see his mother's grave again. He hoped that his father had been laid by her side and given the dignity in death he deserved and had been sorely denied in life these last years.

Perhaps the Blessed Virgin has drawn a line under my failures and given me a clean sheet of parchment on which to write my future, he thought.

He lay with his hands folded behind his head staring out through the stable doors, he had a clear view right down to the sea, and he saw in the distance the glow of the new day as it gently caressed the French coast. Yawning, he briskly rubbed his face with his hand, rolled over, and pushed himself to his feet.

'Ahhh!' He winced in agony; his leg was as stiff as a board from the blow last night. 'Dear, oh dear,' he groaned, and rubbed the muscle trying to overcome the numbness. 'How can having no feeling in my leg be so painful,' he grumbled. He limped outside rubbing his leg as he went, and tipped last night's water from the bucket, filling it afresh from the horse trough, and gave himself a quick wash. He had shaved and washed thoroughly last night; all he needed this morning was to clear the sleep from his eyes. He felt his clothes on the line, they were still damp, they would have to do; they'd dry soon enough once he was dressed.

He made sure Ares had water and hay then went tentatively to the hall to see what mete was on offer. He met the Inn Keeper with a horse by his side; he smiled and bowed most graciously to Richard.

'Ah Sir, good morrow to you, I was making my way to the stable in search of you this very moment, your friend told me you would be there. What do you think?' he asked, smiling, and turned, gesturing to the horse, 'I have found you a fine pack animal, as you asked,' he patted the animal he was holding.

'Mmm... so it appears, how much coin? It looks a fine beast, perhaps it is beyond the depth of my pocket.'

'First take time to inspect her and if you are satisfied, then we will talk of a price.' Richard opened its mouth and looked at its teeth, felt its legs and examined its feet.

'Not bad,' Richard didn't want to sound too enthusiastic.

He told Richard his price, they haggled, and the deal was done. Richard was very satisfied, it wasn't cheap, but he wanted a good animal and it was sturdy, as the fellow had claimed. It was too much to expect Ares to carry all his armour, weapons, belongings, and him as well.

'I will see that she is stabled next to your fine horse while you break-fast, perhaps it will be love at first sight.' The man laughed at his jest and Richard smiled.

'Thank you, aye, break-fast,' Richard would normally eat heartily at such a meal, when available, for one never knew what mete would be on offer for the rest of the day. However, this day his appetite was somewhat curtailed at the thought of the company. He entered staring into the gloom of the hall to see if Sir John was yet there. He was so concentrated on that occupation he walked straight into Sir John's daughter; he automatically took her arms in the collision.

'How dare you touch me, unhand me.'

Richard paused for a second, 'Forgive me my Lady, I am at fault, I was distracted.'

'Is there some doubt? You appear to make a habit of such ineptness.' She turned to walk into the hall.

'You will be pleased to have your necklace once more, it was a pleasure to return it,' he said as she marched off, trying desperately to bring some civility to the exchange, if only for Sir John's sake.

She turned back towards him narrowing her eyes. 'Do not boast to me of your chivalry, for you do not impress me, I see you for what you are. You did not return it as you put it, do you take me for a fool? You made my father purchase it. I would expect nothing more from the likes of you. What care I anyway, I have many such trinkets, it was of little consequence.'

She turned and flounced off in the direction of her father's table, leaving Richard at a loss.

'Phew, she likes me… Too much of that sweet lady's company and I will say goodbye to chivalry, for I will be forced to take a hazel switch to her backside.' In the light of this moment's exchange, he decided that he would sit alone and forgo the pleasure of Sir John's company. Perhaps I would be safer taking my chance alone on the road, he was forced to wonder.

He was just about to sit when Sir John stood and beckon him to join them. Richard hesitated, and then wearily trudged over to their table.

'Here, sit next to me Richard, you honour us, move up Gervase, make space for Sir Richard, he is to be like a son to me for the debt of honour I owe his father.' Gervase looked up to Richard with pure loathing and reluctantly made room for him on the bench.

'You are generous Sir John, but I will not trouble your kind hospitality overlong,' Richard responded quickly hoping to retrieve something from Sir John's well intentioned, but imprudent remark. He could see, what Sir John appeared to be oblivious to, that the noble statement he'd just made, had not only taken the lid off a wasp's nest but also rattled a stick inside for good measure.

It seemed as if Sir John was determined to ignore the silent tension and he talked and laughed as if he'd not a care in the world.

Richard wondered how an innocent sea crossing to his home could turn into such a maelstrom of impending doom, with jagged, spray-lashed rocks, blocking any hope of beaching his future on soft sand

CHAPTER 5

After the morning's meal, which broke the night's fast, Richard and Sir John oversaw the loading of their pack animals.

Richard was very satisfied with his purchase; the gentle little rowan was the antithesis of Ares, thoroughly biddable and well mannered. Richard patted her and she all but smiled. She was more than happy to stand and be loaded with Richard's plate armour and mail. He had bought some pieces of his equipment and won others. His gorget, pauldrons, and breastplate he'd had made especially for him, they needed to fit perfectly, or they would not serve their purpose. The cuisses and greaves he'd taken as trophies, they were held in place by straps around the back of his legs so there was some adjustment to take up any discrepancy. His helm was a visible display of his good fortune. It was of extremely high quality embellished with gilding and etching; the craftsmanship was unparalleled. It would have cost more than the rest of his armour added together. Even the Marshal himself owned to coveting it. It had been a part payment of ransom, after a tournai, for the release of one of Henri de Bourbourg's sons. His hauberk he'd left home with, it was a gift from his father on his knighting and it had lasted him well, but what really turned heads was his surcoat with its two pales of green and yellow, faced with a rampant red lion on his chest, this marked him out as one of the Marshal's men. That coveted badge alone set him apart from other knights.

Richard took great care of his armour and weapons, ensuring that they were always wrapped in oiled skins to give protection from any inclement weather. They were the tools of his trade, and expensive to replace. As well as loading his armour onto his palfrey, he had also to pack his spare clothing, bedding, dried mete, and two leather costrels of small beer for the journey. All that was, or might be needed, he must carry with him.

He smiled sadly; for he remembered his father once saying to him that *he* was yet small beer, when he'd tried to lift his father's sword and tumbled over. His father had lifted him from the ground and took him in his arms saying, "One day you will be a man my son, but know *this* – I will never love you more, or less, than I do at this moment," and he'd kissed him. Strange why that should suddenly come to mind he thought, I could have only been four or five.

Thankfully, Ares seemed to have accepted their new companion, which was a welcome outcome. Richard didn't want to endanger their previously harmonious relationship.

The sun was well in the sky before the loading was complete; once Richard had finished his packing; he'd helped Sir John's men. This was an ideal opportunity to get to know the other knights and men-at-arms that were part of the band of travellers. He was perfectly at ease with these men, after all, it was an ingredient of his daily life mixing with such fellows. They talked and laughed freely together, they all wanted to know about his time with the great Marshal, what was he like as a person? Was he as good as they'd heard? What weapons did he favour? Richard was surprised that William Marshal's fame was so widespread. The difficulty for Richard was that they were looking at him in the glow cast by his connection to the Marshal, this could be quite a load to carry, for he was a poor reflection of the man he held in such high esteem.

There was no sight of Gervase or Julianne until the work was complete. Richard noticed that Sir John kept glancing towards the hall entrance, but neither he nor Sir John made any comment about their non-appearance.

They must have been watching the activity because as soon as the work was completed, they appeared. The mood between them and their father was frosty to say the least.

Once they had set off, the party was about twenty souls, Sir John brought his horse alongside Richard's, it was sometime before he spoke and Richard left him to his thoughts. Gradually he appeared to relax and began to engage Richard in conversation; their talk was general and light-hearted. Sir John was clearly impressed by Richard's friendship with "The Marshal". The Marshal's model of knighthood and chivalry was becoming the standard to which young knights aspired, and were judged by. Sir John wanted Richard to relate every detail of his time as part of William Marshal's elite band of warriors. Richard actually felt a little embarrassed at the generosity of Sir John's opinion.

It was warm, Richard stripped down to his white linen shirt, which was loose fitting, ideal for this hot day. If he'd been travelling on his own, he would have needed to be dressed at the very least in his hauberk. This was good, he enjoyed Sir John's company, but his son and daughter were proving determined to make their travel unpleasant.

Sir John studied him, as they rode. He was a strikingly attractive fellow, and no mistake, such an easy friendly manner. His skin was tanned, and his hair was bleached by the sun. His eyes were sparkling blue; they were the blue of a lapis lazuli gemstone ring Sir John owned. Sir John assumed that his nose had been broken at some time, it was slightly crooked, yet it did not distract from his beauty, yes that was the word, he was more than *merely* handsome. His mouth turned upward ever so slightly at the ends, which gave his face the appearance of constantly smiling and when he did laugh it exposed beautiful even white teeth. Aye, this acorn did not fall far from the tree, he was the double of his father. A fine catch for a Lady… or, son-in-law, he thought.

Richard was quite at a loss as to know how to repair the damage, he couldn't really understand what the issue was, and neither Gervase nor Julianne seemed willing to even attempt to resolve it. He wondered if perhaps he had touched at their vanity and for him to be here, rubbed salt in that wound. The brother no doubt felt ashamed of his dishonourable behaviour. She may well be angry that she had been caught taking a second glance at him, if that's what she was doing. He was sure that a girl of her beauty was usually the one being admired and she never wasted her time looking at a man. In spite of her churlish manners and foul temper Richard had to concede he found her very attractive, he would even go as far as to say, more than any woman he'd ever known. No accounting for taste, he thought, and smiled.

Sir John made it known to Richard that he had organised a banquet to celebrate the return of his children, it was to be a surprise, and he hoped that it would break the ice. This was the only time he referred to the cool atmosphere. He told Richard that he would also meet Sir Guy Molineux, Julianne's suitor.

'From what I can tell he is besotted with Julianne, but I have a fancy that it is not reciprocated; she keeps him dangling like a fish on a hook. He is a courtier, and seems popular with the King, but you can never tell with Henry, there must be some gain to friendship for him and I can't see much gain in a friendship with Sir Guy. But! There would be some advantage for me to have a son-in-law in good favour with the King. You can tell me what you think when you meet him.'

'Ha! You jest Sir John, I'm afraid my opinion may be of little or no account, I'm not the one to judge courtiers, unless I meet them on the practice yard at the end of a lance or the edge of a sword.'

Sir John laughed. 'I wish them well if they want to marry, but I need someone whom I know will take care of those who look to me as their Lord and protector, come the time I go to meet my Maker. The responsibilities God has seen fit to set upon my shoulders I do not take lightly. Alas Sir Guy does not match up to the image in my mind's eye, of a man suited for such work.'

'You have a son; he will marry and carry on your line.'

'Mmm… yes, I have a son,' Sir John repeated in a flat voice. He had reservations about Gervase, and in his heart of hearts, he was unsure that a match with Sir Guy, would bring with it happiness for his daughter. He turned slowly, and cast his eye over Richard.

'Mmm,' he said again to himself. 'What do you think of Julianne, be honest?'

Richard turned to him; it was some time before he responded to his question. 'She is very beautiful, feisty, and yet there is a tender side. I saw that on the boat when she first thought her brother troubled, though the tenderness very quickly evaporated when she learned of the jewel. I think she is insecure for some reason, or why would she have to constantly prove that she is so strong and above the feelings of lesser mortals? She seems to be protecting a vulnerability.'

'Interesting, very interesting Richard… You are a fascinatingly astute fellow, for someone to whom fighting and its physical nature is a way of life.'

'My mentor would say brute force might win battles, but not wars. You must understand your enemy, and he would tap his head with his finger.'

'I would like to meet this Marshal…' Sir John paused again for some time, twisting and chewing his lip, eventually he said in a quiet voice whilst staring straight ahead, 'Her mother was attacked and murdered when Julianne was five; she witnessed it. She never cried or talked about it, I tried, but to no avail… She is very close to Gervase and mothers him, he's weak, and she protects him. I'm not much of a father I'm afraid.'

'I'm indeed saddened to hear such a tragic tale as this Sir, forgive me. You must think me overly harsh, in the light of what you have this moment told me.'

'No, not at all, your assessment was perfectly correct. I merely wanted you to perhaps, understand a little behind the façade she displays. Julianne has done herself no favour by her outrageous behaviour, underneath her cold hard exterior she is very sensitive and caring, just as her mother was, possibly she fears her sensitivity, perceiving it as weakness.'

Richard didn't know what else to say, Sir John had been very frank. He had no need to share these very personal and no doubt painful things.

They rode now without speaking, Richard felt awkward, he didn't know what to say, neither it seemed did Sir John. Richard was relieved when an opportunity presented itself to move the conversation on.

'I recognise this road Sir John,' Richard said, suddenly standing in his stirrups and pointing. 'If I recall correctly there are woods ahead. Perhaps I ought to take two of your knights and ride on before our party to make sure that there is not trouble lurking.'

'Yes, that was on my mind too, you do that Richard, I do not need to counsel you to be watchful.'

'I must make some preparation I fear I am too scantily clad for such work. I will only put on my gambeson and hauberk that will be sufficient.' Sir John signalled to two knights and they came to him.

'Go with Sir Richard and see that the way ahead is safe,' they nodded, turned their horses and waited for Richard. As he was about to follow, Sir John touched his arm, 'Do have a care,' Richard smiled and the three cantered away.

CHAPTER 6

When they neared the wood they slowed to a walk, and Richard asked the names of his two companions.

'Sir Raymond,' said one of the knights, 'and this is Sir *Tristram*.' They both gave a polite nod.

Richard smiled, 'Sir *Tristram*, well, we will come to no harm with a knight from the famous "Round Table" with us,' said Richard, they all laughed.

'Ha, that was in another life,' Sir Tristram jested, 'but I think it is we who have a knight from the Round Table to ride with us.'

'How so?'

'The news has spread quickly that you are a friend of the great Marshal, no less,' said Sir Tristram. 'Only the finest are chosen to be one of his knights.'

'You are kind Sir, but I was merely fortunate, I was in the right place at the right time.'

'And humble too, a man with all the knightly virtues,' said Sir Raymond.

Richard smiled, 'Aye, well that's as may be, but we have work to do. We will take turns of leading. I will go first; you stay a hundred paces or so behind me and we will make our way steadily so as not to create too much noise. If there is trouble one of us must ride back to warn Sir John and two of us will delay any followers. Agreed?' They nodded and Richard rode on ahead of them.

The track was well used by the look of the ruts. The ground was wet; the leafy canopy was preventing the warmth of the sun's rays ever reaching it and drying the ground.

They had been riding for some quarter of the hour or more when Richard heard a faint screaming and shouting somewhere ahead of them, it sounded like a woman's voice. He raised his arm and brought his horse to a standstill, removed his helm and cocked his head to listen. He glanced back to Sir Raymond and Sir Tristram, Sir Raymond raised his arms as much to ask, "What's the problem?"

Richard raised a finger, indicating that only one of them should join him. Sir Raymond rode steadily to his side.

'What is it?'

'Listen.'

'I hear it, it sounds like trouble, not too far beyond us, around that bend in the track's my guess.'

'Aye, mine also.' Richard signalled to Sir Tristram to keep his distance and he nodded that he understood the instruction. 'I'm for seeing what's afore us.'

'Aye, I am of like mind.'

'We will ride cautiously until we know what we face,' Richard said leaning forward onto the garçon of his saddle. The two knights released their lances from their fastenings and settled them under their arms, each positioning his hand securely against the vamplate; they lowered them for action and gently nudged their horses forward at a trot, with Richard leading the way. When they rounded the bend, they saw five villains attacking what looked like an old man and woman on a wain. One of the men intent on this mischief held their horse; the woman had just been dragged from the cart fighting and kicking for all she was worth, she cried out as she fell heavily to the ground, and lay still. It flashed through Richard's mind as he rode towards them, that the soft ground might well have worked in her favour.

Richard spurred Ares, and he instantly sprang forward, Sir Raymond followed. The men looked up at the sound of the pounding hooves, and froze in panic at the sudden appearance of these two knights galloping at full tilt towards them; their lances lowered for battle. The men just stood, unable to move, their fear had resigned them to their fate.

Richard shouted over his shoulder to Sir Raymond, 'Take the one to the right.' The next second Richard connected with his target. Such was the force of the impact; his lance was driven straight through the pathetic creature trembling in his path. Richard immediately released it for fear of being vaulted from the saddle by the trapped lance. He unhooked his war hammer from his waist feeling the wicked curved square pick as he withdrew it. It was second nature, all his movements were instinctive, thinking took time, and in conflict, time was a stranger. If one needed time to think, one would quickly meet its constant companion, death. He turned Ares in his own length and rode once more to the wain, he noticed Sir Raymond had also dispatched his opponent, and like Richard, had in one well-practised movement, turned his horse around to face the mêlée once more. Richard rode straight at one of the robbers who held up a club. In a split second's distraction, his eye caught sight of the woman with a villain, intent on murderous revenge for this interference into his business, iniquitous though it was.

He grabbed the fallen woman by her thick hair, and was about to slit her throat. Richard effortlessly adjusted his direction to the man, the ruffian glanced towards Richard, in that single glance his eyes had beheld their last glimpse of this world, for in the next breath of eternity the square spike of Richard's war hammer was driven viciously through the top of his skull and down into the soft tissue of his brain. He instantly dropped the woman and she fell forward into the brush. The man gave the most horrific scream and his whole body shook violently, his eyes bulged, and he tumbled on top of her, with the war hammer still lodged in his head. The two remaining men ran for their very lives into the darkness of the forest. Sir Raymond made to follow but thought better of it; the undergrowth was too dense for a horse and rider. Richard slid from Ares and dragged the monster of a man from the trapped woman. She was terrified, screaming beyond hope of reason. Richard attempted to wrap her in his arms she struggled frantically flailing her fists at him. He suffered the blows and eventually managed to secure her arms. She stared up at him, 'Sir, I cannot fight you I have no strength left, do as you must and may God forgive you.'

He spoke gently to her then gradually she calmed and clung to him weeping. 'My good lady, you judge me harshly. Neither my companion nor I mean you any harm. We are outriders for a party of travellers, making our way northward such as yourselves.' She hesitated and he tenderly wiped the tears from her cheek with the soft leather of his gauntlet. 'Let me help you to your feet and see what further support we can give.' Richard stood and offered his hand to the young woman, as she made to stand. Sir Raymond coughed, and Richard turned to him, he pointed to the old man who'd fallen back over into the wain and shook his head. The girl saw him too.

'GRANDFATHER!' She shook free of Richard and stepped to the wain clasping her face in her hands.

'A wicked tragedy dear lady, he must have struck his head when he tumbled from the seat,' Sir Raymond speculated, and looked at Richard and then to the girl.

'It is our regret that we could not have done more. May I ask your name,' Richard asked, once again wrapping his arm around her. She turned to him sobbing.

'But for you – we would *both* now be dead, do not upbraid yourselves. I'm called by the name of Esther and my grandfather is called Jacob of Clairvaux, we are Jews and we were travelling to York, many leagues north of here, to be reunited with family.'

'I know York well enough. How may we be of assistance?'

'But you are Christians you will not want to associate with us.'

'I think my Saviour and his Blessed Mother were Jews. I imagine He would want us to help one of His own, what say you Sir Raymond.'

Sir Raymond hesitated for a moment, 'Yes… of course.'

Richard could see Sir Tristram in the distance, standing in his stirrups desperately endeavouring to make sense of what was happening. Richard waved to beckon him and he rode to them.

'You have all under control I see my friends. Good day my lady.' Esther acknowledged his greeting.

'Sir Tristram, return to our party, make it known to Sir John what has happened, and that we will wait here until they come.'

'Be watchful they might have friends and return. I will be as quick as I can.'

'Aye we will.' Tristram turned his horse and galloped off at speed.

'May I call you Esther?' She nodded, 'What do you want us to do?'

'Grandfather needs to be with our people so he can be cared for. They will perform the Taharah; it is our rite of purification. He must be ritually bathed and then dressed in Tachrichim, our traditional burial garments. I am bound by the love I had for him, to do as he would have wished.'

'We make for Canterbury this day; will you be able to find such people there?'

'Yes, I should think so, but there are none known to me. Grandfather seemed to know everyone, but I have never been to England before.'

'Fear not we will help.'

'You are a kind man, I think. You know my name, but I do not know yours.'

'Forgive me, my name is Richard and this is Sir Raymond,' she looked at Sir Raymond who was still sitting astride his horse and she bowed her head.

'Come Sir Raymond and we will lay out the old gentleman in the back of his cart, and cover him while we wait.' Sir Raymond dismounted and helped Richard.

'Thank you for doing this for me, and your offer of further help, do not think me ungrateful, but I will go, I do not want to be the cause of difficulties between you and your friends. It is ever so with my people'

'There will be no difficulties, we will wait, and I will ride with you on your wain once our party arrives.'

While they waited, they dragged the bodies of the attackers into the wood. They walked back to where Esther sat on a grassy knoll, she was quietly sobbing with her head in her hands. She heard them, turned to the sound, and wiped her eyes on her scarf. They joined her and sat either side of her; Sir Raymond laid his hand on her shoulder.

'How are you feeling now Esther?' He asked.

She jumped slightly at the surprise contact and tried to smile. 'I don't know what I am feeling if I'm honest. Perhaps we should have buried those men.'

'I think that the wolves in this forest will soon take care of such kindred spirits,' he answered.

'I was neglectful Esther; forgive me,' said Richard. 'I have not inquired if you are hurt. Were you harmed during the attack?'

'Not really, when I tumbled from the wain I landed on my arm, my shoulder carries some dull pain, and my elbow is grazed, but that is all,' she replied, showing her torn sleeve and the abrasion, at the same time she instinctively massaged her injured shoulder.

Sir Raymond suddenly stood, drawing his sword, 'Ah, it is our party, praise be.' Richard rose too, Sir John was leading the group and rode to them. Richard took the rein of his horse and Sir John slipped from the saddle.

'You're not hurt Richard?'

'No, we are both well, they presented no resistance. We were compelled to act with such force for the sake of these poor travellers.'

'Thank God, we came as speedily as we could.'

Sir John now turned his attention to Esther and bowed, she acknowledged him with a slight curtsey.

'This is Sir John FitzWilliam, who leads our company,' Richard said quickly.

'Good lady.'

'My name is Esther, Sir.'

'Dear child it pains me to see you subjected to such wilful evil as has befallen you this day.'

'Thank you, Sir, your knights have been kind, their arrival was most timely.'

'To where do you travel?'

'She was travelling far to the north, York, Sir John. I have told her we will escort her to Canterbury, so that her grandfather can be treated with all the respect befitting his faith,' Richard quickly jumped in, committing Esther to their help.

Sir John glanced at the covered body in the rear of the wain.

'Alas, we were too late to prevent the death of Esther's grandfather.'

'They would have killed me too, but for your knights, as I have said, Sir.'

Gervase pushed his horse forward to them and dismounted.

'You must let me drive the wain for you my Lady.'

'Thank you, Sir, but I am not a Lady, I must make it known to you… we are Jews.'

Gervase, looked to his father, 'I care not, I see a beautiful damsel in distress and that is sufficient for me, is that not so Father?'

'Err, yes, yes, quite right Gervase.' His father said, more than a little surprised at his son's chivalrous conduct. She looked at Richard, almost as if she needed his assurance. Richard gave a nearly imperceptible nod of support.

Richard looked in the direction of Julianne she never spoke but appeared genuinely concerned. Gervase passed the rein of his horse to a servant, and took Esther's hand helping her onto the wain.

'Let us make haste and clear of these woodlands,' commanded Sir John remounting his horse. Richard did likewise mounting Ares. Esther stared once more at Richard and he leant down to her.

'You will be quite safe Esther, I will ride alongside you with Sir Raymond, there is nothing to fear.' She seemed content with Richard's assurance, though in truth he was as much a stranger as all who surrounded her.

CHAPTER 7

On arrival at their lodgings in Canterbury, Gervase announced that he would take Esther to find some of her people and hopefully a Rabbi, before dark. His father nodded, Richard dismounted alongside Sir John's horse and spoke quietly to him.

'May I offer a suggestion, Sir John?'

'Of course, one moment, Son.'

'Perhaps Gervase should be accompanied, both for propriety and safety, Sir.'

Sir John glanced at Gervase, 'Yes, that would be wise, I should have thought of that myself. You are right Richard.' He looked to his son; 'Richard has suggested that you take some men with you for safety Gervase.'

'Richard has suggested has he! He is in charge now I take it. Aye, and whom does he suggest, don't tell me, himself no doubt.' Sir John closed his eyes and shook his head in despair.

'I think,' Richard responded quickly, 'it would be prudent if I stayed here and helped with the unpacking, I have my own to attend to and I do not expect you and your men to do that for me.'

Sir John was about to say it would not be a problem, but thought better of it. 'Perhaps.'

Richard continued, 'it would be better to send Sir Tristram and Sir Raymond with Sir Gervase, Sir.'

'Aye…' Sir John replied, breathing a sigh of despondency, and instructed the two knights to accompany Gervase and Esther. Esther looked once more at Richard he could see she was clearly uneasy.

He tried to reassure her with a smile, he went to her and said, 'Fear not, if you decide to return, I will be here.'

'Oh yes, you have nothing to fear with the noble Sir Richard on hand. He knows what's best for everyone; he freely blesses us all with his advice.' Esther looked at Gervase, and then to Richard, her brow furrowed, sensing that she was the cause of this undercurrent and it distressed her. Richard could have cheerfully strangled Gervase. Esther did not need his petty aside; she needed to feel secure and safe after the day's trauma.

Gervase set off suddenly tugging on the left rein so the wain would veer towards Richard, a strut supporting the side struck Richard's arm, he grimaced at the sharp pain, and Gervase smiled.

Sir John saw the deliberate wickedness and stiffened. 'Dear oh dear, I'm sorry Richard, I don't know what to do with that boy.'

'Think nothing of it, Sir John, a mere accident, perhaps the horse was startled.'

'Richard, you know as well as I the truth of it.'

'All the same, better to let it pass. After all, there is no harm done. I suspect that he is embarrassed over the necklace incident, I may well have felt the same once I had time to reflect, if I'd made such a foolish transaction.'

'You're being magnanimous to my son, and I thank you. I hope you are right,' Sir John replied watching the wain disappear up a narrow street.

Up until this moment, Julianne had stayed some distance from her father, but her horse was now next to where they were standing. Richard, against his better judgement, went to Julianne and offered his hand to her, attempting for some reconciliation. She hesitated and then to his total surprise she reached for him, he took her by the waist and lowered her from the saddle. In this contrary moment, he'd clearly lost grip of his senses, for he nearly kissed her. He was quite unable to read the oddest look she gave him, and then abruptly she returned to type.

'The Jewess seems taken with you; no doubt she is familiar with your kind. I have heard all about you tournai knights and their revelry with such women.'

'My Lady, do you practise at being offensive, or does it come naturally? Treat me as you wish, but do not extend your contempt to that lady, for such offence is uncalled for and unworthy of you. I think that even you, especially you, will have some understanding of her loss this day.'

'Oh, and what do you mean by that! I will speak to those below me as I wish, and will brook no instruction from the likes of you.' She pushed him aside and stamped off. Richard clenched his fists so fiercely his knuckles turned white; he could not move; he was so angry.

Richard never saw Julianne again until the evening meal, and she sat as far from him as it was possible on the long table. Her brother never returned, which made Richard uneasy. He prayed that he was taking care of

Esther and was mightily thankful that Sir Tristram and Sir Raymond were there too.

'I thought that Gervase would have returned by now, Richard,' Sir John said.

'There must have been some problem. At least he has two good knights with him.' Richard left the group as soon as he could with the thin excuse that he was tired from the days adventure. All at the table stood and bowed and he left, needless-to-say, Julianne just glowered at him then pointedly turned away. A bolt from the blue struck him, and he realised why. She had been touched with a new experience, and for the first time he guessed, and felt fearfully vulnerable.

Yet another sleepless night lay ahead for him, he resolved that he would take Gervase to task if he hurt, or *allowed* the girl to be hurt.

'Yes, by God, I will give Gervase the thrashing he so soundly deserves, but no one it appears, has ever dared administer.'

Richard arose before daylight, washed, and went to see if all was well with his horse. As always Ares was delighted to see him, even his new friend seemed pleased. There was just enough light from the new day for Richard to see what he was doing, so he reached down and took some straw into his hand and began to groom his horses. He always liked this work, he knew for some it was burdensome, but for him it was a labour of love. The sun was up when he heard the clatter of hooves in the yard. He reached for his leather jack and sword, which he'd removed for the warm work.

Richard buckled his sword to his side as he stepped out from the stable into the yard, and was a little surprised to see Esther with Gervase, Sir Raymond, and Sir Tristram.

She saw him too and smiled. He went to her, raising his hand in greeting.

'Are you surprised to see that I was able to accomplish this work, without you?' Gervase asked with his usual underlying challenge. Richard ignored him, and spoke to Esther.

'I did not really expect to see you again. I imagined that you would stay with your own people. Nevertheless, you are welcome.'

'They were all kind, but strangers. We laid Grandfather to rest, as is our custom. I didn't know what to do, Sir Gervase has been very kind and suggested that I come home with him until I can decide my future, so I have returned.' Gervase was obviously pleased with her praise, and his expression made sure that Richard understood that he was not the only one capable of chivalrous deeds.

'Have you eaten?'

'Not this morning.'

'Come Esther, I will see to our mete,' Gervase offered, quickly climbing from the wain and coming to help her down, before Richard could contemplate doing so.

'Will you join us Sir Richard and I will have a chance to thank you for all your kindness?'

'We do not want to interfere with this important man's work Esther, he has our lives to organise.'

Richard frowned and ignored the taunt. 'Thank you, but Sir Gervase is quite correct we must be about the preparation for the day's travel. We will have time yet to talk if we are to journey together.' She looked disappointed, but bowed. Gervase took her arm and led her quickly into the hall.

Richard turned to Sir Tristram and Sir Raymond who had dismounted. 'Good to see you safe and home, did all go well?'

'Yes, it was straightforward, we quickly found the Jewish quarter and they sought out a Rabbi. They saw to our needs whilst they did what needed to be done. While we were there we learned of the furore, apparently King Henry has had Roger de Pont L'Évêeque, the archbishop of York, along with Gilbert Foliot, the bishop of London, and Josceline de Bohon the bishop of Salisbury, crown the heir apparent. This was a breach of Canterbury's privilege of coronation, and Becket is threatening to excommunicate all three. They say the King is beside himself with fury. This battle with Becket will end badly, I'm sure of it.'

'Aye, the talk has been of nothing else since we arrived. From the gossip going around it sounds like they are as wilful as each other, and, though it pains me to say it, I think the King has the right of it.' said Richard.

'Ha, you will go far with that cry of support, for what it's worth I am of like mind. It's difficult for Henry to rule, ever needing the yea or nay of the Church. Those who claim subservience to the Church get away, *literally,* with murder, and the King is helpless. Becket seems to want the King to be subservient to him, and that is never going to happen. As Sir Tristram says, this will end badly; there is no other option, unless Becket catches a fatal flux and dies. It would be no good if Henry died, the next king would still be stuck with Becket. No, some tainted mete and a dose of dysentery for the beloved Archbishop is the way ahead,' they all laughed.

'That aside we have our own mistral to weather,' said Sir Tristram changing the subject. 'The young master seems quite smitten by the Jewish lady, can't blame him she is a fine beauty, and has a pleasant nature too. I could welcome such an acquaintance myself, but value my life too much to compete with Gervase. The problem lies I fear, in so much as she is not blessed with the same attraction, which does not bode well, but what do I know.'

'You know as much as I, Sir Tristram,' said Sir Raymond. 'I am of a like mind to you my friend, I think that I will put some space between our good master and that relationship.' He looked to Richard, 'If I may say so, Sir Richard, I would advise you to do the same, but I feel it might be a little more complex in your case.'

'How so?'

'I will say no more, other than she was very interested in knowing all about you, and that did not go well with our dear Lord, watch your back.' With that curious advice, they bowed and led their mounts off towards the stable. Richard's eyes followed them as they walked away, wondering what was their meaning. He didn't have time to dwell on it, for he saw Sir John coming from the hall, he smiled and greeted Richard.

'A fine day Richard, we must make haste and take advantage of this day's blessed weather. I am much relieved to have Gervase back, and the young lady has come with him. He seems excessively attentive to her needs. Perhaps I am too harsh on him.'

'Indeed Sir,' he responded, but Sir Raymond's strange comments troubled him, and he glanced once more to the stable where they'd taken their horses.

There would be a further two days of travel, Sir John informed Richard, before they reached their destination of Tattershall, north of the Wash, where Sir John's castle was situated.

On the final two stretches of their journey, Gervase rode one day on the wain with Esther, and on the next day, he rode with her on horseback, though she never ventured far from the wain and her belongings. Esther made the most of this freedom to speak to Richard and came alongside him. It was clear that Gervase was not pleased and held back sulking. Esther seemed oblivious to his annoyance or was mindful to ignore it.

'You have avoided me for the better portion of the past day Richard, have I caused some offence? If I have, I am the most wretched of sinners, for I owe my life to you.'

'You exaggerate Esther, I played only but a part, and no more than Sir Tristram and Sir Raymond.'

'Oh, I know such, and I have thanked them, it is only you whom I find never still long enough to speak to. Whatever you say my lasting memory will be that frightening man with a knife to my throat, and I a moment from death.'

'It was merely how the event unfolded and it was I that was on hand. As to any offence, fear not you have in no way offended me I assure you.'

'I thank God for that,'

'From my observations I mean, from the brief moments we have been in each other's company, you are the gentlest of ladies. I doubt you have any offence within you.'

'Ohh, I am observed, am I?' She laughed, 'And I thought you a man of good judgement.' Richard smiled at her.

'We are friends then?'

'It is ever my wish.'

'May I ask a question of you Sir?'

'You may, but can it be answered, that is a horse of another colour.'

'Is there some grievance between you and Sir Gervase?' He turned to her and she stared intently into his eyes.

'Ha, it is no secret I fear, we started our acquaintance badly and he appears to think I mean him harm.'

'And do you?' she looked disturbed.

'Not at all, I hardly know the fellow; we but met four days past. I fear he is angry at this moment because you are talking to me.'

'Surely you are mistaken,' she turned to look at Gervase and smiled, but he did not return it.

'In all honesty he is not easy to be with. I feel a little oppressed by his attention. How ungrateful am I when he has been so kind, and to great extent troubled himself on my behalf,' Richard smiled, 'Why do you smile? It is the truth; he has been very kind to me.'

'Forgive me, I'm sure he is the most noble of gentleman.' She looked quizzically at him, trying to make sense of his expression, which was at odds with his words.

With a quick shake of her head she went on, 'However, I am sad indeed if any disquiet impedes our friendship, for you are, I think, easy company. Sir Raymond tells me you are a famous brave knight and all look to you as an example of how to conduct their lives. They say this is because you are a friend of the great Marshal, whom even I have heard of, is this really so?'

Richard laughed, 'I am truly of no importance believe me, both Sir Raymond and Sir Tristram are my equal, they are fine knights too.'

'So, they have lied then!'

'I must beg for mercy my dear girl; your brain is too sharp for such a lackwit as you see before you. In this mêlée of words, I yield and offer ransom.'

'Now I know for sure that you be a spinner of untruths, for a lackwit you most certainly are not. As for your punishment, I will think on the price of your ransom,' and they both laughed. As they laughed, Richard was even more conscious of Gervase; he could almost feel his eyes burning into his back, and this light-hearted moment, for him, was abruptly tainted. Esther sensed his sudden change and she too ceased her mirth, furrowed her brow, and looked at him. Richard's tone was quite different now; all smiles were gone from his face as he spoke.

'Do not think I tire of your company Esther, nothing could be further from the truth, but perhaps you would be wise to return to your new friend for your own sake as well as mine. I should not wish to be the cause of any distress to you.'

She nodded as much to say that she understood. 'Thank you once again for your kindness Richard and this brief time of conversation. Is it permitted to call you Richard or should I always call you Sir Richard?'

'Perhaps in company "Sir" Richard would be most judicious.'

'Sir Richard it will be then. I will say good day to you, and thank you for this moment to express my gratitude, which is sincere,' Richard smiled at her, and she gently tightened the rein of her mount, allowing him to ride ahead.

Gervase came immediately to her side.

Richard noticed as he slowed his horse once more to an easy gait and glanced back, whatever Esther had said to Gervase, it appeared to restore his previous good humour, and then just as abruptly his scowl returned.

'What was that fellow saying for himself? Was he speaking poison of me?' Gervase's question had more the tone of interrogation, than one of passing interest.

'He really is a very gentle good man, Gervase. I felt I must take this opportunity to thank him once more for his bravery. There has been little or no chance since I was attacked, for he always appears to be working.'

'You are too generous. Do not be deceived, he is a surly fellow, both my sister and I have found to our cost.

You may ask her if you doubt my words, but alas, our father is taken in by his wiles, he even now seeks to rob us of our inheritance. I hope no harm is done before Father sees his foolishness. You must not make too much of his... help, he did nothing that I would not have done for any maiden in distress, but most especially for you. No doubt, he boasted of his association with William Marshal, we knoweth not the truth of why he left the Marshal's company. I suspect he was compelled to do so by some miserable dishonour, that's if the surcoat he wears even belongs to him. He most likely won it at dice or stole if from some unfortunate he murdered.'

Esther was horrified at Gervase's tone, she couldn't believe such things of Richard; there was real hatred here, of which she wanted no part. She was upset; any laughter was now a distant memory. She wondered what distorted wicked thoughts were going through Gervase's mind, but she tried to smile and be gracious thinking, perhaps, because of some misunderstanding with Richard, he was concerned for her well-being. Gervase has been very kind, I should dearly not wish to hurt him, she thought. She wondered if she might be the instrument to bring them together and the putting to rest of this confusion.

CHAPTER 8

Sir John raised his arm and the column came to a standstill, he waved Richard to his side and gestured with his hand.

'My home Richard, and yours for as long as you wish to stay. I will always have a place for the son of an old comrade. What do you think?'

'A fine home, Sir John.' Before them, Richard beheld a substantial, well-positioned castle. The ditch surrounding the structure, of what he judged had originally been of a typical motte and bailey construction; was now filled with water. Riding towards the castle drawbridge and gate, Richard could see that the walls were stone, suspecting that they would have once been timber, and there was the fine stone keep too. Sir John told him that he'd managed to retain the administration rights to the Forest of Dean, which eased the burden on his purse.

'I have been more fortunate than your family Richard, but that is thanks to my brother as I told you. It is my delight to share what I have with you.'

'I hope that I might earn my keep while I am with you Sir John.'

'There will ever be work for the likes of you, Richard.' The entourage rode into the yard and began dismounting. Sir John called for his son and he disappeared leaving Esther by her wain. She quickly took the opportunity to speak to Richard. She appeared slightly disconsolate.

'Sir Richard, I must ask a favour and I do not know who to turn to, you are the only person I really trust.'

'What about Gervase?'

'Yes, he is very attentive, but… well let me leave that for now.'

'I will do whatever I am able.'

'I have some coin on the wain and I am worried that it may be stolen, I don't know what to do.'

'Show me quickly before there are eyes with the time to pry.' Esther took him to the wain and pointed under some rugs to a small wooden coffer. Without hesitation, Richard pushed the rugs to one side and quickly removed the chest. He walked past Esther, as he was passing, he whispered, 'don't let us be seen conversing, I will see to this. Fear not we will talk soon and I will explain. Have you the key safe?'

'Yes.'

'Keep it safe and this moment to yourself,' and he walked off to his packhorse and placed the chest amongst his belongings. At that moment, he saw Sir John and Sir Gervase leaving a building and striding towards the activity. Sir John came to him and Gervase went smiling to Esther.

'Are you being attended to Richard?'

'Yes Sir, may I ask Sir John if you have a strong room where I might for safety, keep what few things of value I have.'

'I have such a room Richard, but I alone have a key, are you at ease with that?'

'Of course.'

'Then come, I will take you there first so that you may be free to continue your unpacking.' Richard followed him into the keep, Sir John told him he would allot a personal servant to both Esther and him. They climbed up a narrow spiral staircase to a door that must have been near the top of the keep, Richard guessed by the number of steps they had climbed.

Sir John spoke again, in between gasping for breath; it had been quite a climb.

'I have arranged for two rooms… near to each other… so that you may keep an eye out for Esther's well-being… I fancy some space between her room, and Gervase's room would be a wise thing.' Richard made no comment. 'Forgive me Richard, would you wait outside, it's not that I distrust you, but I never allow anyone in here.'

'That's quite in order Sir.' Richard set down Esther's coffer and his saddle-bag. Sir John unlocked the door and reached down for the bag and coffer. Richard noticed Sir John's surprise at the weight, but he made no comment, inside the door, he saw him set the two items on a small table and light some sealing wax.

'Your ring Richard.'

Richard removed his ring and passed it to him.

He sealed both the coffer and the bag, by melting wax either side of their openings, with cord across the joint, and pressed Richard's ring into the hot wax.

'I have sealed both of these Richard, with your personal seal, you can be assured that no one will have tampered with them when you retrieve them. Are you quite at peace with this arrangement?'

'I could not ask for more Sir.'

They walked from the keep onto the courtyard and Richard saw a servant standing by his baggage. Esther looked nervously in his direction. Gervase went to his father and sounded to be arguing with him. Richard nodded surreptitiously and she smiled.

Gervase flicked his hand in disgust as he left his father and strode to Esther's side.

'Father has given you a room, against my wishes, near that fellow,' he gestured in Richard's direction. 'If he gives you any trouble or annoyance, you must inform me immediately and I will have his hide removed.' Esther sighed, whatever was he thinking?

Two servants came to Esther, 'My Lord has sent us to you my Lady to take you and your belongings to your rooms,' the girl said, and they bowed.

'You, boy, see to the baggage, I will take the lady to her rooms.'

'Sir, my Lord wants to see you immediately, he sent me to tell you L-Lord. He is in his workroom in the hall,' the boy stammered, he seemed terrified.

'You must go to your father Gervase, this boy and the maids will attend to me, I will see you once I have washed and settled.'

'Humph...' was all he said and stormed off in the direction of the hall. Esther was relieved; this might give her a moment to talk to Richard alone.

Richard looked around the yard and wondered where Julianne was; she had disappeared the instant they had arrived. This is going to be fun, he thought.

Richard's new servant was called Alwin, a bright young man in his late teens; he was all that Richard could wish. Not the dregs of the castle that no one else wanted, and Richard took an instant liking to him. Sir John obviously wanted him to feel that he was an honoured guest.

'Who has been robbed that you might attend to my needs, Alwin?'

'I have served as one of Sir John's servants, Lord, he is a good master.'

'Aye, I imagine that be the truth of it. I will try to be such, Alwin,' Alwin bowed.

Alwin organised a tub for him and servants to fill it, there were even new robes laid out for him whilst he'd bathed.

'This is all very fine Alwin, you are treating me like a king.'

'I was told that you are to be treated as such Lord.'

'By whom, Sir Gervase no doubt?'

Alwin ceased his sorting of Richard's baggage, and raised his eyes, 'No Sir... it was not my Lord's son.' Richard smiled to himself, that was an interesting look from Alwin, he thought.

Once he was bathed and dressed in his new robes, Alwin led him to the hall for the evening mete. Richard felt uneasy, trying to prepare his mind for the unexpected. He had waited hoping to go down with Esther, but she was nowhere to be seen. If he were being honest with himself, he wasn't sure, if it was actually to support *her*, or to be supported *by* her, "Coward" he thought to himself as they made their way along the dimly lit passages.

When they entered, he was impressed; it was a very fine, spacious hall. A place intended to make an impact, even *intimidate* insecure visitors. It was clearly the visual manifestation of how this lord wished to be perceived. A man of affluence, taste, educated, a sportsman, and of course, devout. This hall spoke of all these attributes; the walls were plastered and finished with white lime wash, which reflected the light from the fire and candles, no stark stonework here, which absorbed the light, making for a dark gloomy atmosphere. To add further decoration, the white walls were lavishly painted with fine hunting scenes in red, orange, and yellow ochre's, there were even touches of expensive blue pigment used.

At the far end of the hall, where the Lord, his family and honoured guests sat on the raised dais, there was a splendid tapestry hung as a backdrop to the high table, depicting stories from biblical passages with the Blessed Virgin and Child seated above the place where Richard imagined Sir John would be seated. He noted that the Christ Child's hand was raised as if in blessing upon this lord and all who were invited to share in his benevolence. Everything displayed in this hall, every depiction was meticulously thought out and was a story with significance. The eye would be drawn to them and the narrative read, and understood. It was all very different from his home as he remembered it. However, this was the world he lived in, the victor took the spoils, crying made not the slightest difference. One must be very careful to pick the winning side. Kings did not favour those who stood against them, or their mother, in this King's case. Sir John had been very fortunate, very fortunate indeed, and *yet* he would have given all this up for friendship, but for his father's insistence that his friend disown him. Such as this, is what set people like his father, Sir John and William Marshal above other men, and Richard could not help but wonder if he were such a man, would he sacrifice all at the feet of honour?

He grimaced at one scene on the tapestry of a severed head being held aloft, John the Baptist he guessed, a man chosen by God but not accepted by God's children. He hoped this was not prophetic; there were some unsettling parallels too near home for his liking.

Richard was distracted he hadn't noticed Sir John, who welcomed him with a warm embrace. With him was a stranger, whom Sir John introduced as Sir Guy Molineux.

So… this is the courtly suitor, well not at all what I expected, thought Richard. The fellow bowed with great style, clearly a man who frequented the court and was well versed in presenting an image, which would never offend, yet leave one in no doubt that one was in the presence of a man of importance. He was pleasant enough; someone who was without doubt proficient at conversation devoid of any content, fortunately, he didn't require any response from Richard, who hoped that he smiled, or frowned, at all the correct places in the discourse. Though the man wanted to give the impression that he was only concerned with Richard, Richard was conscious, that his eyes told a different tale. They were constantly on the move scanning those who entered.

'Ahh, *Julianne*,' Sir John broke into Sir Guy's mindless flow. She had now deigned to honour all with her presence. Richard had to concede; she was truly beautiful. Whatever her wilful nature, her beauty, he would *not* deny. She was dressed in a light linen chemise shaped to her waist, with a golden belt resting on her hips and tied loosely at the front, the ends hanging nearly to the floor. The under garment was covered by a rich red over tunic edged with a golden border enhanced with fine embroidery. Her hair was braided and swept around her head reflecting the light and taking on the appearance of a circuit of gold. At her neck, she wore the emerald, which had belonged to her mother.

Sir Guy scuttled to her side, bowing with exaggerated flourish and kissing her hand, any courtly politeness of begging to be excused by Richard, before rushing to the side of this goddess, suddenly a mere inconsequential irrelevance.

Richard was surprised when he saw them together; Sir Guy was only slightly taller than Julianne. Now that he could study Sir Guy at a distance, Richard thought that he was lacking some exercise by the look of his shape. He was compelled to smile; in his opinion, the poor fellow would be fortunate if he were rejected by Julianne. They would both be fools to commit to such an unfulfilling future, which would make neither happy, but then again Richard thought that perhaps he was wrong, and such a relationship would suit both parties very well.

Not all married for love; to some such a sacrament was more of a pragmatic contract, a vehicle for advancement. It had ever been so with kings, of which King Henry was the perfect example. He was reputed to have loved Eleanor, but he did his coffers no harm by the connection, she may not have been so loveable if she'd been poor.

With such a marriage, Sir Guy would be able to display a wife who would make him the envy of all his peers. Such a wife could well be a great advantage if one wanted advancement at court. *She* would have position and status without the added complication of feelings disturbing the waters, *and,* all the better to look down on the likes of me, Richard thought, and smiled again, but this game had changed he was certain.

There was no chance to speak to Esther she was the object of Gervase's total attention, relationships might well be made in heaven, but they were often played out in Hell,

Richard thought. He could not help comparing the two ladies, Esther was beautiful too, that was without doubt, but she was a total contrast to Julianne. Her dress was plain, simple colours, no flourishes of sparkling gold. She was dark whereas Julianne was fair. *Her* beauty shone from her nature, gentle, kind, ever willing to see the good. Too good for the likes of Gervase, he would crush her.

'No, I will never allow that to happen,' Richard swore under his breath.

Sir John insisted Richard be seated on the high table next to him, Gervase sat at the other side of his father, and next to him, Esther. Immediately to Richard's left, "Oh what joy" he thought, when he realised that space was to be occupied by Julianne, then next to her, Sir Guy. When he looked at Julianne, she did not appear to be overwhelmed by the delight of Sir Guy's company, not until that is, that she saw Richard looking in her direction, then she was positively gushing towards the poor innocent, laughing, and touching him.

'Ha,' his life had depended for too long on making the right judgement, and he would wager his life on his understanding at this moment.

It was an excellent meal; Julianne was careful not to make any physical contact with Richard even though they were in such close proximity and she certainly never spoke to him. The whole situation would have been amusing, but for Richard's concern for Esther. He glanced several times past Sir John and she looked to be struggling with the excessive attention from Gervase. However, as far as Richard was concerned, he enjoyed the conversation with Sir John, and Sir John appeared to be enjoying the time with him.

Halfway through the meal Sir John stood and announced that there was to be a feast and dancing on the morrow's night. This was received with cheers and banging on the tables by those dining, even Gervase seemed pleased, however, his pleasure was not reflected on Julianne's face.

When Richard returned to his room, he sat by the fire with a cup of wine. He was alone, Alwin had taken his clothes to be washed and had left Richard to his thoughts. He rolled the cup back and forth in between the palms of his hands, trying to assemble all his thoughts, when there was a knock on the door. It didn't register at first, there was another knock, and he pushed himself up and went to answer the door. He opened it, there stood a maid.

'Yes.'

'Beggin' your pardon Sir, the lady Esther wonders if she might speak to you in her room for a moment?'

Richard, hesitated for a second, then nodded and closed his door, 'Lead on.' The maid showed him to Esther's room and waited outside.

Esther stood when he entered, 'Thank you for coming Richard, I'm sorry we never had the opportunity to talk this night. I wondered what had become of my coffer, here please be seated,' she offered him a seat by the fire. Richard paused then took the seat offered, he was uneasy, concerned as to the wisdom of such a meeting, Esther seated herself opposite him.

'I'm not sure Gervase would find this meeting to his liking, Esther.'

'Maybe... but he has been quite good company tonight, perhaps he is happy now he is home.'

'I would wish it so, but I will reserve judgement if I may, I do not want to be the one to test that understanding. In any event, you ask about your coffer. It is safe for the time being in Sir John's treasure room, I pray that you can find peace in that. He is the only one with access, he did not even allow me inside, and he sealed your coffer with my seal,' and he lifted his hand to show her.

'Thank you, it is family wealth for which I am alone responsible. It is all I have in the world now.'

'What about your family in York, what are your plans?'

'What family there are, are the children of grandfather's brother, I have never met them. You see, my mother was Jewish, and my father was French, so I have always lived on the periphery of my people. My mother and father were killed with my sister, Miriam, when a mob set fire to our house. I escaped with grandfather. He said we would return to his family in York where no one would know I was not wholly Jewish, and that's where we were going when he was killed.

Richard listened to the tragic story; he didn't know what to say. He hoped that his concern showed in his face for it was sincere.

'Really, Richard I feel quite alone. I can't stay here forever; I don't know what to do. I do hope that Gervase has softened towards you so that we may talk and be friends. Pray God that we have not always to speak in secret, if that is the case, well I can't think on that.' Esther's eyes filled with tears and she brushed them away with the heel of her hand trying bravely to stop her chin from shaking.

'We have the feast tomorrow let us not rush ahead. You are tired and our woes always look their most formidable at such a time. I want you to take strength from the truth that I am your friend, and I will take care that you come to no harm. You know I am a great knight, *you* told me so,' she tried to smile. 'Let us be brother and sister, we will care for each other for I have lost everything too, my home, my parents, just as you have, but neither of us are penniless.'

'I'm sorry, forgive my self-pity, I didn't know that you too were alone.' He stood and took her hand, raised her from her chair and embraced her and she sobbed quietly against his chest.

'I'm sorry Richard,' she said wiping her face, 'I suddenly felt very alone and your kindness touched me. You are God's gift to me,' she whispered looking into his eyes.

'I will leave you now, do not be afraid.'

CHAPTER 9

It was the day of the feast; Richard spent his time trying to keep out of everyone's way. He wasn't looking forward to this evening, his mind was racing, trying to second-guess and be prepared for every eventuality. He walked to the stable, stood at the door, took a deep breath, and went to Ares; Ares heard him, turned, his mouth full of hay and bobbed his head. Richard stepped over to him ran his hand along his back and tugged affectionately at his ear.

'Hello old friend, it's all a mess I've led us into. Perhaps we should just saddle up and sneak away, take our chance and forget this brief interlude.' He sat on the low wall of the manger, rested his arms on his knees, and hung his head. 'You know Ares; our friend William Marshal has a lot to answer for. He's landed me with a conscience, and the sole purpose for a conscience the best I can see, is to make life complicated.'

Bright sunlight slowly lit up the stable as the door was pushed open.

'Richard, you're alone! I thought that I heard you talking to someone.'

'Oh Esther, you startled me! I was deep in thought *and* having a conversation with a not too intelligent person.' Esther looked around wondering whom he meant. Richard smiled, 'Forgive me, dearest Esther, I have confused you now. I meant that I was discussing our predicament with *myself*, I think Ares was showing some interest, though it was difficult for him to give me his full attention in the middle of his midday meal.'

She laughed, 'Oh, and I thought that it was only I, who was slowly going mad,' she laughed again. 'I saw you walking in this direction and I assumed that you were coming to see your faithful friend. I hoped that we might have a moment to ourselves, if we could only spend *some* time together to speak without the relentless pressure… You are the only stranger here who perhaps feels a little intimidated as I do, and neither of us have anyone else to turn to. I feel so wretched as I say this, because everyone is trying so hard to be kind, I only wish they would let me *be* for a second. I honestly don't think I can go to the feast tonight. I could scream sometimes. You are the only one who talks to me as if what – *I* – might want, is of the slightest concern.'

Richard smiled, 'Mmm, who knows, you might enjoy it tonight. I must be honest too, I came here in a similar frame of mind, though perhaps I am not subjected to *quite* so much kindness as you,' she laughed.

'Then you may be more fortunate, I will trade places if you wish.'

'Kind – as I will assume is the intention of your offer…' they both smiled again, '…to be subjected to Gervase's endless fawning would I fear be worse than being subjected to his endless loathing.'

'What you assume to be so, believe me I'm sure *is* so.'

'My poor little mouse, I have found over the years that it helps to discuss my problems with Ares. He's very wise you know, *and,* I like to be sure he's well and has all he needs, that provides some light distraction.'

'You really love him, don't you?'

'Who, Gervase?'

She threw her head back and laughed so heartily there were tears in her eyes, 'No – I meant Ares.'

'Ah, well – we have spent many hours together, when death served over a cold grave, was all the day had to offer, believe me those times make for a close relationship. Yes, I love him, when you love animals, they love you, all very simple. One can learn a lot from animals, particularly horses.'

'It is good to be with you Richard you cannot imagine the release. Would you like to go for a ride, I am at a loose end everyone seems busy, even Gervase has left me in peace this day.'

Richard smiled, 'Why not, we will get to know what Sir John's estate had to offer. I'll call the lad and get you organised with a mount. I'm feeling better already, just at the thought.' Richard was about to call the stable lad when another shadow entered the stable through the now open door, Esther turned, and her heart dropped.

'You're there Esther, I have been looking for you, I have arranged a gown for you, one of my sister's. She *also* wants you to feel welcome. Come, we must go.'

'Actually Gervase, I was about to go riding with Richard.'

'Come, we have no time to linger; I will take you riding when you are done, this is *my* home and I know all the best places. But first the dress, I want you to shine for all to see.'

Gervase spoke as if Richard wasn't there. Richard smiled at Esther, gave a slight nod of his head, Gervase took her arm and steered her out of the stable and away from Richard, before she had a chance to argue.

Richard sat once more on the wall, reached into the manger, took a stalk of hay, and began to contemplatively chew on it.

'Poor Esther, just we two once more Ares; come we will go for a ride on our own, no one it seems has found *me* a dress to wear this night,' Ares nodded, Richard smiled, 'I'm sure you understand every word I say, my dear friend.'

'Can I help you, Lord?' A young voice startled him.

'Aye, John isn't it? I'll go and fetch my gambeson, if you will saddle Ares. Take care and talk to him, he's uncomfortable with strangers.'

'You're too late with your advice Lord, we's already made friends,' he said laughing.

Richard laughed too. 'You are honoured indeed, John,' and he patted him on the shoulder, as he left.

Richard returned to the stable, thanked the stable lad, mounted Ares, who skittered a little and trotted towards the main gate. Richard needed to take some of the tension out of his muscles and he was sure some vigorous exercise was what was required. They'd clattered their way steadily over the wooden drawbridge, but once outside the walls they set off at full tilt. Ares' ears were laid back, and his tail streamed out behind him. The cold air was bracing and bit into Richard's cheeks, but he felt exhilarated.

They galloped for ten minutes or so and gradually they slowed to a gentle trot, both Richard and Ares were puffing and blowing. 'Phew, that was good.' Richard steered Ares in the direction of a small stream, where a flock of sheep was trying to eke out a meal from the sparse winter's covering of grass, they looked up and scattered before him, Richard drew Ares to a standstill and patted his neck.

'Mmmm,' he sighed mindlessly brushing some flecks of mud from his thigh.

'What to do, I feel in a bit of a trap, old boy, but for Esther I would pack up this night, and make back to Aquitaine and find William Marshal. We had some difficult times, but naught like the place I find myself in at this moment.' He couldn't leave Esther to her own devices and Sir John would be saddened if he said it was too difficult with his children. He didn't want to be responsible for splitting up a family. Wearily he turned Ares and made his way back.

Outside the castle stable, he sat for a moment, and then slowly slipped from Ares saddle and the young stable lad came to him. 'I'll see to him Lord; he'll be shining like a new boot when you sees him next.'

'Aye, I'm sure he will, thank you John, I can see he likes you. You're honoured indeed.'

Richard watched as the lad led Ares into the stable. He pressed his hands to the small of his back and stretched. Looking to the door of the keep, he slung his gambeson over his shoulder and set off in the direction of his room.

'Ah, Sir Richard, the lady Esther's been asking if you'd returned from your ride.'

'Did she say what she wanted, Alwin?'

'Said it didn't matter, she would see you tonight at the feast.' Richard hesitated for a second, shook his head, and asked Alwin to organise a bath for him.

When Richard entered the hall for the feast, he immediately caught the eye of Sir John.

'Ah Richard, good to see you, I have neglected you this day forgive me, it has been hectic. This is when a man needs a wife.'

'Do not concern yourself, Sir John, I have been riding and enjoying the sights. This is a fine holding, a beautiful place.'

'Thank you, come with me to our seats there will be music while we feast and dancing afterwards, Julianne is a fine dancer. Do *you* dance?'

'Yes, one would not have lasted very long in the palace at Poitiers if one could not dance, though I am no courtier. Perhaps Sir Guy will help me with such skills.'

'Aye – that fellow could charm the birds from the trees. But come, mete first.'

The seating arrangements were the same as the first night. There were many new faces, beautiful women by the score. They were seated before Julianne appeared, followed by Sir Guy. Their relationship had moved on in leaps and bounds, Julianne actually gave Richard a curt nod as he stood when she came to her seat.

After the meal as Sir John had promised, the dancing began, several ladies were introduced to Richard by Sir John and every one a beauty, at one-point Richard was in conversation with three at the same time. His mood lightened, he was actually beginning to enjoy the evening, and he was pleased to see that even *Esther* was allowed to expand her circle of acquaintances by dancing with other men. He was not sure what all that meant; perhaps some boost to Gervase's pride to see others desiring *his* lady. Poor Esther, at least she appeared to be happy. Unlike Julianne, who was at this moment looking in his direction, with an extremely miserable countenance.

'You are attracting quite a following tonight, Richard. No doubt word has spread of your fame.'

'Your daughter does not seem to be enjoying herself quite so much.'

'Don't you know why? Ask her to dance.'

'You jest, have you no care for a friend's life.' Sir John threw back his head and laughed. Their conversation was interrupted and Sir John excused himself, leaving Richard on his own. He saw that Julianne was also standing alone. Richard smiled, hesitated and went to her and bowed.

'May I share this rondel with you, my Lady?'

She seemed so shocked that she bowed and offered him her hand. None too soon, for as Richard took her hand Sir Guy returned, he bowed as they took the floor.

'May I say how beautiful you look my Lady Julianne?'

'One of many you have danced with tonight.'

'Julianne, might we not be friends, I am sorry if I have given offence, it was not my intention.'

'You – offend me! People of no consequence do not offend me.'

'I imagine not, the problem for you is that I am of consequence to you.'

'You flatter yourself.' She made to pull free of him and return to Sir Guy, but he held her tightly.

'I'm going to tell you something, that you will have to have to face up to sooner or later.'

'You are a soothsayer now? I wish to end this dance and return to Sir Guy.'

'I am not a soothsayer, but I can see with my heart. We are in love with each other.' Her mouth almost dropped open; she could only stare at him.

'You – love – *me*!' She gave him the strangest look, and he was certain, and she knew it, but she quickly composed herself. 'Not if you were the last man on earth.'

The music ended, he bowed, and she curtseyed. She strode quickly to Sir Guy's side, taking his arm and kissing his cheek.

Richard smiled, 'Julianne you are so predictable, and he, the lamb to the slaughter. Whatever you have said to Sir Guy he has swallowed it hook line and sinker for he looks exceedingly pleased.'

Julianne almost dragged Sir Guy to her father. Richard frowned, as he watched, Sir John seemed to be frowning too.

'What is she up to now,' Richard said to himself, intrigued by the intensity of their conversation. Sir John lifted his hands in a gesture almost of surrender and then stood on the dais and called everyone to attention.

'It is my pleasure to announce my daughter's betrothal to Sir Guy Molineux.' There was loud cheering and clapping.

No wonder Sir John looked flustered, this had clearly not been expected, or Sir John would surely have mentioned it thought Richard. Dowries and contracts couldn't have been discussed, this is my fault, 'Dear oh dear, you foolish girl. Your wilfulness and pride I have greatly underestimated, fool that I am.' Julianne made sure he saw her looking at him this time, he knew that she was putting him in his place. 'You fool,' he said again to himself.

A young woman came to his side, 'Are you not happy for Sir Guy, Sir Richard?' He was distracted.

'I beg your pardon my Lady.'

'You do not appear to share the joy of the happy couple, perhaps you would like to dance?'

'Why not, my Lady Margaret, isn't it?'

'I am flattered, that you recall my name; you have attracted a great deal of attention this night. Your fame has spread quickly round this assembly.'

Richard danced with the Lady Margaret. He thanked her politely, made his excuses, and waked to the door, he'd had enough of feasting to last a lifetime. Someone took his arm just as he was about to leave; he turned to see Sir John.

'What do you make of that, Richard?'

'Very good my Lord, they have known each other for some time, you told me.'

'Richard, don't let this happen.'

'Ha, I am a humble knight with little prospects, what can I do? I will beg your leave to go, Sir John.'

'Certainly,' he said sadly, squeezed Richard's arm and returned to the feast. Richard glanced once more into the room before he left and noticed Julianne's eyes upon him; there was no smile now. Perhaps she had realised the price she was going to pay for that hollow victory, he thought as he turned, and left.

CHAPTER 10

Several weeks had slipped past since the day of the great feast, most of Richard's days were spent working with Sir John, training men or inspecting his holdings on his estate, some were quite large, others were no more than a single hide.

The land seemed fertile and the animals were healthy. Sir John's main concern at this time of year was that his people had shown due concern and prepared wisely for their winter provisions and he inspected their stores diligently. Mete was often in short supply and it was easy to neglect preparation for the future when your family were hungry today. From what Richard could glean, Sir John cared that his serfs had ample provision of both meat and cereal.

Richard could see that Sir John was not a Lord whose only concern was the short-term filling of his coffers. He clearly saw that to look after those who served him would prove to be the surest way to sustained riches. Richard knew that some Lords ravaged the land for every penny and became the poorer for it. They sold all their grain and next season there was none to sow. Greed made for a poor return in the long-term, and flogging those who were starving would not add one single groat to a coffer, or ear of barley to next year's harvest. Alas, the latter type of Lord seemed the more prevalent. He thought perhaps in time their kind would give way to more enlightened masters.

At first, he was concerned by the attention Sir John was affording him, fearing that there may well be repercussions for both him and Sir John. He need not have troubled himself, it seemed that Sir Gervase was totally occupied with Esther, and Julianne was fully distracted by her forthcoming wedding. They only congregated briefly at meal times and not always then, one or another would often be absent. From what Richard saw of Julianne, she was unusually reserved, none of her normal hostile quick wit, she seemed very subdued. He knew he should have been glad of the change, but he was not. He was sorry for her, she had boxed herself into a hellish place, and this could be her lifetime's hope. No doubt, it was her wilfulness, which had brought this state upon her, but he could take no delight in that for he knew *her* life, and *his* life, were as one, for better or worse.

The days after the feast were a drudge to him; he tried to avoid all; he didn't want to engage in incidental conversation. The only company he tolerated with any equanimity was Sir John's, he would have liked to spend time with Esther, but that was never possible. He knew that this situation couldn't last he was ever aware of Esther's increasing entrapment, which only added to his suffering and feeling of despair. He wrote to William Marshal to explain his current predicament and asked if he had any advice, the constant complication was Esther; he couldn't leave her to fend for herself, he really didn't know which way to turn.

He remembered his father's last words to him before he left for Normandy. He had held the bridle of his horse and looked to him; their gaze was held by the intensity of the moment. "A man is not measured by his years, Son. You will not wander far from the right course if you remember always to *earnestly* desire the Lord's path above all others, for the alternative is a way most fearful to man. Do this, and *He* will make straight *your* paths. I have not much in a worldly sense Richard, as you well know, and I have many concerns for the people who look to me for their care, but I am at peace with my Maker and believe me, that is a fine place to be".

His thoughts drew him to the small castle chapel; he went in, hoping to avoid the priest, Father Francis, he wanted to be alone. I want to hear from God, not be patronised by that fat sanctimonious turd, he thought to himself. He dipped his fingers in the holy water at the door, crossed himself, genuflected, walked to the chancel steps, and knelt.

'Blessed Mother of Christ, pray for me a sinner,' he paused unsure how to proceed. 'This is such a moment of which my father spoke, show me the way, I have a fearful responsibility for Esther, a child of Abraham, and because of my concern for her I feel I must place her before *my* wants, Amen.'

After praying he remained on his knees for some time, wanting to say more, but powerless to assemble his thoughts. He knew he didn't consult God often enough, and felt ashamed to come to Him only now when he was desperate. I don't suppose God will give my problems a second thought, why should He, most of the time I never think of Him. I wish I could ride with Him or even fish with Him. He liked fishing I seem to recall; just the two of us, but there always seems to be some priest blocking His door who will take my message to Him if *he* thinks it suitable, or he might pass it on to the Blessed Virgin, she probably gives it to an angel. Such a convoluted route, no wonder He never answers my prayers, not so I've noticed anyway, they probably got lost on the way to Him. Richard stared around the church just in case a shadowy guardian of the holy order of priests was listening to his iniquitous thoughts and was about to wreak a terrible vengeance upon him. Gervase could well be his weapon of choice.

Thinking once more of Esther he was unable to recall when he had quite so deliberately placed someone before himself, and yet, strangely, he felt that he was without a choice, something *in* him was compelling him to do this. Was this what William Marshal had meant, when he'd said, "When you find true honour it will become your very nature, and empower you to do what is right. If one has to decide to be honourable one will fail, we must be empowered by our hearts not our minds".

He crossed himself, stood, glanced once more at the large wooden crucifix, and fleetingly wondered why the risen Lord should forever be portrayed in defeat. He thought that an empty cross would have proclaimed His victory over evil much more vividly, which was the message he needed to hear, even better an empty tomb. He shrugged his shoulders what did he know; priests didn't encourage their flock to question. He had found that out very early in his life when he had been severely flogged by his father's priest for saying the host was no more than stale dried bread.

He dipped his fingertips once more into the holy water as he left; he crossed himself and reverently closed the narthex door. Striding towards the keep and his room, he felt unaccountably at peace even though his understanding of the way forward was no clearer.

On entering the keep he met Julianne, he bowed, as did she. She hesitated, as if she was about to say something, but she must have thought better of it and walked on without a word. He turned to watch her go, as she was about to set foot on the stair at the other end of the passageway, she glanced back towards him and their eyes met. He dearly wanted to go to her and take her in his arms, but in the blink of an eye, she was gone. He lingered for a moment longer, 'No – Julianne has decided! I must accept that it is God's will, though I will never understand it, she is lost to me, help me Lord.'

It was early, before sunlight when Richard heard knocking on his door.

'Lord, Lord,' a voice called. Richard couldn't quite make sense of the knocking at first, the voice called again.

'One moment, I'm coming.' Richard rubbed his eyes and slipped on his breeches, picked up his dagger and opened the door. 'Alwin, why in the name of the Mother of Christ, are you knocking at my door at this hour of the night?'

'I'm sorry Lord; I was instructed to bring you this immediately. It's a dispatch that has in the last few moments, been given to me; the rider has ridden from London this night, and is in the hall as we speak being given mete. I think he waits in the event you wish him to carry a reply.'

'From London you say, but no one knows of my residence here!' Richard took the document from his hands. 'Fetch me water to bathe Alwin, and mete too, while I read this.' Richard seated himself at his table and lit a candle. He pressed the edge of his dagger under the seal, at the same time examining it; it looked like the King's seal, in the name of Christ what would he want of *me*. He had seen the seal once before on a document the Queen had given to William Marshal, it was of an armoured knight on horseback, his sword drawn. Once opened, he could see it *was* from the King himself; he was surprise that the *King of England* had even heard of him. The letter was commanding his loyal servant, Sir Richard Maillorie, on the recommendation of Queen Eleanor, to make haste to his court at Westminster and be of service to his King and Lord.

This can only be of William Marshal's doing, thought Richard. He stood, 'Mmm, there is much to think of.' He donned a robe, walked to Esther's room, and knocked; her maid came to her door.

'Awake your mistress I must talk to her, it is urgent.'

'Who is it, Matilda?' He heard Esther call out.

'Lord Richard, Ma'am.'

'One moment Richard.' She slipped on her robe and went to the door. 'Enter my Lord, be seated,' she was taken-a-back to see Richard so dishevelled, which added to her immediate anxiety. 'Whatever is it Richard, are you hurt in some way?'

Richard bowed, 'No, I am well, I have not time to sit Esther, I have been summoned by the King and must go immediately to his palace at Westminster.' She pressed her knuckles to her mouth.

'Fear not, I will not leave you here, you must come with me, if it is your wish to do so, if you are to come you must dress now and pack. The King will expect me to respond to his instruction without any delay. I will speak to

Sir John and I am sure he will give permission and allow you to take your maid.'

'Thank God, oh thank God; fear was my first thought that you might be leaving me to my fate. I will ready myself and make my way to the hall as you ask, but if you take me, will I not merely be an additional burden to you?'

'No, ready yourself and wait here, I don't want you to be accosted by your friend. Esther you are no burden to me, the dear Lord has placed our lives side by side and I will be thankful. I don't understand any of this, but I trust Him, that in whatever condition I find myself He is able to keep me.'

'I think the sun will be well up before we need fear a meeting with Gervase, he was in his cups last night and had to be carried to his rooms.'

'How tragic, just the same, wait here; girl, see to mete for your mistress and have her things packed, quickly to it.' The girl scuttled off at a pace. Richard met Alwin and servants with the bathing water he'd asked for. 'Thank you Alwin, this will be sufficient I do not have time to fully bathe; a wash will have to suffice this day. See to my belongings and pack for yourself too, I will ask that you might come with me.'

Alwin smiled, 'Thanks be, I'm honoured Lord. I will see to mete for you this very moment, and for the journey.'

'Thank you, you are a fine fellow Alwin,' Richard patted his back. 'I will return in a short while, then I will bathe, but first I must see Sir John.' With that, Richard hastily made off in the direction of Sir John's rooms.

Richard knocked on the door it was Sir John who opened it, which startled him; he was equally surprised that Sir John was fully dressed.

'Richard.'

'Sir John!'

'I knew it would be you.'

'But how?'

'Ha, do you think that a messenger from the King of England might arrive here in the middle of the night and I would *not* be informed, I recognised his seal as soon as it was shown to me?'

'Of course not, how foolish of me.'

'It was I who sent Alwin to you with the document. Might I ask what was in the said correspondence?'

'Certainly – I have been ordered to go to the King in London who is at the palace of Westminster, directly. I have favours to ask of you Sir John.'

'You are like a son to me Richard, I will do aught I can for you, with some regret, for I will be saddened to lose your company.'

Richard hesitated, 'Sir, I think Esther should come with me; she is overwhelmed by Sir Gervase's attention, it has been relentless since she came, and she needs time to think on her future. She will need a servant; would it be possible for us to retain the services of Alwin and Matilda for the time being?'

'All shall be as you wish Richard, anything I can do for you I will. I must implore that you take Sir Tristram and Sir Raymond with you, for the sake of safety. One thing do I beg, that this remains your home and you will return when you can.' The two men embraced.

'I will need coin; will you take me to my saddle bag Sir?'

'I will if you wish, but it may be wise to leave it where it is safe for the time being, until you are clearer what is to be demanded of you, it will be an added concern to travel with a large amount of coin. I would advise the same for Esther, I assume the coffer was hers, but my advice is subservient to your wishes. I have coin here for you. You have worked hard and asked for no reward, take this and shame me not,' and Sir John reached to him with a leather draw purse in his hand. There was so much activity in Richard's mind at this moment he could only stare at it. 'Take it – you have earned it, and more,' Sir John shook the bag.

'But Lord…' Richard was confused he had too much to think on, 'Very well, I will take this, but only as a loan until we meet again.'

'Nonsense, but if you must, though in truth I am not good with coin and I forget easily,' he smiled. 'Go now ready yourself and *I* will see to your horses and men.'

Richard quickly prepared himself; Alwin was delighted to be going with him. He helped Richard dress in his hauberk and plate armour, he knew as well as Richard that being so few they must be prepared for any aggression towards their party. He ate the mete Alwin had fetched him as he dressed.

Esther was ready and waiting when he went for her. There will be hell to pay when Gervase finds out we have gone, he thought, but he made no mention to Esther of his fears, no doubt she was fully aware without him needing to say aught.

They made their way to the courtyard like thieves in the night. It was a cold but a bright morning, the frost sparkled on the stonework as the new day's light touched it. The horses pawed at the hard earth and snorted plumes of steam from their nostrils. Richard took Esther's hand as she stepped from the mounting block into the saddle, then he went to Sir Raymond and Sir Tristram and offered his hand to each, they smiled and nodded.

'I can only apologise for the untimely disturbance of your night's rest,' he offered smiling.

'We will tell the King of your wilfulness when we see him. No doubt he will be filled with remorse for sending for you at such an hour,' they all laughed. Richard went next to Sir John and they embraced once more.

'Remember this is your home Richard, write and tell me your news, you will try to attend Julianne's wedding?'

'I will Lord, and thank you, my father had the best friend a man could wish for in you.' Richard mounted, there were eight in total in the party, and they set off, with a final wave from Sir John.

CHAPTER 11

They travelled south, it was a well-worn route and the journey of a few weeks past had refreshed Richard's memory.

'We will have to stop somewhere tonight, and with an early start we should make London the next day. However, I think that we'll stop short of the city on our second night, and make our way to Westminster in the daylight of the following day, what do you think?' Richard asked his companions.

'Aye better travelling through cities in daylight as thee says. There are fellows there who'd steal your horse from under you if you were distracted for but a breath,' offered Sir Raymond smiling.

'How are you Esther?' asked Richard.

'It's wonderful to be in the fresh air even though it is cold. I seem to have been looking constantly over my shoulder for weeks. I don't know how I would have survived if you had left me behind.'

'Our lives have become intertwined for the while. I have had less agreeable soul mates these past years believe me Esther. The Blessed Virgin has been generous to me this time,' they both smiled.

It was indeed cold, but there was no snow. The ground was hard which made for easy travel. They rode, when it was possible, at the edge of the tracks to avoid the ruts left from wagon wheels. The ruts were filled with ice, it would be dangerous for a horse to step on the ice, which perhaps covered a deep rut, it could result in a broken leg, and that wasn't worth the risk.

Sir Tristram had fallen behind to watch their rear and Sir Raymond had ridden ahead. Richard twisted around in his saddle when he heard Sir Tristram galloping towards them. Sir Raymond must have heard him too for he turned his horse and looked back to them. Tristram drew his horse slipping and sliding to a standstill alongside Richard and Esther.

'What is it Sir Tristram?'

'There are riders coming up behind us, no more than a league I would think. I saw them from the brow of that hill,' he pointed. 'I recognise the lead horse…'

'*And?*'

'I fear that it's Sir Gervase and riding as if old Beelzebub is after his soul.'

'Hell's teeth,' Richard said beating his fist on his thigh. Richard waved to Sir Raymond and he cantered to join them.

'Trouble?' Sir Raymond called as he neared them.

'The answer to that question is yet to be known, but I suspect it may well be yes. We will ride into that thicket and await their arrival. That will give us the upper hand of surprise. How many were they?' He turned again to Tristram.

'Only six to my sure reckoning.'

'You fellows are all armed with swords,' he turned to their servants come squires, 'but stay behind us if there is fighting, I pray that there will not be, we knights will face that eventuality first.' They steered their horses to the thicket then brought them round at the edge to face the road, and waited.

'Don't be afraid Esther, whatever happens I fancy *you* will be safe,' Richard said leaning over to her.

'What comfort is that if you are hurt or worse?'

'Here they come, it is Sir Gervase right enough; in truth, I feared he might put in an appearance. I will ride out to challenge them when they come closer, the rest of you hold back.'

Suddenly Richard burst from his cover onto the road and drew his horse to a standstill. The surprise caused a moment of equine panic with horses colliding.

'Why all the speed Sir Gervase, is there some problem?' Richard noted that they must have left in haste for they were not even wearing their hauberks. Once Gervase had pulled his horse under control he pushed next to Richard.

'*You* are the problem; you have abducted Esther.'

'Nonsense – we left with your father's blessing on the King's business. Which is more than I warrant *you* did.' Richard looked now to the other five riders and spoke in a very calm unequivocal voice. 'You – would do well – to measure any actions with a thought to *your* Lord and *your* King's pleasure. To invoke their *displeasure* may not bode well with you.' Richard hoped by focusing their thoughts, they would consider mindfully where their loyalties lay, and not be prepared to take such a risk of angering Sir John never mind the King, and certainly *not* for Gervase's petty vanity.

'Ignore – *him* – he is of no account,' Gervase snarled and looked around for Esther, seeing her in the thicket he called to her, '*Esther* – you are safe now, come to me.'

'She stays!' Gervase turned to Richard, and in blind fury, he leapt for him. He had no facial protection whatsoever and Richard struck him a savage blow to his face with his armoured hand at the instant he left his saddle. The blow stopped him in mid-air, his nose collapsed blood splashed over his face and he crashed heavily to the ground in between his horse and Richard's. Richard quickly pulled Ares away for fear he might trample Gervase, for that was what he was trained to do, to fall at his feet usually meant sudden death.

Richard turned to the other riders with Gervase and fixed them with a look of flint. They sat frozen in their saddles and *not* because of the cold morning. Richard had judged them rightly; they were not taking any risks to their well-being for a fool like Gervase. Esther remained in the thicket, but Sir Tristram and Sir Raymond had moved forward to lend gravity to Richard's threat. Richard was moved that these two men were prepared to stand with him, a relative stranger, against five other knights who they had known for some time.

'I suggest you pick up our friend and tie him over his saddle until you get home, make sure he is wrapped in his cloak, he should be kept warm. Explain to Sir John exactly what happened, then make yourselves scarce for the next… *year*,' they laughed, 'because this fellow is going to be in a great deal of pain when he awakes and not in the most affable of moods.'

'We were ordered to come, what could we do? He was beside himself with rage when he found out you had gone with the lady and *wisdom* was a lost friend to him. Sir William mentioned that he should at least don some more clothing; he was still in his cups from the night past. He pushed Sir William to the ground, and that is unacceptable treatment of a brother knight.' They dismounted and went to Gervase, one of the knights knelt, he looked up at Richard.

'Looks to me like he may have broken his arm in the fall, what a fool. There's also a deep gash to his cheek, it must have been from a rivet on your gauntlet. He is in a bit of a mess. We had better strap this arm the best we can for the ride home.'

'We will leave him in your capable hands – Sir Thomas, is it?'

'Aye.'

'We have a goodly way to travel and no time to waste. I trust you will tell the truth of this meeting.'

'Aye we will, or we will be taken for the fools we are, for ever getting ourselves caught up in this madness.'

Esther had never moved apart from straining her eyes in an attempt to see what was happening. Richard signalled to the group and they set off never looking back.

'This – will not end here Richard.' Esther said nervously to him.

'No, I fear not. Returning to Tattershall will be an interesting experience.'

'I have been nothing but trouble for you since we met. Pray God that it does not cost you your life for this day's work. Perhaps I should ride back with them – at least you will be safe.'

'I think not. I see little hope of reconciliation I'm afraid.'

CHAPTER 12

'We'll stay at Iledon, it's set on a hill just north of the city on Essex Street, dead ahead of us. I know the place, Sir Richard, I think it will serve us well.'

'I bow to your superior knowledge, Sir Raymond, you lead the way.'

They rode into the yard of the inn and two ostlers came to them. 'I will go in and see that they can accommodate us,' Sir Raymond offered, sliding from his horse. Richard smiled at Esther while they sat peacefully waiting; the only sound was the horses chomping on their bits.

It wasn't long before Sir Raymond returned and waved to them. 'We are welcome, and there is mete on the spit.'

'Excellent.'

They dismounted, Richard offered a hand to Esther, she leaned forward, and he took her by the waist and lowered her to the ground.

'See to the horses and baggage, Alwin.'

On entering the inn, Richard was informed that they only had one bedroom left, which would be suitable for him and his lady. His party would have to make the best of the floor in the hall. Richard smiled at Esther.

'Fear not "My Lady" it will be my pleasure to vacate the said room for your comfort.' She looked a little concerned at the arrangements, but managed a smile, the others laughed heartily at her discomfort. 'All is good, Esther, never fear. We will feast and talk, sleep and be on our way, first thing on the morrow's light. We must find lodgings in Westminster for you and the rest of our party thus we cannot linger here come morning.'

'Oh dear, I am a constant burden.'

'No, you are not, it is a privilege to be of service to you, really.' Alwin and the other two servants, Martin and Stephen came and helped the knights remove their armour and hauberks. Each was relieved to have the weight off their shoulders, for a few moments after being relieved of the burden Richard always felt to be floating.

They sat at one of the long tables and their mete and ale was set before them. The inn was busy, like-minded people wanting to rest the night before entering the great city. Three knights from the West Country were pleased to make themselves known to a man wearing William Marshal's device on his surcoat. Richard had to answer the usual questions, before they were able to move forward their conversation. They were *also* on their way to the palace of Westminster, one Sir Reginald Fizzurse was from Wilton in Somersetshire, another Sir William de Tracy from Brandninch near Exeter and the third Sir Richard le Breton from Sampford Brett in Somerset. They had ridden together; it appeared the King had need of loyal knights at this time. None of them could shed much light as to the exact reason why they had been summoned.

They speculated that it was something to do with the King's ongoing battle with the Church, the embodiment of which at this time manifested itself in the Archbishop of Canterbury – Thomas Becket. The consensus of opinion was, that Henry wanted to be sure in whose favour the balance of support weighed heaviest. Every move he'd made up to now he had been compelled to back down, but Becket was stubbornly intransigent. They all agreed that they had never known Henry try so single-mindedly to meet anyone halfway, and subservience was not a position suited to kings and certainly not this King. Even the Pope was reluctant to lend support to Becket at the risk of alienating so powerful a king as Henry, yet – Becket doggedly persisted. To a man, they thought Becket a fool, and a proud fool at that, who'd forgotten that pride and falls dwell in very close proximity.

'We will leave you gentlemen and retire to our beds,' Esther stood and beckoned Matilda who was sitting at a nearby table.

The men stood too and bowed to her. 'We will be at the foot of the stairs if you need us, Esther, God give you peace and rest this night.' The men returned to their conversation on the politics of the day and inevitably, there were more questions about the Marshal and the tournais; it was late before the room settled down for the night. It transpired that Sir William de Tracy was actually related to the King; his grandfather was one of Henry the First's illegitimate children. Richard wondered why, having come from the southwest they were now north of London, but apparently, they had first travelled to Sir William's manor in Cirencester, and made their way from there. Now they were of like mind to Richard and the other travellers, intent on completing their journey in daylight. All three were zealous supporters of the King, and staunchly opposed to the Church's oppressive power and greed, which affected their purses.

The new day made itself known by the hustle and bustle of those working at the inn. They had filled a tub with hot water so that the sleepers could wash, which they did. Esther had been privileged in so much as *she'd* been taken water to her room. They ate and dressed as quickly as they could.

'We will ride with your party Sir Richard, if you are content to have our company.'

'You would be most welcome Sir William, to arrive at Westminster accompanied by one of the King's cousins would do us no harm. The difficulty is, that only I was invited by the King, so I will have to find rooms for my party before I make for the palace.'

'Oh, fear not, the King would not expect you to arrive on your own, there will be ample accommodation for all. Westminster is a place of constant activity.'

'It was much the same in Poitiers when I stayed with the Queen. In that case we will indeed travel together and rejoice at the future fellowship with new-found friends.'

There were ten in Sir William's party, which made a formidable band of eighteen when they assembled. It was a fine frosty winter's morning, all were in good spirits, the air was alive with hens clucking, dogs barking, and the voices of excited people laughing and talking.

The palace of Westminster was a stone's throw from King Edward's great project, the Abbey. In his day, the palace lay an easy distance from the ever-growing city of London, and was delightfully situated, surrounded with fertile lands and green fields. The river, which ran close by, bore abundant merchandise and wares of every kind, for sale from the whole world to the town's people living on its banks. Since the palace had been built, the city had spread ever closer. The palace had always been a fine building of wattle and daub, but those walls were now being replaced with stone, and the original palace was being enlarged with new wings. It was without doubt splendid, a home fit for a king and this visual statement of wealth and power was finished off by the red clay tiled roof, rather than thatch. Tiles were expensive, a sign of status, much safer, less likely to catch fire.

They rode into a large courtyard, there were soldiers everywhere the activity was manic. Servants came to attend to their horses and baggage. An elderly steward approached Sir William.

'We are here at the King's command, and we need rooms. Do you know who I am?' The man looked ill at ease. 'I'm Sir William de Tracy a cousin of the King, my great-grandfather was King Henry the First so I expect your finest rooms for my party,' and he gestured to his friends, of which included Richard's party.

'Certainly, my Lord, I will show you your rooms you were expected.'

'And the King?'

'He is not here at present he is out hunting, which he does most days. He is expected to return this forenoon, Lord.'

'See to it that our presence is made known to him when he arrives and we are notified directly, your ears will be the penalty if it is not done,' the poor fellow's eyes nearly dropped from his head at the threat from this burly knight.

'Yes, yes, my Lord.' The steward trotted nervously alongside Sir William he even stumbled twice nearly tumbling to the ground, it was so comical Richard was compelled to laugh.

They were shown to their rooms, which were small, only large enough for a single cot, a table, and chair. Their servants could sleep with them or if it were wished, they would be housed in the communal servant's quarters. Richard and Esther wanted Matilda and Alwin with them and both seemed pleased with the arrangement even if it was cramped. Fortunately, Esther's room was all but next to Richard.

'I'm not sure about this Richard; I feel once more to be merely swept along with events. Thank God we are near to each other.'

Richard stared down at his boots and stroked his chin, 'Mmm, I don't know how to say this Esther, but for now – it may be wise to major on the – Norman side of your heritage. Forgive me I do not mean to offend or hurt you.'

'I understand, it seems that for the whole of my life I have not quite fitted in. When I was with my grandfather's people I was always on the outside, now in truth I know not where I belong. I am not slighted by your suggestion, for I know it is meant in kindness, and concern for me. What about Sir Raymond and Sir Tristram they know the truth?'

'I will have a word with them; fear not, you are safe from that quarter. Believe it or not Esther, but in the short time we have known you – we have all grown to love you.'

'Really, and you?'

'Of course, me.'

CHAPTER 13

Richard was uneasy, he wanted to get the meeting with the King over and done with. He was sure the King didn't know who he really was, he may not be so eager to have him by his side once he knew that his family fought against his mother.

It was in the early evening when he was summoned. He was with Esther.

'I will pray for you Richard,' and she embraced him.

'You have a way of transferring love and kindness into one's soul, I have never known anyone like you. Thank you Esther I am indeed blessed by knowing you.'

'Ha, I think you are over generous, but nevertheless, thank you for your kind words.'

He leant forward and kissed her cheek, turned and left. She watched as he closed the door and lifted her hand to touch the place where he'd kissed her.

There were people everywhere, but he noticed as he followed the servant who'd been sent to fetch him, as he neared where he assumed the King resided, the numbers became fewer.

Finally, he was standing outside a formidable pair of large oak doors, and he was instructed how to approach the King. Once through the door he'd to stand and wait until the King commanded him to come forward. He'd not to look him in the eye, to bow low from the waist, when he came level with the two guards stood in front of the dais, then kneel until he was told to rise, and only speak in response to the King's questions. On leaving, he must bow once more from the waist and walk backwards until he reached the door, bow, a dip of the head would suffice at this point, and leave.

Richard took a deep breath; the servant knocked on the door and as if by magic, they swung open, he glanced at the two guards, and walked in, his heart was pounding against his ribs fit to explode from his chest. The King was engaged in some conversation with a courtier standing on the step below him.

So, this is the great man, Richard thought. He appeared, though he was seated, a man of medium height, so that neither would he appear great among the small, nor yet would he seem small among the great, but he was a strongly built man of leonine appearance. From what Richard had heard, he was possessed of an immense dynamic energy and a formidable temper. He had the red hair of the Plantagenets, grey eyes that grew bloodshot in anger so Richard had been told, and a round, freckled face. His hair had undoubtedly been bright red at one time, except that with the coming of old age grey flashes had altered that colour, somewhat softening the flaming head he was known for, if not his temper. As to his hair, he was in no danger of baldness, but his head had been closely shaved. His head was spherical... his eyes are full, guileless, and dove-like *at this moment*, Richard thought apprehensively. They reportedly burned like fire when his temper was aroused, and in bursts of passion, they flashed like lightning – if the reports were to be believed, and from what he beheld – Richard had no reason to doubt them. He has a broad, square, lion-like chin by the look of it. Even seated as he was, Richard could see his curved legs, a horseman's shins. His chest was broad, and he possessed pugilist's arms. All his countenance and appearance announced him as a man strong, agile and bold...

The Queen had told Richard that he, *"Never sits, unless riding a horse or eating... In a single day, if necessary, he can run through four or five day-marches and, thus foiling the plots of his enemies, frequently he mocks their schemes with the surprised suddenness of his appearance... Forever in his hands are a bow, sword, spear and arrow, unless he be in council or in books."*

After what seemed an eternity, Richard heard the King laugh, then turn in his seat and looked towards him, at the same instant assuming a sterner countenance, and a courtier beckoned him forward, he was startled, inclined to say, "Who me?" The courtier signalled him once more and he walked towards the King who studied him with penetrating eyes, all the time massaging his chin, as much as Richard could see with his head lowered. He bowed when he reached the two guards as he'd been instructed, and knelt. After what he supposed was the proscribed length of time to kneel before a king, he was told to rise. Richard was not certain, but he did not think it was the King's voice. He was convinced at this moment that standing before the Almighty enthroned on the judgement seat would be no more terrifying than this.

'Mmmm, I hear great things about you, Sir Richard, from both the Queen, who is a fine judge of character, and the famous William Marshal, whose coat I see you proudly wearing, high recommendation indeed. No one else here can claim such *deserved* privilege.' Henry cast his eye around those stood near him and the intensity of his gaze caused them to lower their heads and fidget nervously. 'You have an interesting lineage I understand, I have it in my mind that your father fought against the Empress Matilda, what maketh *you* of such a thing?'

He knows me after all; and has had me brought here to make sport of me, as a cat with a mouse. 'My father fought for the man anointed before God. Though it brought him no advantage, I know he placed his honour before personal advancement, and I would pray that I might be so virtuous. That much I have learned from the Marshal, my Liege, and from what I've heard you are such a man.'

'By the blood of Christ, you are bold Sir knight; I'll give you that. You pray do you, and to whom does your honour submit, your King or your church?'

'If I may quote my Saviour, Lord, I give to Caesar what is Caesar's and to God what is God's.' The King was silent, and an uneasy quiet swept over the room... Suddenly the King laughed raucously, and the tension was released, and those around him, one by one, began to laugh.

'Sir Richard, you are an impudent fellow, but you intrigue me. Will you swear fealty to me? I will always have a place for honourable men, with wit and courage such as yourself.'

'You are my anointed King and my life is yours, so help me God.'

'Come place your hands betwixt mine and swear fealty to me. Or does your loyalty lie with that gutter snipe from Cheapside, who wishes to set himself above *me*, and me the rightful King of England – *his* vassal?' Henry's smile was no longer upon his lips and his face was turning redder by the second. Richard moved nearer the King, knelt, and placed his hands before him as he'd been instructed. Henry was distracted now and hesitated, as if his mind was preoccupied, he glanced once more at Richard's outstretched hands, leant forward, and took them between his.

'I swear fealty to you as my Liege Lord.' While Richard's hands were yet held within Henry's a voice cut unexpectedly across Richard's oath taking, clearly fired by Henry's thinly veiled reference to Becket. Suddenly the air was stifling; a mistral at the mention of Becket's name had blown through the room, and heated thoughts and passions.

'My lord, you will have no peace nor quiet while Thomas Becket lives…'

Richard was sure this was the voice of Sir William de Tracy, but he dare not look around to see.

It was apparent that even a passing reference to Becket was enough to stab a fiery poker of red-hot fury into Henry's vitals and these words had blown a rush of air into the smouldering embers, which were now glowing brightly.

Henry released Richard's hands and he moved back to where he'd knelt moments since. Henry's mood had suddenly taken on a different tone, heads were bowed his voice was passionate, heated, trembling with fury. This was the renowned Plantagenet temper ever merely a spark away from igniting.

'What idle and miserable men have I encouraged and promoted in my kingdom, faithless to their Lord to let me be mocked by a – lowborn cleric.'

There was silence… then Richard heard movement behind him; there was the sound of a chair being knocked over, he knew not what or who it was. He remained on his knees. He fearfully imagined that Henry's impassioned outburst would only be understood to mean one thing to a knight who respected him, and suffered too at the hand of the Church. The room was now fearfully quiet; Richard heard several footsteps, and doors opening and closing. Henry sat red faced, pounding his fists rhythmically on the arms of his chair. Richard doubted that Henry would be able to understand how his outburst could be misunderstood by loyal knights. He might grasp the gravity once he'd calmed, but then it could well be *too* late. Someone touched Richard's shoulder he almost jumped; he cautiously stood, bowed, and backed away from the King. Henry was oblivious to him; he was in a darker place at this moment. Richard left; the guard closed the door behind him with great care. Once on the outside, Richard leaned against the door and breathed deeply. He was certain a storm had been unleashed this day that would blow such wrath as never before seen, straight from the jaws of Hell. Woe betides those who sail too near the rocks on this wind.

'Who were the fellows who left before I came from the room?' he asked the guard, flicking his head in the direction of the hall.

'I know not them all Lord, only but two, Sir William de Tracy and Sir Hugh de Morville, there were four in total.'

'De Morville, I am not acquainted with him!'

'He be from the North, Lord, some place called West Moreland. That be all I knows, he came a week past. Sounds to be some trouble in there Lord.'

'This day has spawned a storm that could destroy this kingdom,' Richard said and left the two men in a fearful silence, shaken by his words; their eyes followed him as he walked away.

Richard returned to his quarters, when he entered Alwin, who was busy burnishing and oiling his armour, smiled.

'Leave your work Alwin, and bring Sir Raymond and Sir Tristram to me.'

'Do you know where they be Lord?'

'No – find them – it is urgent.' Alwin left immediately, Richard went to Esther's room, and knocked, Matilda answered and curtseyed. Richard ignored her, and stepped into the room, Esther was sitting on the bed. 'Esther, come to my room, I must make known to you this news.'

CHAPTER 14

Richard strode purposefully to his room and Esther followed.

'Be seated Esther,' she sat as commanded wondering what it was that was so troubling to him.

'A fearful thing has happened which I am convinced will have the direst consequences.'

'Whatever has occurred, did you cause some offence to the King?' She sat motionless, apart from her eyes, which were alive with foreboding. Before he could respond to her question, there was a rattle on his door and Alwin's head appeared.

'Lord, Sir Tristram and Sir Raymond are here.'

'Show them in.'

'We know what you are going to say. It has spread like wildfire around the palace.'

'What is it?' asked Esther.

'It is said that four knights, three of whom travelled with us in Sir William's party and another, Sir Hugh de

Morville, all fervent supporters of the King have left Westminster for Canterbury to – slay the Archbishop – Becket.' Esther lifted her hand to her mouth.

'Has anyone attempted to prevent them, do you know Sir Raymond?' asked Richard.

'Not as far as I know. Most, I suspect, are keeping well out of this exploit. What have you heard Richard?'

'Less than you, Tristram, I have this minute come from the hall where this poisonous barb was given life. I'm sure; once the King's outburst cools, he will be as horrified as the rest of us.'

The palace was a place frozen in fear, for now, even the King seemed unnaturally calm. Those dwelling within the palace compelled to venture out from the safety of their rooms to traverse along the murky dark passages, did so with light, nimble feet. None of the previous day's hustle and bustle, laughter, and trivial chatter was to be heard this day; any words were now said in guarded whispers.

It was the 30th of December when the news reached the palace – Becket – was *dead*, killed – apparently, when he was about to listen to vespers. An eyewitness, Edward Grim, told that the knights had placed their weapons under a tree outside the cathedral and wrapped their cloaks around their armour before entering to challenge Becket. The knights informed Becket he was to go to Winchester to give an account of his actions, but Becket refused. It was not until he rebuffed their demands to submit to the King's will, that they retrieved their weapons, and then rushed back inside to where he was waiting and struck him to the floor.

They had reached Canterbury Cathedral on December 29th. One of the knights approached the Archbishop, and struck him on the shoulder with the flat of his sword. It seems that they were reluctant even then to kill Becket, hoping that he would see the impending catastrophe and consent to their demands, but he stood firm, and after the first blow, their threat became an irrevocable reality, they attacked and literally butchered him.

It was reported that they cleaved open his skull spilling his brains onto the cathedral floor.

Henry was *appalled* when he heard the news; he knew that his words would be accredited as the warrant for this heinous assassination. Even worse, to those who hated him, "His *hand*" would be the hand that delivered the blow to Becket's mitred head. As an act of penitence, he donned sackcloth and ashes, and starved himself for three days.

'What of the four knights, is there any news, Richard?'

'Little or none Esther, I have heard that they have fled north to De Morville's homeland, but no more. They will almost certainly be excommunicated; Hell is their future, what a fool troublemaker Becket was, but he may have played his most deft card in death. It will be a difficult battle for Henry now, Becket was formidable in life, he may be invincible in death.'

Slowly the palace assumed *some* normality, Richard never saw the King. None but his closest advisers were permitted in his presence. Richard was given work training the young "Would-be knights" and he employed Sir Raymond and Sir Tristram as his helpers. He spent whatever free time he had with Esther. The news was of no surprise, all in Europe had deplored and condemned Henry's part in the death of Becket. There was talk that the once embarrassing, previously shunned, Archbishop, was now to be made a Saint.

Richard was sweating and dirty; he removed his helm and made his way from the practice yard. He was looking down removing his gloves as he walked.

'Good day Sir.' Richard was startled and looked up to see the smiling face of Sir Guy Molineux.

'Sir Guy,' Richard bowed and was about to walk on, Sir Guy touched his arm. 'Forgive me did you want something?'

'Indeed Sir, it is my Lady's wish that you attend our wedding this next fortnight.'

'Lady Julianne wants *me* to attend her wedding!'

'Most certainly.'

'Whilst it would be a rare honour indeed, to be present at such an occasion, I doubt the King will give me permission.'

'Fear not, I am a man of influence I will see that you have the necessary consent.' He smiled at Richard, bowed, and walked away. Richard was flabbergasted and could only stand and watch him go.

CHAPTER 15

There was a knock on Richard's door; he was at that moment writing to Sir John FitzWilliam, he glanced up as Alwin answered.

'It was Sir Guy Molineux's servant with a message,' he said passing it to Richard.

'Mmm,' Richard took it from Alwin and unfolded it. 'It is my authorization to attend his wedding. He invites me to travel with his party, the day after the morrow, that is it decided then, we will be travelling north, Alwin. I will make this known to Esther.' He stood, pushed his chair back, and went out.

He met Matilda carrying a robe, 'Where's your Mistress, Matilda?'

She curtseyed, 'She is in the tiltyard, Lord, with Sir Raymond, and Sir Tristram watching the training, she was cold and sent me to fetch her robe.'

'Very well, take me to her.' The two made their way in silence to the yard, when he stepped from the door Esther saw him and waved.

'Richard, Alwin said that you were working this morning.'

'Aye, I was, but Sir Guy has kindly secured me permission to attend his wedding and we are to travel north the day after the morrow.' Esther looked nervous.

'Will I be expected to go?'

'I imagine so *but* – you have not to my knowledge been given a formal invitation, which affords you the perfect excuse should you wish not to attend.'

'I will not go then. What exactly does Sir Guy do for the King?'

'He has something to do with the treasury, he probably sorts all the King's coin into neat piles, knocks them over then counts them again. I imagine such labour would suit him well.' Esther laughed at the picture Richard had created in her head.

'You will take good care of Esther.' Richard asked Sir Raymond who was standing nearby, watching two young men practising at the pell. He turned to the voice. 'You will give care to Esther's safety? If I leave for a few days to attend Lady Julianne's wedding.' Richard repeated.

Sir Raymond smiled, 'Sorry Sir Richard I was distracted; she will be safe. I am more concerned for your well-being. You will be riding into the lion's den; I suppose you have considered such a danger?'

'He's right Richard, must you go?'

'I'm afraid so, I promised Sir John, and it would trouble me sorely to hurt him, and *he* will need support.'

'Should one of us not go with you, Richard?' asked Sir Raymond.

'No, I will have enough on my mind. I want to be sure that Esther is safe. Alwin will be with me, besides I will have Sir Guy to protect me.'

'Ha, all will be well for you then,' laughed Sir Raymond reaching forward and repositioning the sword arm of one of the two men practising. 'Keep your arm up. I know you're tired, but battles are tiring places. If your arm tires in the field, you will get to sleep forever. That my dear boy is why they make the wooden sword you now hold twice as heavy as your real sword, so that you arm will grow stronger. Now do it again and next time you lower your arm, I will strike you with *my* wooden sword. Do you understand?'

'Yes Lord.'

'God in all His mercy, these fellows will never be fit for battle.'

'You are a hard man Sir Raymond,' laughed Richard.

'Perhaps he needs a rest,' Esther offered. Sir Raymond glanced at her, and furrowed his brow.

'Be this a mother's voice, I hear, Sir Richard? It's a mother's tears I wish to spare,' Richard smiled.

'We will leave you and walk by the river,' Richard bowed and Esther took his arm. 'There will be some positive aspects to travelling with Sir Guy, I will be able to learn if he has any knowledge as to the King's frame of mind – now that the Archbishop is no longer with us. I have only seen him once since Becket's – death. I did hear some rumours about Ireland, but nothing more. I have found that Sir Guy loves to impress with his closeness to the seat of power, and confidentiality is not one of his virtues. A smattering of thinly veiled flattery and he will tell all. Perhaps that's why Henry tolerates him, he can tell him whatever deep secret he wants everyone to know, and be sure that it will be spread far and wide.'

'Surely not Richard.'

'My dear Esther, you are so generous; you never have a shadow of a dark thought about anyone. From what I have heard, and have seen, the King is as wily as an old fox, and twice as cunning.'

The morning they were about to leave, all were assembled in the courtyard waiting for Sir Guy who eventually came dressed in a fine suite of plate armour. He acknowledged Richard and Esther, who was standing next to him.

'He offered me charge of his knights but I declined, making the excuse that Sir Granville was senior to me, and it would be an offence to him. In truth, I didn't want my position to be complicated when we arrive at Tattershall.'

'You will be careful, Richard.'

'Fear not, *you* take care.' The horses were anxious to be off, bobbing their heads and skittering at the slightest disturbance. Eventually the word was given and there was the sudden cacophony of clattering hooves and jangling harnesses. Richard reached down and took Esther's hand and Sir Tristram slapped Ares' rump.

'Farewell, God speed,' Sir Raymond called as he released Ares' bridle. Richard was at the rear of the group and turned to wave as he went from the yard onto the track, which went east for a league along the riverbank before it turned north.

Sir Raymond placed his arm around Esther's shoulder, 'Fear not Esther, Richard is no fool, and Sir Gervase is not half the man of him.'

'I know, but Richard will not have his own interests at heart, he will put Sir John first, I know he will. That will make him vulnerable.'

Sir Raymond didn't respond; he merely gave Esther a gentle squeeze. He knew as well as Esther, that Richard's concern for others was his Achilles heel – as well as his strength, and one day it might cost him his life. He was an easy man to love, no one in the practice yard commanded respect and genuine affection like him. He had seen the young knights grow in stature when he praised them. He was even able to rebuke them without damaging their spirits, they simply wanted to do better for him; it was in him, part of him, his sincerity shone through. He would take time to visit any who'd been injured, knew all by name, little details about their families or their homes. It wasn't his coveted surcoat, which set him above other knights; it was the man inside the surcoat. Perhaps he was more like the Marshal than he knew.

It was a warm day, as they made their way north, the cold damp of winter was behind them now.

Richard's mind was drawn to the death of Becket and he couldn't quite believe how little impact it had had. He had expected public disorder, even civil war. There had been voices of outrage but nothing more. Perhaps those in power had breathed a sigh of relief but couldn't own it. While he was lost in his contemplations a horse came alongside him and he looked up and saw Sir Guy.

'Sir Richard, a fine day, is it not?' Richard looked up to the blue sky. 'A fine day for a wedding.'

'How are you liking your work at the palace?'

'I'm happy, the work is familiar to me, it's what I have done most of my life.'

'The King knows of your work and he is very pleased, you should know this. He is preparing a force to take to Ireland and wants you to be involved in the planning as one of the leaders. The King himself has commissioned me – with the task of informing you of his wishes. What say you to that?'

Richard stared at Sir Guy. 'I am surprised, I didn't think the King knew the first thing about me.'

'Believe me, the King knows all about you and chooses to favour you.'

'Tell me what you know of this expedition.'

'I am not the best person to ask about the details, but the King has had problems with the Irish for years. The Irish kings have changed and the Anglo Normans feel now under threat. There are other interesting things happening, developments of which you will be unaware. King Henry has been unjustly treated over the death of that traitor Becket. The treatment sorely troubles the King and he wishes to show his loyalty to the Church by bringing the rebellious Irish in to line with the true head of the Church, Pope Alexander.'

'Mmm, am I to understand that the Pope endorses this mission?'

'Yes indeed, he has authorised it. I must leave you with your thoughts for now. I have to socialise with others in my party, my work never ends, and you have much to consider I think, good day Sir Richard.'

Richard watched him go, full of bonhomie to all. There goes a man who will keep well clear of the places where heroes grow, if Becket had come out on top, he would have been Becket's man. That fellow is the antithesis of all that is dear to the Marshal. He will need every one of his skills once he is wedded to Julianne *but* that has not happened as of yet, Richard thought.

CHAPTER 16

Little had changed to the scene since the first time Richard had approached Sir John's castle. However, this day found him even more troubled than on the day of his first sighting. With good reason, he thought, as they rode steadily towards the barbican towers, knowing that there was bound to be trouble from Gervase; that was an inescapable certainty. What form it would take was the only unknown factor to the equation.

In another life, dealing with Gervase would have been a simple straightforward matter; he'd known many a spoilt rich man's son in the course of his time with William Marshal. Richard knew if it came to facing Gervase man to man, he was superior to him in every way. That eventuality would not have troubled him in the slightest "In that past life", but his life now was so much more complicated. It had become so the moment he saw that beautiful girl on an innocent Channel crossing. Was he in love with her then – surely not – but he was now, and this was no feeling to inspire a minstrel's ballad. This was like living in a hellish turmoil of swirling, debilitating, confusion – without end. What in God's holy name was he even doing here? He could have been safe in London where he was wanted, honoured, even loved, but no, he was drawn to the candle flame like the moth on a summer's evening – ever closer, and yet closer. Even the scorching heat's warning of impending doom did not deter him, he fluttered ever nearer until a tortuous death was the only release on offer from the inescapable tormented attraction.

Was he afraid as he neared the flame? Yes, he was afraid, he had yet time to turn and flee; his future was in his own hands – too late. He was awoken to *Reality* – as the sound of their horse's hooves hammered onto the drawbridge, *time,* had chosen for him. Before he could assimilate the moment, Sir John was on the steps of the keep to greet them. Richard was sweating, his eyes scanned every inch of the yard for sight of Gervase; he was nowhere to be seen. He noticed there was no sign of Julianne either.

'Mmm,' Richard whispered under his breath.

'Sir Guy – Sir Richard, a welcome to you both,' Sir John greeted them with his ever-warm friendly smile.

The troop dismounted in clouds of steam rising from the weary horses. Sir Guy bowed and shook Sir John's outstretched hand.

'Julianne is in her rooms, Sir Guy, you're early.' Sir John beckoned a servant to take him to the Lady Julianne. He watched Sir Guy walk off and he turned to Richard and embraced him. 'Richard, come with me, I am delighted to see you. No doubt, you have much to tell me of your adventures in these turbulent days.'

'Aye and good to see you once more.' Richard was distracted; he was concerned as to the whereabouts of Gervase.

'You look well, the life is suiting you, weight stays clear of your frame. They've found use for your talents; I'll warrant.'

'Err, yes – you look well too my Lord. I thought your son might be here to greet Sir Guy's party.'

'We didn't expect you until tomorrow, Gervase is away hunting he will be home some time soon. You can never tell; it will depend on how goes the hunt.' As they passed a servant, Sir John told him to bring wine to his chambers. 'You and I will have a cup of wine before you divest yourself of your mail. You will be ready for a drink no doubt; travelling is thirsty work.'

They made their way into the keep and up the stone staircase to Sir John's apartment. The guard on the door opened it as Sir John and Richard approached.

'Here, be seated, dear friend, I see you wear a new red surcoat, bearing the two golden lions of the Plantagenet family, the King's man now. I hope you have taken good care of your old one.'

'Aye, it is safe enough,' he smiled uneasily; he knew he shouldn't have come. 'Who knows I may have use of it again.'

'The King would have lost some of his sound judgement if he were to lose you, no – there will be work for you there as long as he lasts.' A servant entered with a jug and two goblets. 'You may leave us; I will serve Sir Richard myself.'

The servant bowed and went to the door; he was about to close it when Gervase entered, pushing the servant roughly to one side.

Both Sir John and Richard stood, Richard felt for his sword but it wasn't by his side, he'd left it at the door on entering as good manners dictated. Gervase drew his sword.

'You entertain this *traitor* who assaults your only son, and treat him as if *he* is an honoured guest.'

'Gervase, put up your sword, Richard is unarmed, don't shame me or yourself.'

'It is you who shame *me* after the way this kidnapper abducted someone under your protection and he drinks wine at your table, no doubt he is here to discuss ransom, that's how his sort make their coin.' Richard laid his hand on his dagger and backed against the wall.

'Gervase, I *command* you, put up your sword!' He lowered his sword but came on nearer and nearer to Richard. He removed his leather glove and lashed it across Richard's face, the metal studs raking his cheek, throwing his head against the wall.

'I challenge you to mortal combat, you see, I am a man of honour.'

'I will not fight you!'

'Coward…' and Gervase lashed his face once more splitting his lip. Blood was now dripping freely from Richard's chin.

Sir John grabbed his son by the arm but he struck Richard once more, having whipped his head viciously from side to side with each blow, and another gash appeared, this time below his eye, Sir John pushed him away, and stood before Richard.

'Guards throw this dog outside into the gutter where he belongs.' The guards grabbed Gervase; it took three to subdue him and they dragged him cursing and screaming from the room. Richard never moved; he was dazed from the blows; he simply lay back with his head against the wall. Sir John took his arm and led him to his chair. The servant who'd brought the wine was cowering behind the open door.

'Don't stand there shaking, get water and a cloth for Sir Richard.' Richard never moved, 'Richard, why didn't you defend yourself?'

He looked at Sir John, 'He's your only son, would you have me kill him, and you, my friend, never!'

'He is dead to me, for the shame he has inflicted this day.'

'He's hurt, confused, feels he's a failure in both your eyes, *and* his sister's.'

'He's dangerous, that I can see, but can you? Give that to me, girl.' A servant had brought a bowl with hot water and some cloth; the girl passed the bowl to Sir John. 'Lift your face to me so I can clean it, it's a mess, but the blood's probably making it look worse than it is. It will turn black and blue but you'll live. How does that feel?' Sir John asked as he began to bathe Richard's face.

'Actually, I can't feel anything at the moment it's quite numb, but thank you.' Sir John straightened himself and set the bowl on a nearby table.

'Drink your wine,' he said, filling Richard's goblet and passing it to him. They both sat staring into their wine unsure what to say.

'I think it would be wise if I went. I was dubious about coming for this very reason. I should have listened to the voice in my head, if I had, it would have saved you this embarrassment.'

'I don't know what to say Richard, what I feel is beyond sorrow. I have faced certain death in my time, but I have never felt the burden I do at this minute, the shame and regret is unbearable.' Sir John sat with his head hung down as if he carried the whole world on his shoulders.

Richard reached over to him and laid his hand on his back. 'There is nothing *to* say my friend, I hold you not culpable for this sadness. I will go while there is still light, and pray the Blessed Virgin for the peace of this place and restoration of your family.'

'*Perhaps* you are right, it would be selfish of me to expect you to stay and place you in an intolerable position. I will walk with you to your horse, but this pleases me naught, this is the blackest of days.' Sir John rose from his seat, stretched out his arm, offered Richard his hand, and drew him into his embrace. Richard collected his sword and buckled it to his belt. They walked together down the spiral staircase without a word.

Sir John held the door onto the courtyard open. The door from the keep was deliberately small and low, if the keep was attacked the undersized entrance made defending it easier. Richard nodded politely, ducked below the lintel, and stepped through the opening and into the daylight. Without warning, he was struck with a vicious blow from a sword to his right arm. Only by the miracle of some intrinsic sixth sense, did he manage to avoid his head being cleaved in two. The strike was so ferocious it separated some of the links in his hauberk, and cut deep into his sword arm. Richard spun round to face his assailant; he was not surprised to see Gervase's spiteful, gloating smile. He circled Richard, who with great deal of fumbling, managed to draw his sword from its sheath. It was difficult, his arm was weak from the force of the blow alone, never mind the cruel gash, his fingers were struggling to grip the hilt.

Sir John shouted, 'Cease this madness NOW, before it's too late.' Gervase was deaf to everything but his all-empowering blinding hatred. He swung his sword again. Richard managed to react more from instinct than intention, with barely enough control and resistance to parry the blow, he was struggling to lift his arm in any resolute way. After he'd deflected the blow his sword tip dropped to the ground, he was unable to raise it then he caught sight of the blood running from below his hauberk sleeve at his wrist and into his hand. It felt sticky between his sword hilt and the palm of his hand, he needed both hands to lift his sword, but that was limiting, the hilt was too small to grip it properly with both hands. Gervase was confident now – *overconfident* and prowled like a wolf at the kill. The only chance Richard had at this moment was to appear broken and defeated, hoping that Gervase's overconfidence may make him complacent, and such a lapse would be his downfall. Gervase lifted his sword, and swung at Richard's unprotected head, the light flashed off the polished blade as it cut through the sun's fading rays. Richard pushed against the ground with his foot and twisted, he felt his ankle give way, but the movement was sufficient to deflect the stroke; he was on his knees now. Gervase came forward, leering, enjoying every second of his triumph, he slowly lifted his sword to deliver the coup de grâce, clearly making the most of this sweet revenge which would rid him once and for all of his nemesis. Richard dredged up every drop of his strength, felt for his dagger, and without warning sprang, driving the blade into Gervase's thigh. Even in this perilous second, he had chosen to disable rather than slay his enemy. Gervase gasped, screwed his eyelids together as the red-hot pain flashed into his brain. He stumbled two steps backwards dropping his sword and grasping at the wound, losing his balance he fell heavily to the ground. He was dazed, and cried out in excruciating pain, but still he tried to rise, Sir John placed his foot calmly onto his son's chest and Gervase slumped back defeated into the dust. Sir John turned to the guards who were now at his side fearing for their Lord's life.

'See his wound is cleaned and bound, put him on his horse with mete and drink and this coin,' he took his purse from his waist, and passed it to the guard. 'Take him from me, he is banished from my home and lands. If he ever sets foot on my lands again, he is to be taken and hanged.' Richard was in too much pain and confused to argue with this dreadful punishment by a father to his son.

Sir John knelt down by Richard's side, and took his head in his lap. 'You can't go now, you need to be attended to.' He called more men, 'Help this knight to his rooms and send for my chirurgien. *You* are my son now – all I have is yours.'

CHAPTER 17

The two men supported Richard to his room, one carried his sword and helm, the other acted as a crutch, he had definitely twisted his ankle in the fray, and it felt weak. He desperately tried not to make a fuss, he could walk, but felt faint, and his head was throbbing. He thanked the two men for their kindness, but he was sure he'd have managed better on his own; gentleness was definitely not one of their attributes. Alwin came to him as they lowered him onto his bed; he hadn't even had time to unpack, he was waiting for instructions as to where they might be housed. As soon as he'd been told of the fight, he rushed to find Richard. They'd said that the Lord's son had been banished.

When he entered the room, he was shocked to see the dire condition of his master.

'You can leave now, my servant will help me undress, thank you once again for your help.' The two men acknowledged him and left.

'You will have to stand Lord while I remove your hauberk, do you think you are able to do that? I will be as quick as I can, let me help you.' Alwin took his arm and Richard groaned as he stood.

'My ankle is a problem too; I must have twisted it.'

'We will attend to that when I remove your boot.' He told Alwin the tale as he loosened the straps of his hauberk.

'It is going to hurt, Lord, as I pull this over your head.'

'Just get on with it and don't worry.' The cut to his arm was deep into his shoulder muscle. He knew it would be a while before he could use his sword arm again. He took a deep breath as Alwin lifted his arm and began to ease his mail over the wound, some of the torn jagged links hooked into the cut. He felt faint and stumbled, in that split second Alwin pulled the hauberk over his head and held him or he would have fallen. Alwin manoeuvred him onto a chair, he felt sick.

'I will get water Lord, the wound needs washing.' At that moment, Sir John and his chirurgien entered the room.

'Ah, thank you Alwin, you have undressed Sir Richard. This is Bernard de Lacy, my chirurgien, he will tend to you, Richard.'

'My Lord,' he said bowing and carefully taking hold of Richard arm. 'Mmm, I will have to stitch this.'

He took out a bottle of spirit, and Richard reached for it, thinking he was to drink it to numb the pain. 'No, no, no, this is not for drinking,' and he swept the stone bottle clear of Richard's hand. 'This is to prevent the wound turning putrid. I have found drinking alcohol to be the very worst thing when the body is in shock, as yours undoubtedly is at this moment.'

Richard looked at Sir John as much as to say, "Are you sure this fellow knows what he's doing?" Richard knew it was common practice to give drink to dull the pain, the more the better.

'Ahhhh,' he called out in agony and nearly leapt from the chair when the spirit was poured onto the wound, it was so numb afterwards Richard never felt a thing when he did stitch it. This man's an incompetent fool, whatever was Sir John thinking about, he thought, but he was too weak and disorientated to argue, *and* panting like a dog trying to get some air in his lungs before he fainted.

'It's a deep cut,' Richard already knew that, he had looked at it; it was like the open mouth of a fish. 'It will be a while before you are able use this arm, Lord, but I'm sure if you are mindful of it, you will make a full recovery. I have taken great care not to overlap the flesh, which will be particularly important when I tend to the lesion on your face. With such care it will heal neatly, perhaps a *small* scar,' he shrugged his shoulders, 'but no more. I'm ashamed of those in my trade when I see some of you fellows with such unsightly scars, no need, no need.' Richard was in so much throbbing pain, he could only nod.

The chirurgien turned to Alwin, 'Bring him a large ewer of small ale he should drink plenty, "*No*" strong drink! On that, I am most insistent. You are very fortunate Lord, no main blood supply has been cut, and in time, your muscle will heal. You must rest it; your arm will need to be supported for some while, to allow the wound to repair. It would be the worst thing possible to reopen the cut just as it starts to bind itself. Now the cut below your eye, perhaps two small stitches and one at your lip.' He quickly and painlessly stitched Richard's cheek and lip. 'Very good,' he said stepping back to admire his work. 'I will leave you now.'

'Th-thank you,' Richard said, sorry for his early doubts. The man bowed and was about to leave.

'My Lord's ankle is injured too.' Alwin interrupted.

'It is nothing, Sir, a mere sprain,' Richard said brushing it off as inconsequential with the flick of his hand.

The chirurgien hesitated, knelt, and once again removed his bag from his shoulder.

'Which one is it?'

'The right.' He carefully eased Richard's boot over the damaged ankle.

'Mmm… not broken, I think. Though it can be difficult to be certain with this severe swelling,' he felt gently around the bones and joint with his thumbs. 'Can you move your toes?' Richard wiggled his toes in response. 'Very good, I feel certain it is only sprained, I say *only* sprained, – sometimes a break heals more quickly than a sprain. You see these sinews,' he pointed with his finger, 'they hold the joint in place, they have been overstretched and will not perform their work because of that. They are thin and take a while to repair, not much blood gets to them. You must rest it until the swelling recedes, thereafter gently begin to move it, or it may stiffen and be a constant weakness. Your servant was right to make this known to me. I will bind it, but you must give it rest at first. You young fellows think you are indestructible and to some extent you are, but when you get to my age, these wounds will return to haunt you if you do not let the body repair itself in its own time. What does the scripture tell us! That we are fearfully and wonderfully made, and never was there a truer thing said.'

Richard had never heard any chirurgien like this man before. 'When the swelling recedes, I will inspect it again.' He took a bandage from his bag and wrapped it several times around the swollen ankle and under the foot. He nodded, clearly satisfied with his work. 'I will leave you now and return later, perhaps on the morrow. Is that all I can do for you?'

'Yes, thank you.'

'You are most welcome; it is a great privilege to be able to help those who are suffering. Good day to you, *and* no strong drink for a day or two.'

'Thank you… what a strange fellow,' Richard said, more to himself, than anyone else when the chirurgien had closed the door. He turned his attention to Sir John, 'How's your son, Sir John?'

'Come, I will help you to your bed.' Sir John ignored his question. Clearly, the dishonour was more than he could tolerate and he wanted to remove his son from his thoughts. Richard would not mention Gervase to him again, Sir John had made his decision, and he no longer knew Gervase.

Richard could not imagine how he would cope with all the pain laid at the door of this most honourable of gentleman. "I should have foreseen this, it is my fault to own as much as Sir John's, but this is worse than I ever thought possible," and he cursed himself for his folly.

Dishonour was the worst punishment that could be inflicted upon a knight, worse than death, it was a *living* death, and he knew Sir John was feeling dishonoured, as if Gervase's behaviour was a direct reflection of his own honour. Yet, in spite of the terrible blow Gervase had dealt his father, his father had treated him honourably even as he banished him. Richard wondered how Gervase could have lost sight of all that was right and noble, and turned such aspirations into jealousy and envy with this father as an example.

'And what did you think of my rare treasure, Bernard? He is the very best, he can snatch life from the jaws of certain death; I have seen him do it many times. I could see your doubts; he learned his trade from an Arab, an infidel no less, when he was on the crusade. You won't find a better man to care for you. Worth his weight in gold.'

'I have to say he was very quick and efficient. I never felt a thing when he stitched my arm or my cheek.'

'You should sleep, Son, you have had a long ride today. I have much to do; I must see Julianne and talk to Sir Guy to make him feel welcome. I'll see what I can wheedle from him of the gossip from court.'

'There will not be much wheedling required, keeping awake is the difficulty I am ever faced with.' They both laughed.

'Rest as you have been told, I will leave you now, ah, here's Alwin with your drink,' with that Sir John left.

Richard awoke early on the morning of the wedding. His face was badly swollen; drinking was a problem with his damaged lip, whatever he drank spilled from his mouth down his chin and his right eye was all but closed. This was nothing to the sorrow he felt. Julianne is going through with this folly, even though she knows that it's a mistake. He couldn't believe she could be so wilful as to condemn herself to such a life with that shallow courtier, merely to demonstrate to him, that *he* was wrong. She would be destroyed; he slammed his fist into the bed, jerking his wounded arm, 'Ahhh', he fell back onto the pillow, he was sweating. 'Damn her for the fool she is.'

By now she will know all the details of the day's madness, he thought, at least her father will have told her the truth of it. Who knows how she will respond.

Alwin entered with hot water for Richard to ready himself for the wedding.

'Have you heard aught of Sir Gervase?' Richard asked as Alwin bathed him. Alwin took some time to respond. 'Come on, out with it, Alwin.'

'It's not for me to spread rumours, Lord.'

'Granted – now make this the exception.'

'I have heard that our Lord and the Lady Julianne had a fearful exchange, she has given permission for Sir Gervase to live with her and Sir Guy at his castle.'

'Oh… and what did Sir Guy have to say to that?'

'He was shocked and unsure about the wisdom of such a thing. He knew King Henry would hear about the treachery sooner or later and be furious about your treatment. He is very loyal to those who are loyal to him, and Sir Guy fears he may be tainted if they are seen to have given support to her brother. However, he gave way to Lady Julianne.'

'Now there's a surprise, what else was said? Come on, out with it fellow, this is like drawing blood from a stone.'

'I heard the Lady Julianne asking the chirurgien after your health… it was strange.'

'Strange – in what way?'

'No one else was there, she did not see me.'

'Alwin – *what* was strange?'

'She seemed to be genuinely concerned.'

'Mmmm.'

Alwin dressed Richard and tied a linen sling around his neck to support his arm.

'How's that, Lord?'

'Oddly, it's my face that hurts the most. It must be a fearful sight.'

'Not really *Lord*… I think it a marked improvement.'

'Ho, ho, ho, and I thought that Sir John loved me. I see now that I merely presented an opportunity for him to rid himself of a worthless servant, on a poor innocent such as myself,' Alwin laughed.

All gathered in the courtyard to watch the marriage ceremony performed, servants and guests alike. They would be married outside on the steps of the narthex as the Church dictated, and then they would celebrate the mass in the church. Julianne was wearing a gown of red damask made even more striking by its simplicity. She wore no adornment, apart from her emerald; her beautiful thick golden hair was braided and interwoven with flowers. She was breathtaking; he could forgive her for anything. She looked innocent, a lonely lost child; there was no ugly harshness or unkindness in this woman before him, she was without equal, gentle, serene, all of these things and more. Her beauty would stand alone above all others of her sex.

'Dear Mother of Christ be merciful to her,' he prayed.

Sir John caught sight of Richard and waved him to the front. Julianne turned and saw him, she stared at him, without shame; in that single moment there was no one else there, only them, as it was always meant to be. There was a cheer and the spell was broken, *suddenly* she looked terrified like a fawn he'd once seen standing by its dead mother, who'd just been slain by a hunter's arrow, it trembled terrified of the unknown. It was as if she was begging him – to do what – what could he do? Perhaps – she was merely shocked to see his swollen face. In truth, he was sure he was no pleasing sight to the eye. Normally, if she cast an eye in his direction and he saw her, she turned quickly away, but not this time. The priest had to speak twice to her to attract her attention and Sir Guy twisted his head to see what had distracted her, but she turned to the priest, and he never saw what she was looking at, *thankfully*.

After the mass, they all assembled in the main hall for the marriage feast. First, they were introduced to the new bride and her knight. Sir Guy was fully preoccupied just being Sir Guy, all courtly and charming, diverted at this moment by the attention of Sir Mark FitzWallen.

Richard raised Julianne's hand to his lips and kissed it, she never lifted her head. In a soft almost inaudible voice she said, 'I'm *sorry* – will you ever forgive me? What you said was true.' and he was jostled on, no time to respond to her. Sir Guy took his hand, but was obviously feeling uncomfortable, not that Richard noticed. Sir Guy was concerned as to how Richard might respond to him having given sanctuary to his enemy. He knew Richard was in favour with the King, and Julianne's support for Gervase could well damage their future at court. Nothing was further from Richard's thoughts at this moment. He was oblivious to every word Sir Guy spoke; he couldn't hear a single thing, only *her* words were in his head.

He had to get away he couldn't suffer this torment. He was gasping for air, suddenly struggling just to breathe.

'Richard, where are you going?' Sir John spoke to him, as he was about to leave.

'I must apologise, my Lord, I feel not well, forgive me, I need air *and* quiet.'

'I will get help for you.'

'No need Lord, you be about your business you have much work this day, I will be well enough. I have Alwin, he is the best of men.' Richard left the proceedings with Alwin. Once he was clear of the hall, he turned to make sure no one was watching, then said quietly to Alwin, 'Fetch me my cloak, I am going for a ride.'

'But Lord!'

'Just do as I say, Alwin.' He bowed, turned, and went in the direction of Sir Richard's rooms. Richard made his way to the stables, and ordered a horse saddled, not Ares, he didn't think he could manage him.

'Help me up, boy!' It was a struggle and painful but he managed. Alwin came with his cloak and stood on the mounting block to fasten it around his master's shoulders.'

'Do you want me to ride with you, Lord?' He asked anxiously.

'NO!' Alwin didn't even think to argue; he'd never before seen this dark side to his master. Richard set off more quickly than he should have, he knew this was foolish, but he needed to get away and this was a gentle horse. He didn't see Julianne watching from the hall doorway, she called out in her head, "Take me with you", and almost ran after him as he rode towards the castle gates, she willed him to turn – but he did not.

CHAPTER 18

Sir John was furious with Richard when he returned, he had sent men out looking for him, he feared that either Gervase had ambushed him or he'd been thrown from his horse and was lying injured in a ditch somewhere, possibly even dead.

Richard was quite taken aback by the attention when he rode into the castle, Sir John actually ran to his horse to help him down.

'Richard, Richard, where did you go? I have been beside myself. Whatever were you thinking about, you could have been killed or more sorely hurt than you already are?'

Richard was quite surprised by all the worried faces. 'I apologise Lord; I did not anticipate the causing of such grief. I never imagined that I would be so missed.'

'You clearly have no idea what you mean to me. Fortunately, Alwin had sense enough to come straight to me with his fears.' Richard narrowed his eyes and stared at Alwin, Alwin ignored him.

'Alwin take your master to his rooms.' Alwin came to Richard's side, he actually did need the support, his ankle was unexpectedly weak after its work in the stirrup.

'Thank *you* Alwin…'

'I'm pleased to help you, Lord.'

'I am referring to this fuss you have brought upon my head.'

'I think that work was all to your own credit Lord.'

'If I wasn't in so much pain at this moment, I'd have you flogged, I might even have done it myself,'

'Careful Lord, these steps are steep, someone with a damaged ankle could easily fall, and I'm not strong,' they both laughed.

The night seemed never-ending as Richard stared up at his ceiling. He was tormented by thoughts of Julianne on this her wedding night, and her words to him in the hall went around and around in his head. What was she sorry for, he wondered. Eventually, he heard a cock crowing somewhere in the distance, and a shaft of light entered the darkness through a gap in the shutters, it sparkled against the dust floating in the air. He didn't want to face what the new day might have in store for him. I'm as old as I've ever been this day, and I will never be any younger, life is dragging me along and I have no idea where it is taking me. Father used to say "Life should be determined by our hopes not our fears". Fine words, but not so easy to bring to life when all seems so hopeless as it does this day.

There was a knock on the door and Alwin walked in with mete on a tray. 'I thought you may wish to eat in here Lord, Sir John is on his way to see you.' At that second, Sir John walked into the room.

'Ah – Richard, I have just spoken to Sir Guy, he is in the hall at this moment breaking his fast, and in fine spirits, *no* sign of Julianne. He tells me they will not return to London for another three days so that you might have more time to recover. It seems he would not leave you to travel back on your own, too dangerous.'

'What a noble fellow…'

'Indeed, indeed.' Sir John talked casually about the wedding, and what plans Sir Guy and Julianne had made. They would travel to London then he would take her to his estate, the King permitting.

The day for the return journey came too quickly for Richard; he'd managed to avoid any contact with the newly married couple. He sat on a mare Sir John insisted he have, and Alwin was commissioned with the work of leading Ares. They were all awaiting Julianne; eventually she came down the steps and embraced her father. Not the happy carefree bride one would have expected, Richard thought, and felt a pang of sorrow for her, or was it for himself.

He'd had no contact with Julianne, as they travelled, apart from the occasional glance and only a brief polite word with Sir Guy.

When they had stopped for the night Richard had kept well away from the rest of the party, and ate and slept in the stables, not that he was hungry *or* able to sleep.

On one of the fleeting occasions he'd spoken to Sir Guy, Sir Guy said he hoped that *his* predicament with regard to *Sir Gervase* would be made known to the King with some sensitivity for the difficult position he'd found himself and *he* would not forget such a kindness.

'Fear not Sir Guy I will speak supportively of your part, if I'm asked to give an account,' Richard assured him. Poor fellow, was all Richard could ever think when he saw him; no, he would not make life anymore of a trial to Sir Guy, life had that already in hand.

Richard rode some distance behind Julianne and watched her hips sway gracefully – even sensually – to the movement of her horse, as it ambled slowly on. There was a cloud of resignation about her, as if happiness was all but a memory. What did it matter to her, what did anything matter, she appeared as if she was dead to feelings now. Yet still he would have liked some time alone with her, to simply be a friend, they had never once had such a moment. The pain of that need was a miserable thing.

She rode on in silence speaking to no one. As he watched her, he wondered what was going through *her* mind, was she thinking of him, as he was thinking of her? Sir Guy had tried several times to engage her in conversation. She appeared to totally ignore him, and never once so much as turned her head. It was as if she'd – never *even* heard him. After a while, he'd given up and moved on to converse with others. Richard shook his head in despair; any vain hopes were all passed now, to cling to such a futile dream was a road to disaster, life had dealt a miserable hand, and that was all there was to it. His mood now swung between anger towards her in one moment and the deepest sadness in the next.

Never was he so glad to see the palace of Westminster. They rode once again alongside the river Tamyse, with the sight of the red roofs of the palace in the distance.

Their party had been noticed; Richard could see the sudden activity. He knew the news of their sighting would have been made known. As he neared, he could see his three friends there to greet him and his spirits lifted.

They came quickly to his side, their smiling faces changed abruptly to ones of concern when they saw his yet swollen face and arm in a sling. Sir Raymond helped him from his horse and Richard carefully removed his arm from its support so that he could embrace each in turn.

'A jolly wedding, I see from your face,' Sir Tristram smiled.

'Richard, *what* happened,' Esther asked taking his arm, and pushing Tristram none too gently, her brow furrowed with concern.

'Let us go inside and I will make known to you of my adventures.' Richard glanced up to see Julianne looking at him, he nodded, and she was swept away in the melee of activity.

'Some good news for you here Richard,' said Esther, 'you have been rewarded for your work by being given a grander apartment. Much larger, your things have been moved there. So, you will not have to mix with the likes of us in future.'

'Oh, not next door to Sir Guy, God spare me,' they all laughed.

'No, you will have to forgo that joy, but at least we will all be able to go there now and be seated whilst we hear your saga.' She said laughing once more.

'I'd better inform Alwin or he'll take our belongings to my old room. You two go ahead Sir Tristram will show me the way to my new luxurious apartment.' Richard stopped and touched Tristram's arm, 'Tristram come with me.' Esther nodded and walked off with Sir Raymond.

'Are you well Tristram you look troubled?'

'I'm glad of this moment to speak in private with you Richard. I'm concerned for the well-being of Esther.'

'*Why* – what has happened in my absence?' all revelry now gone from Richard's face.

'I have heard rumours from France. Something they are calling the Blois affair, where a person "Is reported" to have seen Jews throwing the bodies of murdered Christians into the river Loire. Despite the flimsy basis for the murder accusation, the populous and the authorities have accepted it, and religious and political leaders have stirred up hate. The Count of Blois has ordered the arrest and execution of over thirty Jews. This talk is rife in the Palace, do you see why I'm concerned?'

'Mmm, I do, you are right to draw my attention to this so quickly. Thank you Tristram, there is only one thing I can do to completely ensure her safety for good.'

'You know more than I for I am at a loss, but by God I will cut down any who threaten her.'

'You are a noble fellow Tristram… but there is another way, and mine to do.'

They saw Alwin organising the unloading of the pack animals and Tristram told him where Richard was now to be housed. Richard spoke little as he and Tristram made their way to his new accommodation. Tristram glanced at him; his face was furrowed in thought.

'It's here Richard – *Richard* – it's here.' Richard's thoughts were far away from concern about a new room, he was thinking about the rest of his life.

'Ah, sorry.' Tristram opened the door and Richard saw that mete and wine had already been fetched for him.

'Be seated,' Richard directed them, they sat waiting for him to speak. 'A fine room, ideally suited for my purpose,'

'So, tell us about your trip north, Richard,' asked Esther.

'My trip north, aye – my trip north.' That was a lifetime ago now, but he began to tell them of his journey and the meeting with Gervase. They were very sombre as he recounted the tale, fully aware of the gravity of what had happened. They sat quietly when he'd finished, he said, 'We should eat, someone has acted very quickly to attend to my needs.' He smiled at Esther, 'or this fine mete will go to waste. We must not risk causing offence to our Lord the King's kitchens.'

Slowly they began to relax, Richard was told that the King was not there, he had crossed the Channel to raise support and an army from amongst his nobles in Normandy, Flanders, Gascony and Anjou.

'We are to ride to Newnham on the Welsh border and join up with his army from France, from there, sail to Ireland. As far as we understand, you are to be one of the commanders. Apparently, "Strongbow" as he was known, the once Earl of Pembroke, had made the mistake of supporting Stephen during the "Tempus were" or the anarchy as it was commonly known, and as a result, Henry had deprived him of his Earldom of Pembroke. Much in the same way, in which you Richard have lost *your* inheritance. Therefore, Strongbow's fortunes were on the wane and he was in severe need of coin.' Richard listened intently to Raymond.

Raymond also told him that, apparently, the Earl of Pembroke had gone to Ireland to escape his creditors, while Gerald of Wales claimed that Dermot of Leinster wanted him because he had a great name, rather than great prospects. Even so, he had much to lose by moving to Ireland, and he was only finally persuaded when Dermot offered him the hand of his daughter, Aífe, in marriage and the prospect of succeeding to Leinster on Dermot's death. Henry has now taken notice and is resolute in his intention to quash any alternative offered by these Norman renegades. He is determined to assert his Lordship over the whole affair, thus his recent departure.

'Interesting times, are they not,' responded Richard.

'We will leave you now Richard to make yourself familiar with your lavish apartment, we have yet work to do.'

Richard was once more distracted by his thoughts and paying no attention to his friends, he tapped his fingers nervously on the table, he had other pressing issues on his mind at this moment, they stood and turned to leave, he looked up.

'Oh – Esther, would you stay for a moment, please?' She sat once again and turned her eyes apprehensively to Sir Raymond and Sir Tristram. Tristram shrugged his shoulders at her unasked question and left. Richard seemed to be concentrating on the drumming of his fingers.

'You are troubled, Richard, do you wish to share or ask something?'

'Esther – this no doubt will be a surprise to you and you might not wish to hear this...'

She stopped breathing; he was sending her away she knew he was. '*Please* Richard, don't send me away, I'm sorry if I have offended you in someway, I'll do anything.' He was shaken from his thoughts and stared at her.

'What are you talking about Esther? I'm not sending you away, on the contrary. I want to ask you – would *you* – consider – marrying *me*?'

Esther was literally struck dumb, and she almost fell from her chair... Richard raised his eyes to her; she could only stare at him, she was *absolutely* – dumbfounded.

'*Richard* – my dearest Richard, I have loved you from the first, but thought such a thing as being your wife impossible, *do you* love me? I always felt that you had some feeling for Lady Julianne, but never me, not as a wife.'

'You know I love you I have told you many times. We are the dearest friends, is our time together not always one of happiness? Many married couples would wish to have what we have.'

'But is it enough to want *me* for a wife?'

'I have thought on all this and I am asking you just that, to be my wife,' he smiled and stood, taking her in his arms, she lifted her lips to his and he kissed her.

She looked into his eyes; still able to feel the warmth of his lips on hers and that warmth swept over her whole body. 'I want you to hold me forever, never let go of me. Yes Richard – I will marry you, and gladly, for I *love* you more than life itself.' He was taken aback; he'd never given her a thought, certainly not, as far as her being his wife. He felt ashamed and unworthy. He wondered could an honourable deed ever be a sin.

'It might be difficult, you are not a Christian, I don't know how such a thing works. I can't ask you to renounce your faith.'

She laughed, 'Though I was brought up in the Jewish faith, my father was a Christian, I told you,' he nodded, 'and he had me baptised when I was a baby, this has always been one of my difficulties with grandfather's people, until now. Now it is a blessing.'

'And would you be happy to put aside your faith?'

'Grandfather said, "We must learn to bend with the wind if we are to survive. Thus, it has always been with my people, and always will". I will bend because of my love for you, but I will not forget.'

'We will need permission from the King, I will attend to that when I meet him in Wales.'

Julianne was lost to him, and he *did* love Esther, she would be safe as his wife from any persecution, he would make this work, he knew she would be the best of wives. Yes, he loved her; "I must think on that, it is I, not Esther, who is the fortunate one". He also knew all Hell would be let loose when Gervase found out. Sooner or later, I will have to kill that man and so it has been from the beginning.

CHAPTER 19

'We must not speak of our betrothal, Esther, until I have spoken to the King, we will need his permission. To make our intentions known without his endorsement, may well anger him.'

'I understand, but you have made me so happy it will be difficult, may we at least tell Tristram and Raymond, they have become my dearest friends?'

Richard thought for a moment and smiled, 'Yes, I think so; perhaps we should mention our thoughts to Alwin too. Servant he may be, but he is as close to me as anyone, and that is as it should be with a truly good servant. Let us simply tell of our intention to seek the King's permission making it clear we will do nothing against his wishes.' She reached up and kissed his lips and he smiled down at her. 'Come, why do we linger.'

They told Alwin first, he was clearly delighted then Matilda, Tristram, and Raymond. Only Tristram hesitated, staring unsettlingly into Richard's eyes.

At the first opportunity, Tristram spoke quietly to Richard.

'You are the noblest and kindest of men Richard, your decision to marry Esther came very quickly on the heels of what I made known to you. We all love you both, and wish for your happiness, this be the noblest thing you do, and an act of the purest love. I will pray for you both, do I need to beg you never to hurt her?'

They walked on quietly for some time before Richard spoke, 'I hear you my friend and thank you, for these are the words of a friend. Fear not, I love Esther and will never hurt her, I realise I am the most fortunate of men.'

'I will say no more, but to wish you the richest life together. I would have married Esther myself, but she only ever had eyes for you, yet it seemed that you never noticed. You don't suppose that her eyes are defective in someway,' Tristram smiled. The moment lightened and Richard pushed Tristram with his shoulder and they both laughed.

Over the next weeks, there was little time for Esther and Richard to be alone because of the frantic work assembling an army. Typically, Henry had left instructions as to who was to lead his English forces south and those, he had named were all minor nobles and knights such as Richard. Henry would make sure that only the men he knew who were "His" men would be given power. The Barons were furious that their historical right to rule and lead was taken from them but none dare challenge the King.

Richard would take Esther with him to Newnham near Pembroke on the river Cleddau where they were to meet the King.

On the morning of the departure, Richard went to help Esther onto her horse. She kissed him affectionately on the lips, it must have been clear to any who noticed that this show of love was not the kiss of a mere friend. As she released him from her arms, he saw Julianne watching them. It was an awkward moment for him, but why should he be so angry that she had seen them? She had made her decision in the full knowledge of her feelings and his life was now with Esther. Yet he knew for certain, that kiss would be a knife turned in Julianne's innards and that pain would not find easy relief.

When he returned, with the mercy of the Blessed Virgin – *and* – King Henry, Esther would be his wife.

His simple life was now very complex, it appeared that whatever he did people were hurt, never was it his intention to be the instrument of delivering such an outcome. Because of him, Sir John's son was estranged to him; Julianne had married a man she could barely stand. Sir Guy could be in fearful trouble from Henry for sheltering Gervase and now Esther; the potential for destroying her was his future, and that was without the reckoning of Gervase's part. It seemed to Richard that every turn he took, his life became more complicated however well intentioned he might be.

On the face of it, his life was one of fame and fortune, he was to be blessed with a beautiful wife, who loved him, and even the King had seen fit to honour him, he was a man who had everything. Yet he knew every blessing that had come his way was now qualified with the word, "BUT"…

The two armies were to meet outside Newnham, then once assembled a delegation would ride and meet Rhys ap Gruffydd. The English army made camp and waited, riders reported that Henry's army would be there within the next two days. Preparations were made to receive and accommodate the King.

Once the King was sighted, the troops were assembled to welcome him with the leaders before them, of which Richard was one. The King was at the head of the army he'd raised from his growing empire, and he rode into their midst. The soldiers cheered and the leaders knelt.

Henry beckoned Richard, he rose and walked to the King's horse and bowed. 'Sir Richard, you have done well, I am not a man who likes to be kept waiting, so it pleases me greatly to find my army ready and waiting for me.'

'You honour me; I am only one of five who have been responsible, my Liege. They deserve as much credit as me.'

'Mmm, did *I* not know this?'

'Forgive me, I mean no impertinence.'

'It is nothing, your humility does you credit. Have you accommodation for me?' Henry asked.

'Indeed Lord. I have seen to that and mete too, might I show you?'

'You appear to think of everything, I will see all five of you, come show me.' With that, Henry leapt from his horse, smiled, and rubbed his hands together; he even did a little jig. Yes, Henry was in fine spirits. Richard gestured to his companions and they came forward, bowed, and walked to the King's tent. Not that he really needed to be shown to it, for it was clearly visible; it was larger, and more splendid than the rest. Now that he was present the magnificent bright red royal standard with the two golden passant Plantagenet lions had been raised, with all its underlying heraldic symbolism of the noble, fearless warrior, and of course its Christian connotation of the

Godly "Lion of Judah", was flapping majestically in the wind for all to see.

'This is fine my good Generals, everything seems to be as I remember it.' Henry glanced around, 'Ah, mete and wine, more than I need you will join me?' He sat at the large table, 'Be seated gentlemen'. Richard had made sure that the seat for Henry was raised above theirs, so they would not be on the same level as him, but Henry seemed relaxed and at ease.

Richard knew Henry was very sensitive about such detail. Though he would talk to anyone, he often ignored rank much to the annoyance of those with rank, but one would be wise never to forget who he was.

'What news of Rhys ap Gruffydd, no doubt he knows we are here. Is he crowing and as defiant as ever, for I mean to crush him once and for all, he and his family have been a thorn in my side for years. What say you to that sport?'

'I have already met with him, Lord. I wanted him to be quite clear that we are here in great number, I may even have exaggerated a little,' Henry smiled. 'I did not want him attempting to waylay or harass our army, by the type of warfare at which the Welsh are apparently masters. We have not time to be delayed. If we are to make our way to Ireland before the winter, our time is limited. I did all I could to inform myself of the Welsh and their tactics before we set off. I know fine well the value of understanding one's enemy. To blindly face a foe and have any subsequent battle decided merely by numbers seems a very unimaginative way to conduct a campaign. I learned that in the tournais, we often succeeded against superior odds because we studied our enemy and planned our tactics to make the most of our resources.' They all made sounds of agreement and Richard continued, 'It has been made known to me of the problems with the Welsh terrain – it's high mountains, deep and narrow valleys, forests, rivers and marshes. I was told that it was a difficult and dangerous undertaking to lead an army into the Welsh interior, which would cost us an unnecessary loss of men. Therefore, I wanted Rhys to know of our overwhelming strength *and* resolve. I have ordered every third man to light an extra fire in case he sends spies after dark. It will do no harm to have such spies return to him with the fearful news of our great army. Fear is a dreadful story teller, the giants get bigger with every telling.' Henry laughed, but was greatly interested in all Richard said; this was not his *first* encounter with Rhys and his family.

'*And?*' The King asked.

'I listened; he was defiant at first, as you so rightly said Lord, I imagine he was trying to intimidate me. I made no commitments on your behalf, but I reminded him of how you dealt with Hugh de Mortimer at Wigmore,' Henry smiled again as he remembered. 'I refreshed his memory, though I could tell he knew well enough. I told him de Mortimer was no fool he surrendered to you; you took his castle from him then immediately gave it back to him, thereafter he has been loyal to you, and was the richer for it. Rhys was less belligerent now and sat silently for some time, staring into his tankard of ale.'

'Ha, you are a shrewd fellow Sir Richard, no wonder my Queen spoke so highly of you. I met your friend, William Marshal, while I have been away, he asked after you, he will be joining me in the near future, and you can renew your acquaintance. You think Rhys would pay homage to me as his Overlord?'

'I do. Might I ask if you have enjoyed the roasted boar before us Lord?'

Henry was for a moment bemused by the sudden change of subject. 'Oh – yes, very fine, I like nothing more, plain simple fayre. No man could ask for better.'

'That was a gift from Rhys ap Gruffydd, to "His" King, were his words.'

'Ah – was it now! And you Gentlemen, do you believe that this fellow has at last come to his senses?'

'Yes, Lord, we have spoken together. Sir Giles was with Sir Richard at the meeting, and was of the same opinion as Sir Richard,' Sir Giles nodded. 'We consider that a peaceful settlement would place us in a stronger position when we face the Irish. Perchance if it did not go well for us in Ireland, we would find ourselves with hostile forces before and behind us. Even if we are, and pray God that it be so, victorious in Ireland, we may well yet have a depleted force on our return, and the prospect of facing a hostile reception would not be to our liking. If we do battle with Rhys ap Gruffydd now, we will lose men. Yet, if we overcome his forces, they could merely disperse and reassemble to face us when we return. Of course, we must not forget we have Rhys' son as our hostage, ever a powerful bargaining piece.'

'I can tell you have given this much thought. I am minded to follow your advice; what you say suits me perfectly, war takes much coin, you have done well. Organise another meeting, I will see of what stuff this fellow Rhys ap Gruffydd is made. God willing, he has learned from the past that he will have not rest whilst I am on the throne of England.'

The King rose and the men bowed and made to leave, the King came to Richard and looked quizzically at him, 'Richard – did you have to wrestle Rhys to the ground to make him see sense?'

'Forgive me Lord, I do not understand…'

'Your face man, and you carry an injury to your arm if I'm not mistaken.'

'Ah – a misunderstanding, Lord, no more.'

'Mmmm, never forget, Richard, I know every hide in my kingdom and everything that happens on it. We will talk further this evening when we have mete, I will make known to you my Norman Generals, but *you* are no stranger to them it seems.' Richard looked astounded. 'See to that envoy, and arrange a meeting with Rhys.'

'Yes, Lord.'

An envoy was sent with the King's instructions; all they could do now was wait. Richard told Esther, Tristram, and Raymond of the outcome of their meeting with the King.

Afterwards he took the opportunity of the hiatus in the planning and negotiations, to walk with Esther among the soldiers; ensuring all was as it should be. It was October now and they could not expect the weather to favour the well-being of their army indefinitely. Decisions had to be made quickly; they needed to cross the Irish Sea before it worsened, it would be next year before they returned, all being well. The leaders had arranged for ships to sail up the River Severn from Dartmouth and meet them at Newnham. Some men sailed with them, but the bulk of the army had come overland, if they had to face a battle with Rhys ap Gruffydd, their options were ever greater on land.

Richard could see that the ships had arrived. The sheer number of them must be making Rhys ap Gruffydd think. He would not know they were all but empty, with only the sailors required to sail them onboard. Richard smiled at the thought of what must be going through Rhys' mind with what he imagined was a sea force on one side of him and a massive land force on the other. They met again with the

King in the afternoon and discussed the campaign. The whole activity seemed to generate life into the King, he was a man of action; there was no doubt about that in Richard's mind.

The King was in high spirits as they left; the planning had gone well. Just as Richard was about to step from the tent, the King called to him. He paused, lowered the tent flap with his arm, and came back in. The King had the strangest expression on his face, somewhere between a smile and a frown; Richard was quite unable to read into it what he was about to say.

'Yes, my Lord,' he said hesitantly.

'Richard, I am delighted with all you have done. I am a generous man and never more so than to those who serve me well. You have worked hard, a King needs such men as you, and I wish to reward you. I have found a bright young wife for you, with a fine estate.' Richard's face dropped; Henry looked bewildered he'd assumed such an offer would delight Richard. 'You do not seem pleased.'

'I am overwhelmed by your kindness, Lord, I have only done, be it on a grander scale, what I have been doing in France. The tournais main purpose is to give training for such as this, as you no doubt know.'

'Well, I wish to reward you, and yet you look troubled! As if I'd forced a poison chalice upon you.'

'It is difficult for me, Lord. I have recently asked a lady if she would be prepared to be my wife, a lady whom I love. She is here with us, it was my intention to seek your permission to marry, I have made no formal announcement of betrothal, not before I had your sanction, but that aside she has consented to be my wife.'

'Ah – I see. Does she have property?'

'No, Lord, she is the ward of Sir John FitzWilliam from Tattershall.'

'I know him, a good honest man of honour, even if he has lacked some wisdom in the past. He has a son, has he not?' Henry captured Richard's gaze for a brief moment.

'Yes, he has a son Lord. Sir John was responsible for the rescue of the lady of whom I speak, when her grandfather was murdered. She is a merchant come farmer's daughter.'

'A merchant's daughter – I can do better than that for a loyal knight, make her your mistress.'

'My Lord, I am your most loyal servant come what may. I am bound to you by honour not for profit. It is this same honour, which must put this lady before any advancement. I know you Lord, to be a man who sets the greatest store by loyalty and hope you will understand my difficulty. If you make me the poorest knight in your service, I will still be loyal to you, for I have sworn such.'

The King was quite at a loss, 'I hear the same voice as your friend, William Marshal. I know not if such loyalty be a blessing or a curse, and I have thought on it believe me. Men who can be bought are the easier to measure, people such as you, and the Marshal, are something quite different. It has already cost me dearly for *one* such fellow who was above coin, but his principles were not for loyalty to me. You have unsettled me, I will think on this, you may go, I must thank you for your honesty, and your promise of loyalty. I take that as no small thing from a man like you.'

'My Liege,' Richard bowed from his waist and left, he knew the King was watching his back as he went.

CHAPTER 20

Richard made his way towards his tent, his brow furrowed deep in thought as he walked. He was troubled as he considered the exchange, he'd this moment had with the King. He paused at the entrance, took hold of the pole that held the tent flap and rested his head on his arm.

'Mmm.'

'You sound troubled Richard.' He was startled and almost jumped.

'Esther, I never heard you!' He reached for her and she came into his arms, laying her cheek on his chest, he pressed his lips to her hair and kissed her head.

'I saw you leaving the King's tent, I waved, but you seemed very deep in thought.'

'Sorry – I never saw you. Yes, *I am* troubled. The King wants me to marry, and it is his pleasure to gift me an estate.'

'*And…*'

'It is not *you* he has chosen to be my wife,' He felt her stiffen and her breathing all but ceased.

'I told you that I loved you… and I do, more than my own life. You must obey the King's commands, forget me,' her head never moved and she made no other sound, but he felt a tear run onto his hand and he tightened his grip on her.

'I – turned down his gift.'

'You *what!*' She pushed herself from his chest no thought of hiding her tears now. 'Richard, Henry would think it an insult; you can have no idea what he will be planning now. I am not worth it. You know of his fierce temper when he feels slighted, you have told me so. Please go back to him, tell him of your error, for mercy's sake.'

'My honour would never allow me to, the Marshal has put his spell upon me,' she wished he had said his love would never allow him to, 'and you only will be my wife, I will beg on the streets before I fail you.' She once again rested her head on his chest.

'Richard, Richard, your honour will be the death of you.'

'Then I will die at peace for there is no better way to face my Maker than to die an honourable death.'

'In truth, I would rather have you alive and dishonoured, death is death, when I see the dead, I know not whether they were honourable or dishonourable, they are just cold empty shells. You men set such store by your honour is it not simply *pride* with a different helm, and is pride not a sin? You will never be completely mine, not as I am yours, you are a man above ordinary men, like your Marshal. The man you are is the man I have loved since the first time you held me, so I will try to love your honour too, though it worries me sorely. Was Henry very angry?'

Richard was puzzled, and more than a little disturbed by what she said, was he simply a man filled with exaggerated pride?

'Err, no – on the contrary he was fearfully calm. I fancy his mind was turned to his once friend Becket. He still feels the pain of that great sadness. I believe he loved Becket, which is why he was so sorely wounded that Becket betrayed him. Becket transferred his love for Henry to his God and Henry was unable to cope with that deficit. Becket made it worse by continually rubbing Henry's nose in his rejection with his constant confrontations with him. If Henry had said white, Becket would have said black, but then my loyalty lies with Henry. As to our problem, he said he would think on our conversation, and bade me good day. Henry is a passionate complex man who gives loyalty and love, and perhaps naively expects that those around him will see life as he does.'

It was dark and yet the envoy had not returned. The King and his generals were seated in his tent, ten in all. Mete had been set before them and as they ate Henry introduced them to each other. When he introduced Richard, he made a big play of them already knowing him and they clapped. Richard shuffled awkwardly in his seat. He was sure they were confusing him with the Marshal.

Whilst they talked informally, they made the most of the opportunity to get to know each other, they laughed and were enjoying newfound comradeship; Richard did his best to relax.

Henry was laughing too and appeared to be delighted with the unity and company of his men, he caught Richard's eye and gestured with a flick of his hand for

Richard to join him. He took the seat offered next to the King.

'No sign of this envoy?'

'I have given orders that I am to be informed the moment he arrives.'

'You think him safe?'

'I do, I told Rhys, that we would be sending such a man and he guaranteed his safe conduct, reminding me that we had his son. I imagine there is much talk amongst his council and that will take time to run its course.'

'Yes, that's the truth.' The King took his knife calmly between his forefinger and thumb, and tapped the hilt lightly on the table looking pensive. 'This lull has given me time to think on our conversation this forenoon,' he paused once more and lifted his eyes to Richard. 'You are a bold fellow and no mistake, I will meet this lady you speak of, bring her to me.'

'Now Lord?'

'Now!' Richard stood and went to fetch Esther.

She was shocked when Richard came hurriedly into her tent and told her the "King of England" commanded that she be presented to him. 'But Richard, I am not suitably dressed, I am wearing naught but my travel clothes, not fit for such a meeting.'

'The King is not a man over concerned with clothes, it is *you* he wants to see and he will see a beautiful lady, no more than that.'

'I must at least wash and attend to my hair, dear, dear, I'm all flummoxed.'

'Do it then, but quickly.' She washed, faced him, and straightened her dress with her hands.

'*Perfect,*' he said smiling, and embraced her.

The tracks between the tents were now becoming too hazardous for light courtly shoes with the constant traffic and the dampness.

'We must see to it that you have some more practical footwear for the winter ahead of us, in Ireland. From what I hear it is a fearfully wet and boggy place.' Esther was compelled to lift her dress clear of the mud as she tried to avoid the worst of it. She lowered her head as she entered the King's tent; all heads turned to her she felt her face flushing. Richard took her to where the King was seated; she curtseyed and remained so until the King bade her rise.

'My, Richard, and I thought you driven by honour, now I see such beauty I am not so sure that it was *honour* that made you so bold. What is your name good lady?'

'I am called Esther, my King.'

'And where does Esther hail from?'

'I am French, my father was a yeoman farmer, but he and my mother and sister were killed in a fire. I am now under the guardianship of Sir John FitzWilliam, a very kind gentleman.'

'What does he think of your proposed marriage?'

'I do not know my King, Sir Richard said we were to do nothing without your say.'

'I have great plans for Sir Richard; he has proved himself a man of immense worth to me. What think you on that?'

'I know no other man so worthy, save *you* my King,'

'Ha,' Henry laughed. 'You will do well at court; let me say this then, Esther… it is my pleasure to grant the wish of Sir Richard.' She staggered and fell back into a chair.

'You may sit,' Henry laughed once more, he was in good fettle this day and amused by Esther's confusion, Richard couldn't move, he was flabbergasted.

'Forgive me my King,' and she made to rise, Henry lifted his hand and bade her stay where she was.

'Perhaps you will be more pleased by my decision on the morrow than you appear at this present time.' He was suddenly distracted by voices when the envoy they'd been waiting for came into the tent. 'That is all good lady, you may go now!' The king said.

Richard offered her his hand and kissed her lightly on the cheek. He beckoned a servant and instructed him to see Esther to her tent.

'Go now; we will speak later; it appears that my head is to remain upon my shoulders. However, at this moment we need to know the news this fellow brings,' he nodded towards the man who'd just entered, 'which may also be of some note,' he smiled at her and tenderly touched her cheek with back of his hand, she kissed him and left.

The messenger bowed and knelt before the King, who bade him rise.

'What news, fellow?'

'The Welsh Prince has made known to me his desire to meet with you, my Lord, at *your* pleasure.'

CHAPTER 21

The following morning a rider was sent to Rhys ap Gruffydd's stronghold to arrange a meeting. He returned before half the morning was gone, leapt from his horse and ran panting to the King's tent. The King and his Generals were sitting at the table, studying maps of the area both of their current position and their intended destination in Ireland.

The messenger knelt, 'Stand and come forward with your news,' the King instructed him.

'My Lord, Rhys ap Gruffydd will be here within the hour.'

'Good news, assemble guards to welcome him, let him see that I honour him and think him not an enemy.' Two of the leaders left the council to do as he'd ordered. 'Have his son brought nearby; I am of a mind to demonstrate my magnanimity – if he is prepared to accept me as Overlord. I want him to know that this is the better option than war.

He can rule in peace with my support. What say you Gentlemen?'

'We agree to a man,' Sir Thomas of Kent said, and heads around the table nodded in agreement.

'Richard organise mete and drink, not ale but our finest wine.' Richard left to attend to the King's instruction. There was a buzz of excitement about the two joined armies; the news had spread as if by wildfire around the camp that the Welsh rebel, Rhys ap Gruffydd was coming as a guest of Henry's.

Whisperings were rife; most speculated it was a trap, some said laughing, that when he arrived, he would dismount from his horse dangling at the end of a rope.

Esther was at her tent and as excited as everyone else. Her world was a beautiful place since she'd met the King the night before and he'd consented to her marriage to Richard.

Richard had written to Sir John for his permission to marry, inline with his rendering of the tale of Esther's history, and Sir John's given part. A rider was despatched that night with the King's permission and they hoped that he would return in the next few days so they could marry and travel to Ireland as man and wife.

The King paced back and forth outside his tent, talked with all who came near, he even went briefly to speak to Esther. Of course, she was a beautiful woman and he was no different from any man, he liked the company of beautiful women and Esther laughed with him. Up until this point Esther had merely been a camp follower, now she was to marry one of the Generals, a lady favoured by the King. The Ladies who'd travelled with their husbands were unsure of her, but she was beautiful, and reluctantly they welcomed this mysterious woman; because of whom she was to marry, she was now part of the elite. Richard had given her a ring that had belonged to his mother, which he'd always worn on a gold chain around his neck. The ring was a heavy gold band with a large ruby set in it. It had belonged to her father, it was really a man's ring, but his mother had it altered to fit her finger. Esther was overwhelmed when Richard had drawn it from his neck, slipped it from the chain, and placed this precious family heirloom onto her finger.

'I have never known such kindness before; I have forever been on the outside. I realised that was how it would always be for me, second best, but not now, with you Richard, you make me feel that I come first.'

'Hmm, I pray God that I never fail you Esther, I will try always to set you above other considerations in my life.' God help me, I love this woman. Help me forget Julianne. Please, please dear Mother of Christ, pray for me a sinner, he begged as he held Esther.

'You have already set me above your life when you tested the King, I never imagined that anyone would do such a thing for me, and for no return. I have nothing but my life and that is yours.' He held her and kissed her forehead, her eyes, then her lips – he did love her.

'RIDERS COMING.' A man appointed as a lookout shouted. Richard jumped onto the stump of an oak tree they'd felled for firewood the night before.

'It is Rhys ap Gruffydd I see him, there are… ten of them – wait – he has stopped, they are talking together, what are they up to? No, he comes on alone, he has left his guard behind.'

'Ah, a man who knows how to play mind games too,' said the King.

It was only moments before Rhys came into view. He was much the same build as the King but whereas the

King had red hair flecked with grey, Rhys had jet-black curly hair showing much more grey. He smiled as he drew his horse to a standstill, it skittered a little, and he dismounted, falling to his knees before the King.

The King reached to him and Rhys placed his hands in a prayerful pose, which the King understood well, Rhys was declaring his subservience to him. Henry took the offered hands in between his and Rhys ap Gruffydd swore fealty to Henry as Lord.

'Rise, Prince of the Welsh and dine with us, we are honoured to have you amongst us, your friends. Have you not a guard?'

Henry knew fine well that Rhys was only Prince of *South* Wales, which he had clearly established since the Norman rebel leaders left their lands in Wales for Ireland. Henry *also* knew that flattery suited rulers well.

'I have Lord, but I wished to show that I know you to be a man of your word and I left them a league back.'

'Sir Richard, have them join us, and Richard – bring the Prince's son, they should be reunited.'

'Yes, my Lord.'

Henry had invaded South Wales in 1163, stripped Rhys of all his lands, and taken him prisoner. A few weeks later, he was released and given back a small part of his holdings. Rhys made an alliance with Owain Gwynedd and, after the failure of another invasion of Wales by Henry in 1165, was able to win back most of his lands. He was no fool; he knew this new alliance would strengthen his hold on his newly acquired domain. He was constantly under peril from his family in the north; with support from Henry or at least peace, he would be able to focus his attention on the northern threat.

Henry was equally conscious of the advantages of having a peace with Rhys; it suited him well at this time. Rhys was to pay a tribute of 300 horses and 4,000 head of cattle; in return, he was confirmed in possession of all the lands he had taken from the Norman Lords, including the Clares. Rhys said he had at this moment 86 horses, which he could gift, but Henry agreed to take only 36 of them and remitted the remainder of the tribute until after his return from Ireland. Henry was more than happy to have rulers such as Rhys within his empire, but they *must* be subservient to him.

Rhys' son, Hywel, who had been held as a hostage for many years, was returned to his father and they embraced.

'I see that you have grown, I hardly recognised you. You have done well on good English mete; the air must have suited you. I can tell the King has cared for you and for that I am thankful.'

Richard wondered how Hywel would readjust to the more basic Welsh court he'd described to him, having grown accustomed to the life and luxuries of the English court.

As they negotiated, they ate, and scriveners made a record of their agreements, eventually a covenant was drawn up and their seals were affixed to it. Darkness had fallen before the Prince left. Richard liked the man; he was affable and laughed heartily at the good-humoured joking throughout the meeting.

Richard thought Henry and Rhys' were of an age. Sir Guy had made known to Richard that Henry was born in 1133, which would make him thirty-eight last March.

Hywel seemed almost reluctant to leave, he had grown attached to Richard, they had regularly practised together on the tiltyard, but it was not so at the beginning.

On one occasion Richard was standing with Esther watching him at the quintain, thrice he'd been unhorsed.

"Dear oh dear, would you excuse me Esther?" Richard walked to where Ares was tied swung nimbly into the saddle and reached for a lance from the rack.

"Here boy, watch me. You are allowing the impact of the strike to cause you to lean back. You must determinedly resist that natural tendency. If you lean back at the moment of impact that *also* reduces the force at which the blow is delivered. To carry the blow with maximum power one needs to lean *into* the moment of impact." and he put spur to Ares and rode at the quintain, striking the target perfectly in its centre, and avoided its spinning arm with ease. He dismounted and Ares was led away, he told Hywel to do it again – and again – he was unhorsed. Richard had shaken his head in despair, even Esther had laughed and Richard shouted, "This is going to be very painful until you do as your told". All the other young men around laughed too.

Hywel remounted spun his horse round and charged full tilt at Richard. Richard pushed Esther to the ground behind a timbered screen, and stepped back into the line of the charging horse, as Hywel thundered towards him. Esther screamed. At the last second Hywel drew his horse to a skidding standstill, his lance only inches from Richard's chest. Richard cast his eyes down at the end of the lance, even though it was not tipped it would have seriously injured him, he was only wearing his favoured loose linen shirt. He walked to the side of the horse and dragged Hywel from the saddle, all who watched feared for Hywel's life. To threaten the life, of not only a *defenceless* knight and he their Lord, but a lady too, was to face a certain flogging.

All were dumbfounded at what happened next. Far from throwing him to the men-at-arms for punishment, Richard wrapped his arms around Hywel and embraced him like a lost son.

"*Forgive me*, Hywel, I was *wrong* to mock you. I am ashamed that I did such a thing. You will make a fine knight."

Hywel was in tears and Richard hid the young man's face in his arms so that he would not be shamed. There was a lasting bond forged that day. Esther had only been able to sit back against the protective hoarding trembling and in tears. She simply could not believe this man; he had never flinched although faced with serious injury perhaps even death, and *"He"* had begged for forgiveness. He was no ordinary man; she shook her head in sheer disbelief at what she'd just witnessed. It was no wonder that he was so loved and that these young knights worshipped him. She could well understand how someone weak like Gervase, would let his *envy* turn into hatred for such a man as Richard, for Richard was all that Gervase was not.

Rhys and his men were about to leave the day's council and return to the Welsh camp when Hywel touched his father's arm, turned his horse, and rode to Richard's side; he was standing next to the King. Hywel reached down his hand to Richard and he took hold of it.

'*You* – are the *greatest* knight, I place *none* above you.' All who stood nearby heard his affirmation. Richard said nothing but bowed. Hywel rejoined his father and rode off, all were silent at this overt act of homage; even the King was clearly struck by the sincere love in this spontaneous demonstration of affection.

When the Prince left, Henry continued the council meeting with his Generals. He was filled with energy after the day's excitement and was not for sleep. The talk of their future invasion of Ireland eventually concluded. The contented assembly of knights, carried on into the morning with feasting, and drinking. Their Ladies were invited to join them and with them, Esther. This was her first such occasion and there was much light talk of her forthcoming wedding. In the midst of the frivolity, Richard was plagued with thoughts of Julianne, which no amount of drink would obliterate.

CHAPTER 22

Richard had managed to get himself to Esther's tent with Alwin's help. Though he felt exceedingly ill, he was certain he had not disgraced himself. He was able to escort Esther despite the fact, that he knew he was morose and struggling to form words in his mouth. Every ounce of his willpower was required to present the appearance of a sober human being, he was able to bow to all he met, not that he recognised them.

As soon as he stepped from Esther's tent, he all but collapsed. 'Never again Alwin, I have never felt so ill in all my life. Never again, never again, I don't think Esther realised, do you Alwin?'

'It has been my observation Lord, that people in their cups have a way of looking more drunk by trying to look sober. Perhaps she may have had some inkling, but she is too much of a lady to make mention of it. You may have overdone it a little with your bowing, especially to that horse. No doubt the dark moonless night was at fault.'

'Ah – yes, it is fearfully dark. The darkness plays tricks on one's eyes,' Richard hiccupped. 'Have you noticed the movement of things before your eyes?'

'A strange phenomenon, Lord and I imagine you find it particularly prevalent this night.'

He hiccupped once more, 'I do, I do, now you make mention of it, Alwin.'

'I thought so, Lord.'

'You are a good fellow, Alwin, more of a friend than a servant.'

Alwin's observations seemed to sap away the last remnants of Richard's strength, he staggered, tripped over a rope supporting a tent pole, shot out of Alwin's grip *and* in the same movement one of his boots, and landed in a heap of his own vomit which had preceded his flight through the air by a fraction of a second. Alwin had to bite his lip for the sight was, to say at the least – comical, he had seen jesters at the court tumble with less humour.

Esther must have heard the noise for she looked from her tent. On seeing Richard, she ran out and knelt by his side.

'Alwin, go and find Sir Tristram, or Sir Raymond, we ought to get him into his tent before any of his men see him, he looks very ill.'

'I will manage, Esther.' Alwin turned him over and dragged him by his feet into his tent whilst Esther held the flap open for him.

'Careful Alwin, his head is banging on the ground.'

'Fear not Esther, judging by the smile on his face he appears thoroughly amused by the whole experience.'

'ALWIN, this is not a moment for levity!'

'No, ma'am.'

Once inside the tent Alwin manhandled him onto his bed.

'Find some warm water, Alwin, I will undress him, he needs to be washed.'

'*But…*'

'Just do as I say, he is to be my husband and I have seen men before.'

'My Lord may not see it like that, but I will do as you order.' Alwin returned in a short while with a bucket of warm water and Sir Tristram.

'Esther, I see you are coping admirably with our noble Lord.' Esther only glanced up at him; the look was such that he immediately removed the smile from his face. Richard was stretched out on his bed as naked as the day he was born. At a first glance the deathly pallor could have led one to believe he'd passed on, until that is – he burst into a non too melodic singing of some bawdy song, managing with some skill to sing in two keys at the same time. Fortunately, he was struggling to remember the words and kept having to restart again, both Tristram and Alwin were compelled to laugh until Esther rebuked them and they apologised. She was growing more furious by the second.

'Give the bowl to me, I have no inclination for your jesting, you are no better than he.' Esther was clearly not amused; she pushed them out of her way and began to wash Richard. Alwin, now contrite, helped, they dried him and wrapped him in rugs for he was shivering uncontrollably.

'The decision is yours Alwin, you may stay with us and protect your master's virtue, but I am about to slip from my dress and lay next to him to keep him warm. The night is frosty and he may catch a fever, he is sweating and keeps throwing off the coverings. Or do you wish for such work?'

'Coward that I am, but I do not want my master to awake and find himself naked in *my* arms. He may misunderstand my good intentions. I will go to my humble tent which is next to this, call if I am needed.' Although she was not in the mood for humour, Esther had to smile at the vivid scene in her mind of Alwin holding his naked master.

Esther undressed lay down next to Richard, and fell fast asleep.

It was daybreak by the time Esther was awoken. There was a great deal of activity outside their tent. At first, she couldn't understand where she was, then a hand touched her and she sat up and screamed. Alwin ran half dressed into the tent, his dagger drawn, Esther pulled the rugs up to cover herself.

'Where is my Lord?'

'He has fully recovered, *believe* me Alwin,' the rugs covering her had obscured Richard from view.

'Leave us Alwin; your master apparently has the constitution of a horse, and Alwin – I would appreciate your discretion, I am here only because of *your* cowardice.'

'Indeed, ma'am.'

There was some movement under the covers and Esther moaned, '*Go* Alwin, quickly!'

'Are you sure, ma'am?'

'*Yes, she is,*' he heard Richard's voice answer from below the covers.

Richard pulled back the tent flap, the sun was well up, he looked up at the sky and blinked, perhaps he was not as well as he thought. He straightened his gambeson and ran his finger around the neck it was strangely tight. Once his eyes came into focus, he saw directly ahead of him Sir

Tristram, Sir Raymond, and Alwin sitting on a log facing his tent and grinning like fools.

Richard coughed and ran his finger once more around the neck of his gambeson, which seemed to have suddenly tightened even more.

'Can I not leave you to your own devices for a minute but you are shirking your duties.'

'Forgive us, Lord, we await your instruction.'

'There is work aplenty, we must pack and see to loading an army onto these ships. There is not a day to waste. Has the King risen yet?'

'No, it seems our leaders to a man are in no hurry this day.'

Richard had to keep opening and closing his eyes to try to bring some sense to his head, it was pounding.

It was midday before Richard saw Esther once more; she was packing her things and his, with the help of maids. Richard, no more a mere humble knight, had now a whole retinue of servants to do his bidding.

Esther was gradually beginning to realise how important he'd become. She was no longer marrying some insignificant stipendiary knight, but a leader in the King's army, a man who conversed daily with the King of England. She was unsure what was expected of her; she had no idea how a person betrothed, to such as Richard, should conduct herself. People she did not know now bowed to her, even people with rank. Lady Julianne would have known how to behave, she thought. She wondered how long it would be before the rider returned from Tattershall with permission for them to marry, then she panicked once more, what if Sir John refused…?

CHAPTER 23

The work for the past three days had been frenetic. Richard had never stopped, labouring night and day with the preparations for their mission. Esther had been busy too, but not *so* busy, that she did not have time to worry as to the whereabouts of the rider, who was hopefully, bringing Sir John's permission for her and Richard to wed. She had been convinced that he would have arrived before it was time to set off for Ireland.

It was a cold afternoon with rain in the air, not much wind. Once they set sail, their travel was painstakingly slow. There had been a heavy mist in the morning and all were cold, wet, and miserable. This was an army, which was in low spirits as they set off to subdue and assert authority over the Irish. The leaders knew this would need to be addressed very quickly when they landed.

Weather played a large part on morale; Richard knew this fine well, as did the other leaders. He was impressed with those Henry had appointed, they worked well together, all sensible good men. Henry's idea of appointing men because of their ability rather than their assumed right through rank, undoubtedly had contributed to his success as a commander.

Richard and Esther stood at the stern of the ship watching England disappear into the distance. Neither had made mention of the disappointment, but Richard was keenly aware of how upset Esther was, as he stood silently with her at this moment clinging to his arm.

'Fear not, my little mouse,' she cuffed a tear from her eye. 'The rider will come,' and he took her in his arms and kissed her wet face.

'You knew what was on my mind, I have never made mention of it, I have seen so little of you these last days.'

'I am sorry for the neglect. There has been much to plan. We sent a ship, and soldiers, before us yesterday to spy out the land. With luck, they will find us a safe place to land and make camp. We are to land at, or near, the oldest town in Ireland, called Waterford.'

'Why is this so important to Henry?'

'The main reason is that Henry does not want another Norman power established in Ireland to challenge his authority. The Norman Lords, who are there now, are to some extent rebels and no friends of Henry. They were supporters of King Stephen against Henry's mother, the Empress Matilda. After losing the protection of Muirchertach Mac Lochlainn, the High King of Ireland, who died five or six years past, Diarmait MacMurrough was forcibly exiled by a confederation of Irish forces under the new High King, Rory O'Connor. MacMurrough fled first to Bristol and then to Normandy. He sought and obtained permission from King Henry to use the latter's subjects to regain his kingdom. Having received an oath of fealty from Diarmait, four years past, Henry gave him letters of authority. MacMurrough was sure he'd obtained enough support to invade. In addition to Henry's patronage he had also formed an alliance with the once Earl of Pembroke, Richard de Clare, who like his father, is commonly known by his nickname Strongbow, but this was *not* to Henry's liking.'

'Ah, you have mentioned him before.'

'The first Norman knight to land in Ireland was Richard Fitz Godbert de Roche, four years ago, but it was not until sixty-nine that the main body of Norman, Welsh and Flemish forces landed in Wexford. Within a short time, Leinster was conquered, Waterford and Dublin were under Diarmait's control. Strongbow married Diarmait's daughter, Aoife, and was named as heir to the Kingdom of Leinster. This latter development caused consternation to King Henry, who feared the establishment of the rival Norman state in Ireland, which I mentioned previously. Accordingly, he resolved to visit Leinster to establish his authority once and for all, and that's what he intends to do now.'

'Forgive me Richard; you must think my tears very trivial, when you have such great concerns of state on your mind. All that is in *my* head, is the document from Sir John.' Richard turned her to him and wrapped her in his arms pressing his lips to her head.

'My dearest Esther, perhaps what you are concerned about is *all* that is truly important. A few people of position, who are perhaps only anxious about their own power and wealth, compel us to fight and kill each other. It has been my observation that the ordinary person has only simple everyday concerns, mete, warmth, family, and love. The majority of people do not want to kill each other, or assert themselves; they just want to *live* their lives.

Perhaps it's fear that drives us when it should be love. I'd hoped that we followers of Christ may offer an example to the heathen, but I am heartily ashamed when I hear the stories of how we behaved on the crusades. I don't know the answers,' he shrugged his shoulders, 'it has been so since Adam was a boy. I'm afraid I only try to behave rightly in the small place where God has placed me, and no doubt fail miserably even with that humble commission. I will leave that judgement to others wiser and more Godly than me.'

'Sir Richard Maillorie, did I tell you that I love you?' And she reached up and pressed her lips to his.

'Trust me, we will hear from Sir John and we will be wed. I don't know when it will be, but it will happen.'

The fleet sailed slowly up the twisty river Suir to Waterford, there was a tension amongst the soldiers and their leaders, wondering what they were to face.

Before the landing, there was a meeting on the King's ship with the forward party, which was sent ahead, and now came to give their report.

Henry listened to what was said. It seemed that the people of Waterford were afraid that Henry intended to wreak the same terror on the town as in the August of the previous year, when they were invaded by the Norman, Strongbow. Henry turned to his leaders, they paused, and one by one, they offered a similar opinion.

The consensus was that Henry should present his arrival as one who has come to liberate the town, not to subjugate it, and thus garner the support of the people and their leaders against the rebel Normans from Wales.

Richard was convinced at this time that for Henry to enter into a conflict in Ireland would be an unnecessary drain on his coffers.

It was decided, and ambassadors were sent to meet with the leaders at Waterford and deliver Henry's offer. He would be declared Overlord, and the present authorities would administer the country, with him as their Lord. In return, Henry would ensure stability, and freedom from constant upheaval. He knew that this was a poor country and such unrest brought with it a terrible cost for the disadvantaged.

The ambassadors returned with the agreements for such an outcome. When Henry disembarked from his ship, he was to be the first English King to ever set foot on Irish soil. Henry entered the stronghold in a blaze of pomp and grandeur to the cheering of Waterford's citizens. There would be a cost to Henry's benevolence, but for the time being, such detail was forgotten.

After the meeting with the leaders, Henry beckoned Richard.

'Richard, a word,' Henry said leaning close to him.

'Yes, my Liege.'

'We will march on Dublin within the week, their resistance crumbles before us, but I need to see and be seen. I do not want to sail home and have to return within the year to face a worse problem.'

'I understand this Lord.'

'Did you see another ship arrive today?'

'Yes, I ordered it watched and sent soldiers on board. It was an English vessel they had brought missives purportedly for you, I know not what they were, but I ordered that they be brought to you. Was that done, Lord? By God, I will have someone's head if it was not.'

'Peace Richard, they came to me. Let me ask you something, and I want you to answer without fear,' Henry smiled, 'not that you ever speak with anything other than with boldness.' Richard looked pensively at Henry, 'Tell me what you thought of Thomas Becket?'

'Lord, in truth, I did not know the man, my opinion was formed by rumours and the opinions of others perhaps even less well informed than myself.'

'And what is that opinion?'

'For the little value of it, I thought Becket an arrogant fool who was blinded by his position; I heard that even the Pope struggled with him. His death, though almost inevitable, was a terrible tragedy. I do apologise if I offend you Lord, for I have heard that he was your friend, and that you loved him and I *do* know how saddened you were that such a thing happened.'

'You are a strange man Richard, from anyone else I would hear a flatter's voice, but not with you. You are honest to a fault.' Henry drew his eyes together and furrowed his brow as if assembling his thoughts before he spoke.

'The correspondence made known to me that Papal legates have been sent to England to investigate the death of Becket.' Richard listened intently as Henry spoke in a whisper. 'I want you to return home immediately and meet them as my appointed envoy. I do not want to be imagined as distraught with guilt and fear, thus rushing home in panic, but I do want to be seen as supportive of such an investigation and I think you are the person to present a favourable balance. Do you understand?'

'I do my Lord, but are you certain I am such a man?'

'I have watched you and you have shown yourself to be equally able to use your brain as your sword.'

'Of course, I will do as you wish, I am your servant.'

'No doubt you will be a married man when we meet next, I will be sad indeed to miss the performing of the Holy Sacrament,' Henry's face was now transformed and he laughed. However, Richard's face was sombre and Henry slowly ceased his humour realising that something was amiss.

'About my marriage Lord, all I have said is the truth, but I am troubled.' Henry's face was expressionless now. 'I must make it known to you that Esther was brought up in the Jewish faith, though she has been baptised a Christian. I do not want my neglect to be used to make advantage against you at some time, by persons who would wish to harm you.' There was still no expression on Henry's face, Richard could feel his heart pounding fit to burst, and still Henry stared at him.

'Mmm,' Henry eventually spoke, 'And did you imagine I was without such knowledge Richard?' Now it was Richard's turn to present a completely blank face, and Henry smiled. 'You did not need to make such a thing known to me. Your integrity risked losing my blessing, yet you placed your heart bare before me. I will not forget this demonstration of deference to me as your Lord. You have touched my heart believe me. I gave you my blessing, in the full light of my knowledge and I give it once more,' and he reached to his hand, and removed from his finger a large gold ring, on which was mounted a deep orange cameo stone with his crest carved into it. 'Take this, and wear it, you are my man.' He took Richard's hand, slipped the ring onto his finger, and kissed him on either cheek. 'Go now to Canterbury; find out about these legates, the truth of it seems vague in the letters. First, see my treasurer, he has been instructed to give you funds. Take with you the men you want and God willing we will meet again soon. Read the documents carefully, it is my pleasure to honour you, I will say no more.'

Richard looked bemused, but bowed, and went to find the man with the King's purse. He had been expecting him. As well as the coin he'd been promised, he was given letters. One the King's authority to represent him, Richard could only stare at it, a document to represent the King of England. He shook his head then rolled it up and placed it into the leather wallet. There were two other documents, one authority from the King to marry Esther and another a wedding gift. He was to hence be known as Lord Richard of Aylesford in Kent, and a description of his holding, which included a stone-built castle. Richard could imagine Henry's smile, knowing, full well, how shocked he would be.

'Will that be all my Lord?'

Richard slowly lifted his eyes to look at the man, 'Quite.'

'Our master is a generous man, is he not?'

'Quite.' That was the sum total of Richard's vocabulary it appeared. He rolled up the other two documents and placed them in the wallet, slipped the carrying strap over his shoulder, bowed and left.

Richard found Sir Tristram and Sir Raymond sitting by a roaring fire feasting on roasted mutton.

They stood when they saw him approaching. 'You've decided to spend the evening with the rabble have you Richard?'

'Chance be a fine thing; we have work to do – in England.'

'In England – have we not but come from there these past days?'

'Well, we are to return now, seems like the good folk of Ireland worry if they will have enough sheep to feed you two,' they laughed. 'Pick twenty, no, thirty of your best men and have them taken back to our ship, we sail on the first tide. I will meet you there.' He bowed and disappeared into the darkness.

As he was being rowed out to his ship, the cool breeze blowing on his face began to cool his brain as well as his cheeks and he was able to absorb, in some measure, the enormity of the evening's business.

'Phewwww,' he exhaled a long breath, the Queen was right when she described the boundless energy of the King. I wonder how Esther is going to like being Lady of the manor. The smile slowly fell from his face, and he thought of Julianne, a life robbed of all this in a moment of petty childish pride – just *one* moment – the price of such a gesture was indeed a high one.

CHAPTER 24

Esther went on deck when she heard the guard call out the watch.

'STRANGERS APPROACHING, to your posts.'

She'd wrapped herself in a large hooded cape at the sound of the voice to protect herself from the biting wind and salty spray, which was whipped over the side of the ship stinging eyes and cheeks alike. She leaned over the gunwale trying to see whom it was that approached. Only to be told by a guard to stand back for fear there was danger.

All that told of an approaching boat was the glow from a light and the rhythmic splash of oars. Gradually straining eyes caught sight of flickering water from the sliver of moonlight, which touched the edges of the water broken by the oars. Apart from that, the night was pitch black. Esther was excited, she *knew* it was Richard and her heart leapt with relief to know he was safe.

'We're friends, the King's men, carrying Lord Aylesford, we want to board.' Richard smiled he knew they would not have a clue who Lord Aylesford was. The ghostly lantern swinging from a post at the bow of the small craft made it difficult to see those onboard. All that could be seen was intermittent splashes of yellow shimmering light cast by the lantern onto the moving hands of those rowing.

'Come into the light of our vessel so you can be seen, we have archers so beware,' the guard called back. Esther squinted trying to see, and was rewarded with the sight of a waving hand, gradually Richard's face came into the light cast from the ship.

'RICHARD,' she called excitedly, returning the wave. 'Put up your arms it is your Lord,' she called. The small craft drew alongside the large ship, Richard was offered a hand, and he leapt onto the rope ladder and clambered lithely up and over the side onto the deck, bowing to Esther with a smile.

'Return and fetch the others as soon as they are assembled,' Richard called down to the boat below.

'Aye, aye, Lord,' a voice came from the darkness as oars pushed the small craft away from the ship and once more shrouding it in darkness.

Richard embraced Esther, 'Come to my cabin, one moment, wait here, I must speak quickly to the Master then we will talk.' He turned and spoke to the ship's Master, William FitzHerbert, who bowed.

'My Lord.'

'William, make for Dover on the first tide.' The Master hesitated, 'Is there some problem?' demanded Richard.

'I have written orders, Lord, which state I am to remain here until the King issues new commands.'

'Do you know who I am, William?'

'Yes Lord, I knows well enough, you sailed with us. You are one of the King's commanders.'

'Read this,' Richard withdrew the King's letter of authority from his wallet, lifted it closer to his eyes to be sure it was the correct document and passed it to the Master.

The Master held it to a lantern so he could read it; he looked at Richard and returned the document. 'Your servant my Lord Aylesford,' he said bowing.

'William, do you see this?' Richard showed his knuckle and the large gold ring with the King's arms upon it. 'When I speak you will never question me again, for it is the King you are obeying, *is* that clear?'

'I'm sorry my Lord,' the Master bowed once more and Richard went to Esther's side.

'What was all that about Richard, who is Lord Aylesford?'

'Come to my cabin and I will explain.' The sailors all bowed with respect as he passed them.

His quarters were cramped; there was a very small cot, he couldn't even lie straight out in it, and there was a three-legged stool. Esther was only just able to stand upright; Richard had to move around doubled over. He offered her the choice, and she seated herself on the cot and leant against one of the ribs of the ship, Richard sat on the stool facing her.

'*Now*, tell me Richard, what of that odd exchange between you and the Master.'

'I am at a loss as to know where to start… First, let me introduce to you Lord Aylesford.'

'I don't understand!'

'ME – my little mouse, the King has elevated me and now you are to marry a Lord, a man of property who lives in a castle with a fine estate in Kent, though I have yet to see it I assume it to be so.' She could only stare at him. 'You, my dear Esther, are to be Lady Esther of Aylesford, the *grand* Lady of one of the King's favoured knights,' and he showed her his ring.

'That's the King's ring, I have seen him wearing it.'

'It is indeed, he gave it to me, are you not pleased?'

'Well, yes, of course, I think so; I don't know *what* I really think. I simply can't assemble my thoughts they are afloat on the high seas as we have been these last days.'

'We are to leave Ireland on the first tide hence the interaction with the Master, you have the moment past been privy to, and make for Canterbury via Dover. Our lives seem to go around in circles. This is where my new life began and such a journey is now to birth me yet another life.'

She smiled as she saw the possibilities. 'That *means* we will be able to marry, praise be to God, no waiting in Ireland until next year. That is all I need to know.'

Richard laughed, 'I have in my wallet,' he touched the leather document bag at his side, 'the King's written authority to marry. I will send two riders north to Tattershall as soon as we land at Dover. With them a missive humbly requesting permission from Sir John, for you and I to marry, and would it please him to send such consent to Canterbury as soon as possible. I will also make known to him our change in fortunes.'

Richard knew that it was important for a lady to be seen to have someone of prestige with authority over her, so that she belonged, and Sir John had by default, taken on that role.

'What about Tristram and Raymond?'

'I have been given authorization to take whomever and whatever I need for this expedition, and they will be joining us before this night is past.'

'Why are we going to Canterbury, and not London?'

'Ah – I will explain all when Tristram and Raymond arrive. Come, Lady Aylesford, let us stretch our legs.'

'First sit by me and kiss me. Such would not be appropriate on deck and I have sorely missed you. You cannot believe how much, your joyous news – *almost* – makes such a discrepancy worth it.'

'Ah, Master,' Richard said as he came from his cabin onto the deck.

'Yes, my Lord,' the Master bowed nervously.

'William, be at ease. I apologise if you thought me a little abrupt when we spoke earlier; you acted perfectly correctly. With your kindness we will make no more mention of the encounter, I have much on my mind, but that is not your concern, forgive me.'

'Thank you, my Lord.'

'When is the next favourable tide, William?'

'The sixth hour of the day, Lord.'

'Very good, perfect time; I wish to be informed when you make sail. Within the hour we will be joined by thirty souls, soldiers, knights, and two Captains, see to it there is mete and drink for them. Have you ample stores for our voyage?'

'Aye, Lord, we will reach Dover in two, maybe three days God willing, and we were restocked this day, expecting that we'd be here for a long stay.'

It was not an easy voyage the wind drove them perilously near the rocks as they rounded the Lizard. The ship had, with creaks and groans, listed and thumped against the deluge of water with such force, they all feared that it would be torn apart at any moment and its wooden walls would be their coffin. Nausea lurched in the bellies of all, even the most resolute of sailors.

It was Christmas Eve when they arrived at Dover and they were greeted with flurries of snow in the air. All were relieved to be once more on dry land, some were so ill they needed to be carried ashore, Matilda, Esther's maid being one of the afflicted. Three horses had been lost overboard and the rest like their masters were clearly relieved to be on dry land. Fortunately, this ship was designed for the purpose of transporting horses, and was fitted with a ramp for easy unloading.

This voyage had more than tempered Richard's love of sailing. He almost stumbled; so unsure was he of his legs when he lifted Esther onto Ares. He steadied himself took a deep breath and led him up the hill, away from the jetty. This hill held some lasting memories for him, particularly as he passed the inn where he'd first met Sir John, and had been introduced to his family. He hoped that the sharp stab of pain that followed the most fleeting thought of Julianne, would not be his to own for life.

Accommodation was found for them in Dover castle, no longer was Richard to be a man who slept in stables. The King's warrant in his possession appeared to breakdown all doors that it touched. The custodian would go to any length to see that Lord Aylesford and his Lady were contented. This time Richard had a room as well as Esther. His apartment was lavish, with a large bed, and wall coverings of rich red and gold. In the centre of the room, there was a large oak table with a dozen chairs *and*, most welcome of all – a blazing fire.

Ideal thought Richard for he needed to talk fully with Sir Raymond and Sir Tristram about the work he was commissioned to undertake. Such conversation had been limited onboard the ship because of the space and lack of privacy. However, Richard had not wasted his time on the voyage, he'd used the occasion to acquaint himself with the men that Raymond and Tristram had selected, and he was now familiar with all their names.

They feasted on goose that Christmas Day, first having attended mass in the Saxon church nearby. Richard had taken the opportunity to ask the priest about his marriage. The priest had reassured him that the King's permission was all he required. That meant it did not necessitate Sir John's approval, however he felt that for his peace he needed such. He discussed his feelings with Esther and she reluctantly agreed, for she neither wished to offend Sir John who had shown them both great kindnesses. It was during this conversation Richard made known to Esther, that King Henry knew of her connections and upbringing.

'I am relieved that you made such known to the King, it would have forever been a darkness hanging over us and I am only too familiar with such a way of living. I never want our future to have any unsaid darkness, such a thing holds only death not life.'

Richard smiled bravely.

They walked alone around the castle grounds in the afternoon. 'I am sorry that I have no gift for you on this day, Esther, but I will make this neglect right in due course.'

'Richard, my life feels to be filled with the most incredible gifts already, I could not wish for more.'

'Aylesford is but a day's ride from Canterbury; as soon as we are married, we will ride there. We need to make ourselves known to all, and I am anxious that we do this immediately. It does not take long for anarchy to settle in. Overseers may well take the opportunity to make some coin for their own pocket. Uncertainty in life breeds insecurity and fear; I want to establish the rule of law as soon as possible for the sake of all. I have sent the two riders, I spoke of on the voyage, northward with a letter to Tattershall, and will expect them within a day or so of our arrival at Canterbury.'

'I will have to prepare for our wedding as soon as we arrive in Canterbury, what will we do for coin, we have none?'

'I have coin but it is the King's, I will use it and then replace it once I have what is mine, from either our estate or what was left at Tattershall.'

Richard, Raymond, and Tristram sat around the table in his room and he made known to them what was expected of him at Canterbury.

'Have you any idea who is in charge in this interim period before a new Archbishop is appointed?' Neither knew for sure, any more than he did.

'Who wrote to the King, do we know?' asked Tristram.

'That correspondence came via Canterbury from the Pope himself.'

'The Pope will be the head at this time, but there must be someone who has daily charge of administration. It is my thought that Richard a Benedictine monk, from Dover, will be making the decisions. I heard that he took charge of the burial of Becket; they had been working closely together for some time. It appears he has a sharp legal mind with an eye to his future, he was reported to have had some discussion with the Young King Henry, that can have only been with an end to causing a fissure between father and son.'

'Thank you, Raymond, I hear the Young King Henry is hankering after more power, but his father is reluctant to give up his hold. There will be trouble from that quarter and in the near future, of that I am certain. I know that the

King hoped to secure his dynasty by having him crowned as King-in-waiting, but that good intention might be a dog that is not content to sleep in his basket until King Henry the Second departs this earth. He may well rise up to bite him in the vitals, if he is truly his father's son. However, that aside, with regard to Canterbury, we will find out soon enough, but Richard of Dover will be a starting point. We will leave on the morrow's first light. The King will expect to be fully informed; I have learned that he wants to know of every detail in his Empire, he has the most incredible memory and understanding. We must all be conscious of this when we inform him of our findings. He will expect to know everything.'

'Might I suggest that I travel onto Aylesford from Canterbury with a dozen men, so that you do not feel under any pressure and can take your time to deal with the King's work in peace. I will establish your authority and get to know the manor and it's structure.'

Richard furrowed his brow, 'Mmm, that sounds to be ideal, this is asking a great deal Raymond. I *am* concerned; the manor is of some importance to the King, it belonged to his great-grandfather William the Conquer, and is part of the King's own estate. We have time to discuss details, I will furnish you with written authority.'

CHAPTER 25

Richard stretched as he walked down the stairs of the keep into the yard, followed by Esther then Alwin and Matilda. He smiled as his eyes lighted on an industrious sparrowhawk sitting on a post, manipulating a piece of carrion in its claws, quite mindless of him. It was tugging at the hard meat whilst balancing precariously on the post, periodically fluttering its wings to keep its balance. Richard placed his hand over his mouth as he yawned again – soon he would be in his own home and the thought warmed his heart.

The sun was beginning its daily passage, its rays flickering through the treetops in the wood beyond the castle. There was a glistening dampness everywhere from the heavy morning dew. He shuddered involuntarily to shake off the sneaky morning air, looking up he knew this would be a fine day. Sir Tristram and Sir Raymond were walking amongst their men talking and laughing as they waited.

'Are we ready?' asked Richard.

'Yes, Lord we were packing before the sun was up. We need to make haste if we are to reach Canterbury before dark.'

'I intend to stay at the castle; we are completely different people from the ones who last stayed in that town, a lifetime ago. The castle is only minutes away from the Cathedral and they will have all the facilities to house our men and horses. You can send a rider ahead when we are nearer, to make our arrival known.'

Richard helped Esther onto her horse and the party set off. Riders were once again dispatched to ensure their safety when they passed through the wooded part of their journey, where they'd first met Esther. She made no comment as they passed the place where her grandfather had died. Richard merely smiled and nodded to assure her he was conscious of her thoughts.

It was dark when they arrived in Canterbury, there were people all over the place, and it had the feel of a carnival. Pushing, shoving, traders in every corner, selling everything one could imagine. Mete, trinkets, and remedies for all ailments. Richard looked at Esther; they had to almost force their way through the throng to the castle.

Richard de Luci, Chief Justiciar for King Henry came to welcome them. He informed Richard that he was there to negotiate the transfer of land, from one Azelitha, to the King, and he would give her other land in compensation. That would then enable the King to strengthen and extend the castle.

'Come, my Lord, your knight made known to me of your imminent arrival on the King's business. As we speak, your accommodation is being prepared.'

'Thank you, let me introduce my betrothed, lady Esther. Sir Tristram and Sir Raymond.' The Chief Justiciar bowed. 'I need to talk with Richard of Dover as soon as possible. Can he be invited to take mete with us this night?'

'I know him; I will see if such can be arranged. Take the Lord, his lady and his officers to their apartments.' He ordered some servants who awaited his instruction.

'The town seems unusually busy, is there some festival of which I am unaware?'

'Ha, you have not been here for some time I understand! It is like this every day, pilgrims come from far and wide, hoping for a miracle. The hand of God has performed many healings of every sort through the saintly Archbishop's prayers to our Beloved Mother of Christ. He will be canonized; it is only a matter of time.'

'Are you referring to Becket?'

'Yes, the beloved of God, the martyred Archbishop, who gave his life gladly, at the altar of Christ. *Even I* have a vial of his precious blood, which I carry around my neck.' He showed Richard the chain, 'to ward off all manner of evil vapours.'

'No doubt your master the King will be delighted to know the regard in which you hold Thomas Becket.'

'No, no do not misunderstand me,' realising perhaps he'd said too much to an envoy of the King. 'I am not one of the people who suggest that our King was in anyway part of his murder, our King himself is a saintly man, yes indeed,' he added quickly.

Hmm, smiled Richard to himself, this is a lawyer who knows how to defend a vulnerable position. 'I see, interesting. So, Becket is now loved by the Holy Church, where he was once an embarrassment to our Father in Rome!' The Chief Justiciar bowed, averting his eyes.

Clearly, he didn't want to engage in this conversation, probably feeling he had said too much as it was. He begged leave to be about his business, bowed and he scurried off, Richard hoped, to organise the meeting with Richard of Dover.

They followed the servants, 'Come with us Alwin and once you know where we are to be settled you can then attend to our baggage,' Alwin nodded. 'Oh, and Alwin, see if you can organise bathing for my lady Esther, hot water and warm towels,' again Alwin nodded.

'Oh Richard, how thoughtful. I am weary with all the travelling; it has been weeks now I am so tired.'

'I'm sorry Esther; perhaps there will be some quiet after I have attended to my commission from the King. There will be work at our new home but that will be different I think.'

'Such a hope keeps me going, to be married and in one's own home, it sounds as a dream.'

'We must find new clothes and footwear; I will send for someone to come to the castle and we will assemble a suitable wardrobe for a Lord and Lady.'

Word was sent to Richard that the meeting he wished for had been arranged. The meal was in the great hall of the castle; Richard of Dover was already there when Richard and Esther arrived. They bowed; Richard of Dover was in his full clerical clothes, Richard smiled and wondered if he had his eyes on Becket's see.

'I understand that you are here on behalf of our noble King, Lord Aylesford!'

'I am indeed, let us be seated and talk as we feast.' Richard gestured with his hand and the priest was seated. Richard took his place and Esther sat next to him.

'You understand Lord I am merely an administrator, a mere servant, under the authority of the Holy Father.'

'Are we not *all* servants, *even* the Holy Father?'

'How true my son, how true.'

Pompous ass Richard thought, a few more of these parasites put to the sword might be no bad thing. 'It has been made known to the King that there is to be an investigation into the death of the Archbishop, Thomas Becket.'

'Indeed, it was I who wrote to our Lord the King.'

'I am here on his behalf, *our Lord* the King, him being in Ireland at this time, suffering the harsh winter weather with naught but a thin tent wall for protection against it, to establish the Holy Father's authority over the Irish Church. As you know the King is a godly man who wishes the Church and its blessing to reach every part of his empire.'

The priest stared at his goblet. Richard was unsure what he knew of Henry's campaign, but it was now this priest's choice to question the King's sincerity, if he dare. He must have thought better of picking up the gauntlet Richard had thrown down, and decided against contradicting his rendering of the truth of King Henry's visit to Ireland. Richard smiled to himself, now he had the measure of *this* priest.

'I know that the King be a godly man, and I am sure he will want to help in anyway he can. The investigation is to be held in May at Avranches in southern Normandy.'

'In *Normandy*, the King naturally assumed that it would be here in Canterbury, and *not until* May!'

'Yes, such is the will of the Holy Father.'

'I will make this known to my Lord; will he be expected to attend?'

'It is the wish of the Pontiff.'

Richard was now compelled to think. 'Mmm, I can say no more on this until I hear from my Lord. To make change to our conversation, would you be able to give Christ's blessing to my marriage in the week hence? I have much to attend to on my estate at Aylesford, and I need my wife by my side. We would have wished for more time to organise such an important sacrament, but time is ever in short supply in the temporal world where I must work out my salvation in fear and trembling, is that not so?'

'Ah yes, I understand, Lord, you are no doubt a busy man, and it appears that our Lord the King is well pleased with you, Aylesford is a fine manor. I would be delighted to accommodate and offer the Lord's blessing to a servant of our King. A small donation,' he flicked his hands and shrugged at the insignificant, 'to the continuing work of Archbishop Thomas would be ever welcome. No doubt, when he is canonized, he will remember those who saw fit to give, expecting naught in return, on the occasions he intercedes to the blessed Virgin for our souls. I will administer the sacrament myself, in one of the small chapels if you wish for a simple ceremony.'

'That would be perfect. Does that meet with your approval my lady?' Esther nodded smiling. 'Then it is decided.'

'May I ask if the King has sanctioned this marriage?'

'Indeed, he has.'

Esther leant closer to Richard, 'What about such permission from Sir John?'

'I am under great constraints Esther; he should have responded by the next week, if he has not, I can wait no longer. Now that this investigation is not to be held until May, I need to make as much use of the time as is possible. No doubt Henry will want to meet with me before then.'

Richard was at his table writing when Esther burst into his room, 'Richard, Richard look who is here,' and she stepped to one side to reveal Sir John FitzWilliam, it took Richard a moment to take in what was before him then he arose laughing and embraced Sir John.

'This is indeed a blessing, a sight for sore eyes.'

'You could not marry but I was there to give away the bride, and so I made haste to Canterbury.' Apparently, the first rider had never reached Sir John, for whatever reason.

'Well thanks be to God that we have you here now, wine for us Alwin, this is the finest gift to have you here.'

'I have brought what is yours, now you have a home of your own,' and he signalled to a servant at the door. The servant entered with Richard's saddle-bag and Esther's coffer.

'Excellent, how propitious, your timing is perfect, my dearest friend.'

Richard arranged that they ate in his room that night and he invited Sir Raymond and Sir Tristram to join them.

'I am honoured that you should consider my approval for your marriage necessary.'

'You have been so generous to us Sir John, and neither Richard nor myself have any family, yet you have made us feel as if we are part of yours,' said Esther.

'You *are* my family.'

Richard knew that the consent for a couple to marry was of greater importance than their consent to each other. It was the signing of contracts and the exchanging of dowries, which sealed a marriage, nothing to do with the Church, only in latter years had the Church insisted on giving a blessing. Their particular circumstances were slightly different from the norm, but having the King's approval and Sir John's gave their union social credibility.

Richard asked after Julianne, the words were from his lips before he thought. He didn't mean to ask in front of everyone, but as the talk around the table passed from one to another, she was all that he could think of, his brain was only occupied with her. He couldn't concentrate on a word that was said.

'Ah, Julianne, she is unhappy, foolish girl. They have been to Tattershall once and it was difficult, why she married that fellow is an utter mystery to me.' The mood changed and all were quiet. 'Let's not think on sad things this night, this is a time for rejoicing.'

Richard wanted to ask about Gervase, but he thought better of it. He tried to join in, and hoped that he managed to hide his heart, which was in turmoil. Esther smiled at him but her eyes betrayed her, she knew. Was this the dark cloud over their lives of which she had talked, which would ruin what they had?

Finally, Richard said that it was late, and there was much in need of attention on the morrow.

'Has accommodation been arranged for Sir John?'

'Yes, I have seen to that.'

'Ah – what a wife you have been gifted with Richard; I miss such support.'

When they were leaving, Richard drew Esther to him and closed the door. Esther stood before him but did not look at him.

'Come my little mouse, out with it!'

'You love Julianne, don't you, not me.' He was lost at her directness.

'Esther, I have chosen you for my wife and I feel to be the most blessed man in God's world. I was merely distressed to hear that she is so unhappy, if what Sir John surmises is indeed true. Are you not upset too by Julianne's predicament? I was saddened all the more because we are so happy and our life is one that seems to have God's blessing at every turn.'

'Forgive me Richard, how selfish I am. Of course, you would be concerned for Julianne and I think only of myself. You see this wretched woman you want for a wife; you are the better person. I don't know what came over me.'

CHAPTER 26

Richard had written to the King in Ireland, and sent two riders with his letter hoping that they would find him in Dublin. He informed the King of his conversation with Richard of Dover, and the arrangements for the investigation. He also made known to Henry who had been appointed to carry out the search for the truth, and that was to be two Venerable legates from Rome, Albert and Theodinus. He had never heard of them, but Henry may well have. Richard added that in the course of his exchange with Richard of Dover, that he had emphasized that he, the King, was at this very moment, risking life, and limb, fighting at the Pope's behest to establish the Holy Father's rule in Ireland. Richard had smiled whilst he penned the words, as he was sure Henry would, for he knew that this version of events was a slightly singular account of the truth. He concluded the correspondence by informing Henry that he would be at Aylesford if he required any service from him, and he would do all in his power to fulfil his command. Richard was sincere in his commitment to serve Henry, he knew Henry was a flawed human being but he liked his straightforward honesty, there was no pretence.

It was three days to the day of their marriage blessing, and there was a great deal of activity. Alwin, in his quiet inimitable way, had found a draper and seamstress. He seemed to have some mysterious ability to do whatever was asked without causing the slightest disturbance. Any desire requested, simply materialised, as if from thin air, merely by the wave of his hand.

Esther didn't want Richard to see what she was to wear; she wanted him to be presented with the complete image in a single second of time. This would be a once in a lifetime moment and she was determined it would be memorable. That morning in the chapel, when he first caught sight of her with Sir John, she wanted *that second* emblazoned onto his memory forever. She was presenting herself to him, the best she could be, and all she had, she was giving to him to love and care for. This would be her offering.

Richard's focus was different from Esther's, even while he was being fitted with his wedding clothes his mind was on other things. He was ever surprised at the flattery and show of such deference to him as if he was the King himself. Richard of Dover, being the perfect example, he could well have been at odds with the King because of the close working connection with Becket. After all, he was the one who had taken responsibility for Becket's burial, but on the contrary, he could not do enough to ensure Richard and Esther had every whim indulged. The more he fawned over Richard the more Richard was convinced he had an eye to the seat at Canterbury.

Richard's thoughts were never far from his new manor, he nervously wondered what would be expected of him. He was not totally without experience he had been brought up a Lord's son, but he had not been the one with overall responsibility, to whom they all looked. He had fears and doubts in himself, he knew the way ahead would be difficult, and was thankful for Esther.

Sir John had brought gifts for them; he gave Richard a beautiful sword. Richard all but gasped as he unwrapped it from the cloth. It was the gift of gifts, to a warrior, an "Ulfberht". All who knew about swords knew about this sword, they were priceless; it must be at least two hundred years old. This sword was perfection – an extension of the arm, so light it floated on air. Richard was convinced it must have been a treasure, which was handed down through Sir John's family, from father to son, but he didn't want to ask.

'It belonged to my ancestor from my mother's family called Magnus Magnuson, a Lord from the north, a Viking.'

Richard was sure this should have gone to Gervase. Richard's eyes met Sir John's, and all that needed to be said, passed between them in that meeting of eyes. This moment was beyond words. Richard swore to himself that this sword would go to a son of Julianne's, he knew it should have been a son of theirs, and that thought burned within him.

For Esther he brought a magnificent sable cape, which reached down to her feet, she was also convinced that she'd been given a family treasure. He told Esther that it also had originally come far, from the frozen lands in the north. She ran her hand across the shining silky pelts.

'It is so beautiful Sir John, I cannot imagine the cost of such a gift, but it's value to me is above price. Thank you,' she said and kissed him.

'It is both of *you* – who have extended your kindness to me, that I value. They are the real gifts one learns to treasure, when one gives their love, such a gift is above price. These trinkets are merely tokens of the regard in which I hold you.'

The gifts were clearly given to reinforce his intention that Richard was now his only son. This was generous and sincere, Richard knew and understood the honour behind such, but he feared the consequences; he could only see that in the end, there would be a fearful outcome. Whilst his gratitude was genuine it was tainted by these doubts, Esther seemed oblivious and was overcome with both tears *and* smiles as she hugged Sir John once more, who looked equally heedless of any hidden dangers.

This evening was all such an occasion should be – laughter and joy – and Richard was determined that he would lay aside all his thoughts and concerns for the King, and the facing of his new home and tenants, at least for the next few days. He was sorry that Tristram would not be there, but he had gone ahead to Aylesford as suggested, to prepare the way for their new Lord and Lady. Both Raymond and Tristram had wanted to be present at Richard and Esther's wedding, in the end they had thrown dice to see who would stay for ceremony, and Tristram had lost.

Richard's servants had fussed about his appearance to the point of annoying him. He was glad at last, to be walking towards the Cathedral, free of their suffocating attention. He was no preening courtier and never would be.

He waited for Esther in the chapel with Sir Raymond at his side. Raymond made idle chatter, saying that he did not recognise this new man before him, but Richard was not amused, and only snorted.

As she walked from the darkness of the entrance to the chapel, she passed into the blazing light shining through a stained-glass window, and it bathed her in flames of brilliant colour. She was on fire with an almost magical glow. Richard's mouth literally fell open. Her dress was unusual, most brides wore bright gay colours denoting their happiness, but Esther's was simple, *white* brocade silk, or so it appeared at first glance. It was as if one was being encouraged to look more closely if one *really* wanted to see her, as she drew closer, he could see that it was covered with delicately embroidered golden flowers. He was compelled to concentrate, to fix his eyes on her *alone*. It was as if it was the first time, he'd ever really seen her, she looked like a princess a queen she was unbelievably beautiful. She saw his stunned gaze and smiled for this was just as she had intended.

They made their vows being sure to say the words, "I do", and not "I will". The latter would be taken to mean that only at sometime in the future they intended to be man and wife. The priest blessed them, yet it was, as it had always been, that the consummation of their union was what made them truly man and wife. They both knew that for the ordinary people few bothered with the Churches blessing, but for Esther with her Jewish background, the ceremony before God was imperative.

Richard had organised a feast for his soldiers they were his family.

The following morning Esther awoke and stared at Richard as the golden light of the new day rested upon his face, a tear formed in the corner of her eye and she quickly brushed it way with the back of her hand.

'You are so beautiful my husband, and I love you, I could wish this moment never to end,' she whispered. Her eye caught sight of a feather sticking from his pillow and she carefully drew it free from the covering and smiled, lightly stroking it under his nose, he unconsciously flicked his face with the back of his hand. Gripping her nose between her fingers to prevent herself laughing and biting her lip, she touched his nose once more, he jerked his head, and his eyes flickered. She was *desperately* trying not to laugh, she again tormented him, his lips this time, brushing them lightly with the feather, he snorted, his eyes sprung open, and he awoke.

'It's you, you tantalizing vixen,' and he quickly turned over onto her and took hold of her wrists, she giggled and thrashed about as he pressed his lips to her neck just under her chin, his beard prickled and she wriggled with hysterical laughter. He raised himself and gazed into her eyes, gradually they ceased their laughing, both merely stared at each other for some time, and – *slowly* – he lowered his lips to meet hers.

CHAPTER 27

It was a bitter cold January morning when they set off for Aylesford, Sir John's party were leaving too. Each promised to visit the other, though Richard doubted that he would go to Tattershall without much thought. He was unsure how he would cope with any accidental meeting with Julianne. It would have to be faced sometime he knew that, but neither he nor Esther were ready for such an encounter. Esther needed to feel secure in their relationship and he was fearful that he might fail her. He knew the power of his feelings for Julianne and was afraid of them, to meet at this time would be utter folly, of that he was sure. He was certain that he should not have gone to her wedding, but went against his better judgement and suffered for the recklessness. His father once said, "The worst thing about any tragedy was that we did not learn from it". Well he had learned, and he would not make the same mistake again.

Richard was in a querulous mood and had been since he awoke. He was trying to be reasonable, but it seemed to highlight, rather than hide his troubled condition. Esther knew he was worrying about his first appearance at their new home. He fidgeted in his saddle staring straight ahead and tapping the pair of gloves in his hand against his thigh.

"Quick Sir Raymond get us on our way before he explodes." Esther silently prayed. She cast her eyes heavenward when she saw Sir Raymond eventually give the signal to move off.

It was evening before they arrived at Aylesford having travelled thirty very *tense* miles. As the castle next to the priory came into view Richard drew his horse to a standstill and Esther came to his side. Raymond was going to halt the men but Richard bade him keep moving.

'We will catch you up Sir Raymond, I just want to take a moment.'

'Are you all right Richard?'

'Yes, why do you ask?'

'Oh… no reason, it's merely that you seem so relaxed and happy!' Turning his face to her, she saw it crinkle into a smile, his saddle creaked as he leapt from his horse, he reached up to her, and she leaned forward into his arms, he lowered her until she was level with his lips, her feet dangled in the air and he kissed her.

'I love you, Lady Aylesford. I'm sorry that I have been such a morose companion on the journey, but I'm afraid.'

'Afraid!'

'Yes, afraid, that I might not be worthy of these people.'

'My dearest Lord Aylesford, that is the very reason I know you will be a good Lord, because you care.'

'Ha, come on then, let's meet our people.' With that, he helped Esther once more into the saddle and they set off at a steady pace towards their new home. It was a fine castle set on a motte surrounded by a deep ditch. There was a village of wattle and daub houses nearby; they were in need of some maintenance by the look of them. To the left there was a Priory of sorts with large vegetable gardens. Workers in the fields at the side of the road ceased their work and bowed; removing what headwear they had, some even waved to Richard and Esther as they rode along the narrow road towards the castle gates. Richard tried to smile, Esther both smiled and waved.

It was dark now but even so, Tristram had made sure that all those in the castle had turned out to welcome them.

Richard slipped from his horse, and a well-dressed overweight fellow, about forty years old, Richard guessed, came forward. Tristram stood further back, he was leant against a wall his arms folded he nodded to Richard.

'Welcome Lord,' the man said smiling and offering his hand. Richard only stared at the outstretched hand and the man withdrew it and bowed. This informality was not how Richard intended to manage his estate, and he did not shake hands with servants. Whatever the regime was before, this was a new start now, with a new Lord and Lady.

'What name are you called by, fellow?'

'I am the Head Steward and my name is Fawkes Gaillart, Sir.'

'You will refer to me as Lord, and this is your Lady,' Fawkes gave a curt nod to Esther.

'May I introduce *my* good lady,' he gestured to a grossly overweight, common looking woman, who was equally clothed in fine garments. Richard nodded. 'And this is my beautiful daughter Geneen.'

Beauty was very much in the eye of the beholder, Esther thought. The girl's dress was too tight, and decidedly immodest, *and* she clearly fluttered her eyes at Richard as she curtseyed. It was enough to distract Esther, she inadvertently tugged at the rein and her horse suddenly skittered, Richard took hold of the bridle and steadied the animal. He reached up to her, she leaned forward to him and he lowered her to the ground, her face was set like stone. He returned his attention to the steward.

'Take us to our rooms first then attend to the needs of my men, and have our baggage seen to, be instructed by Sir Raymond,' Raymond nodded to the steward. Richard paused and looked at the man.

'Yes, my Lord,' he eventually responded without smiling. 'My wife, Sybbyl and daughter Geneen will see to you Lord, and I will attend to your orders here.' Richard nodded; Geneen brushed flirtatiously against Richard as she passed him and smiled. Esther was incandescent with rage. They followed the mother and daughter into the keep and up the stairs without a word.

'These are your apartments Lord,' Sybbyl said, and turned to go. Esther now spoke for the first time.

'I did not tell you to leave, open the door and await my instructions.' The woman froze, 'Now!' She was flustered and fumbled with the door and Esther pushed past her. Richard all but smiled; this was a side of Esther he'd never seen before. She was every bit the Lady of the manor. The mother and daughter stood side-by-side looking very nervous; Richard went to look out of the window, he would leave this to Esther.

'This room is a disgrace, it is filthy, these bed sheets are soiled. One can only imagine what it was like *before* you prepared it for us.'

'Sorry, my Lady, I will have the servants flogged.'

'*I* – will decide who is to be flogged, and might I remind you, that I hold *you* alone responsible for seeing that my instructions are carried out. Where are the keys for the castle?'

'Here my Lady, I always keep them.'

'Pass them to me!'

'But my Lady.'

'I beg your pardon, don't you *ever* dare – *but* – me again, give them to me this instant!' The woman could hardly loosen the keys from her belt such was her trembling and she shakily passed them into Esther's open hand.

'See to this room!'

'Y – Yes my Lady,' she turned to leave.

'And where are you going?'

'To get the servants, my Lady.'

'I told *you* to see to it – you – and this, this, *girl*,' Esther flicked her hand in the direction of the woman's daughter, 'and make sure that it is perfect when I return. Do you understand?'

'Yes, my Lady.'

'Well – what are you waiting for?' Esther's, eyes were on fire as they followed the two women from the room.

Richard turned and made to hug Esther, 'Don't touch me,' he stepped back as if he'd been lashed with a whip. 'I am absolutely furious.' She saw that Tristram had come to their door. 'Tristram – what's going on here? What have you been doing?'

'My Lady – you have *no* – idea. Our good steward, Fawkes, and his lady live here, and they have a fancy, that *they* are the Lord and Lady. The last custodian was a drunken debaucher, from what I have heard, and left them to their own devices. It appears that the King has only actually been here but the once and that was many years past. They dress better than some Lords of my acquaintance do,' he smiled at Richard's muddy clothes. 'You have yet to sample the mete we have to eat, that will be a rare delight for you.'

'This is outrageous, how do they afford such clothes?'

'I suspect, my Lady, that they make free with the estate coin, though I have not yet proof. The good Sybbyl keeps a tight hold on her keys and I have not been permitted free access to all the rooms. I have looked at the estate records and they seem in order. One of the monks from the priory next to the castle…'

'We saw it.'

'… keeps the records, the monk is called brother Cuthbert. I have talked to him, he seemed nervous. He's hiding something, I'd swear on *his* life, but my time has been limited.'

'Thank you Tristram, you have done well in the short time you've been here. I have the keys now and by God I will get to the bottom of this offence. Come show us *this* pigsty Tristram, *Richard*.'

'Oh… certainly my Lady, lead on.'

'Richard, this is not a moment for humour.'

Tristram showed them the castle, but it was not a pleasant introduction, the place was a disgrace. Richard caught the eye of the steward, as he was about to scurry out of sight. He came to Richard.

'You wanted me – Lord!'

'I will eat on the morrow's first light in my apartment, as soon as I am ready, I want everyone from the highest to the lowest, *everyone,* assembled in the main hall, is that clear?'

'Yes, my Lord.'

'I expect you to bow to me, when you answer me in future.'

'Forgive me Lord,' he bowed, but the tone of his reply fell only a fraction of an inch short of insolence.

'Sir Tristram, bring Sir Raymond to our apartment when I send for you. We will eat together this evening.'

'Be about your business, Steward.' Richard watched him go. 'Shall we return to our rooms now my Lady, and see how our new maids are managing?'

'Richard, I'm sorry I spoke to you as I did, but I was so angry.'

'Surely not!' He smiled. 'My gentle little mouse, never. Come, good lady, into the fray,' he said taking her hand. Their room was transformed when they opened the door; Geneen was on her knees scrubbing the floor. They were wet, filthy, and red-faced. Her mother had a large rip in the skirt of her dress. Esther went to the bed and turned back the covers, the sheets were crisp white linen.

'This is as it should be. If I hear of any punishment meted out to servants, because of *your* neglect, you shall receive it twice over, do you understand?'

'Yes, my Lady,' she said defiantly. Esther paused and narrowed her eyes and Sybbyl bowed her head.

'Go now and see we have mete sent to us, and it must be fresh mete, enough for four.' They shot towards the door like arrows from a bow. 'One moment,' the two women could have twisted an ankle they stopped so abruptly. 'Have a tub and water sent to us, and a costrel of the finest wine, whilst we wait *and* inform Sir Raymond and Sir Tristram once we are ready to eat.'

'Yes, my Lady.'

'Well – what are you waiting for?'

'Now, may I hug you?'
'Richard, this is dreadful, *but* we will make this a place to be envied. I cannot imagine what we have yet to discover.' There was a knock at the door.
'Enter!' Esther called.
'A tub, and we are fetching water, my Lady.'
'Set it there in front of the fire and bring more logs.'
'Yes, my Lady.'
The tub was filled and Esther inspected the towels. 'We was told to bring the Mistresses own towels, my Lady.'
'Were you indeed,' Esther glanced at Richard.
'Will that be all, my Lady?'
'Yes, by what name are you called?'
'Margaret, my Lady.' Esther nodded and the girl left.
'She is the first person I have seen since we arrived, who has looked as if she has the slightest concern for her work.'

CHAPTER 28

As they broke their night's fast Richard, Tristram, Raymond, and Esther talked about the extraordinary situation in which they now found themselves.

'You have been here longer than us Tristram, in your judgement, what is the mood of the soldiers and the castle workers?'

'Of course, they were guarded when they spoke to me, reluctant to say too much. I tried not to ask questions, but I presented myself as merely another, if newer, member of their community. Gradually they paid less attention to me and talked more freely, and I listened. They think little of Fawkes and his family and mock their pretentiousness. His daughter apparently has the morals of an alley cat which her mother and father are more than happy to use to their advantage. The arrangement seemed to suit the previous Constable of the castle very well.'

'Well, it does *not* suit me!' Esther asserted.

Richard laid his hand gently on Esther's arm, and smiled at her, hoping to quiet her spirit a little. 'Thank you Tristram, what about you Raymond?'

'I know as much as you Richard, but it caused great merriment when it was heard of our Lady's confrontation with the Steward's wife and daughter. Apparently, they have treated the servants abominably, flogging them indiscriminately for minor infringements. You can imagine how they felt when they heard of this angel from heaven, in the shape of our beautiful Lady, who'd been sent with a flaming tongue to avenge their suffering.' Richard laughed, but Esther was not so amused and sat straight faced, angrily tapping her forefinger on the surface of the table before her.

'Gentlemen, I'm afraid that I do not share your humorous perspective. There has been unnecessary suffering amongst the people here and I understand the helplessness of their position.'

'You are right of course, Esther, forgive us, but this all changes today. I will make this known to our people when we meet them. I will speak to them of my intentions, and what we will expect of them. I pray that you will support us in the work ahead, we will need you, perhaps more than ever, your value to Esther and I is beyond price.'

They nodded, 'As if you need to ask, Richard,' said Sir Raymond.

'Very well, let's see what is before us.'

The four left and made their way to the hall, Richard stood at the front of the dais at the end of the hall where the Lord and his Lady were normally seated to feast. Esther, Raymond, and Tristram were seated behind him. The room quickly stilled.

'Let me introduce myself, I am your new Lord and this is my Lady,' he turned to Esther, 'and these knights are my senior Captains. Whenever they speak to you, they speak as for me, and they will be obeyed as such. You will find that I am a fair Lord, but! I will not tolerate any form of insolence from anyone. You will care for each other as from my example. If you who are shown kindness then demonstrate meanness of spirit to one below you, I will punish you severely. If anyone of you have grievances which can't be resolved, one of us here will pass judgement, and you have my assurance that you may come to us without fear.' There was a murmuring and nodding of heads in approval. 'I am one of the King's generals and will be away from time to time, but you will not be neglected. Your Lady will represent me and will be obeyed without question.' Richard glanced to the stony faces of Fawkes and his family; if looks could kill, he would have been struck dead on the spot. 'All soldiers and knights will meet with my Captains and they will give you your orders. Your Lady will meet with her servants and make herself known to you, male and female alike. She will also make known to you what will be expected of you. I will be visiting every farm and hide on my estate. This work will begin today. This castle is a disgrace...' Richard allowed the words to hang in the air, 'but that is past, we will transform it together and we will be proud to call this our home.' Richard was cheered, he held up his hand and gradually they stilled. 'Soldiers go to the yard and be instructed by your Captains. Servants remain here and your Lady will speak to you. Master Fawkes, you will come with me to my new workroom.'

Fawkes stood nervously, no doubt wondering what Richard was going to say to him. He followed Richard; several steps behind him, Richard never looked once to see where he was. Richard waited at the door of the room he was going to make his place of work. Fawkes quickly caught up to him and opened the door for him, bowing as he did so.

Richard took a seat behind the table, wiped his hand over the tabletop and looked at the dust on his hand, he said nothing but lifted his eyes, which were as shards of ice, and stared at Fawkes holding before him his dust covered palm. Fawkes shuffled uneasily, nervously massaging his sweaty hands together.

Speaking in a frighteningly calm voice Richard said, 'All is past from this day, all is as new,' Richard's intense gaze was too much for Fawkes he had to look down. 'I wish to see Brother Cuthbert *now*, go and fetch him to me.' Fawkes' head was beginning to sparkle with droplets of sweat.

'Lord, he may be occupied at this moment and unable to come.'

'You misunderstand me fellow; this is not a request, but an order. *You* – will bring him to me *this* instant, suppose he is sat on the dung-hole, he will come here with his brais about his ankles if needs must, but come he will. DO – you hear me?'

'Yes – yes, Lord,' Fawkes face was ashen, he was trembling like a leaf.

'The Priory exists at my behest and their funding comes not from the coffers of Mother Church but from this estate. They will do exactly as I command, as will *you*, and *you*, will do well to remember that. Go now and I will see all the estate accounts in the possession of this *man of God* when you return.'

Richard sat for a moment when Fawkes closed the door then he stood and went to the window. From the window he could see the yard and Tristram and Raymond working with the soldiers, he knew it would be difficult at first but they would soon see the benefits. He understood only to well, that most people needed some structure and parameters to their daily lives, for though they might grumble it brought a certain security.

Richard went outside his door just as an unkempt skinny boy was passing. 'Here boy, come to me. What's your name?'

'Martin, Lord,' he said giving the most graceful of bows. Richard all but laughed at this young courtier in the making.

'Well Martin, a task for you,' he stared up fearfully at Richard, 'I want you to find my servant Alwin, do you know who I mean?'

'Was he the tall thin man with the green cape who came with thee yesterday Lord?'

'Yes, that's the man.'

'I'll fetch him Lord,' he said and ran off in a cloud of dust, Richard smiled.

While he waited, he entertained himself watching the activity from his window. The whole place looked to be a hive of industry, men, women, and children rushing hither and thither.

There was a knock on the door, and he spun round, '*Enter.*'

The door opened and Martin came in with Alwin, 'Sorry I've been so long Lord, but he was with our Lady at the top of the keep, I 'as never been there before.'

'Well done Martin,' and the boy bowed once more like the accomplished courtier he clearly was, much to Richard's amusement. He was about to leave, Richard beckoned him closer with his finger, and he came warily, thinking he was about to be struck for taking so long.

'I's sorry Lord, I's been as quick as I could.'

'Don't be afraid Martin, I like you; you must teach me to bow, for I see I can learn much from you.' Martin beamed with delight. 'You have pleased me, stretch out your hand.' Richard took a penny from his purse and pressed it into Martin's none too clean palm. Martin could not believe what he saw; he had never had a penny in his life. He stared at it in his hand, utterly mesmerised. There were actually tears in his eyes and his nose began to run; he wiped it on his sleeve and snorted, Richard pressed his eyes together and grimaced.

'All I ever got from the mistress was beatings,' and he turned and lifted the back of his shirt to reveal some dreadful bruises, old and new. Richard squeezed his fists tightly at the sight.

After a moment when he felt able to speak calmly, he said, 'You are now to be my right-hand man Martin, and you will work with Alwin, he will need a man like you to help him, someone who knows the castle. Now go to your Lady, show her your back and she will have some salve for it. Tell her I sent you and what your new work is to be. Go now.' With that, he bowed once more, turned, and ran out.

'Can you believe that Alwin, did you see that child's back?'

'I did Lord.'

'I detest bullying or wanton cruelty of any sort. I will never be able to work with that fellow, Fawkes. God forgive me for the thoughts in my head at this moment. How old are you Alwin?'

'I'm twenty-four, give or take, Lord.'

'*Really!* I thought that you were much younger. Listen Alwin; I want you to take on the role of castle steward, I will make this known to Fawkes later this day. He is at this moment, fetching a monk to me from the priory, though God only knows where he is. It must be an hour past since I sent him.'

'Lord – I'm honoured that you see me equal to such a task. I pray to the Blessed Virgin I will not fail you.'

'Alwin, do you imagine for one moment, that you could really do any worse than Fawkes? Lady Esther or I will always be on hand to give you our support.'

'Thank you, Lord, you know I will do my best. With regard to the monk, I suppose that he could be anywhere, he may even be ministering to someone sick in the village.'

'That is true, in the meantime Alwin could you send someone to clean this place so it is fit to work in.'

Richard returned to the window and again watched Raymond and Tristram at their employment, there was another knock on the door. 'At last, come in Fawkes,' the door opened, it was two servant girls.

'We was sent by Master Alwin, Lord.'

'Ah, yes, I want this place cleaned. When the Steward comes tell him he is to wait here for me.' The girls bowed and Richard made his way to find Esther.

Richard had his midday mete with Esther who told him of her progress with more than a little pride. She also made known to him how impressed she had been with the girl Margaret he'd met the night previous. She said that Fawkes wife and daughter had been conspicuous by their absence, but for now, she was managing better without their interference and she would deal with them in due course.

After their meal, Richard made his way back to his workroom, rehearsing Fawkes dismissal as he walked. He stood momentarily at the door, took a deep breath, and pushed it open. The room had been meticulously cleaned, there had been lavender sprinkled on the floor, which would be crushed under foot releasing its fragrance, *but* there was no sign of Fawkes. Richard was furious, he had told the girl to instruct him to await his return. He stepped from the room into the passage; a girl with a bucket, nearly as big as her, was passing. She stepped back against the wall and bowed her head so she was not in his way.

'One moment, are you not one of the girls who cleaned my room?' The girl trembled so much the water in her bucket splashed over the top.

'I'm sorry Lord, I will do the room again forgive me. Please do not beat me, please Lord.'

'*What*! Oh, the room, still yourself girl, you have done well, I can see how hard you have worked. How old are you?'

'Me Lord – I be eleven, so me sister says, me mother's dead.' She looked at him – wondering if the room was pleasing to him, what it was she'd done wrong, and began to sob.

'Did you not tell master Fawkes that I wished him to remain until I returned?' The girl was beside herself with fear in case Richard did not believe her.

'He did not come Lord, I waited and waited, but he never come.' Richard was lost for words.

'Be calm child, you are not in any trouble, dry your eyes, I'm very pleased with your work, you are a credit to your mother, she'd have been very proud of you.'

She could only stare at this man with her mouth wide open, no one had ever spoken to her like this, 'I must go. You sit in my room until you feel a little better, don't be afraid.'

Richard left her and strode out into the yard. Raymond and Tristram were talking and turned to the sound of his feet and smiled at him.

'Lord...' they both bowed.

'Have you seen that ill begotten excuse for a steward Fawkes anywhere?'

'Not since this morning – he, his wife and daughter were riding out of the gates making for the priory and dragging a heavily laden pack animal. Loaded with old books and such like, that were no use to you, just as you'd ordered,' said Raymond shrugging his shoulders, 'I asked him what he was about, and that's what he said.'

'WHAT, by God, he's made off, Raymond, take soldiers and bring them back to me, all three of them by their scruffs. I will hang the lot of them, and I want that pack animal, who knows what they have stolen.' Neither Raymond nor Tristram had ever seen Richard so angry.

'I'll get men organised, Sir Raymond you see to the horses,' Tristram offered. 'Phew, I wouldn't like to be in Fawkes shoes when he has to face Richard,' Tristram whispered to himself as he ran to assemble the soldiers.

'Bring them straight to me when you find them. I will be with Esther,' he shouted after them and he stormed off in the direction of the keep.

It was late before the riders returned with tired, steaming, hard ridden horses. Raymond went to find Richard; it was made known to him that he was in his apartment with the Lady Esther.

He knocked on Richard's door, Alwin opened it, and ushered him into the room.

'What news, where are they?'

'I fear Lord that they had too great a start on us, we were able to follow them, but only by asking those we passed, which greatly slowed our travel. What we were told led us to Hempstead, east of here, to a tavern. They had met a knight there, by accident or design I know not. Alas, the Landlord was unable to enlighten us. They talked with the knight; he was by all accounts not the wealthiest knight, nevertheless they left with him, so we were told. I'm sorry Lord. *Oh,* one other thing, when I mentioned your name the Landlord said he'd heard the name of Lord Aylesford mentioned, and that was when the knight had joined them. They been quiet at first, then they all started to laugh, shaking hands and the knight with them.'

'I for one, shall be relieved never to see their impudent faces again, and good riddance to them,' Esther said forcefully.

'Aye good riddance to *them* well and good, but I want to know what was on that pack animal, what have they stolen from me, for this place is without any coin, Alwin has searched high and low. A knight you say, have you a description?'

'The Landlord could not say, other than he was a good-looking young fellow with a limp, he's never seen him before.'

'Thank you, Raymond, here sit, there is mete enough.'

'That is kind Lord, but if I may change and bathe first, for I am tired and weary.'

'Very well Raymond, Alwin will you see that someone attends to Sir Raymond's wishes? Remember who you are now Alwin, you are Steward of my castle.'

'Well, *congratulations* Alwin, if you can stand working for this fellow, he is a fearful taskmaster and ugly too,' said Raymond and they all laughed.

CHAPTER 29

Slowly the castle was assuming a new identity and after years of distrust and fear, the inhabitants to whom this place was all they had to call home, were accepting their new Lord and Lady. Fawkes and his family had seemingly disappeared off the face of the earth much to Richard's annoyance. The thought that they had escaped without any redress of their crimes was ever a thorn in his side. He was sure someone, perhaps the mysterious knight, was sheltering them.

Though they were never mentioned amongst the people, Richard was sure that they had not heard the last of them. Richard had eventually confronted brother Cuthbert and it turned out he'd been blackmailed into keeping two sets of estate ledgers. The fool had been seduced by the beautiful Geneen and discovered by her father. He threatened to make it known to the Abbot if he did not do as he was ordered. The poor innocent fell for the plot like a lamb to the slaughter.

It was some time since Richard had heard from the King, but this morning a servant brought a letter from him. He was going to Avranches in Normandy to attend the inquiry into Thomas Becket's death. The King would travel there with the army of his duchies. In the meantime, his English army would march towards London where Richard was commanded to join them. Before they arrived, Richard was first to go to Westminster to see what truth there was to the rumours of disquiet amongst Henry's family.

Richard knew of the tension between the King and his sons; most did, but Richard had also noticed fissures in his relationship with his wife. They were beginning to delight in disagreement, each championing the causes of different sons.

Henry favoured Prince John, his youngest, whilst Eleanor favoured Prince Richard. Young King Henry was merely tolerated; he showed little interest in the affairs of state unless they interfered with his life. He thought the predominant purpose of the state was to supply revenue to enable him to pursue his interests, no more than that. To compound his entrapment, his father kept him chronically short of funds, much to the annoyance of his wife, Margaret of France, King Louis' daughter.

How far the family troubles had degenerated into rebellion Richard had yet to discover. Personally, Richard didn't take to any of the King's children and shared Henry's concerns for the future of his empire. On one occasion, John had tried to intimidate Richard and belittle him in front of his friends, but it had backfired on him, and John had ended up looking a fool. Richard knew that would not be forgotten and was ever watchful of John. Young Henry looked every inch a King, he was handsome, intelligent and a capable warrior, but self-absorbed. Prince Richard was too fond of male company, for Richard's liking, Richard had never seen him once in the company of women.

Richard thought Henry to be the most astute of men, but when it came to John, he was quite unable to make a sound judgement, or so it appeared.

Perhaps the shortfalls of his sons, was why the King was determined to retain his control of power as long as was possible.

Richard read the missive out to Esther and she listened quietly. 'We are only now getting our home in order after much work, no time to relax and enjoy the fruits of our labour.'

'When will you have to go Richard?'

'Today, that's Henry's timeframe, he expects his commands to be instantly obeyed.' Richard rose from the bed and stretched.

'I may not see you for some time Master.'

'I can't tell, not too long.' Esther fluttered her eyelashes and slipped her nightdress from her shoulder.

'Is this how the beautiful Geneen would do it? I should have asked her for lessons.'

Richard returned to the bed and took Esther in his arms. 'My dear Lady, from what I saw that girl was a complete novice compared to my wife,' and Esther fell back laughing…

'I must get dressed, and go, or is there more you wish to make known to me?' He said, puzzled by her odd expression.

Esther sat up, 'I have been unwell of late Richard.'

He was unerringly silent; there was something about her countenance, he didn't even blink. Esther stared down at her lap as she fiddled with a loose thread on the blanket. Gradually she lifted her head and looked into his frozen face, she slowly smiled. 'I think we are having a baby.' Richard never moved, then slowly he too began to smile and his face lit up.

'Esther – my dearest, I can't believe it.'

'It happens you know...' and she smiled. Richard stood and offered his hand to her, raised her from her bed and he lovingly embraced her.

'You will have to stay here, you will not be able to endure the rigours of travel, if you are unwell.'

'I'm afraid not, but I will hate being separated from you.'

'We are not too far from London, I will return often and perhaps my work will be completed quickly, it can't take too long for I have to return to meet the King's army. When will our child be born?'

'November, I think.'

'I will make for London this day and return as soon as possible. I'll leave Raymond with you; the army will be in our vicinity within the month. I have sent riders to intercept them and have them wait until I join them with orders. If I am expected to be one of the commanders, I *must* return to meet them. The future will be linked to the news in London, I am convinced that is what the King envisages; clearly, he has caught wind of something. I'll take Tristram and soldiers with me.'

Richard made good time; he was in high spirits and told Tristram of his news as they travelled. Tristram was delighted and slapped Richard's back.

'Tristram's a fine name for a baby boy,' he said laughing.

'Perhaps not so good for a girl though,' Richard responded.

Richard's good humour subsided as the palace came into view and he wondered what he might learn that may not be to the King's liking. He thought it strange that Henry didn't trust anyone at the Palace to give an honest account of affairs; he supposed that he should feel flattered or perhaps he merely wanted the opinion of someone not so embroiled in the palace politics.

When they arrived, Richard sat in his saddle for a moment then he dismounted and momentarily rested his head against the leather knee roll of his saddle.

Richard hardly had time to find where he was to sleep before he was introduced to the latest scandals. "Young King Henry" as he was called to differentiate him from his father, Henry II, he was eighteen or nineteen now. He wanted to have control over his own Kingdom but his father would not acquiesce. Richard knew all that, but the final straw was Henry's decision to give his youngest son John three major castles *belonging* to Young Henry as part of a marriage settlement.

Young Henry was furious; this was an unmitigated insult to him and his wife. His father had gone too far. Henry knew he would be a laughing stock if he allowed this insult to go unchallenged. He would show his father that he was a man, and would not endure this treatment.

Richard quickly discovered that the upshot was that the Young King Henry had fled to his father-in-law, the King of France, who was actively stirring up rebellion against King Henry.

There were also rumours that Robert de Beaumont, the Earl of Leicester was raising an army of 20,000 Flemish mercenaries and was planning to invade England on the Suffolk coast in the autumn. Richard thought the number absurd, but clearly, it was an army of some note.

The divisions in the royal family gave the disenchanted Barons the ideal opportunity to remove, or at least undermine Henry's grip and restore their lost powers and fortunes. Richard was genuinely fearful of a full-scale rebellion in Henry's empire.

There was already talk of Barons taking sides. Richard heard that Hugh Bigod, the Earl of Norfolk, was reported to favour the invasion in support of the Young King Henry, but for the time being, he was in his castle at Framlingham on the Suffolk coast waiting. Richard wrote to Henry in Avranches and prayed that the letter got to him. Richard was fully cognisant that the matter was urgent.

He made known to Henry that he would take the English army, add to its number then march into Suffolk and prepare for an invasion in case perchance the rumours were true. Richard wrote that he would await further instructions, if he did not hear from Henry, he would face the invaders, and by the grace of God defeat them. The message was sent to the King with a troop of soldiers, to ensure that it reached him, emphasising the significance of the threat.

'We must return with all haste to Aylesford, Tristram and unite with the King's army from Ireland. This is more serious than I ever imagined it could be. Come let us eat and we will set off on the morrow's first light.'

The atmosphere at the meal was surprisingly relaxed, Richard could only think that the nobles there did not realise the gravity of what was before them. Richard was seated next to Thomas de Lâgrace, during the course of the meal Richard asked him where Sir Guy Molineux was, saying that he'd expected to see him here at this time of crisis.

'Ha...' de Lâgrace said, 'he has disappeared, fled.'

'What, do you *mean* disappeared; I have no knowledge of this? Do you speak in riddles?'

De Lâgrace had Richard's full attention now; suddenly Richard had lost his appetite.

'No riddles my friend, he has disappeared and no one seems to have any idea where he has disappeared to.'

De Lâgrace continued eating unaware of Richard's change of demeanour, then casually he started up again. Yet chewing on a mouthful of mete, he tapped Richard on his arm with the point of his knife as he spoke, 'Our dear Sir Guy has expensive tastes, it appears that he fancied he would help himself to some of the King's coin. Apparently, he has been engaged in such activity for some time; from what I heard he's been selling his belongings to survive. The talk is he may have been blackmailed. No one seems to know what is the truth of it, except as I say, he has vanished.'

'*Murdered*, you think?' asked Richard.

'Perhaps, but that has never been mentioned. No, the talk is he has made off fearful for his life.' De Lâgrace paused from his eating for a moment, wiped his hands and mouth on a cloth, reached to his neck and withdrew a chain on which hung a large green emerald. 'He sold me this, a fine stone, I hope that it's not Henry's,' he laughed. 'I don't suppose he'd be too please if he saw me wearing it, he might think I'd stolen it. Ah – I'll sell it before our noble King returns.' He tucked it once more down his shirt.

Richard twisted his goblet in between his fingers and watched the wine swirl one way – then the other, as he reversed the turning of the goblet.

'Mmm,' he said to himself. 'I'll buy the jewel from you.' De Lâgrace paused and turned to him.

'What will you give me?'

'Name a price.' They haggled and coin was exchanged. Richard studied the stone in his hand, he had to see Julianne, but how – he had no time.

'What of his wife and property?' asked Richard.

'No doubt King Henry will attend to his lands – and his head too, when he returns. As for his wife, a great beauty, do you know her?'

'Yes.'

'Ah… she has returned to her father from what I know, what a waste, what a waste.' De Lâgrace was enjoying the mete and the wine, and was clearly in the mood for idle gossip; totally unaware of the turmoil he had innocently stirred up in Richard's life. Suddenly Richard couldn't hear a word he was saying, he was overwhelmed by the smell of greasy food on De Lâgrace face and fingers. It was all he could do to stop himself being sick.

'Excuse me Sir Thomas, I'll make for my bed I have a long day ahead on the morrow.' Richard couldn't sit here idly chattering when it felt as if his brain had suddenly been removed from his skull and kicked round the hall. He was in such a state of bewilderment he was hardly able to find his way back to his room.

Richard collapsed on his bed fully clothed. He lay awake; sleep would not be his saviour this night he had to see Julianne. Was it *really* only to see that she was safe, or did he now hope for a chance to fan a flame, perhaps this was God's word to him. The thought had not but settled when he heard the Marshal's words ringing in his ears. "*Richard*, never make an enemy of your conscience by trying to massage it to conciliate *your* desires".

His mind was in turmoil he stared at the jewel in his hand. Walter, the personal servant Alwin had appointed to serve Richard, now he'd been given new employment, came into the room to see if Richard needed anything, before he went to his quarters. He asked Richard if he needed some help to undress, but Richard never responded. Walter waited for him to answer, after several minutes standing quietly he shrugged his shoulders and left.

CHAPTER 30

It took two days of hard riding before they saw the castle at Aylesford come into view. They had driven their horses with more haste than was good for them. The adrenalin was still pumping through Richard's veins when he leapt from his horse. Raymond came to him.

'Lord.'

'What news Sir Raymond?'

'We have made contact with our army.'

'Praise be.'

'They are at Hounslow sixty or seventy miles west of here, do you know the place?' Richard thought for a moment.

'No.'

'No matter, I gave orders that they were to camp there until you joined them. I thought it pointless for them to march all this way and have to march, perhaps back the way they'd just come.'

'Splendid Raymond, I will write to the leaders and command them await further instruction from the King. Come let us walk to my apartments I must see Esther; we can talk as we make our way there.' He paused and called to Tristram, 'See to the men, then join us in my apartments.' Tristram nodded. 'Do you know who leads the army Raymond?'

'Indeed Richard, the Earl of Cornwall, William of Gloucester, Reginald de Dunstanville and William d'Aubigny, the Earl of Arundel.'

'Ah, good men, they went to Ireland.'

'They said that they were expecting Richard de Luci the Chief Justiciar to join them from London.'

'I know him, but he is no soldier, however it's good to know who's for the King. *And,*' Richard smiled, 'He has a vial of Thomas Becket's blood which he wears around his neck, that could make all the difference, then again what do you think of Thomas Becket fighting on the King's side, I can see a certain poetry in that.' They both laughed at the irony.

Richard removed his gauntlets and pushed them into his belt then passed his helm to his new squire, Brian.

'Come, Young Henry has fled to France and some of the Barons are planning to revolt in his support. There is an army massing across the channel, 20,000 strong I have heard, but that figure is ridiculous they can't have had the time needed to assemble such a fleet to carry that number. My guess is more like two or three thousand, but what we need to be wary of is those Barons who intend to unite with them, that could grievously enlarge their army. Do you know our strength?'

'I know there are 300 knights and perhaps 2000 foot-soldiers. At this moment the Earls are attempting to swell the numbers.'

'By all accounts they do not expect to come until late in the year, that gives us time. Do you know, it is my inclination that we should not wait but strike first at their own heartlands and make the initiative ours.'

'What, you mean take the battle to them in France?'

'Ha, not quite, I mean to attack Leicester's home that will place him under pressure. For this moment, I pray you will excuse me whilst I greet my wife, I will call you directly.' Raymond bowed, Richard knocked, and Esther flung open the door dressed for outdoors.

'Richard,' Esther threw herself into his arms. 'I have just heard of your arrival and was this very instant coming to welcome you. I am so contented to see you.' She stepped back and pulled a face, '*Richard* – you smell like a horse.' Richard smelt his arm.

'Ha, sorry my love, I have ridden hard just to be by your side. You may as well join us now Sir Raymond.' Raymond smiled.

'*No!* I will send for you later Raymond, my husband needs a bath and a change of clothing first. I don't care what he has to tell of his visit to London.'

'Esther!'

'*Do* as I tell you Sir Raymond.' Richard shook his head and shrugged his shoulders.

'The country is about to fall into open rebellion, *but* it appears as if I must bathe, do as your Lady instructs Raymond.'

'Matilda, organise a bath, mete and drink for Lord Aylesford, in that order.'

'Yes, my Lady,' Matilda said and scurried from the room.

The tub and water duly arrived and Esther bathed him. He enquired as to her well-being and her news. Once she had related her tale, *she* asked what had been the outcome of his visit to London. He told her all about the King's woes and – reluctantly made known to her what he had learned of Julianne's troubles, *but* never mentioned the emerald. He wasn't sure why, it was as if this was part of something else, of which he didn't understand – or didn't wish to.

He was finding the conversation difficult now; really, he wanted to be alone with his thoughts. Whenever Julianne came near, be it merely a mention of her existence and his wits fell apart; it was a hellish painful confusion, which numbed his senses.

'Poor Julianne, poor Sir John, do you really think Sir Guy was robbing the King? Are you all right Richard you suddenly look tired?'

'Aye – I'm tired – living can be tiring. As for Sir Guy, I know not the truth of it. I didn't take him for such a fool. Henry will have his innards torn from him, if it is true. Thankfully that is none of my business.'

'But will Henry not expect you to make known to him all you've learned. Surely it will be of great concern to him if Sir Guy is suspected of pilfering from his coffers.'

'Mmmm...'

'Clamber from the tub, dry yourself, don your clean robes and we will take mete.'

He stepped from the tub and she reached up to wrap a towel around his shoulders, but he took her in his arms, she felt the warmth of his naked body against her, she gasped and pushed herself free.

'It's suddenly gone very hot in this room,' she said and she wiped her face on the towel she held, 'Come dry yourself, dress and eat. Your knights will be here directly.'

Richard met with Sir Raymond and Sir Tristram each exchanged their knowledge. They left and Richard wrote to the commanders of the English army. He would wait until he heard from the King so that he was sure of the King's will before he joined them.

Richard was talking to Alwin in the yard when he heard the guards call out. There was a small troop of knights at the gates, who were unwilling to give their names. Richard made his way quickly onto the battlements.

'What are you good knights known by?' Richard shouted down.

'Richard, open up I would speak in private.' The knight at the front called back. Richard drew his eyes together and hesitated. His eyes suddenly flashed open and he shouted to the guard on the gate.

'Open the gates, make haste fellow,' and he dashed down the stone steps to the yard. The knight leapt from his horse nearly jumping on Richard, wrapped his arm around his shoulder, drew him close, and spoke quietly.

'Say naught and take me to your rooms.' Richard walked with the knight who still kept his arm around Richard's shoulder. Those who watched the scene looked at each other completely mystified. Richard walked straight into his room and told Matilda to leave. She looked puzzled, but did as she was bidden. Esther rose nervously from her chair and looked equally bemused. The knight removed the scruff from his face… it was the King of England.

'*Sire,*' Richard knelt and Esther curtseyed.

'Rise, is that wine on the table?'

'Yes Lord,' Esther answered.

'Might I have a goblet, I'm fearfully dry.'

Esther filled a goblet and passed it to him. Henry gulped it down and wiped his mouth with the back of his hand. 'Ahhh – very fine, very fine, you look surprised to see me Richard!' He threw his head back and laughed at their confusion. 'No one knows I'm in England; the French are attacking me in Normandy and would make capital of it if they knew I were absent. I received your letter.' Esther refilled the King's goblet. 'Thank you, good Lady, I needed to know from your lips what is happening here and speak to you personally so that you are clear what is my will and are confident in my support.'

Richard reluctantly told of Sir Guy, Henry pursed his lips and slammed his fist down on the table. 'Is there no limit to the treachery against me, nothing offends me more than to be betrayed by those I have trusted and elevated. Take his lands Richard and occupy his castle. If he is found he must not be harmed, I will deal with him myself. Make that known Richard. What of his wife?'

'She knew nothing of his treachery and has returned to her father in shame.'

'As well she may. These are traitorous times, thank God I can trust you for your loyalty, Richard.'

'Indeed, you can, my Lord.' Richard went on to tell the King about his army where they were and what he thought was the best way ahead. They were seated at the table, Esther poured more wine, and they talked at length, exchanging their information. Henry was delighted with Richard's plan to attack the Earl of Leicester's home, and it was decided that's what they would do, they would take the battle to the rebels.

'I will return tonight before the French find out I've gone; secrets are ever determined to be free from their hiding place. Have you parchment and a quill? I will write a warrant stating it is my wish that you will lead my army. You are the only real soldier who has any experience of battle, though they are all fine men. They served me well in Ireland, they will control their own troops, but you will have overall command. My throne may be at stake here; I do not underestimate the severity of these times. We need to act quickly and decisively and I can't be in two places at once.' Henry wrote down his orders, melted the red wax beside his name and into it he pressed his seal, held it for a moment then with a slight twist freed his seal and passed the warrant to Richard.

'Take this Richard and may God bless you.'

'What of mete, Sire?' Esther asked.

'Thank you, dear Lady, for your concern, but we came prepared, I will leave you now, my time is urgent, I must make haste and return to Rouen. Walk me to the yard Richard, no bowing to attract attention and I'll be on my way. Good day Lady Aylesford, thank you for your kindness.' Esther curtseyed once more. Whilst they walked, Henry told him how fortunate he was to have found such a wife as Esther.

'Such a soul-mate is a gift from God, believe me Richard you must treasure it, neglect it at your peril.'

Something must have touched him when he'd seen them together, perhaps memories of something *he'd* once had and neglected. In recent years, Henry had been captivated by his mistress, Rosamund Clifford, known as the "Rose of the world", a great beauty. Perchance he was tiring of her offering, or was merely more conscious of its temporal nature. Richard knew her, he'd met her at Woodstock where she lived, and he liked her, she was undoubtedly an extraordinary lady he heard rumours that she was quite seriously ill, perhaps dying another worry for the King to deal with at this time. There was no doubt that she was the love of Henry's life. Richard once again was overwhelmed with thoughts of Julianne.

Henry told Richard that the Queen had taken her leave of the palace at Poitiers, and she'd intended to join her sons, to support their rebellion against *him*. Richard saw by his face how hurt he was. She had ridden across France alone, dressed as a man, but was caught and taken prisoner. She'd been brought to the King at Rouen and was now imprisoned there.

'It is a secret for now.' The King went on to say that her treachery had been a heart-rending blow, and wondered what had happened between them that she would do such a wicked thing against her God anointed husband.

'Aye – we were in love once.'

Richard thought Henry was merely giving voice to the private thoughts within his head, so made no comment.

His men mounted as soon as he strode from the keep, they had remained by their horses all the time Henry had been with Richard, keeping themselves to themselves. Henry squeezed Richard's shoulder, Richard nodded, and Henry leapt into the saddle with all the ease and grace of a man half his age. His famed energy had not yet deserted him, he put spur to horse and left.

When Richard returned to Esther, she was standing exactly where they'd left her, as if the whirlwind, which was Henry Plantagenet, had affixed her to the spot.

She shook her head, 'Richard, I have never been so surprised in all my life.'

CHAPTER 31

'Fear not Esther, Raymond will be here and the castle is well fortified. I have confidence that if you are attacked, that you will be able to stand fast until I can relieve you, but in truth, I think such an occurrence unlikely.'

'I'm sure that you have done all that you can, but you will not be here, try if it be possible to keep me informed of your well-being. Remember that you have responsibility for many lives and keep well clear of the main fighting.'

'Dearest Esther, I will do all to ensure I return, for I have much to return to,' and he touched her stomach, kissed her, and mounted his horse. Raymond lifted his hand to him, as did Alwin, Esther clasped her hands tightly together, and did her best to smile.

'Farewell,' Richard said returning her smile. 'Be brave little mouse,' he gently laid his hand upon her head, turned Ares, and rode out at the front of his men.

It took two days before they rode into a nervous camp and dismounted. Richard de Luci came first to greet Richard; it appeared as if he had assumed overall command.

'Are there quarters for me?'

'Indeed, Lord Aylesford, we have rooms in the town.'

'Ah, well, I will make myself known to the men walk with me. Afterwards I will ride with you to the town and meet with my commanders.'

'Actually, *I* have command of the forces, Lord,' Richard de Luci offered with some hesitance.

'I thank you Sir and I can see you have acquitted yourself with some credibility, but I have a warrant given to me in person by the King, commissioning me with the work of overall command.' de Luci looked at him with some suspicion – for he knew the King to be in France at this time.

'Am I to be permitted to see the *alleged* warrant?'

Richard slowly lifted his eyes to meet de Luci's, and in a fearfully soft voice said, 'Take care lawyer – I will understand this question as one of mere interest, not one intended as a challenge to my honour. The warrant will be shown to *all* the commanders when we assemble later.' De Luci saw discretion as the better way for now and bowed.

Richard walked and talked to the men some of whom he knew and many whom he did not know, but they knew *him* and of him. Richard understood these men it had been his life; he'd slept in ditches and scavenged with such men for what meagre succour they could find. They would slit your throat for the price of a tankard of ale, then give their last crust to a dying comrade. One had to be part of this to understand such contradiction and he knew Richard de Luci would never be able to understand, or inspire these men to sacrifice their lives for him. Life for Richard de Luci's lawyer's mind ran in straight lines, and no such line existed on the battlefield. In such places that endeavoured with success to give vent to the blood curdling cries of Hell, life was measured in heartbeats, right was decided by the strength of a sword arm, quick decisive action, it was not the cut and thrust of words that determined the outcome of a battle.

Richard listened to the men's grumbles he'd heard the same in every language, soldiers were soldiers, under whoever's colours they fought. They wanted more mete, more ale and to know what they faced, they wanted to feel hope seeping into their bones when they heard their leaders.

Richard promised to see they were all fed, he may be able to keep that promise, then again, he may not, but he would honestly try.

The nights were drawing out; each day grew longer. Thank God for the warm weather he thought.

'Come, take me to my rooms.' He told de Luci and they rode from the camp, the men cheered Richard as he passed.

Richard met with the commanders around a large table, ideal for the displaying of maps, and notes, and passed them the warrant from Henry, so that there could be no question of his right to command.

They were surprised that Henry had travelled to England to deliver this warrant in person. They seemed relieved that the decisions would not be theirs, if any future conflict did not go their way they could step quietly back into the shadows. Richard's attitude was completely at odds with that thought; he relished the conflict, pitting his brain against the enemy. He was a soldier not a Lord with distracting considerations. Perhaps he should have been for he was now a man of property with a wife and a burgeoning family. However, this work was part of him, he was a warrior and he feared not the Earl of Leicester, or any such as he, that he might have to face in the days to come. Even if he were outnumbered, he never doubted for an instant that he would prevail.

They marched to the outskirts of the city of Leicester and laid siege to it. Though the fighting was fierce, Richard's forces quickly overcame the resistance. Richard discarding all Esther had implored of him had been in the thick of the fighting. His horse, not Ares, he was thankful that he had decided to take a less conspicuous mount into the fray, was shot from beneath him. He was thrown and stunned, his helm strap broke in the fall, and left his head unprotected. While he struggled to regain control of his senses, he was struck a blow above his ear. He was alert enough to avoid the full impact; nevertheless, there was a serious wound to the side of his head. He fell to his knees then forward onto his face.

The next thing he knew he was in his tent divested of his livery with worried commanders stood gazing down at him.

'Lord Aylesford, how do you feel now?'

'Help me sit up. How goes the day?' Walter and Tristram took Richard's arms and gently eased him into a sitting position. Richard was hardly able to focus his brain, or his eyes.

'The town is ours, but the castle still resists, and we have news that the Scots have marched south and have taken Carlisle.'

Richard lay his head back and groaned, 'I might have known that the King of Scotland, would make the most of this revolt.'

'They say he has united with the Young King Henry.'

'Damn,' cursed Richard. 'You know the tactics we have talked on and practised. Leave a force to contain this castle here, we can't waste time defeating it and take the bulk of the army to rout the Scots. Go first to Carlisle. You will follow my orders as if they were the King's voice. Once you have subdued the Scots. You must return quickly; I will make my way to Tattershall it's only two days east of here. I will meet you on your return; it must be before September if we are to face the Earl of Leicester in Suffolk when he lands. Make preparations to go immediately, speed is of the essence.'

CHAPTER 32

Richard was carried in a canvas sling between two horses, but it was agony. He vomited at least twice and was fearfully ill for the entire two days.

When he opened his eyes, he had no idea where he was or how long he had been there. Before him sat Julianne, her hands on her lap, her brow was furrowed but she managed to smile. He couldn't quite make sense of it why was she at Leicester, he didn't recognise the surroundings. He remembered his horse was hit and it falling, but no more.

He felt weak, he could only gaze at Julianne; he heard the door and shifted his eyes to the sound. He saw Sir John coming towards him.

'Richard, you are awake, how do you feel? We were concerned for your life, thank God for Bernard my treasured chirurgien.'

It was coming back to him now; he'd been taken to Tattershall. Richard tried to speak but his lips were parched. His tongue felt so swollen he could barely move it within his mouth.

'Here Richard, drink this,' and Julianne slipped her hand gently under his head and offered a cup of small ale to his lips. He took several sips, sighed at the effort the simple task required, and then she lowered his head once more onto the pillow. His eyes never left hers he was transfixed by them. He wanted to take hold of her, feel her lips on his, but he was too weak even to move.

'Thank – you,' he croaked. 'How long – have I been here?' She had to lean close to hear him, for his voice was so faint. He could smell her hair, her skin; he willed her face to touch his, she was so near, but it did not.

'It's been nearly two weeks now Richard, we were fearful for your life, you have been so dreadfully ill.'

'Has there been any news from the King's army?'

'Not as of yet, that's not important at this moment, you need to rest and recover your strength.'

'Do you want mete, perhaps some broth, you have never eaten since you arrived, and your men said that you ate naught on the journey here,' asked Sir John.

'I *must* sleep – I will eat when I awake – I'm not hungry. Does *Esther* know of this?' There was a sudden urgency in his voice.

'*No*, be still,' Julianne gripped his shoulder as he tried to rise; his brow was bathed in sweat. 'We didn't know what to tell her until we were sure…' she said, wiping his forehead with a cool damp cloth.

'Don't make this known to her, she will only worry, I will write when I can. Thank you for your kindness,' he said and he summoned up every ounce of his strength and moved his fingers just enough for the tips to touch

Julianne's hand, she bowed and stared at them, then slowly withdrew her hand. Richard's head was filled with questions, but he was too weak and tired to ask them at this moment.

Another week slipped by and another. Gradually his strength was returning, though he was plagued with the most dreadful headaches. They were so debilitating at times he could scarcely see, but this day he felt able to stand. For all he knew, Julianne had never left his side; whenever he awoke, she was there. When he could they had talked, about everything and nothing, it was worth every second of pain to have this time together.

He lay on top of his bed, Walter had helped him dress, and he felt better for it. He raised himself slowly to a sitting position and slid his legs from the bed and onto the floor.

'Lord!' Walter his servant called when he saw him.

'Still yourself Walter I must do this while Lady Julianne is gone from me.'

'She must be very tired Lord; she has never left your side above a moment these past weeks.' Richard sighed.

He had no sooner pulled himself to his feet than Julianne entered. 'Richard, what are you doing?' she stepped quickly to him and took his arm. 'Whatever are you thinking about boy, allowing your master up from his bed?'

Richard reached to Julianne and touched her arm, 'No, no, it is I who am to blame, not my servant. I feel better this day Julianne, come help me walk for a short while in the fresh air; it is a fine day by the look of it. I need to own my legs, to get them moving and feel that they belong to me once more.'

'Are you sure about this Richard, you have never left your bed?'

'Yes, come take my arm.'

She supported him as they walked out the short distance onto the battlements, next to his room in the keep. He was surprised how weak he was. They walked slowly without talking, and stopped for Richard to catch his breath. He leaned against the wall and gazed into the distance. This was the first time he'd actually been alone with Julianne since he was wounded. He lowered his eyes and examined his hands for some moments, building up the courage to speak...

'*Why* Julianne?'

She looked at the ground, lifted her fist quickly to her face, and cuffed away a tear.

'What does it matter? What's done is done,' she said quietly.

'I love you Julianne – that's not done,' he spoke more sharply than he'd intended.

'What about your wife?'

'Is loving – *that* simple – aye, for some I dare say it is?' He was in pain from his head wound and desperately trying to control his frustration.

'Love is rarely simple Richard. I remember our old priest saying, "Love is more than a feeling, it's an act of your will",' she responded quietly, her head still bowed.

He ignored her offering, and stared once more into the distance... 'I am to be a father – Esther is with child.'

'God has blessed your union; mine was cursed from the beginning, what I did was a sin. I have been punished for my wilfulness, nothing less do I deserve.'

He turned once more to face her. 'Is that what God does, wait for us to fall then tramples us into the dirt? If so, I want no part of Him,' he said angrily.

'Don't say such a thing, *He* did not force me to do what I knew was wrong, no – it was my wilful pride,' she lifted her head and looked him in the eye.

'What of Sir Guy?' Richard asked more calmly, out of genuine concern.

'I know naught of him; he was a vain fool. I think he was blackmailed by my brother and a servant.'

'Where is your brother now?'

'I know not, he is wicked. I was blinded by my love for him to what I always knew in my heart of hearts. Perhaps vanity was the downfall of both Guy *and* me.'

Richard sighed and pushed himself up from the wall, reached into his purse and withdrew the emerald. He smiled sadly, took her hand, and placed the jewel into her palm.

'Richard, your life's work seems to be returning this,' she stared at the green stone. 'The colour of envy, no one would envy me.'

He leaned forward to kiss her but she twisted her head to the side.

'No Richard, you are Esther's, I will not make worse my iniquity by destroying your lives.' She turned and walked from him – he stood – helplessly and watched her go.

Shakily, taking support from the wall he made his way back to his room and collapse exhausted onto his bed.

'Might I get you anything Lord?'

'No – thank you Walter,' he gasped.

In the days that followed Julianne never returned to Richard's room, to sit with him, every sound from the door and his eyes brightened, but it was never Julianne.

That moment of open honesty had changed the time together, once said, the words could not be unsaid; they spoke little now, only briefly at mealtimes. The closeness was tortuous for both, Sir John was clearly aware of their problems and it saddened him too.

After such a meal, Richard bowed and was about to leave and return to his room; Sir John touched his arm and embraced him.

'I would do anything to make it different, believe me Son. God forbid, you ever have to experience the pain of being a powerless parent, having to stand by and watch the helpless child you have loved and nurtured, suffering the pangs of Hell, and there is *nothing, nothing,* you can do. I love you both. I am to blame – I could have stepped in and enforced my will. I foresaw all this, but I was weak, God forgive me,' he whispered as his voice trailed away to nothing. Richard tightened his hold on the old man.

'No one is to blame my dear friend.' Richard held him quietly for some time. 'I have been dreading this moment… but I must leave on the morrow, Sir John,' he paused again, 'The documents you sent to me, that some rider brought this day, made known to me that the Earl of Leicester has landed at the head of a large force of Flemings and Normans, both horse and foot. They landed at Walton in Suffolk on 29th of September.'

'Can I help in any way?' Sir John asked as they separated, Richard continued to hold Sir John by his shoulders.

'Keep Julianne here and safe, that is your work now.'

'Do you know where the rebels are?'

'Immediately upon their arrival, they joined forces with Hugh Bigod, Earl of Norfolk, at his castle of Framlingham. I've met him before, he's a powerful and crafty man, and I knew that he favoured this rebellion. Together the earls laid siege to Hakeneck, the castle of Ranulph de Broc and took it. While this was going on

Richard de Luci, Justiciar of England, together with Humphrey de Bohun and the King's army, were wasting their time, and no doubt men, in the north ravaging the Lothian's, lands of the King of Scotland. However, upon learning of the Earl of Leicester's arrival in England, de Luci has made a truce with the Scots, until the feast of Saint Hilary, that's the 14th of January. What a wonderful time of the year to take an army north, to re-engage the Scots, the *fool*. At this moment, he is hurrying southwards. In the meantime, Earl Robert has left Framlingham and set off for Leicester. This is a fearful mess Sir John, I need to join them, we have an invasion to face and by the ineffectual marauding that lawyer de Luci's done in Scotland, I can't trust him in command of this engagement, this must be ended and decisively.'

'But are you well enough?'

'Aye, well enough, some wounds only death will heal,' he said. He lowered his arms from Sir John's shoulders, they nodded to each other and Richard walked wearily to his room, Sir John turned and watched him go.

Richard reached to the handle of his door, and pushed it open, on seeing his servant he said, 'Walter leave me. I will not need you this night, see that all is ready for our journey on the morrow, be sure you are rested.'

'Very well, Lord.' Richard stepped to one side; his servant bowed and left him. Richard watched him walk off then leaned forward, pressed his brow against the cold stone of the door reveal and beat the side of his fist against the wall. He turned at the sound of footsteps on the wooden floor, and stopped, he bowed, and she froze.

'Julianne!'

She hesitated and then continued. He touched her back as she passed, and she stopped and lowered her head. In the past, Richard could have expected a burst of vitriolic abuse, but that Julianne was no more, now she was beaten and broken. He slowly turned her to face him, placing his hands on her shoulders, he swallowed unable to speak so restricted was his throat, her head remained bowed; he could see she had been crying.

'Julianne, I am truly sorry to hear about your husband's disappearance. It has placed you in an intolerable position, I will see what can be done, when I meet next with the King.' She apprehensively raised her head and stared into his eyes, responding to the warmth of his touch as it slowly seeped into her body.

'You think *that's* why I'm upset… it's me who is the fool, not you.' They merely stared at each other then she bowed her head again and whispered.

'Father tells me…' She was struggling to speak, '… that you are going on the morrow… I know we will never see each other again… God keep you safe,' there was no pretence now, no attempt to hide her torment. The tears dripped freely from her chin.

'I have no option, I must go lives depend on me.'

'*Yes* – you are a good man Richard, I know that now, you always were.'

Richard unconsciously lowered his head. This was a moment, which was not determined by thought, but something living and aching within. Julianne responded by lifting her chin. Their lips touched, and then came together, suddenly their world changed, taking on a life of its own. The warmth was overpowering, sensual, there were waves of suppressed passion flooding into her body, she was struggling just to stand; her head was spinning never had she known any feeling like this. The moment was now frantic, and their bodies pressed urgently together. Richard swept her off the ground and cradled her in his arms; she clung to him, her lips fighting for his. He pushed his room door open with his shoulder, carried her through, and then slammed it closed with the heel of his boot. He literally tumbled onto the bed with Julianne still in his arms. Loosening his hold on her, he relaxed into the pillow. She took his face in her hands, stared into it for a second, and then pressed her lips passionately to his. She separated for a moment to enable her to give attention to the buttons of his shirt, she fumbled with them, her hands trembling, all the while pressing her lips hungrily to his. They held each other so tightly she had to push herself free to gasp for breath, fearful of fainting. There were no words, just two people desperately needing each other…

It was still dark when he awoke, he was naked, he reached for her, but – she had gone. Pushing himself up onto his elbows, he looked around the room, then fell back and hammered his fist into the bed. He stared at the ceiling and pressed his hands to his face, 'Dear God in heaven, what have we done! I am in Hell, Julianne, Julianne.'

CHAPTER 33

Richard was seated upon his palfrey; Sir John was there to wish him well. Richard hoped that Julianne might come to say one last word, it may even be goodbye, but she did not.

'Better go Richard, I understand as I'm sure you do, that she will be watching you and willing God's angels to keep you safe.'

Richard was unable to speak; he held his lip between his teeth and jerked his head in acknowledgement. Casting his eyes once more to the castle windows, he put spur to horse and the small troop moved off. As Richard crossed the drawbridge, Sir John heard the most fearful scream, the cry tore into his heart, and he hung his head in sorrow, as perhaps only a father could.

It was midday; Richard had ridden in complete silence. He knew he should have spoken to his men but he couldn't. He was angry with himself. He was sick of being noble, always doing the right thing, thinking of others before himself. That's why he'd married Esther out of concern for her not because he loved her, yet he knew he did love Esther, and she was the best of wives. He understood none of this. Henry had a mistress and none thought the less of him for it. Marriage was a contract for advancement; all parties knew that it was the way of things, nothing to do with love.

What was wrong with him, that he should be different, what made him love so intensely? Love was a curse for him, if he told his friends they would laugh at him for a fool and that's what he was. How could he be so passionately in love with Julianne and yet care so deeply about Esther all at the same time. Even now in his anguish he was concerned that she and his child may be safe and well. Death at childbirth was a common enough thing and the thought of being without her was unimaginable. It was weeks since he had heard from her, he'd written to her and told her of his injury, but there had been no reply. He'd never given it a thought before, now he was suddenly concerned.

He was distracted from his thoughts by dust rising in the distance; he shaded his eyes with his hand trying to see what was before him. Richard raised his arm and brought the troop to a halt. It was as he'd thought, soldiers on horseback.

'Arm yourselves, there are riders coming this way at some speed, no more than us is my estimate, stay behind us Walter. Lower your lances we will move towards them at a steady pace, when I give the order we will charge, keep the line.'

The troop started to move forward, Richard shook his head trying to clear his eyes and see what device was on their banner.

'It is the KING'S banner, they are not rebels.' The riders came on and clearly into view. Richard once again drew his men to a halt. They waited and it was not long before Richard saw the lead rider, he smiled, 'Tristram,' he said to himself.

'TRISTRAM', he shouted, dismounted, and waved. Tristram lifted his arm in response, in seconds he was at Richard's side, and leapt from his saddle; they bowed and embraced. The two parties greeted each other laughing and talking.

'Tristram, a sight for sore eyes.'

'I knew you would be riding this way and thought that it would save time if I rode to you and then I could guide you to the location of main army and thus save you time searching the country for us.'

'How are things?'

'It has been difficult, Richard, but we should mount, and make haste we can talk as we ride.' Richard nodded his agreement and mounted. He waved to the troop and they moved off at a steady pace.

'So, tell me what I need to know.'

'I have been tormented having to bite my tongue. De Luci is so indecisive I could have turned my coat and joined with King William of Scotland and his rebels. There were at least three occasions, when we could have struck a decisive blow, and instead we let the Scots go. I think he was terrified that he may lose men and be so weakened that we had not the strength to face Leicester when he landed. Thank God you are back.'

'How far ahead is our army?'

'We will be with them before the day has passed.'

Richard de Luci did not appear as pleased as the others to see Lord Aylesford. There was a great improvement in his demeanour when Richard praised the way he had brought the army so quickly from the borders of Scotland to face the Earl of Leicester, and had even swelled their numbers. They ate and talked as they marched; time was of the essence. Richard wanted to strike quickly and decisively so the doubters watching and waiting were not sucked into following the rebels.

They first sighted the Earl of Leicester with his army near St. Edmund's, at a place which is known as Fornham, situated on a piece of marshy ground, not far from the church of St. Genevieve. On his arrival, Richard was determined to attack immediately, no discussion with the rebels, listening to, or bargaining with them. He would strike hard, and first, there would be no mercy. Any who wavered on the sidelines would see what the cost was of standing against the rightful King of England and their sworn Lord.

Richard, with a considerable force, rode alongside Humphrey de Bohun. Their strength consisted of three hundred knights, all fine experienced soldiers of the King. They went forth armed for battle to meet the Earl of Leicester, carrying before them the banner of St Edmund, the King, and Martyr, as their standard.

Richard pushed and jostled the ranks into battle array. Shouts went up, *"By virtue of the aid of God and of his most glorious Martyr Saint Edmund, we will destroy the traitors"*. They first attacked the line in which the Earl of Leicester had taken his position. Richard would strike at the head with absolute determination and God willing, end this impudence quickly.

Richard's assault was vicious; the blow was delivered with such swiftness and ferocity that they had overwhelmed the rebels who were so stunned by the speed and intensity they gave only a token resistance. Any opposition was decimated before they could fully comprehend what was happening. Richard's knights had wreaked utter carnage, men and horses lay in heaps of dismembered offal; it was the charnel house from Hell.

The Earl of Leicester was vanquished and taken prisoner, along with his wife. Also taken was Hugh des Chateaux, a French nobleman, clearly here on behalf of the French King. All their might and hope was utterly crushed.

Richard's concern was to now reassemble his army, and await any hostile response from Barons sympathetic to the Earl of Leicester's cause. This was no time to be complacent; they had won a great victory over a force, which outnumbered them; now in that moment of triumph, Richard knew they were vulnerable. He understood that an army is always at its weakest immediately after a battle, even a great victory such as this, they were exhausted the surge of excitement had gone.

Richard left the Lawyer de Luci to deal with the prisoners. There fell in this battle more than ten thousand Flemings, while all the rest were taken prisoners and were thrown into prison in irons, where they were reportedly starved to death. The wounded Flemish mercenaries received the most brutal treatment; most weren't soldiers but poorly equipped farmers who'd been slain on the promise of rich pickings of English wool. They met their cruel and gruesome end when the villagers finished them off in the massacre that followed the battle of Fornham. Richard heard to his disgust that *there was in the country neither villager nor clown who did not go to destroy the*

Flemings with fork and flail by fifteen, by forties, by hundreds and by thousands and tumbled the bodies into ditches to rot. It was said, *"Upon their bodies descend crows and buzzards who carried away their souls to the fire which ever burns".*

As for the Earl of Leicester, his wife, Hugh des Chateaux, and the rest of the wealthier men who were captured with them, they were sent into Normandy to await the King's pleasure.

Richard hated the aftermath of battle; the cries of those wishing life and those wishing death disturbed his sleep for nights after. He saw one wretched mortal with his innards spilled out into his hands, Richard simply rode past him, the human scavengers would alleviate his suffering soon enough. Perhaps in time man would learn a better way, or would this carnage forever be the only way? He was relieved that he might ease his conscience knowing that the torment of the vanquished was laid at the door of de Luci. Though he knew, that he would not have to scratch far beneath the surface of his conscience, to see that he was as culpable as de Luci.

He heard rumours of the Earl's wife that she had been proud and formidable. The Countess Petronella was captured fully armed, carrying a shield and lance. Whilst trying to escape, she fell into a ditch and almost drowned, she would have, had not Simon de Vahull lifted her up, saying: *"Lady, come away with me, give up that idea. Thus, it fares in war, to lose or to gain".* Simon meant that Petronella wished to drown herself intentionally. She left her rings in the mud rather than have them stolen by her enemies.

Roger of Wendover provides further detail, claiming that; *"The countess had on her finger a beautiful ring, which she flung into the neighbouring river, the Lark, rather than suffer the enemy to make such gain by capturing her".*

Richard did return once more to the battlefield to speak with de Luci, as soon as he was satisfied that the uprising had been quashed, "For the present", for he did not know what mischief was abroad in other parts of the country. He knew for certain, come the New Year, the Scots would have to be faced. There were mounds of dead everywhere, blood-soaked heaps of death; they would be a warning to all for years to come.

He told de Luci that he was making for home he was in need of rest. He yet suffered with blinding headaches and nausea because of the blow he received to his head in Leicester. At times, the pain was so ferocious that he literally could not see. He also made known to de Luci that he would write to the King in Rouen and tell him of the victory, encouraging de Luci to write also. It was an uneasy relationship with de Luci but Richard knew he had talents and was loyal; it was merely that they were different people, with *different* talents. They shook hands amicably and Richard mounted and rode off.

When Richard reached the turning south there was a moment of hesitation, for he could just as easily turn north. He sat at the junction, for some time, staring at his hands. Resigned to the demands of honour; he tugged on the left rein and turned southward. He knew that this was more that a mere junction in the road.

"Life is made up of decisions and we must live in the consequences of them," William Marshal said to him once. "That's why I am always guided by my honour, Richard. When all is stripped away, we are left with, only one question, is it right or wrong".

The place in his heart that burned so fiercely, tortured him mercilessly. He often felt that he could hardly stand such was the torment. He knew that choices had to be made and he was certain that he had made the right one, but at this moment, he did not feel any better for it. Julianne was alone and that was a hard thing for him to endure. He had chosen Esther, she had given herself to him without condition, and he did love her.

'Come Tristram why do we tarry? I have a wife and child waiting.'

CHAPTER 34

With every mile they drew nearer to Aylesford, Richard became increasingly eager to see Esther. The speed of the troop seemed to gather pace until his home suddenly appeared before them out of the mist. They had set off this morning before light. His first glimpse of his home welcomed him with the sight of the low autumn sunlight brushing against the top of the keep, washing the tips of the battlements in the glow of a new day.

'Home Tristram, thank God, new day, new future, come on I'll race you,' and he spurred his palfrey on.

'Cheat,' shouted Tristram after him.

Richard was still at a gallop when he thundered over the drawbridge on to the bailey. He turned his nimble little palfrey and it skidded to a standstill sitting back on its haunches. Two stable lads rushed to take hold of his horse and he leapt to the ground followed closely by Tristram.

'What kept you?' Richard laughed. 'Ahh – Alwin,' he had caught sight of Alwin walking down the steps of the keep.

'My Lord,' he bowed very respectfully. 'You were not expected.' Alwin's greeting was delivered in a voice that chilled Richard to the bone.

'No, I dare say, where's Esther? Quick man…' Richard's face was now transformed by a fearful foreboding. 'Where – is your Lady, Alwin?'

'In her room Lord, she will be pleased to see you.' It was not what Alwin said, but that which he did not say, which now fired Richard. Pushing past Alwin, he leapt up the steps three at a time; as he ran, he was possessed by one of the chronic headaches, he'd been subjected to since Leicester. He ran half stumbling up the spiral stairs blinking as he climbed, desperately trying to bring the pounding in his head under some control. He continued along the passage to his room and flung open the door.

Esther was laid in bed propped up on a pillow, two maids scuttled past him closing the door behind them. Esther smiled weakly at him and he walked with leaden feet towards her. She was deathly pale, which was made more noticeable by the contrast of her jet-black hair.

Her voice was weak, 'I thank God you are safe, yet I have been dreading this moment. I didn't want to see you, I'm afraid of your rejection. I have prayed and prayed that the Blessed Virgin would keep you safe, but I didn't want you to come home.'

'What is this nonsense you greet me with?' he whispered anxiously, yet at the same time afraid to hear the answer – she looked desperately sick, even dying. At the tenderness of his words her lip trembled. She was too weak to control her emotions but there were no tears, no, that time had passed.

He knelt by her side, took hold of her hand, and pressed his lips to it. Slowly lifting his head, he stared into her eyes then leaned forward and tenderly kissed her on her brow.

'… Our – baby is *dead*, Richard,' and he took her in his arms. 'Your, your – letter came when you, you were at Tattershall, saying you had been wounded in battle, I was so fearful, I panicked for the feeble creature I am. Any thought that I might lose you,' she trembled, 'there is no pain like it. I think that my foolishness brought on my labour. Our b – baby boy, Richard – he, he was so perfect; it was *awful* – they wanted to take him from me, imagining that the sight of him would do me more harm. As if anything between us could harm me, I held him and loved him. He was strangled by the birth cord. I made Alwin promise me that he would have a proper grave so we might go together. How could I just forget him and pretend that he never was, I saw his face, and it was *our* son. Richard – I'm sorry it's my – my fault, do you despise me? I've failed to give you your son.'

Richard didn't know this feeling or how to give vent to it. He couldn't understand anything that was whirling around inside his head at this moment.

'You are being foolish Esther; there is no blame for you to own.'

His compassion for Esther was suddenly transformed into fury, God Almighty, You could have beaten me, I deserve nothing less, but she is innocent, she is without guile. What sort of Being punishes the wholly innocent by making them share the retribution of the guilty? He raged in his head.

'Richard, it's…' she couldn't speak.

'All that matters, is that you are all right, we will have *more* children.'

'No… Richard you comprehend not; Asseline came from the village, she has delivered many babies, she says… I will not be able to have any more children. There, there was too much damage done to me, I nearly died, it was so awful Richard. I'm filled with shame, I love you but you will not want me now.'

'Dear God, it is I who am sorry. I'm *so* sorry I couldn't get to you. I don't want to be loved. Love is merely God's jest, we grasp, beg for it and He laughs at us for the fools we are. It's His way to distribute suffering. Tell me, what does love, ever bring in the end, but pain and misery? This is *my* punishment, my sin that *you* are made to suffer for, all because you love me, don't you see?'

'But Richard!'

'Esther, there is *nothing* I wouldn't give up for you, so help me God this is the truth, but He despises me.'

'Richard – you are hurt, I understand. I have felt all these things I have been so afraid. I thought you would send me away so you could take another wife, but for me all of this is worth the price of loving you.'

Richard shook his head, 'Then you are a fool Esther,' he said and sat next to her and held her tightly to him. They lay for some time without speaking.

He kissed her, 'I must go for a short while and speak to Alwin, he will be concerned, I will return directly. You have nothing to fear, rest and know you are safe.'

Richard eased himself carefully from the bed, gave a tired smiled and left. Her maids were standing outside the door, and he bade them attend to their mistress. He needed to be alone before he saw anyone; he walked along the passage to some wooden steps, which took him onto the roof of the keep, slumped down in a corner against the battlements, held his face in his hands and wept. He pressed his knuckle to his teeth and bit into it so fiercely he could taste blood on his lips. He was in no doubt that, his sin had caused all this suffering; all this was over his head, 'I'm feeling so small, I no longer understand anything, Mother of Christ pray for me, a sinner.'

Alwin was in the yard with Tristram and Raymond attending to the returning men. Tristram gestured towards Richard as he came from the keep and Alwin turned to him.

'Lord – you have seen my Lady, I am saddened by this, we all share in your grief. The castle has been a place of shadows these last weeks.'

'Thank you, all of you, I am truly blessed to have such friends.'

'I had your son buried as my Lady wished. The priest was reluctant to do as I ordered, he started to tell me his reasons why he could not be laid to rest in holy ground, but I was deaf to him. I told him that I would leave him to think on it, while I dug two graves, one for him, and by God he would have occupied it, so help me. He must have thought better of it and found he was able to adjust his theological understanding, for he blessed the child with holy water and we laid your son to rest with all dignity. The carpenter made an oak box, it was padded with wool, and the mason has carved a small stone with his name upon it. My Lady named him William, after your father she said.'

Richard had to turn his back on them for a moment. He lifted his hand to his face, took a deep breath, and turned to face them once more.

'You are a good man Alwin,' he said in a soft voice.

'I will show you where it is Lord, but I fancy my Lady wants to see it for the first time, with you by her side.'

'It will be as she wishes.'

CHAPTER 35

Richard wrote to Sir John to tell him of all his news, he mentioned that he was still being subjected to the fearful headaches and periodic blindness. He did not make mention of the loss of their son, he couldn't find the words, yes that was the reason, he couldn't find the words. He concluded with a simple footnote, that he would find it a kindness if he, Sir John, would make known to "All" at Tattershall how he missed and thought of them daily. He stared at his letter for some time… folded it neatly and tapped it mindlessly against his chin. Sighing, he laid it once again on the table before him, dripped the molten red liquid onto the join, and applied his ring to the wax. There was so much more he wanted to say, needed to say, he touched the parchment to his lips, rose and called for Walter his servant.

Richard was astounded when his guards called him, no more than a week later, to tell him of approaching riders, and when he went to see what the commotion was about, he saw Sir John, his chirurgien and perhaps a dozen soldiers riding towards the castle. He told Esther and immediately made his way down onto the bailey.

Sir John dismounted and they embraced each other, 'I received your letter Richard and talked with Bernard, he thinks he can help.'

'Really?'

'Yes Lord, I think that the blow to your head has placed some pressure on your brain, hence the headaches. There will be some risks, but the success rate is high. I have done this many times. Some want it done to release evil spirits from their head, I believe not in such things, but what do I know! I leave such appreciation to those who make the other world their life's employment. *My* calling is to ease the suffering in the temporal world.'

'Come to my apartments and you can make this known to us.'

Esther was from her bed now and dressed, though she was weak she was feeling better day on day. They ate together in their rooms, the stairs were yet too much, and the cold debilitated her. She smiled as Sir John entered and he embraced her, as he had Richard, for she was now as a daughter to him.

'God bless you Esther, I am delighted to see you looking so well, we pray for you, and I have also commissioned our priest that he may say daily prayers for you both. These are dangerous days and prayer is a labour suited to we old men. Julianne sends her love; she could not come, though it was her wish, for she is with child. It has transformed her lowness of spirit; she has new life now. It blesses my heart to see her. There is no sign of her wretched husband; he has disappeared from this earth. You know Bernard,' he said gesturing to him.

Esther hesitated, as the pain came afresh like red-hot stab to her heart. Such news would do so for the rest of her life, Richard knew, and squeezed her hand.

'We are thankful indeed, for her trials have been great,' she turned to the chirurgien, 'and my welcome to you, Bernard.'

'My Lady,' he said and he bowed.

'For what do we owe this great pleasure?'

'We have, or at least Bernard has, come to restore your husband to health.'

'Blessed be, for he suffers mightily.'

'Yes, my Lady, I believe there to be some pressure on the brain. Perhaps if you sit, Lord, I may examine your head?' Richard shrugged his shoulders, and withdrew a chair from the table and seated himself. Bernard began to feel around Richard's head especially where he'd been struck.

'Mmmm.'

'What is it?' asked Sir John with some urgency.

'There is a definite indentation where the wound was.'

'And can you do anything?' Asked Esther nervously, fearing that it would be hopeless.

'Most certainly, my Lady.'

'What is it you intend to do?' piped in John.

'I will use trepanation,'

'Which is?'

'I will drill a hole in Lord Aylesford's head.'

'Dear merciful Mother of Christ,' Esther blurted out and collapsed into a chair. Richard stood and went to her.

'*No* Richard, I've never heard of such madness!'

'May I say my Lady, this has been done for many years, and it is a common enough practice.'

'*No*, it is madness, I forbid it!' Bernard looked a little hurt, but only shrugged his shoulders.

'Esther, I trust Bernard.' Bernard bowed to Richard.

'Thank you, Lord, I quite comprehend your Lady's fears, I carry no offence.'

'He will die of the pain, aye, and me with him.'

'He will feel nothing my Lady, bone does not transmit any pain and there is little flesh on the skull. I have drugs from my Muslim friends, which will make my Lord sleep. There will perhaps be a little soreness when he awakes, no more.' Esther looked at Richard then to Sir John and again to Richard.

'When will this be done?'

'As soon as possible, today, now, this very minute would be perfect, my Lady.'

'I'm still unsure.'

'Esther, I am prepared to take this risk, these head pains are hellish.'

'I fear they will only get worse as time passes, my Lady.'

'Will you stay with me Sir John?'

'Of course, dear child.'

Richard and Bernard went into a small room next door where Matilda usually slept when Richard was at home. Bernard took his bag from his shoulder, asked Richard to be seated, and began to mix some potion; he dipped the tip of his finger into the pestle and touched it to his tongue.

'Hmm,' he said. 'Drink this Lord, when you awake all will be accomplished.' Richard was trying to be at ease with what was happening, Bernard's whole outward show was as if he was about to engage in the most trivial of occupations, such as the trimming of his beard. Richard tried deliberately to avoid the words entering, even forming in his mind, "He's about to drill a hole in my head".

'Perhaps it would be advisable if you lifted your feet onto the bed and lay back, relax into a sitting up position I will bind you securely to this bed so that you can't move. It is imperative that you are held quite still. I have this frame, which I designed, to hold the head rigid.'

'Perhaps we should summon servants to help.' Richard suggested nervously, relieved that Esther was not able to see the particulars of this operation.

'A noble thought Lord,' Bernard smiled. 'I have envisaged such a plan myself in the past, but found it to be a most precarious method. It proved to be more of a hindrance than help. Believe me Lord; such assistants have been known to leave the procedure rather abruptly, preferring to lie on the floor, perhaps even fracturing their skulls in the process. You may be able to imagine that this unwelcome distraction, is at the very least unhelpful, when one is making a hole in someone's head. Better just you and me, all will be well.' Richard blinked his eyes… he was no longer listening...

Esther, had completely forgotten her recent suffering, she stood, walked, sat, stood, and asked Sir John repeatedly, the same question, 'How long will it be?' Sir John seated himself next to her and tried to be as reassuring as he could. He suspected that she was not even listening what he was saying.

After what seemed to be hours of waiting there was a knock on the door and, Esther rushed to open it.

'Bernard!'

'Yes, my Lady.'

'Come in, come in, how's Richard?' Bernard entered the room smiling the smile of a man; it might be said, with the mere hint of smugness.

'He is well; the procedure was a perfect success. I have stitched back the skin it must be kept clean, but really all is well.'

'And did you drill this hole in his head?'

'Indeed, my Lady, I suspect that the bone had burst in on the brain, a mere fragment no doubt but one's brain is subject to many humours, to talk in a language you may more readily comprehend.'

Esther lowered herself into a chair and leaned forward cupping her face in her hands, shaking her head from side to side. Sir John went down on his hunkers and took her hands in his.

'Perhaps you should go to your bed and rest for a while, you can do nothing.'

'I will, Sir John.' The next thing she knew Richard was lying next to her, smiling.

'He is quite a remarkable man, Bernard, he tells me that I will have no more headaches now, and with such confidence that I could do no other than believe him.'

Richard's recovery was extraordinary. Sir John stayed for a further ten days. Bernard wished to be certain that all was as it should be, before he left. Richard took the opportunity of Sir John's visit, to show him around his estate. Sir John was impressed; it was considerably larger than his own holding *and* richer.

'Let us rest a while over there. There's a fallen tree,' Richard pointed to a small wood. 'We can be seated while we have some respite before we make for home.' They steered their horses through a gap in the hedgerow and into the sheltered glade and dismounted.

'This is a fine place, the Lord giveth, and the Lord taketh away.'

'Aye…' Richard was unsure as to what Sir John was referring, but the scripture was indeed true. They sat quietly both with questions, but each fearing to wound the other. Richard leaned forward, picked up a stick, and began to prod determinedly at a lump of frozen snow. It had been a mild winter thus far with little snow, only one night, but it remained in shaded places such as the place where they were now seated.

'Have you had much snow up north Sir John?'

'It would please me Richard if you called me John, ours is not a formal connection, you know how I feel about you. In truth you are elevated above me now *Lord*, it is I who should show deference to you,' they both smiled. 'But you ask about our weather. We have suffered more that you Southerners, but only a little.' Richard prodded once more in the snow, staring before him.

'I was wondering…'

'About Julianne?'

'Aye, Julianne – I am a man torn in two – John. I can't stop the ache. I pray, but it will not take its leave of me. What can I do?'

'Richard you need to talk to one wiser than I, but try to take some comfort that Julianne is much happier, she seems to have thrown her love into this child.'

'When is the child due?'

'March – April, she was still with that villain in July, though she is very small yet. I do not concern myself with women's things. She is content and I am happy with that.'

'That eases my pain to some extent, you realise that we lost our baby.'

'You made no mention of it when you wrote, but I thought that must be the way of it. I'm sorry son, but God willing you will be so blessed again.'

'It seems not, Esther was told that she would not be able to have more children.'

'Ahh… that is a hard thing for a man who builds up an estate, all I have I will leave in your capable hands, if the King wills it. I know you will take care of Julianne and my grandchild.'

'Yes, but what about your son, John?'

'Come, we must make our way to your home, it is turning cold,' and he stood patted his horse, led it alongside the log on which they'd been seated and climbed onto its back. 'This horse has grown I'll swear it, or my legs have got shorter, I used to be able to leap onto a horse, aye, and in full armour too. ' He held the rein tight until Richard was mounted, and they made their way steadily homeward.

Gervase was as dead to Sir John, as Richard's son was to him. Richard hoped that perhaps Sir John's heart might have softened towards Gervase, but it seemed not. Whatever happens to life that the journey should be so convoluted? He thought. When I left France all that while since, I had gained enough coin to help Father, we would work together and build up the estate again. Surely a noble employment, with Godly goals, the caring for people's lives, a safe place where they might live in peace. Aye – not to be, it could have been so different. He suddenly wanted to talk to his friend William Marshal. He wondered how his life was; no doubt, he had his struggles too. He was discovering that plans were good, but one needed ever to be ready for the unexpected blow, he had stumbled *and* fallen, more than once, but there was ever a hand to reach out to, if one was not too proud. Aye, he'd fallen right enough – and the ground was hard, perhaps the wounds would heal one day.

They dismounted, unexpectedly Sir John held him in his arms. 'Bless you Richard, God keep you safe, and all those you love.'

'And you too, Sir.'

CHAPTER 36

Richard was happy that Julianne was not alone that she had found some peace and a future, built on something solid for a change.

He prayed that all would go well for her. If there was a God, surely this was His mercy for her; His vengeance could never demand that a mistake, even a wilful mistake, should be held against her for the rest of her life. If there was a God, Richard hoped that *He* was all, and more, than man at his noblest, aspired to be. Alas, in spite of his best endeavours, man was ever hampered by his fallen nature.

Richard knew his love for Julianne would forgive her for anything, even though it resulted in *his* suffering, and he was only too aware that *he* was a poor model of Christian virtue. Surely, God *must* be more forgiving than I he prayed, was it not our wilfulness that put *Him* on the cross? Yet, He willingly suffered for us because of His love. In its own miserable way, is my willingness, to suffer not of that same root? Somehow, he had never seen it quite so clearly before, he could understand now, how love would suffer *any* pain, *any* rejection, indeed it could do no other, for the sake of the loved.

'You are deep in thought my Lord,' Esther looked up from her embroidery. Richard never responded; he remained as he was, gazing into the ever-changing colours of a world on fire, his chin resting on his steepled fingers. She was sitting close enough to enable her to press her foot onto his.

'I'm sorry, Esther did you speak?' He said half turning to her.

'I said, you seem to be deep in thought, are they worth sharing, or was it far too deep for *my* simple mind?'

He smiled, reached to her and touched her knee, 'Humm, now you take me for a fool if you would have me believe my beautiful wife has a simple mind. The very words are laced with female cunning.' She laughed and set down her embroidery, rose from her chair went to him, and sat on his knee.

'I am merely jealous of any part of you, that I do not share.'

'Ah… my thoughts were mindless nonsense. I was thinking about the choices we make, and second chances we are given. Have you any regrets, Esther?'

She pressed her face into his neck and held him; he felt a tremble run through her.

'I'm sorry Esther, that was thoughtless of me, but I would not exchange places with Julianne, if I was forced to choose between losing you or our baby. God forbid that such a hellish, choice would ever be inflicted upon me.'

Esther took a handkerchief from her cuff and wiped her eyes and her nose, she sniffed. 'Aye… hellish, is the word. I envy her hope, God willing, it will come to fruition, and she will hold her child. I pray that for her, but she has not you in her life, she will be alone. She will perhaps never know what it is to be loved, or to love enough, to give up all for that *one* person.'

Richard's heart was pounding, he had to bite into his lip, but he could not hide the tension in his muscles.

Esther lifted her eyes to his face, it was etched with pain, she cupped his head in her hand, and tenderly pressed her lips to his then ran her fingertips lightly across the furrows on his brow. Suddenly he wrapped her fiercely in his arms. She almost gasped he held her so tightly, when he relaxed his hold a little, she laid her head on his shoulder, and stroked his hair.

'Forgive me my dearest knight; I forget in my selfishness that my pain is yours to share; I am not the only one who hurts. *Richard* – Let us sleep together, I need you this night,' she stood, reached out her hand to him and he rose from his chair and embraced her.

'Esther, *you* are above all women, dear God I am not worthy of you.'

'I love you just as you are; we are *all* merely learning to love. You see how you have bewitched me, Lord Aylesford. My Lord, this is the truth, if I walk even from your shadow, there will be no light.'

He tried to smile; 'Now I know you are teasing me, Lady Aylesford.'

They were awoken to a new day by a vicious hammering on their door. Richard's immediate reaction was to reach for his dagger; he slipped on his robe and gingerly open the door.

'Raymond, what in God's blood…?'

'Sorry Richard, it is an urgent letter from the King, a rider waits in the yard for your reply, he has ridden from

London, and the King himself ordered him to wait.' Raymond passed the missive to Richard.

'See the rider is given a fresh mount, and return to me. I will respond to this.' Raymond turned and ran off down the passage.

'What is it, Richard?'

'An urgent message from King Henry.' Richard sat at the table and Esther came to his side resting her arm on his shoulder. Richard broke the seal, laid the parchment on the table, and straightened it with the heel of his hand.

'Hell's teeth, the Scots have invaded, this should have been dealt with by that damned Lawyer.'

'Who?'

'De Luci! He merely jousted with them and let them escape. I am to meet up with Ranulph de Glanvill, I know him, he is a good man, and good soldier. I am to take command of the King's army and ride to the Scottish borders. The King says *he* cannot ride with us, for he has to deal once and for all with this cross, Becket's death has laid upon his back, and that *I* have his *complete* confidence.' Richard lifted his eyes to Esther and gave her a puzzled look. 'Who knows what that means, I cannot imagine what Henry has in mind,' He shrugged his shoulders. 'Dear God – I could be gone for months.'

'I am coming with you; I am your wife and I will be there to care for you. I have learned how precious each moment is, I will not be here longing for you, wondering if I am ever going to see you again.'

'Esther, this will be hard employment; it is a long way, there will be great danger. It will not be a repeat of Ireland.'

'I have this moment told you, I am coming with you, if you forbid it, I will follow on my own. This subject pains me, we will talk of it no more.'

He laughed, so much his eyes filled with tears. 'You infuriating woman, you swore to obey me!' He said wiping his eyes.

'And so I do, when you do as I wish,' she smiled.

'I would flog a man who defied me as you have. I shall have you bound in chains and thrown into my deepest dungeon.' She wrapped her arm around his throat and took his dagger from the table where he had set it and pressed the point to his neck.

'You will yield to me or I will slit your *beautiful* throat,' and she leaned forward and kissed his ear. He took hold of her wrist and dragged her around onto his lap – and kissed her.

'I yield; the Scots will throw down their arms once they get wind of such a she-wolf coming to demolish their army. Get from me woman, I must write to my King.'

He took a clean sheet of parchment and a quill, tapping the feather to his lip; he thought for a moment and then began to write his reply to Henry.

Raymond returned and rattled once more at their door, 'Come!'

'The rider awaits and I have rallied the men. The fellow said the Scots have invaded, no doubt that means we are going to war?'

'*Yes*, we must ready ourselves pack animals, mete, armour. It is imperative that we make haste. Here take this to the rider, I will join you in the yard directly.'

Richard came from the keep to find the yard covered in bundles, men rushing back and forth, with Raymond and Tristram barking out commands. To the unschooled, this would appear as total chaos, but Richard knew that this work was part of their daily preparation. A castle may come under attack at any time and their ability to respond to whatever faced them with speed, was a matter of life or death. Richard stood on the steps of the keep, and cast his eye one final time over his home, as he always did before he left, for he knew that the defence of the castle must not be neglected especially when he was not there. It could be vulnerable when it was learned he was so far away. Not all were delighted with his defeat of Leicester in Suffolk. That in effect, was not only a defeat to the King's sons, but their supporters, and this may well be seen as an opportunity to redress the balance and right perceived wrongs.

He felt confident that what he had put in place would be sufficient. If his home was threatened, and if he lived, he knew he would wreak hell and destruction upon any who dared to come against him.

CHAPTER 37

They made good speed north, the weather was ideal, in fact, the whole of June was fine, little or no rain. Richard had joined the army east of London. They were well equipped and in good spirits, he knew that the weather played a vital part in morale. He was delighted to see his friend Ranulf; in total, they had more than five hundred knights as well as men afoot. This was a fearful force to be unleashed on any army no matter the size and it was reported that the Scottish army was near on 80,000 men.

Both Richard and Ranulf thought that if there were such a great number it could work to their advantage, but neither really believed that this figure was likely. They knew that such a force could bring with it its own shortfalls. Feeding such an army would be nigh on impossible they would quickly impoverish the surrounding lands and hungry soldiers were not happy soldiers. They would most likely be spread over a large area, that too was often a weakness and Richard was a master at exploiting a weakness.

Richard was certain he should never have allowed Esther to travel, but he was glad to have her by his side and never once did she complain.

They set up their camp just north of Newcastle with the city as their backdrop and a place to resource their army. Richard would use the city as a defence if this war did not favour them, they would withdraw into the city, which would make their capture difficult. They may even be able to reform and make a fight back. Once he was confident that their position was consolidated, he sent out spies to locate the Scots and establish a picture in his mind of his enemy's geography.

Gradually the picture was unfolding as one by one the spies returned with their information. They were immediately sent out again so that the leaders were constantly updated about the movement of the Scottish army. At this time, it appeared that the Scots were unaware of the presence of Henry's army, for they did not seem to be making any change to their positions.

Richard wondered because of their vast numbers, if they'd perhaps simply discounted the English threat, and of course, they had their recent experience with de Luci, of the English armies ineffectual tactics.

Richard paced back and forth at the edge of their encampment, he looked a lonely figure, pausing every few steps and massaging his chin. Esther watched him from the entrance of their tent. She understood only too well that ultimately the decisions rested upon him, and he took not that responsibility lightly. The life and death of men for whom he was accountable, weighed heavily upon him.

Suddenly, something changed, he lifted his head and strode back into the camp; he'd made his decision.

He came towards their tent; Esther busied herself so he would not know how intensely she'd been watching, fearing constantly what was going to happen in the next days. He entered, ducking under the decorative canvas pelmet over the entrance and quickly made known to her his intention, she was resolute; he would not see her fear. She was determined not to distract him from his employment by having him worry for her. Her tears would be shed in secret. The rest of the day he was with the other leaders. In the evening he came to her, he was fully armoured and she knew he was going to battle. She tried to still the dreadful tremble, which beset her when she first caught sight of him.

'I am going now Esther to be about my work. I am leaving Tristram here – *if* – perchance I do not return, you must not linger; you will ride south. I have told him this; he will take care of you. Esther, on this I will brook no argument.'

This was not her Richard; this was the commander of the King's army. 'Yes Lord.' She stood on her tiptoes, kissed him, bade him Godspeed and he left. The flap of the tent closed behind him and she fell to her knees.

'Dear Mother of Christ, keep him safe.'

King William had made, what Richard considered a fatal error, that of allowing his army to spread out, just as he had prophesied, instead of concentrating them around his headquarters in the town of Alnwick.

On the night of the 11th of July 1174, a party of about four hundred mounted knights, led by Richard and Ranulf de Glanvill, set out from Newcastle and headed north towards Alnwick.

It was an awesome sight to behold, this force of sheer muscle, power, and death. Great clods of earth were thrown up by the huge hooves of the horses as they rode from the camp.

This was a bold move, which would be either an unmitigated disaster or a glorious victory.

They travelled through the night, God had blessed them with enough moon to see, but not enough to be seen by, *providing* they took care. They made camp a few miles south of Alnwick in a wood, what mete they had brought with them they ate cold.

Richard intended to strike at first light with overwhelming force as he had in Suffolk, and strike at the head, without a head the flock scatter, that was something some priest once said, and the same thought had been in his mind when he fought at Fornham. This small fighting force contained seasoned knights, who had already battled against the Scots.

They reached the town of Alnwick as the sun was rising; the early morning's fog was burning off, remaining only in the hollows. The river Aln was almost completely hidden from view. At first, they wondered if the heavy fog was a bad omen, after becoming disorientated by it first thing that day. On leaving the wood where they'd rested, they almost immediately met with disaster when blinded by the fog they stumbled into a Scottish encampment of some size. By the grace of God, they managed to make advantage of the very fog that had nearly brought about a disaster. Eventually, more by good fortune than anything else, they found King William's encampment on the north side of the river Aln. *King William was only protected by a small bodyguard perhaps sixty fighting men in total.* Richard could hardly believe his good fortune.

Of his four hundred knights, he took but only one hundred of them to attack the King of Scotland's camp, the rest he left to watch for the unexpected. There was no shouting orders Richard lined his men with hand signals. He glanced once more at the line then lowered his arm, as one they put spur to horse and charged. No turning back now, as they burst from the fog, they must have appeared to be the physical manifestation of hell and destruction. *At the sound of the alarm, King William rushed from his tent, and hurriedly prepared to fight.*

It was too late – the English forces were upon them; the fearful pounding of hooves made the very earth shudder and shake. The Scottish King and his bodyguard were faced with the full force of Richard's attack, which struck with awesome intensity.

The fighting did not last long. King William had managed to get to his horse and turn to face his nemesis, but he was ill prepared, his horse was hacked to death while he still sat upon it, he tumbled heavily to the ground and was captured.

'He must not be killed! We are safe while he lives.' Richard shouted when he saw his men roughly treating the King. *Once the King was secured, those of his followers who had not been killed then surrendered.*

Richard had defeated an enormous army with only a handful of knights, in a single engagement. If God's hand was not in this day, then He had never been in any battle, so wondrous was their victory.

Unknown to Richard, at this time, King Henry was seeking the restoration of his relationship with God, if not God, the Church in England.

The council at Avranches had the year previous absolved the King of any blame for the death of Thomas

Becket. *The cardinals were overjoyed at the humility of so great a prince. While numbers joined their tears, gave praise to God, and dissolved the assembly, – the King's conscience being quieted, and his character in some measure restored.*

Richard was told Henry had returned to England, home from Normandy, which he'd already known before they'd set off. Now in England, King Henry was able to throw the strength of his presence against his sons, who were expected to arrive with the Flemish forces and once again attempt an invasion and usurp his throne. On this occasion, Henry would rally the heavenly hosts to the defence of his kingdom.

Henry, ever the political player, knew he needed the Church behind him to undermine his sons claims. He had gambled that Richard would defeat the Scots and, in the meantime, he would throw himself before God and he knew Richard's victory would be seen as confirmation of God's forgiveness. Richard had formed such an opinion when he heard the news, then wondered if perhaps, he was beginning to think more like Henry than Henry himself.

Henry, remembering how much he had sinned against the church of Canterbury, had proceeded thither immediately he had landed, and prayed, freely shedding tears, at the tomb of Thomas, the blessed bishop. On entering the chapter of the monks, he prostrated himself on the ground, and with the utmost humility entreated pardon; and, at his urgent petition.

He, though so great a man, allowed himself to be corporally beaten with rods by all the brethren in succession. On the following night, in a dream, it was said to a certain venerable old monk of that church, "Hast thou not seen today a marvellous miracle of royal humility? Know that the result of those events which are passing around him will shortly declare how much his royal humility has pleased the King of kings."

Richard learned this from that most reverend and simple-minded man, Roger, Abbot of Byland, who, while relating it, said that he had heard it from a trustworthy person, who was coincidentally staying at that very time in Kent. *"He who touches the mountains and they smoke, Psalm 144:5. Soon after clearly made known, by a notable proof, how much He valued that devotion of that smoking mountain; for on that day, and, as it is said, at that very hour in which that mountain gave forth smoke at Canterbury, the divine power overthrew his most mighty enemy the King of Scots, in the extreme confines of England: so that the reward of that pious work might not seem to have followed the work itself, but rather to have attended it, so that no man might be suffered to be in suspense on this point."*

This prince, departing from Canterbury, hastened to London, and having sent his military forces forward against Hugh Bigot, he made a short stay there, having been let blood. When low! In the middle of the night, a very swift messenger, sent by Richard and *Ralph de Glanville, knocked at the gate of the palace. Being rebuked by the porter and the guards, and ordered to be quiet, he knocked the louder, saying that he brought good news on his lips, which it was positively necessary that the king should hear that very night. His pertinacity at length overcame them, especially as they hoped that he came to announce good tidings. On being admitted within the door, in the same manner he over-persuaded the royal chamberlains. When he was introduced into the royal chamber, he boldly went to the king's couch, and aroused him from sleep.*

The king, on awaking, said, "Who art thou?"

To which he replied, "I am the attendant upon Lord Aylesford and *Ralph de Glanville, your faithful liegeman, by whom I have been sent to your highness; and I come to bring good tidings".*

"Richard my friend and *Ralph! Are they well?" asked the King.*

"He is well, my lord," he answered" and, behold, he holds your enemy the King of Scots, captive in chains at Richmond."

The King astonished at his news, said, "Say on", but he only reiterated his words. "Have you no letters?" he asked.

On which the messenger produced sealed letters, containing all detail of what had been done. The King, instantly inspecting them, leaped from his bed, and, with the deepest emotion, rendered thanks, moistened with pious tears, to "Him who alone does wondrous things". He then summoned the people of his household, and made them partakers of his joy. In the morning came also other messengers, reporting the same; but only one, that is, he who had come first received the gratuity. The good tidings were immediately made public, amidst the earnest acclamations of the people, and the ringing of bells in all parts of London.

CHAPTER 38

'I would like to go to Tattershall on our way home Richard,' Esther suddenly announced as they rode south. 'I know that the sight of Julianne's baby will be painful for you Richard as no doubt it will be for me. God willing it will have been born by now.'

'Are you quite sure about such a visit Esther?' Richard continued to look ahead. 'Will you really be pleased for Julianne?'

'I have moved on. I in truth want to talk to her, I'm happy for her.'

Richard had the gravest doubt about the wisdom of this, it was so much more complicated than Esther ever imagined. Richard was not sure how he would feel about Julianne or how he would feel about her giving such affection to Guy's child. Perhaps he would be overcome with envy. The truth of it was that he could not assemble his thoughts in any sort of order. At this very instant he even wished that he'd been slain in the recent conflict, death where is thy sting, he thought.

'*Please* Richard.'

'If it is your wish,' he said sternly.

They left the main force and Richard made his farewells to his friend Ranulf and watched them ride away.

On the next day's leg of their journey, Richard barely spoke and at any opportunity rode off alone. His whole manner disturbed Esther to the point that she was now unsure herself of the wisdom of this visit. She attempted to tell of her doubts to Richard, but he lifted his hand and bade her cease her talking.

On entering Sir John's castle, she was inexplicably trembling with fear and trepidation, and had no idea why.

Sir John was as always, 'Welcome, what a joy for me, what news? I hear of a great victory, and to my son the victor's laurels.'

Sir John reached up to lift Esther from her saddle and she threw herself into his arms and clung to him.

'It is a fine thing Esther to feel so wanted, I have missed you too.' He decided to ignore Richard's strained face.

'Come, I will take you to meet my beautiful grandson.' Richard nodded to Tristram bidding him to see to the men and Tristram returned the gesture, signifying he understood. Sir John led the way followed by Esther and then Richard.

Julianne, who was sat by the cot, rose to greet them and curtseyed.

'May I lift him out to show him to his uncle and aunt.' Julianne nodded. Sir John picked up the sleeping child, 'Here Esther hold him.' Esther took him to her breast, kissed his forehead and smiled, removed her glove and offered her knuckle to the lips of the eager child, who instinctively sucked on it. She smiled again; Richard's severe countenance never altered; he neither spoke nor made eye contact with Julianne.

'Who do you think he favours, Julianne?' Esther asked.

'He is the double of his father,' she whispered.

'I can't see any of that fellow in him, he was dark and William is fair,' Sir John interrupted.

On the mention of the name, "William", Richard looked at the child. He was compelled to agree with Sir John, he could see no likeness to Sir Guy whatsoever. He was suddenly distracted by Esther's expression; she was staring most oddly at him.

'He was late in coming; they said over a month, there must have been some mistake. I hardly slept for worrying, women have no idea how we men suffer,' Sir John laughed heartily.

'He's a fine child… Julianne…' said Esther.

Richard turned, he couldn't take anymore of this, and left, without a word, all eyes turned to him. He was struggling for the very air to breathe.

It was some time before Esther joined him on the ramparts. When she saw him, he was leaning on his elbows, staring out from the battlements whilst absentmindedly crumbling some moss between his fingers, which he must have picked loose from the stonework.

He glanced briefly at the sound of her feet on the gravel, and then returned once more to his contemplation, she touched his shoulder.

'Sorry Richard, perhaps we were wrong to come. He's a fine child that must be difficult for you, I'm sorry that you felt unable to stay. Say something Richard. Do you want me to go and leave you to your thoughts? Perhaps you will talk to Julianne on her own, she was distressed when you went, she said nought, but it was in her eyes.'

He now turned around to face her and leaned with his back against the wall. 'I have never felt as small as I do at this minute it all goes over my head. Esther, I know nothing at all, except that *I love* you, I don't understand anything, it was more difficult than I ever imagined seeing that child, but where does it say we must be happy? For I see more sad people than ever I see happy ones, I have much to thank God for, and so I will...' Suddenly he peered over Esther's shoulder to the courtyard below, and jerked her to one side. She stumbled and nearly fell to the ground so fierce was his movement.

'*Richard!*' He wasn't listening, something had happened. He ran along the ramparts and jumped down the steps onto the courtyard barely setting a single foot to them, but he was too late. The man leapt on to his horse and galloped past him knocking him to the floor. Esther was only able to watch this sudden inexplicable change of mood. Richard got up, dusted his hands, and went to Julianne, who was yet standing where she'd been talking to the man. He took her by the shoulders and violently shook her.

'What has that fellow to do with you? Tell me.'

'Richard you're hurting me,' he stopped, she bowed her head, 'It is Gervase's servant. I don't know where he came from, Gervase brought him home one day to Guy's castle, when he stayed with us. That was a mistake, I never realised how wicked he was.'

'Do you know his name?'

'Fawkes.'

'*Fawkes*, I knew it. What's he doing here?' She continued to stare at the ground Richard stepped back from her and viciously kicked a nearby dog. The dog yelped and ran off with its tail between its legs. 'I'm *listening*, Julianne!' he said returning once more to her.

'He's – blackmailing me, he wants money or he will tell Esther – about us,' she spoke so softly he could hardly hear her.

'How does *he* know anything about us?'

'His daughter works here, I didn't know who she was, just another servant. She has found out everything. *She* knows more than you do. I am afraid of her; she is evil she has threatened o… my baby.

'What do you mean, *she* knows more than me, what nonsense is this…?'

Julianne ignored his question. 'Fawkes and Gervase were blackmailing Guy; Gervase had discovered that Guy had been taking coin from the King. Guy was terrified and was compelled to get money any way he could. Once they'd started, they wanted more and more. I knew none of this until Guy ran off, he left me a letter explaining it all and asking for my forgiveness. I challenged Gervase, but he only laughed at me for the fool I was.'

Suddenly they were distracted by the sound of a scream. Richard spun round and they both looked up to where they heard the scream; Esther was no longer to be seen. Richard ran back up the steps to the ramparts, running as if his very life depended upon it. He could hear Esther shouting; once he reached the place where he'd left her, he stopped for a second and listened to establish where the shouting was coming from.

'*Please* Gervase, don't.'

'But I love you, you are everything to me. I know you want me; I have money now and it's all for you.'

'I'm begging you, please Gervase; I *don't* love you I'm married to Richard.' Gervase held Esther tightly lifting her off her feet. She struggled in his arms; he was trying to kiss her. He'd been drinking, and his breath stank, she was revolted. He was dressed as a servant; he must have stolen into the castle in disguise. What had she ever done to warrant this kind of treatment?

'Get off me, let me go, you're drunk.' She twisted her head from side to side, desperate to avoid his advances. She managed to free one hand and struck him in the face, splitting his lip. He was surprised; he lifted his hand to his face, dragged the back of his hand across his mouth, and then glanced down at the streak of blood on his knuckles. His face seemed confused, taken aback that this woman, who was everything to him, and surely felt the same as he, had done such a thing.

The moment gave her enough freedom to push him away and he staggered back as she broke free of his hold. He was shaken by both her strength and aggression. She was afraid now, he was frighteningly still; he raised his eyes from his hand, and glared at her. This was not the look of undying devotion; his face was shrouded in a sinister darkness.

She screamed and backed away as he came slowly towards her, there was no love in his eyes now.

'It's *him* you love isn't it, you've never loved me, you deceived me?' He shouted in utter contempt, spittle spraying from his mouth.

'Gervase I've never deceived you, please let me go, I'm sorry I didn't want to hurt you, I kept trying to tell you.'

'Why him, he has everything, everything that was mine by right, it's I who needed you? You love *me* he's confused you, he's evil, he has destroyed everything. If I can't have you no one will.'

'You are quite *mad*.'

There was the sound of running footsteps and someone stepped into the room, Gervase turned, it was Richard, sword in hand, Esther breathed a sigh of relief. Gervase drew his dagger, and made a grab for her, but hampered by his limp he yet carried from the stab wound Richard inflicted, he was too slow. He'd mistimed his move, and she took hold of Richard's outstretched hand. Gervase reached for her, but Richard pushed her behind him. As he turned back to face Gervase, Gervase drove his dagger into Richard's chest. Richard staggered, Gervase paused for a second grabbed at the door and disappeared.

'Richard, Richard.'

He shook his head, 'I'm all right.' He rested against the wall, 'It's nothing.'

'Don't be foolish, I can see fine well it's serious,' the door swung open and Alwin dashed in.

'Alwin – Richard's been stabbed, he needs help.'

'*NO,* I'm all right! Where has he gone?'

'*WHO!*' shouted Alwin; he'd hadn't seen Gervase.

'*Gervase*, he's stabbed Richard.'

'He has lodgings in the town. I've this moment spoken to Lady Julianne; she has found out that he's living nearby. She's saddling a horse and about to set off to find him before he does anything else stupid. She instructed me to find you.'

'Too late for that, but we must stop her, he's mad, who knows what he might do. Do you know where this house is Alwin?'

'Yes, Lady Julianne told me.'

Richard was thrown for a moment; he could only stare at Alwin. 'What are you doing here, Alwin, where's Tristram?'

'Lady Julianne wrote to me. She said she needed to see me, she had something for you, she was in danger, and could not tell her father. As for Tristram he's gone to a nearby farm to look at a horse.'

'Never mind all that now, take me to this house, *now* Alwin.'

'No – Richard, please God no! You're not fit to ride; your wound needs attention; please make him stay Alwin. You will kill yourself.'

'I will *kill him*, I must, this has to end now. Do as I have told you Alwin.' Richard pushed himself away from the wall. He was forced to gasp and crushed his eyes tightly closed; the pain had gripped him when he moved. He reached for the door swung it open and left, followed by Alwin.

'Stay here my Lady; lock this door, in case he's still here, or has some other mischief planned.'

Alwin shouted to a guard when they came out from the keep door, 'Have any riders left?'

'Aye two, Sir Gervase and Lady Julianne seconds afterwards, both riding like they were possessed.'

'Quick Alwin, bring Ares to me and a mount for yourself.' Richard panted struggling for breath, and leaned against the stable wall desperately trying to keep himself on his feet. If he fell now, he knew he would never rise, and Gervase would have won. He would do this even though he knew it was going to be the death of him. 'God give me just enough strength.'

Alwin and the stable lad came out with the horses. 'Bring Ares to the mounting block.' Richard steadied himself and with a supreme effort, he mounted Ares.

'Here Lord push this cloth into your jacket and over the wound.' Richard took the rag and did as Alwin had said, even though he knew it was a waste of time, he was done for, but he had no strength to argue. Without another word, they set off. Richard was wobbling from side-to-side he could hardly hold on to the reins, one of his feet fell from the stirrup and dangled free.

'This is madness Lord, stop, and turn back as my Lady suggested.' Richard never responded it would have required energy he simply did not have. Alwin leapt from his horse and pushed Richard's foot back into the stirrup. His horse had drawn to a standstill and lowered its head to feed on the lush grass, Richard didn't even seem to realise he'd stopped. Once back on his horse Alwin took Ares' rein and led Richard, expecting at any moment he would topple from the horse but by some miracle, he stayed on its back.

'That's the house there, Lord,' shouted Alwin, 'There's Lady Julianne's horse outside it.' It was a large yellow timbered house; Gervase must have rented it; Alwin leapt from his horse and took hold of Ares' bridle.

'Quick help me down, Alwin, I can't manage.' His speech was rough and laboured. Once he'd dismounted Alwin held him for a moment until he was able to stand on his own.

'Let's get inside quickly, who knows what that madman is up to.'

They heard Julianne and Gervase arguing, their voices sounded to be coming from somewhere above them.

'Take my arm Alwin, with your support I'll manage the stairs.' Alwin wrapped his arm around Richard and they stumbled towards the foot of the stair. A door to the side was flung open banging against the wall and Fawkes leapt for Alwin who was nearest to him. In one smooth movement, Alwin drew his dagger and drove it mercilessly into Fawkes' fat gut, without even altering his step. Fawkes staggered, staring in disbelief. Alwin eased Richard to one side, Fawkes groaned, his legs gave way, and he collapsed onto the floor in a cloud of dust.

'Come, Lord,' Alwin said quite matter-a-factly, as if his action was merely part of his normal daily activity, and they climbed the stairs.

Alwin kicked the door open where they heard Julianne's voice. Gervase glanced at the intruders, drew his dagger, and grabbed at Julianne, bundling her towards them, forcing them out onto the landing. Alwin and Richard backed away, Richard manage somehow to draw his sword.

'*You,* you've taken everything, my sister loved me she always put me before everyone else, until you bewitched her, well you'll never have her, she's mine.'

He was holding her with some difficulty because of the dagger in his hand; this was a repeat of the scene with Esther. Julianne twisted and he lost his grip, he tried to adjust to her change of position, but in the awkward movement, their bodies came forcibly together, and his dagger blade – pressed into her chest.

There was a moment of complete stillness, as if eternity had missed a beat. Julianne just stared at him, took a deep breath, lifted her shoulders, went limp; and she slipped free from the knife into a heap on the floor.

Gervase stood, yet holding the knife, traumatised by the magnitude of what he'd done. Richard dropped his sword, and it clattered onto the wooden floorboards as he fell to his knees taking her head in his arms.

'You *wretched* madman,' Richard snarled up at him, 'get some help.' Gervase never moved, he was trembling and cried out.

'*Julianne, Julianne,* I never meant to hurt you, I love you,' suddenly his mood changed. 'This is *your* fault, *you* did this, *you've* killed her. You've taken everything from me.'

In a split second, his insanity once more possessed him, and he lunged at Richard. Richard leaned back still holding Julianne and reached for his sword; Gervase came forward and lifted the knife to strike. Gervase – *stopped* – motionless, groaned, and stared in utter disbelief at the spearhead sticking from his middle. The spear had entered his back with such force it had been driven all the way through his body. The dagger dropped from his hand, and he grasped hold of the bloody spear point. He turned, half stumbling and saw Alwin, he'd torn a spear from a display on the wall and thrown it. The length of the spear shaft sticking from his back unbalanced Gervase and caused him to stagger backwards tumbling headfirst over the balustrade, there was a moment of silence then a dull thud as he hit the stone floor below.

Alwin rushed to Richard's side he was still holding Julianne in his arms. A trickle of blood ran from the side of her mouth.

'Richard' – she was gasping for breath – 'I love you,' she reached to him and frantically gripped his shirt. 'Take this,' she tugged the emerald free from her neck and passed it to him, it was covered in blood. 'Remember me,' her face twisted in pain and she squeezed her eyes tightly together, then she relaxed – all but her fingers, which continued to hold him. She stared again into his eyes, 'William, William – is – yours,' she whispered and coughed; more blood bubbled from her mouth. He wiped her lips with the soft leather of his glove, 'I – named him after your father, tell him – tell him, how his – mother only ever loved his – fath – father, he was every – everything to her…' Her eyes blinked rapidly and gradually closed, her fingers released their hold on him and her head rolled slowly to the side. Richard pressed his cheek against hers and held her to him.

'Julianne,' he whispered into her ear.

CHAPTER 39

'Lord… she is dead. *Lord, Lord,* let me help you,' he said again, lightly shaking Richard's shoulder, trying to get his attention.

Richard couldn't hear anything; he was struggling for breath; he was becoming more conscious of the burning pain in his chest. Blood was oozing from his wound. He stared into Julianne's face, hesitated, then his eyes were drawn to her blood-soaked gown, she was at peace now. Alwin eased Julianne free from Richard.

'Wait…' Alwin laid her carefully on her back, straightening her limbs.

'Alwin – *your cloak* for her head, don't hurt her, please – don't – hurt her,' his voice trailed to a whisper.

'Yes, Lord,' he removed his cloak, folded it, gently lifted her head, and slid it underneath for a pillow.

'Alwin... see to it no one touches her, I *must* get to the castle, assist me. You will return and care for her, promise me.'

'I don't have to promise Lord... she will be cared for.' Alwin helped him to stand.

'Lord, you can't ride like this, your wound needs attention, stay here I'll get help.'

'Alwin, we both know the truth of this wound; I must get back to the castle that's all that matters now. We will ride together on Ares. You will needs hold me, for I am fearfully light-headed and I may not be able to stay in the saddle without help.'

'Never fear Lord, on that, I will hold you, but so help me I doubt the wisdom of this.'

'Tush, you fuss too much. I have no choice; *I* must go to Esther I simply have to. My cloak, Alwin, help me.' Alwin shook his head then reached to aid Richard with his cloak, he removed it with difficulty. Alwin could see how even such a simple task crippled him. Richard took it into his hand, leant on the balustrade, and lowered himself to his knees by Julianne's side; his eye caught sight of the twisted body of Gervase on the floor below them. He bent forward holding his wound and tenderly pressed his lips to hers, laying his cheek one final time to hers.

'Why did this beautiful human being have to pay the cost of that evil person's envy, why, what a waste,' he repeated, staring at her face. His body jerked and his hand trembled as he tried to gently touch the back of his fingers to her cheek. He lifted the edge of his cloak, took one last look, a bead of sweat dripped from his nose onto her face and trickled down her cheek, he removed it with his knuckle and slowly lowered the cloak to hide her face forever.

He took a deep breath and wiped his brow with a sweep of his forearm, reached again to the balustrade to help him to stand, glanced once more at Gervase's distorted body below.

'I pray you rot in Hell for this day's work. An eternity of torment will not wipe clean this wretched evil.'

Alwin stepped to him and took his arm. As Richard turned, he coughed violently, doubled over and almost fell as the pain wracked his body, he felt so light-headed, he would have fallen but for Alwin.

'Lord you must rest.'

'*No* – I will have all the rest I need soon enough. Take me to the castle, I *must* see Esther,' he said struggling to speak. 'I must, suppose I die trying.'

Alwin lifted Richard's arm over his shoulder and held him by his wrist, wrapped his other arm around his waist and gave him what support he could. They staggered down the stairs, Alwin was sure they would stumble and fall. Richard was much bigger than Alwin, and he was struggling to support him. However, in spite of Alwin's fears they made it down the staircase.

At the foot of the stairs, they saw Fawkes wife kneeling over her husband.

'You've murdered my husband!' She yelled at them.

'Woman, get from this place, and run as fast as you can, for when I return, I will be returning with a hemp collar for your neck,' Alwin barked at the terrified woman. She stood, glanced once more at her husband, and then ran from the room. Alwin and Richard continued into the yard where Ares was obediently waiting. Ares raised his head and snorted when he saw them.

'Your horse will be well enough here, you can come for it later,' Richard mumbled.

'Yes Lord.' Alwin lifted and pushed Richard into the saddle, he just had to ignore Richard's cries of torment, and he climbed up behind him. All the while Ares stood perfectly still, which was contrary to his usual disposition.

'Here Lord, put my jack around your shoulders, you must keep warm.' Alwin removed his padded jack and laid it over Richard's shoulders; the warmth actually was quite soothing. Alwin saw the sweat standing on his brow and shook his head, he was fearfully pale, but said nothing; he knew well enough the effort it had taken Richard to climb onto Ares back.

'Bless your – kindness, *my* – friend,' Richard said gasping. Each word was *coughed* out, more than spoken. Ares was uncannily patient, as if he understood the gravity of the situation. Alwin tied his belt to Richard's to make him as secure as he could, reached around him, and took the reins, and they set off at a steady trot. Alwin kept looking over Richard's shoulder he could see he was in agony, but he made no sound. Alwin was thankful that they had not far to go.

'As soon as we get there, summon help to get me to my room. *You* go and find Esther, and bring her to me. Don't tell her how badly I'm hurt, there is little enough time to waste.'

Alwin held the door; Richard's eyes wearily opened at the sound, and he beheld Esther. She stood on the threshold, visibly trembling, she looked as if she was about to turn and run; her face was drained of colour.

'She's dead Esther' he said in a tired voice. She could only stare, endeavouring to understand all that was before her. She came fearfully towards his bed, white knuckles pressed fiercely to her lips. Her legs gave way, and she slumped down in the chair next to him and gasped for air, she had been holding her breath since the door had swung open, and she'd first seen him lying on the bed. Nervously she reached to him, she noticed her fingers trembling, and curled them into a fist trying to steady them. She saw that his face was bathed in sweat; he weakly smiled and reached, over laying his hand on hers. Her eyes brimmed with tears, and as his hand touched her, the tears spilled over, streaming down her face.

She bowed her head, '*Richard…*' she said, struggling to speak.

'You have *always* been by my side Esther,' he whispered softly, he raised his hand and tenderly lifted her chin in the crook of his finger, the effort of that simple act took all his strength, he grimaced. His arm dropped lifelessly onto the bed, but yet he managed to smile, even his *eyes* smiled.

She eased herself onto the edge of her chair then leaned forward laying her head on his arm; her body shook with spasms of sobbing. He tenderly stroked her hair and pressed his lips to the top of her head. She took a deep intake of breath in an attempt to control her shaking.

'Richard… I, don't know how to say the words, this is more than I can face, there is no life without you, you've never understood.'

He smiled. 'I know now Esther; you and I were always meant for each other; I've been such a fool can you forgive me? I never meant to hurt you.'

'Please, please don't say it…' she buried her face in her hands. 'I've always known that. God forgive me, I'm sorry for all your hurt. I tried not to be jealous, I knew how hard it was for you.' She made to hug him and he groaned, and coughed once more. For the first time she saw how much blood there was, his shirt was saturated; it was everywhere, soaking into the bed linen. She abruptly ceased her sobbing and stared in horror at her blood-covered hand. '*Richard,*' was all she said.

'Don't be anxious for me Esther, please care for William, you know he is my son, don't you?'

'I know, it doesn't matter, love makes *everything* right, it keeps no record of wrongs, I will love him.'

'The sword, the sword, to my son,' he whispered, but she couldn't make out what he said.

'Richard you need help, I must call someone,' she swung round frantically and saw Alwin who was yet standing at the door.

'Alwin, for mercies sake get help.'

His only response was to slowly shake his head, but he went nevertheless as he'd been instructed. Richard gently touched her arm.

'Still yourself my dearest Esther.'

'God no, there must be something…'

'*No* – stay – don't trouble yourself Esther, everything's all right I'm not in any pain, let me have this time with you and our love.' He smiled staring intently into her eyes.

'But Richard, my dearest, no, no, this can't be happening…'

'I love you Esther…' she could hardly hear his words, but through her tears she could see it clearly written on his face. She knew what was between them didn't need words. She touched her tummy and felt a flutter of the child living within her; he didn't know, she'd never told him.

'Richard, listen, I *must* tell you this…'

He couldn't hear her… ever so silently a long breath slipped slowly from his lips. They no longer had the strength to cling to the smile, his eyes alone now held his joy, as if by his last reserve of willpower, he had directed all his strength to burn his love into her soul. While there was an ounce of life in him, he would behold her face, his eyelids flickered one last time, and gradually... they closed. His body relaxed, and his head sank peacefully into the pillow. All his strength, to touch, to feel, to hold, to caress... left this gentle, noble, warrior's hand. His fingers relaxed and opened. In his palm the light touched the edge of a beautiful stone of green...

"It was the colour of envy."

CHAPTER 40

Sir John and his chirurgien, Bernard de Lacy, dashed into the room, Esther's head was laid in Richard's hand she was weeping and beating the bed with her fist.

'It's too late, he's dead,' she looked up through swollen eyes.

The chirurgien went to the opposite side of the bed.

'He's not dead Lord, he is still bleeding, his heart must yet be pumping. He has passed out because of the great blood loss; he may still die but there is yet hope.' The chirurgien tore open Richard's shirt. 'We must stop this bleeding if he is to have a chance. There is no blood in his mouth' he said pressing his fingers into Richard's mouth and examining them, 'which is a mercy. I take from that blessing that his lung has not been pierced. That would have been fatal.'

Esther's head was spinning she was shaking like a leaf in a summer storm, what were they saying! The wound was exposed now and, *yes*, praise be, there was yet blood being pumped from it. The chirurgien poured alcohol over it, Sir John knew he swore by alcohol for preventing wounds going putrid, and then he stitched the wound. It was a relatively small wound. He wiped the cut saying,

'We seem to have stopped the flow of blood, it is in the Blessed Virgin's hands now.' Richard groaned. 'If he comes around, we must try to get him to drink as much as he can, people who lose a great deal of blood are always thirsty I have noticed.'

Esther's merely sat staring; she was unable to make sense of what she beheld.

'Alwin undress your master, carefully, I will send help to you. Wash him and make him as comfortable as you can. We will leave them to their work Esther, here girl let me take your arm we will go to the chapel and pray,' ordered Sir John. 'He will live, he will live.'

To be continued...

BOOK TWO

Driven by Honour

Chapter 1

Recovery

Richard's eyes flickered – gradually opened – and closed again. They were expressionless, as was his face. Esther stared without daring to breathe, her heart pounded against her ribs fit to burst, whilst she waited, waited and waited. She could hear the whooshing of blood and the rhythmic beating of a pulse in her head. Feeling faint, she took a deep breath, and unconsciously drew her forearm across her brow.

His eyelids were striving to respond to some basic survival instinct. Slowly they opened once more, and she *knew* his brain was trying to make sense of the light, as the silent intruder crept into his consciousness. She gently squeezed his fingers and he responded by rolling his head – slowly – on the pillow to face her.

'*Richard…*' was all she said in a whisper. He stared at her for several seconds endeavouring to smile. His lips were dry, he touched them with his tongue, and they felt rough, he could feel loose flakes of skin. She saw him trying to speak.

'Here, Richard,' and she set a cup of small-ale to his lips. A little ran over the dry fissures and into his parched mouth, but most ran down his chin, which she gently dried with a cloth.

His eyes never left hers. He was frighteningly thin; he'd had no solids for over three weeks. Fortunately, in calmer moments when the fever relaxed its grip, they had been able to get him to drink. In all that time she'd barely left his side, watching his every movement, sigh, and groan.

'Esther…' he spoke softly and her eyes filled with tears.

She gave a weak smile, 'God has spared you; thanks be to the Blessed Virgin. Try to drink a little more Richard, Bernard, you remember Bernard?' He made the slightest gesture of acknowledgement with his eyes. 'Well, my dearest, the most precious Bernard insists that you drink,' and she once more offered the cup… 'There, you did better that time.' He again ran his tongue over his encrusted lips.

'What – about – Julianne?' He whispered in a ragged voice.

'She has been laid to rest – next to her mother.'

There was no reaction shown on his face, *or* in his eyes, which stared wearily beyond her. There were memories in the deepest recesses of his heart, but his senses had erected a barricade, preventing even him access. He would not have the strength to go there, not now, perhaps sometime in a distant future, but not now. He acknowledged his understanding with no more than the slightest facial movement, and focused once more on Esther's eyes.

'I love *you*,' Richard said, *fearing* her rejoinder.

His words *tormented* the deep, dull, ever present pain. She'd forgotten to put on the face that she kept in an invisible bag at her waist. The face that welcomed and smiled, that said I'm all right, I can cope with anything. She'd been caught off guard, and the tears overflowed, running silently down her cheeks. Lowering her head, she tried to discreetly brush a drip from the end of her nose.

Responding in a soft trembling voice she said, 'for me – there has never been anyone else, but you…'

His eyes begged for forgiveness, 'I'm sorry.'

'Yes...' she said, struggling to reply, and stared down at her hand resting in his. It was some time before he spoke again.

Suddenly he coughed, 'Ahhhh,' his body writhed in agony, he screwed up his face and gasped for breath. The involuntary muscular spasm had clearly tortured his wound.

Esther was distracted and instantly stood, unsure what to do. 'Can I do anything?'

He shook his head – trying to steady his breathing.

Once he had calmed the sudden trauma in his chest, he asked, still panting, 'How long – have I been ill?'

She sat down again before responding.

'That's in the past, *all* is in the past now, I want to forget. I thought that you had died, there was blood everywhere, you won't remember.' He shook his head; he was struggling to make sense of anything at this moment. 'Thank God for Bernard, he saved you. He stitched the knife wound and stopped the bleeding, but you had lost a great deal of blood, we owe him your life. I have been so afraid. Sir John's been here constantly, I don't know how I would have managed without him.'

Richard gently tightened his hold on her hand. 'And, Gervase?'

'I know naught of him, Sir John has never mentioned his son, I heard whispers that he was dead. I asked Alwin, but he only shook his head and bade me not to mention him to anyone.'

Once again, Richard's face gave only the slightest hint of understanding.

'Drink a little more, then perhaps you should lie quietly, there will be time to talk when you are stronger.' Esther carefully raised his head in the palm of her hand, set the horn cup to his lips and he sipped the nectar.

'Yes… you're right…' he drank as much as he could and she lowered his head onto the pillow. 'I'm so tired – I must sleep. Thank you Esther…' he relaxed, and his eyes closed; she tenderly touched his sunken cheek with the back of her hand.

'You will live, Richard, you have much to live for.' Esther stood, placed her hand in the small of her back, and stretched. A hand startled her as it touched her shoulder. 'Sir John, I didn't hear you!'

'Sorry child, I have been standing by the door for some time. You were talking to Richard; I didn't wish to disturb you. It was enough to know that he was with us once more.'

'I'm so relieved, I can hardly think, I am beyond tiredness, I know not what I feel. Forgive me Sir John; the world I once frequented is now a stranger to me. I have dwelt for so long where there has been no night or day, only a never-ending sameness, trapped in this womblike place, fearful of being delivered into a hellish world without Richard.'

'It will change now, believe me, why don't you go to your room, bathe and sleep?'

'But what if he wakes and needs me?' Sir John took her in his arms and pressed his lips to her head.

'Esther, you will better serve him if you are refreshed by sleep. You can do no more; thank God, he is recovering. Do as I say, I will sit by his side. He will come to no harm.'

Sir John turned to Margaret, Esther's maid, 'Take your lady to her room, see she is bathed and cared for.'

Margaret nodded, stepped forward, and took Esther's arm. Esther offered a token resistance then went, childlike, with her servant. In truth, she was indeed past mere tiredness. Her head was as dull as dust unable to comprehend one moment from the next, and thankful for Margaret's support.

'Oui, perhaps you speak the truth of it, Sir John,' she said as Margaret led her away.

Sir John watched them go then sat down next to Richard and gently clasped his hand.

Chapter 2

Reflection

They were alone now, the room was quiet; all that could be heard was Richard's deep, steady, breathing. Sir John rested his forearms on his knees, hung his head, weighed down with bitter sadness, and sighed. His world was a heavy load of shame and regret now, and it was pressing down upon him. He tried to close his mind to all that had happened, but, in the silence of the room, he could not avoid the memories infiltrating even his most resolute of defences. He had lost all he'd loved; no matter how he tried to expunge Gervase from his thoughts. Gervase was *his* son, and Sir John was ashamed that his flesh and blood had caused all this misery.

Gervase had been driven to the point of madness by obsession, hatred, and his envy of another man. Sir John was not sorry for himself; feeling he deserved all that was now his constant companion, but he *was* sorry for those who were innocent and yet suffered – because of *his* son's wickedness. *If* only he hadn't spoilt a weak son… *If* only Julianne hadn't been so afraid, yes *afraid*, some would say

"Wilful" but he knew – that was merely a mask she wore to protect herself. It was so – ever since she had been witness to her mother's brutal murder.

'Aye, *if, if,*' but he had another son now, and he loved Richard as much his own flesh and blood, be that right or wrong. It could have all been perfect, he thought. He'd known from the very beginning that Julianne had loved Richard, and he had loved her, but in spite of his certainty, *he* had sanctioned her marriage to Sir Guy.

In all this sadness, he could yet find some goodness, it was as if God had seen his suffering and had sprinkled a little hope in the form of his precious grandson, William. He was certain now; William *was* Richard's son, though no one had said it directly to him. He'd half suspected the truth of it, as soon as he'd seen William next to Richard. He didn't know how he could have been so blind, but, then he thought that perhaps his eyes saw what he wanted to see and it was merely wishful thinking, now he was sure. In the midst of Richard's fevered ramblings, he had promised Julianne that he would never fail *their* son, and thanked her for him. Sir John now understood the looks of sadness, which had been etched into Esther's face, it was all clear now, *she* knew and he was in no doubt of that either.

Esther was the most gracious person he'd ever known; she would make no mendicant of those in need of grace. He loved her as all did, and was keenly aware of her silent misery. It was indeed a merciless thorn to torment her heart, she'd never mentioned it, but yes, she knew. How simple it was for us made of mud and clay to pass judgement and apportion blame, to what end? Bitterness and un-forgiveness, that was not the path to life and its riches, he knew that the key to this dungeon door was on the inside.

'Dear Mother of Christ I have one prayer, that all this anguish and sorrow stops here, that love and forgiveness prevail, and my grandson does not have to pay the price for others *humanness*. If punishment must be meted out then set Your vengeance upon my head, for that is where the debt was accrued.'

He stared quietly at his feet, his heart wept but there were no tears, he had cried all his tears in the quiet of the chapel when he'd sat in vigil by Julianne's body. He would suffer no one else near that night; he wanted that time alone with her. There had been much to say. He'd held her hand and stared at her peaceful face, she looked for all the world like the little girl he'd sat with night after night while she waited for sleep, fearful of the dark after her mother died; she wanted no one but him. He talked to her of those times, and memories, her first riding lesson, how proud he was of her. He loved her more than life, he wondered if he'd given her too much love, and it was to compensate for his neglect he'd spoilt Gervase.

'Ah... too late now, too late now,' he whispered and reached again to hold *Richard's* hand.

Sir John must have fallen asleep; *he* was tired too. He began to stir, stretched and rubbed his thigh, a wound from a fall many years past seemed to be bothering him of late.

He'd been young and reckless, misjudged a fence during a hunt and been thrown. His leg had never troubled him much over the years, but these past weeks a dull persistent ache had returned to haunt him and his foot was ever cold, it was worse first thing in the morning.

'A new day,' he said to himself, stretching once more and yawning, he glanced towards the window, he could see the sun's rays splitting the shutters, 'I must have slept most of the night, and Richard too, thanks be to God. He has clearly turned a corner.'

He heard a cough, and carefully turned his now stiff neck to the sound, 'I have brought some warm spiced wine for you, Lord.'

'Ah, Margaret,' Esther's servant was standing by the door with a jug and a goblet on a tray, 'how kind of you, a welcome thought.'

'Shall I fetch mete too, Lord?'

'Yes, something simple, some bread and cheese will suffice for now. Has Lady Esther awoken yet?'

'Not yet, Lord.'

'Good, good, let her sleep as long as she wishes.'

Sir John stood and stretched, then he walked cautiously, yet rubbing his leg, and opened the shutters, it would be a fine day, he thought.

Chapter 3

New Beginning

Once Richard began to eat, he recovered rapidly, he was weak, but that would not really change until he was able to begin some physical work.

He was growing ever concerned about his estate; he'd written to Alwin, Raymond, *and* Tristram, who had now returned to Aylesford. They in turn had responded assuring him that all was well. He was becoming restless, which was a sure sign of his improving health.

Richard glanced up as Esther entered, she was carrying baby William, he appeared to be content with her, she was his mother, and he was clearly secure in her presence. What was more important to Richard was that *she* appeared to have accepted him. Once he was able to use his brain there was one thought that dominated all thoughts and that was, how would Esther be with Julianne's child, knowing *he* was the father?

Every time Esther referred to him as, "Your Father", when talking to William, he felt awkward. He was not sorry for what had happened between him and Julianne, but he *was* sorry that he had hurt Esther, more than hurt her, betrayed her. She had never mentioned his treachery; she was someone who only seemed to know how to love, that was her nature. In someway that made what he had done all the more despicable. He felt, if – *only* – she had rebuked and shunned him, or refused to accept William, such chastisement and the subsequent sorrow *might* in some small part, have assuaged his guilt. How could she believe him now when he told her that he loved her? Would "I love you", sound hollow, naught but words?

Not since he'd recovered had he said the words, he couldn't bring himself to say them. He did not recall Esther – having said the words either – now he thought on it, but he *knew* she did love him. Not for one moment had he ever doubted her love.

They had not been as man and wife since he had recovered and he dreaded facing such an occasion, guilt was an exacting master. He would have to talk to Esther about what had happened, and try to explain, but thoughts of how and when, and what to say overwhelmed him.

He needed to clear the air if they were to move on. She had once said that she could not live with a cloud hanging over their relationship, in that instance she was relieved that he had told King Henry of her Jewish background. This was a different cloud, but it would cast a long shadow if it were not dealt with soon, and honestly.

Then there was Tristram, he wondered if he knew about William, he thought *Sir John* would understand, perhaps even be pleased, but Tristram, that was a different matter altogether. He had once promised Tristram, and sincerely too, that he would *never* hurt Esther, such an easy promise to make, but nigh on impossible to keep. Tristram had accepted his assurance, but now, he had clearly failed, where would that sit on any future oath? His word might now be worthless – as far as Tristram was concerned and who could blame him. Both he and Tristram were knights and they had a very simplistic view of an "Oath". A knight gave his word and that was that, to even question such an offering was in itself dishonourable, but now it had been made crystal-clear to Richard that life was not quite so black and white. He wondered what his friend William Marshal would have to say on this, he always had such an unambiguous view of right and wrong. He would often say, "When one has to make a decision, if all is stripped away, there is but a simple choice, is it right – or is it – wrong?" Richard prayed that his friend would always walk a path where the world and its choices presented themselves so obligingly.

He cast a face of hopeless despair to Esther as she neared him, but she smiled the smile of someone with the clearest conscience, and offered William to him and he took hold of him.

'He grows heavier by the day, Richard; he will soon be too much for me to carry. You look troubled, does your wound distress you?'

'Aye, more than you could ever imagine, as surely it will for the rest of my life.' Esther furrowed her brow, unsure what was his meaning, but decided against asking, and her face once again beamed.

In spite of all that troubled Richard, he couldn't help but smile as he looked at his son. At this second, he held part of his love for Julianne. He must drag himself from this distress in his heart, it was agony, but he didn't know how to do it.

'Do you love him, Richard?'

'Well… yes, yes I love him, who could do any other than love him!'

'For sure *I* do, he is so like you. Perhaps he has Julianne's eyes, she had the most beautiful eyes, did she not?'

'Aye…' Esther, please don't say these things, he silently begged, is this how you intend to punish me.

Esther hesitated for a moment… 'Do you mind – if he calls *me* Mother?'

Richard was speechless; I am not equal to this game he thought. 'I know not what to say to you, Esther. My whole world has been built on those two revenants, honour and chivalry, but next to you all I hold dear – are but shadows sent to torment me, me who undoubtedly knows naught, not even the *first* thing of real honour.'

'Richard, I loved you just as you are, not a saint, but a man above men and to me you will always be so. I told you once that I thought a knight's precious honour, and straightforward worldly *pride,* were easy bedfellows. Does not the Holy Scripture tell us, that it is the *meek* who shall inherit the earth? Perhaps the Blessed Virgin is teaching us both how to be – *less*. I understand your anguish, for your ordeal is that of a *noble* man, a man who cares, and I love that man and what's more, I know that *he* loves me. Perhaps you did not at first, not as *I* loved you, but I am in no doubt now.'

'Esther, what can I say?'

'I was brought up with Grandfather's people; Jewish people are ever a people of faith trusting God. He once asked me to fill a bucket of water at the well. I said, "But Grandfather the bucket is full of holes. Never mind he said, do as you are bidden." By the time I reached him, the bucket was empty. He told me to fill it again, once more it was empty by the time I reached him, and again I complained that the water had all run out of the holes. "Yes," he said, smiling, "but see how clean it is on the inside. So, it is with life, God will allow life's trials to wash us clean through the weaknesses, or holes, in our lives, *if* we trust Him and not our own strength. Our inclination would be to block up the holes, but then our troubles would stay within and turn us sour".'

'Esther, you have the answers before I know the questions.'

'Ha!' She laughed, 'I know very little, my dear knight, only what is on my heart, but I want to hear the words that are on *your* heart Richard, for they have *never* been more important than they are at *this* moment.'

He lifted his head and looked directly at her, what did she mean, "At *this* moment"? Since he'd been wounded, he had not been able to look her in the face, not consciously anyway, she smiled at him, glowing, angelic.

'I am not a *complete* fool,' he said, 'I love you and so it will be until death parts us, that's the truth on my heart. It will be clear to *any* lackwit that I do not deserve you. You are wrong on one thing though, when you say I did not love you at first, I did, but I just did not realise it.'

She lowered herself and knelt at his feet and he wrapped his arm around her, she offered her lips to him and he kissed her. 'My heart is as full as my arms at this moment, my dearest Esther.'

'Room for *our* child too I hope?'

'Ah… that is ever a tender place. For Julianne to call her son William as you did ours… that must be a hard cross for you to bear, as it is for me.'

She looked at him with compassion. 'I'm sorry that you think of it so, perhaps I did too at first. God in His wisdom saw fit to take *our* William to Himself, but He has given us another William to love, and so pour a healing balm onto our sadness. No, I talk not of that dear treasured memory, but of another child that now quickens within me even as I speak,' she stared into his eyes and smiled as if her face had that moment been gilded by a golden shaft of light. 'My poor Richard, are you not pleased? In truth you have the look of a man who has lost a purse filled with gold and found one filled with pebbles. Richard… speak to me, or I may think you not *beyond* joy as I surely am.'

'But, but… you said that you could not have any more children!'

'Does the Mother of Christ not understand the loss of a son; she has seen our suffering and it has been her pleasure to bless us?'

Richard lifted his head and shouted out with joy, so suddenly that William nearly jumped from his lap and began to cry.

'Careful Richard,' Esther laughed, 'you are crushing us both.'

'Thank you, God of all mercy, Jesus, Mary, Joseph and all the saints in heaven, it is I who is beyond joy, my most precious wife.' He paused and looked at her, 'Who knows of this miracle?'

'And, pray, whom would I tell before the father of my child? *You* are the first to know, I have had to keep this bliss to myself, can you imagine what such an occupation has done to a heart fit to burst? Especially when I thought such a thing not *ever* possible.'

'WALTER are you out there?' Richard called, his servant nervously opened the door, and two eyes appeared around the edge fearing what he might find. He'd heard the shout and had trembled.

'*Yes*, Master…'

'Come man, fear not, an angel has brought glad tidings of great joy, go quickly and bring Sir John to us.'

'Is all well, Lord?'

'Better than that, make haste man and do as you are bidden.' Richard turned laughing to Esther and William, hugging and kissing them once more.

'Poor Walter, never have I seen him so confused,' Esther said and laughed too. She took William into her arms and gently attempted to soothe him. 'There, there, you are to have a brother, or a sister to play with,' and she lifted him above her head and his tears were replaced by giggles.

'I must write to Alwin, and the *King*, I want the world to know of my joy.' Esther laughed at Richard, his response to her news pleased her more than she could have ever imagined.

Chapter 4

William Marshal

'Do you think it wise to go riding, Richard?' Esther asked, holding Ares bridle tightly as if any final decision would be hers to make. Richard smiled down at her.

'Tell me, how can I – an armed mounted knight, tremble in fear at the mere words of a slip of a woman?'

'Tremble with fear, I think not! Just so long as you remember it is I who have the impossible task of caring for my child's foolish father who is without the wisdom to be concerned for himself,' she laughed.

'There has to be a first time Esther, I have been working in the tiltyard to build up my strength. I know fine well that I have a way to go yet. I will be careful, *and*, I have your spy Walter with me,' he glanced at Walter. 'I do not intend to ride far so fear not.'

'I will hold you to account when you return Walter so take care of this foolish fellow, it's no good looking to your master, he will not be able to protect you if you incur *my* wrath.' Richard laughed; Walter looked nervously from Richard to Esther.

'You, my dear wife, need concern yourself with *your* own well-being, you are more important than I am. Go and rest, I will have returned by the time you awake.' Esther released the bridle, stepped back, the two horsemen put spur to flank and moved off.

She watched them ride under the barbican towers and clatter over the wooden planking of the drawbridge. She continued to keep them in sight until they were swallowed up by the countryside. Turning back towards the keep she saw Sir John coming down the steps, he smiled and acknowledged her with a wave of his hand.

'Where is your maid, Esther?' He called as he neared and narrowed his eyes.

'She is busy Sir John.'

'*Esther*, her work is to be ever by *your* side, if she needs help with other work, she will have help, but attending to you *must* be her priority. Here take my arm and I will see you to your rooms. It cannot be long until your confinement, has that place been prepared?'

'Yes, though I dread being shut up in the darkness and quiet for all that time. How is it that the peasants manage to have children without even ceasing their day's labour, yet we "Ladies" so called, must be shut away until we are delivered?'

'I do not know the answer to such a question, but you will have the best of care, for your health and that of your child, are ever in my thoughts.'

'You are so kind to me,' and she reached up and kissed him.

'You think so, do you? It is only the measure of the regard in which I hold you.' Sir John was not over-comfortable talking on such matters and changed the subject. 'I saw Richard riding out as I stepped from the keep... We must let him go Esther, it's difficult for you, I understand that, for it is equally worrisome for me.'

'I know you speak the truth, Sir John, but I will never forget that feeling when I thought that I'd lost him,' and she involuntarily trembled at the thought.

'Being the man he is, he will be like a caged animal if we try to prevent him. He is a warrior; it is all he has known and worked for since boyhood, and he is no ordinary warrior at that. I'm surprised the King has let him have all this time to recuperate.'

'Did you know Richard has had documents from the King? His friend William Marshal is in London, he has returned from France at the King's behest.'

'Yes, Richard told me. Let us stand for a while before we attempt these stairs.' Sir John was out of breath. Esther had noticed of late that it did not take much exercise before he needed to rest. So as not to draw attention to his affliction she thanked him for thinking of *her* condition, and he smiled.

'I wonder what brings the famous William Marshal to Henry's court, did Richard say?'

'I think it is something to do with Young King Henry, but Richard was unclear.'

Sir John glanced up the stair and sighed, 'Come, Esther not too quickly, I don't want to tire you.' She smiled and thanked him again for his concern.

'How do you feel Lord?' asked Walter as they rode side by side.

'I'm beginning to ache a little, I will no doubt suffer for this pleasure on the morrow, but it will be worth the misery to have been out in the fresh air. We will ride as far as that thicket then turn back,' Richard pointed to some willow trees ahead of them which had been coppiced, probably for renewal of the castle's basket-wear. A flock of sheep scattered before them, noisily bleating at the disturbance as they rode past and continued towards the wooded stream. Richard was suddenly aware that Ares was uneasy, it was a sure sign if Ares ears began to twist and turn that all was not well, and, he had learned from experience that he should be prepared for trouble. Richard stretched out his arm to his side and motioned to Walter to slow their pace and they steadied their mounts.

'Is there some problem Lord, are you unwell?' Richard brought Ares to a standstill.

'Whoa, steady boy,' Richard whispered to Ares, patting his neck.

'What is it Lord!'

'Shush, listen…' Walter did as he was bidden, 'there is some trouble ahead, can you hear it?'

'We must turn back Lord, for the sake of safety. You are not protected or well enough to engage in any such activity. Think of my Lady, Lord.' Walter panicked; his horse clearly sensed his unease and danced nervously sideways.

'Control that animal,' Richard said sharply, 'and your wits too, there might be those ahead of us in need of help,' Richard said turning angrily to Walter and rebuking him, 'we must see what disturbance there is. Could your conscience feast peacefully over this night's mete not knowing what we had turned our backs on, thinking only of our own safety? For sure, mine could not, *you* may return if you wish, I must see what is before us.'

Walter was plainly unhappy, 'I dare do no other than stay by your side, but if I might say so I think this foolish, Lord. I can hear both Sir John and Lady Esther's voices in my head. They will be furious when we return, *if* we return,' he spoke under his breath, fearing to challenge Richard. Not that it mattered, Richard was not listening; he had already pushed Ares towards the sound.

Once into the woodland Richard saw a single knight being set upon by at least a dozen villains. There were forever displaced hungry people living beyond the law in the protection of the forests. Richard galloped full tilt towards the action with Walter's mount hard on his heels. He could see the knight had been ambushed and unhorsed, but he had managed to gain his footing and was now resolutely defending himself with his back to a large oak tree. The attackers were mostly armed with cudgels and quarterstaffs, but at least three had swords. The odds were not in the favour of this knight, even though he appeared brave and able. He was armoured, but there were too many set against him and he was suffering serious blows, it was only a matter of time before he was overwhelmed.

'Gallop straight into the mêlée, WALTER, don't ease your pace,' Richard shouted over his shoulder. He knew from experience, that charging horsemen were a fearfully intimidating sight. He drew his sword as he neared, yelling at the top of his voice hoping to generate as much confusion and panic as he could. Ares pounded into the midst of them, great clods of earth were being thrown into the air from his enormous hooves. Richard swung his sword with the consummate skill of a seasoned warrior and completely removed the top of a man's unprotected head, blood, and detritus splattered in every direction. In the continuation of the same scything action, he severed the arm of a second man, who immediately collapsed to his knees and fell headfirst into the waterlogged ditch at the side of the track. If he did not bleed to death, he would surely drown. Walter was less successful with his sweeping untutored slashes and did not so much as break the skin of a single assailant; in fact, on his second sweep of his sword it flew from his hand into the undergrowth. However, his horse had compensated for his deficit, wreaking havoc as it plunged into the mob, trampling at least two men to the ground, who were now curled on the track in a writhing, bloody, twisted mess. By the time they had turned their mounts to charge again there was not a villain to be seen, save the two whom Richard had dispatched, and another five, either already in, or on the threshold of purgatory, having been trampled under the pounding hooves of their horses or slain by the knight. A moment of remorse touched Richard, as he noticed that one of the wretched bundles of rags lying before him was a young woman. They steadied their anxious steeds and pushed them towards the knight, who now cautiously removed his great flat-topped helm.

The knight smiled, 'your servant Sir, I was about to…' He paused; 'I know well that ugly face,' he said, 'There is only one man who would boldly ride un-panzered into such a mêlée, intent on blighting a fellow's amusement?'

'WILLIAM!' Richard shouted then coughed, jumped from his horse without thought and crumpled to his knees in agony, he groaned. The knight quickly knelt and Walter leapt from his saddle to aid Richard. Richard couldn't speak he was struggling for breath. The rush of adrenalin had momentarily obliterated thought for self or sense of pain, now his awareness had returned in surfeit.

'Are you hurt Richard?' Richard was unable to answer, he only groaned, he was as pale as a sheet. Walter turned him over onto his back, resting Richard's head in his arms and the knight loosened his scruff and gambeson.

'What ails your master, has he suffered some blow? He is without marks or signs of blood, as much as I can make sense of what I see.'

'My Lord is recovering from a serious wound, he has been very ill; he should not have done this. I tried to tell him.'

Richard grunted in annoyance.

'Well thank God for his bravery, for he has saved my life, aye, and not for the first time either.'

'I'm all right, don't mither me,' Richard grumbled, some colour returning to his cheeks, he tried to raise himself, but slumped back onto Walter's lap. 'I will be well once I have stilled my breathing. I did not recognise you, where's your surcoat?'

'Ah, I didn't want to be recognised and draw attention to myself.' It took several minutes before Richard was even able to sit up.

'Have we aught to drink?' Richard gasped. William went to his horse, took from his saddle a costrel of ale, and passed it to Richard. He took it and gulped greedily to slake his thirst, wiped his mouth with the back of his glove and passed the leather flask back to William.

'Help me stand and heave me into my saddle, we must get clear of this place for fear those fellows have second thoughts, and return emboldened.' Sir William and Walter took hold of Richard and raised him to his feet. 'Ahhhh…' Richard groaned, then his eye caught sight of the dead woman, 'Hold a moment,' he stared at her, 'It's Geneen, Walter!'

Walter now looked at the bloody mess, 'Aye it is Lord, she were a servant at the castle; I thought I'd not seen her for some time. Did you know her Lord?'

'Aye, and this is justice, she was from a nest of vipers. Come let's get this over with.' They lifted Richard as carefully as they could into his saddle but he was clearly in agony.

Once seated, he took several deep breaths and tried to settle himself, 'Here, pick up my rein Walter, and lead me,' he said gasping for breath. 'I need to get back to the castle; I can't manage. Did you retrieve your sword Walter?'

'Aye Lord, I have it here,' Walter said rather sheepishly, patting the scabbard at his side.

William knelt by one of the bodies; it had been his servant, he lifted him up and laid him over the saddle of his waiting horse.

'I must see he has a proper burial in your churchyard.' William said then leapt onto his great white stallion. This animal on its own would have been worth a lifetime's coin for his pitiful attackers, Richard thought, glancing towards William as he mounted.

'Steady Tournai,' the poor beast was obviously distressed, but never flinched, William held him tightly and spoke reassuringly, and he quickly calmed. 'A slow pace fellow,' the knight called to Walter. 'I will ride at your master's side to steady him.' Richard was unable to move in harmony with the motion of Ares and each step shook every one of his aching joints. 'I was on my way to see you Richard, but this was not the meeting I had in mind.'

'Aye, aye, it was not what I expected either when I left for this morning's gentle hack. There will be hell to pay when I get home, what I have to face will pale *your* recent encounter into insignificance.' Richard held his side and lent forward gripping the upstand of his saddle before him. He was thankful for the high cantle and front of his war saddle, for it fulfilled the occupation of its design, to hold him from being unhorsed in battle. William reached to his arm.

'Still yourself for now, save your strength.'

'This is naught, I am right enough. I will need *you* to rescue *me* William when my wife hears word of this morning's employment. The greatest knight in Christendom, will be as but a newly fledged squire when faced with her wrath.'

'You intrigue me, she must be a fearful harridan indeed,' William laughed.

'My Lady is the kindest person you will ever meet my Lord,' Walter said, not in the slightest bit amused.

'Ignore my servant William, he is in her paid employment,' Richard gasped and William laughed even more.

Sir John saw them enter the castle and it was clear to him there was something amiss. 'Dear God in heaven,' he exclaimed as he made his way to Richard's side. He called for servants and they lowered Richard to the ground. 'Carry him to his room, no! Not to his room, his lady will be distressed, take him to the chapel, the priest has a bed, lay him there. I will send for my chirurgien, Bernard,' and he bade a boy fetch him.

'I am well; only let me rest for a minute. Hell's teeth, don't let this be known to Esther,' Richard lifted his head in a moment of panic.

Sir John turned to Richard's servant, 'Walter, make your way to Lady Esther's rooms, wait outside and make sure no one tells her of Sir Richard's condition, make haste man, your life on it.' Walter bowed and ran off towards the keep.

The servants carried Richard to the priest's room and Sir John pushed the priest out, none too gently. It was not until Sir John had cleared the room, did he really take note of the tall knight standing at the door.

'Tell me, in God's Holy name, what wickedness has befallen my son, and whom pray are you, Sir Knight?'

The knight bowed, and set his helm and gauntlets on a nearby chair. 'I am Sir William Marshal, tutor in chivalry to the Young King Henry, Sir.'

'*The* – William Marshal?' Sir John asked in astonishment.

'I am not sure I understand your question Sir, but I am a good friend of Sir Richard, and have been so for several years, we met in France, perhaps he has made mention of me.'

Sir John was further distracted when he saw Bernard entering the chapel, 'Where is he, Lord?'

'Oh… in there!' Sir John turned and pointed, then followed Bernard into the small room. The priest hovered uneasily behind William Marshal.

Bernard examined Richard, 'He is well, Sir John, he has merely overtaxed himself, he must rest for a day or two, no more than that and he will be fully restored. I will mix a potion of willow leaves, that should set at ease his muscles.'

'I will be well directly, just let me rest here a while.'

'Richard, you will do as Bernard says or so help me, I will tie you to your bed and sit on you, is that clear?' Richard was forced to smile. 'Sir William stay here and see my orders are obeyed. I will go, and pray that I can break this news to Esther without causing distress.'

'Sir John, I beg you, I feel better now, please allow William to support me and I will go to Esther, then I will lie on my cot for a month if you order it. You know as well as I, Esther will be distressed and I too, for I will fear for her.' Sir John paused and looked to William Marshal.

'Perhaps he is right Lord, I will give a shoulder for him to lean against and with one other to help he will make it.' Sir John looked at Richard and then to Bernard.

'Perhaps that would be best Lord,' reassured Bernard. 'I am thinking of Lady Esther too; she is too near her time to be disturbed by such a shock.'

'Very well, but have a care.' Sir John called for help and Richard was gently lifted to his feet.

Chapter 5

Young King Henry

William and the servant half carried Richard up the spiral staircase to his rooms. He endeavoured not to complain for it was difficult for them to negotiate the tapered steps. When they reached the door of his rooms, Walter, who was standing nearby, as he'd been instructed, came to aid them.

'Has anyone been to see your Lady?' Richard gasped.

'No Lord, Margaret her maid came from the room with clothes for washing, she told me Lady Esther was asleep. She has since returned and is once more with Lady Esther, but she is all I have seen. She asked what I was doing and I told her that I had been ordered to see no one came to speak to her Ladyship. She was plainly curious, but no more was said.'

'Excellent, now step back, I need to do this on my own.' William and the servant cautiously released Richard; he sagged slightly then straightened. 'Ahhhh,' they reached once more for him, 'No, leave me be! I must do this, *only* give me a moment.' He took a deep breath, 'Hell's teeth, I feel as if I have been trampled by a horse.' He leaned against the door reveal whilst he composed himself. 'I will enter first then send Esther's maid to fetch you, just abide here until she comes, it will be but a moment. Open the door Walter.'

Esther was now sitting by the fire; she looked to the sound of the opening door and a smile lit up her face. Richard clenched his teeth and stepped slowly into the room, trying to casually return her smile.

'Richard, I am so relieved that you are home,' Esther said and then narrowed her eyes. 'Are you well Lord? You look awkward.'

'I'm fine, still yet diverted by my unexpected good news.' He walked with some difficulty to the nearest chair and carefully lowered himself onto the seat.

'Are you injured?' She stood and came to him.

'It's a long while since I have been on a horse and believe me, I am fearfully stiff, no more than that.'

She laughed, 'I have no sympathy.'

'Oh… is this not the lady who has cared so devotedly for me these past weeks that I hear?'

She laughed again, 'and, what is the good news you have hobbled here at such speed to bring me? Let me guess, you will not be riding horses in the future, but sitting by my side with your arms outstretched wrapped with wool usefully employed by helping me wind it into balls?'

'In truth that is a pleasant thought, but no, when I was out who should I meet on his way to see me? None other than my old friend, William Marshal.'

'What, "*The*" William Marshal?'

'You sound like Sir John, that was his reaction. Yes, "*The*" William Marshal, at this very moment he awaits your pleasure at our door.'

'Margaret, show in Sir William,' Margaret did as she was bidden, the door swung open and Sir William Marshal entered, he bowed and Esther responded in like manner.

'This is, "*The*" William Marshal, my dearest friend and mentor.'

William laughed, 'How could a man live up to such an acclamation? It is I, who am honoured. Richard told me how beautiful his lady was, but he did not do justice to such a damsel as I see before me.' Now it was Esther, who was embarrassed and laughed awkwardly.

'I see not my husband before *me*, but I hear the same courtier's voice, he learned well from you, Sir.'

'Please, my Lady, call me William, I pray that this meeting will merely be an extension to the friendship which is already so dear to me.'

'Indeed *William*, and you must call me Esther. I pray you will forgive my husband; he sits because he is stiff from this day's ride, which he undertook against my wishes, I might add. *Margaret* bring refreshment for us, do you wish for mete, William?'

'No, thank you kindly, I will wait until this evening.'

'Walter, I see you there, ask Sir John to join us. William, come, be seated.'

'My Lady… Esther, might Walter help me remove my hauberk before he goes?'

'Forgive me William, of course. Walter do as Sir William asks.' Walter stepped forward and knelt to undo the leather straps then eased the heavy mail hauberk over Sir William's head.

'Ahhh… that feels better.' Sir William wriggled his shoulders and rubbed his arms.

'I will see that this is cleaned, Sir.'

'Good fellow.'

'Once we have talked, I will organise a tub for you to bathe, if that is to your liking, William.' Esther suggested.

'That would be perfect Esther.'

'Your arm William,' asked Richard. Esther watched suspiciously as William helped Richard nearer the fire.

Once they were seated Esther said assertively, 'Now we will have the truth of this,' and she pointed to Richard, whom she could clearly see was in some considerable discomfort. Neither spoke, but gazed at their feet.

'Not both at once!'

Richard spoke hesitantly, 'It was nought of consequence, Esther.'

'Good, so tell me!'

'I must speak for my friend,' Esther shifted her attention to William, she gazed so intensely he was compelled to cast his eyes past her. 'I was attacked in the forest south of here and outnumbered,' Esther took a deep breath, 'Richard and his servant rode into the mêlée and the villains, who were yet able, ran off. I fear that if he had not acted so promptly, I would have been overwhelmed and may even have been killed. I might add that he showed great courage and disrespect for his own well-being to come to the aid his friend. He is forever driven by honour as you will no doubt know.'

Esther drummed her fingers on the arm of her chair, looking first at William and then to Richard. '*And* – are you hurt, Richard?'

'No only stiff, I am ordered by Sir John and Bernard to rest for a day or so, no more,' he answered quickly.

There was a knock at the door and Sir John entered with a goblet in his hand. 'A drink from Bernard, Richard.'

'Be seated Sir John,' he did as Esther bade, passing the drink to Richard, which he sipped pulling a face.

'Ah, vile witches brew.'

'And how will we punish this offender, Sir John?'

'He must stay in bed; I think that will be sufficient.' They all laughed, apart from Richard who pulled a face.

'We are honoured to have your company Sir William; all are familiar with your exploits.'

'Perhaps my friend exaggerates and has misled you Sir! I have heard tell of some of these noble deeds of daring, and I do not recognise any of them, but they make for good tales and are worth the hearing,' William shuffled awkwardly, embarrassed at the attention.

'More than Richard speak highly of you. When chivalry or honour is spoken of, your name is first on the lips of all knights. You are the yardstick by which knights measure themselves.'

William laughed, 'is that so? I think that the King has yet to hear of such extravagant praise. He has made known his opinion of me and it is somewhat less endearing.' William took the goblet offered to him by Esther's servant and nodded to her. She gave drinks to them all, then bowed and withdrew.

'What is your meaning William?' asked Richard.

'Ahh,' William stretched out his legs, 'It's a long tale. I was commissioned by the King to tutor Young King Henry when he came to France. The King hoped that I might be a good influence on the young lad. He is capable, able, and fine company, but all he thinks of is play. He spends coin as if there is no tomorrow. It is said that he has been spending three hundred marks a day on the tourney and I am of an inclination to believe it.'

'Phew,' Sir John was visibly shocked at the vast amount.

'When you reckon a knight's pay at eight pence a day, that's about eighteen marks a year, and to aggravate the King even more, in the recent rebellion by his sons, I was honour bound to fight with the Young King Henry against his father, that did not go well with *The* King. Not his son John of course he was too young to fight at the age of nine, even for a Plantagenet,' William laughed. 'I don't like him I must say; he is a thoroughly spoilt, wilful brat who should have been drowned at birth, and spared us all future suffering. Mark my words he is dangerous.' Richard cast his eye towards Sir John who'd lowered his head and stared at his feet, clearly drawing the comparison to his own son who had caused so much wilful suffering. Esther touched his hand. William hesitated and glanced at Richard, what had he said? There was a sudden undercurrent of dark water here, that he'd inadvertently stepped into, but he was content to ignore it.

'Why, honour bound?' asked Richard. 'Is not your honour first and foremost to the King, Henry the II?'

'King Henry had me swear fealty to his son.'

'So… you and I were enemies in the recent rebellion, William!'

'Aye it appears so, you acquitted yourself with great credit I hear, defeating the Earl of Leicester at Fornham and taking the Scottish King prisoner north of Newcastle, and on both occasions against the odds. Henry speaks highly of you.'

'Thank God we did not meet on the field of battle, by the grace of God we were spared that conflict of honour,' Richard said. 'What has the King said to you, he allowed you to come here, so he has not yet demanded your head be removed?'

William smiled, 'Not yet… He blamed me for instigating the rebellion and causing his son's recklessness.

I managed to make him understand that controlling young Henry was no easy task, I made mention that his mother the Queen generally overrode me if I stood against young Henry. I think he already knew the truth of it, for he gave a snort of derision at the mention of the Queen's name. As far as I know, the Queen is at this moment held prisoner in Rouen. Not in some dark dank cell, you understand. She lives in comfort so I've been told, but guarded and a prisoner nevertheless. Such knowledge is only spoken of in hushed voices and Henry made no mention of it when we met. He wants me to return and continue, suitably chastised, I must assume I am redeemed and forgiven.'

'Mmm,' Richard was thoughtful.

'Is this merely a visit to reacquaint yourself with an old friend or is there more of which I wish not to hear?' asked Esther.

William looked at Esther and gave a slight smile. 'You have the measure of me good lady.'

'So, tell me, and do not dissemble your answer,' Esther said tapping her foot on the tiles and looking very serious indeed.

'The King has asked me to take Richard to Westminster if he is well enough, he has need of him, I have letters for you Richard from the King.'

'Where are these documents?' asked Esther frostily.

'In my saddle-bags, this reunion has not started in the manner I'd imagined, but I fancy from the way he talked the content does not require urgent attention. Your injury is known to the King, he showed genuine concern. He worries and needs to know all that is about him, so he is well informed and in control. One of his strengths – and *weaknesses*, but I am convinced that he will never relinquish power to his sons.'

'I will see that your personal belongings are brought to your room Sir William,' offered Sir John.

'And that a tub is organised to bathe and refresh you after your troubled journey. When we meet tonight perhaps you will give me the documents?'

'Indeed Richard.'

Richard beckoned his servant, who had now returned and was waiting in the shadows. 'Walter, with Sir John's permission…' Sir John nodded, 'show Sir William to his rooms.' They stood and William squeezed Richard's shoulder.

'You rest, as you have been bidden, Richard, we will talk later, and, you my Lady, do not worry. Henry asked to be remembered to you, so take comfort that he has you in mind. You have clearly made an impression on him,' William said kindly and Esther smiled as he left to be shown to his room.

Chapter 6

Henry II

Neither Esther, nor Richard went to the hall for the evening meal; food was brought to their chamber, which meant that they were both able to rest. Esther was uncomfortable now and tired easily.

Richard knew Esther had slept, but *he* merely lay on his back and stared at the canopy above him.

He cast his eye to Esther, 'I'm *sorry* if I caused you distress, Esther.' he said when he saw her stirring.

It was some time before she responded, 'How do *you* feel?'

'Eased, I think Bernard's foul potion has helped, strange my adventure today started at the sight of some coppiced willows. I thought the work had been done for the making and repairing of castle baskets, but on second thoughts it was probably Bernard making his cure-all brew,' Richard jested.

'I will not hear one word against Bernard.'

'No, I'm sorry, and I am thankful for him, I will forever be in his debt.'

She didn't respond but simply lay silently, comforted by the warmth of his body next to her, she touched his hand, and he closed his fingers gently around it.

Like Richard, she now lay on her back and stared at the beautifully woven canopy overhead. 'Please Richard, do not leave me until I have been delivered of our child, I am so fearful, I need you here.'

'It is my certain intention to be by your side, whatever work is set before me in these letters from King Henry. If, that is their purpose to give me some employment, I will write to him and beg that I might be allowed to remain here with you before I attend to such occupation. The country seems settled at *this* moment so by God's grace there will be no urgent work. However, from what I hear, the problems with Henry's children are not going to go away, William said as much confirming the rumours.'

'I know well and good what he said, but they are not your problems, you have a family and an estate to concern you. There are people there who rely on you for their daily bread. Are their needs not as important as the King's wants?'

'Esther, you know as well as I – sitting at home while the nation falls apart is never going to be an option for me. All I have is at the King's behest and I have sworn to serve him. It is in my peoples best interests that I serve the King well, they will benefit too.'

'That… may well be the truth of it, but I will die if I have to face – alone – the anguish I was subjected to last time.' Richard carefully eased himself into a position where he was able to wrap his arm around Esther; he drew her to him and pressed his lips to her brow. She was glad of the reassurance and began to weep.

'Forgive me Richard,' she sobbed, 'I understand that I am being foolish *and* selfish, but I seem to cry at the slightest thing of late. I don't know why, perhaps it's fear. I would rather die that our child might live. It is the most hellish thing to look upon one's dead child.'

'God in heaven, don't say such a thing, no child could be worth losing you. I comprehend clear enough that I deserve to be punished, but I pray it is not at the expense of others. All I have, all the wealth and position take from me Mother of Christ, but spare my dearest, dearest Esther.'

Suddenly a voice broke into their miserable thoughts, 'My Lord, my Lady, I have brought mete and drink.'

'One moment Margaret,' Esther wiped her eyes. She reached up, opened the heavy drapes around their bed, and slid her legs over the edge of the mattress. Margaret and another servant were standing nearby with two large trays of food.

'Sir William begs that he may come to see you after he has eaten, my Lady.'

'Set the mete on the table I will tend to our Lord's needs myself. Tell Sir William we will see him when he is ready.'

'Yes, my Lady.' They placed the trays on the table, bowed, and quietly left.

'I'm sorry to be such a trouble to you, can you manage? I'm sure I can sit at the table, Esther.'

'No! You bide where you are, I can manage well enough, you are to rest,' she scowled at him.

'Well I think it ridiculous; I will suffer more stiffness if I lie here.' He sat up, bit his lip, and squeezed his eyes together at the sharp pain, which shot through his chest.

Once the pain had calmed and he was able to relax his breathing, he continued. Gingerly he lowered his feet to the floor and stood.

'See, I am well enough,' he said defiantly.

'Richard!'

He slowly made his way to the table and sat down.

'You are so wilful, do you think such determination sets my mind at rest, for I assure you it does not?'

'Once we have eaten, I will return to my sickbed and not leave it without your yea or nay. Now may we change the subject? What did you think of "The" – William Marshal?'

Esther turned to him, 'he is like you. There is an energy, which radiates from him just as it does from you. If he were a complete stranger and I knew not of his fame, I would yet know I was in the presence of a man of some note, everything about him, the way he walks, his noble bearing, gentle clear voice of authority all make him out as a great man, and you are his brother. No wonder you are such friends, but he makes me afraid, as you do.'

'*I* – make you afraid! God forbid,' Richard suddenly twisted towards her and groaned at the abrupt pain.

'*Yes*, you make me fear, for your life is not important to you, you would sacrifice yourself on the altar of honour, and gladly, for you think that such selflessness be the measure of a man.'

Richard leaned forward and stared down at his food, moving it mindlessly around on his plate with the point of his knife… 'I'm sorry Esther… I cannot change that, and would you love such a man who cared more for himself than the well-being of others?'

'I have told you I love you as you are, but that very love also makes me fear. Let's not dwell on the unthinkable, we must eat, though in truth I have little appetite, I have some discomfort, something I have eaten has not agreed with me.'

'Try the wine it's good, what does the scripture advise? "Take a little wine for thy stomach's sake",' he smiled glad of the opportunity to change the subject.

She laughed, twisted her face at her disquiet, and adjusted her seating, for she could not find a comfortable position on the chair no matter how she tried.

When they had finished eating, Richard was true to his word and climbed back onto their bed. No sooner was he settled than there was a knock on the door and Margaret showed in William Marshal, Esther noted that he had a leather document wallet in his hand.

Esther, with some effort, stood and bowed.

'Sit my Lady, there is no need for such formality amongst good friends, I'm not disturbing you, I pray?'

'Not at all, here, sit by me,' instructed Richard. William pulled up a chair by the bed and handed the wallet to him.

'Some wine William?' asked Esther.

'Indeed, thank you,' and Margaret filled a goblet and passed it to him.

Richard proceeded to open the correspondence; there were only two letters. He looked again in the pouch, no; there were only the two. He broke the seals and unfolded them both. One gifted him Sir Guy's Castle, (which had been for a short time Julianne's home) for his loyal service to the Crown, and the other was a more personal letter from the King. He stared thoughtfully at the first document for some time then laid it on the bed next to him. The second letter he read out. It was a kindly letter of concern. The King wished him a speedy recovery and prayed that he would soon be able to join him, for he was ever in need of his counsel.

'He hopes that I will speak firmly to Sir William Marshal,' Richard cast his eye to William and they both smiled. 'I am to express my disappointment that William Marshal took up arms against his rightful "Liege Lord" and in doing so betrayed his friendship with me, ever the King's most loyal subject. So, there you have it, William, consider yourself admonished.'

'Is that what *you* think Richard, that I behaved dishonourably?'

'Does it matter what I think, William?'

'Yes.'

'A man cannot serve two masters, is that not what the Holy Scriptures tells us? Henry sent you to serve his son, Young King Henry. What the King did not bargain for was that the Young King would rebel against him, his father. Young Henry is a Plantagenet as is his father and the Holy Mother herself would be sore challenged to dissuade a Plantagenet once he has set his mind to a course, no matter how ill advised. So, my friend, it is a tight rope you have been placed upon, damned if you do and damned if you don't.'

'It is such a comfort having your opinion made known to me,' said William and they all laughed.

'You might take some comfort from knowing the King *you* are sworn to serve, should by all natural course outlive the King whom *I* am sworn to serve, and then it will be *I* who is on the wrong side of the sharp point of honour and you will be admonishing me.'

'You are fools the pair of you, these men of power are not driven by honour and see you for the easy game you are, that is the truth of it. Would Henry, young or old give up all, on the hallowed altar of honour? Not a bit of it, honour is merely a distorting summer haze, to keep you lesser mortals in order.'

William's eyes widened, 'Mmm, what a low opinion you have of all we hold dear, my Lady,' he smiled, though her words had touched a nerve. It was true that the older he got the more complex the whole question of divided loyalty became.

Esther once more adjusted her seating position. 'You will find that loyalty, as Richard has this moment confirmed by what he read to us, is judged from the position of the viewer…' Esther was about to continue her opinion when she suddenly gasped and slipped from her chair onto her knees. William quickly went to her, and Richard endeavoured to raise himself from his bed.

'Esther!'

Esther groaned, 'Dear Mother of Christ, it is the child! God help me, I have yet another month before it is my time,' she gasped.

'Are you sure?' asked Richard.

'Yes, yes, get Margaret she will organise the midwife,' she panted, 'I can't go to the room prepared for my confinement; there is not time. Richard loosen all that is tied about my person, I must not have any bindings that might fasten my child to my womb, then lift me to the bed.'

He raised himself trying to ignore his pain, to do as she commanded. With only one hand, it was difficult labour undoing the laces at the back of her gown, for he needed his other hand to steady himself against a chair. He was about to sit back on the edge of the bed before he fell to the floor, when she spoke sharply once more.

'My *shoulders* too!' He hesitated; at a loss to see how cords tied at her shoulder, could make the slightest difference to a child inside her, nevertheless he did as she bade him.

She even loosed the bindings from her hair, and the lush thick folds tumbled down her back. For a single breath in time, he was in another place, consumed by her beauty, but he was abruptly drawn once more into the moment, as her cry grasped hold of his senses.

'William, can you lift Esther? It is beyond me, I'll instruct Margaret.'

William carefully lifted Esther and laid her on the bed. 'What now?' He asked, completely at a loss.

'It's no good I can't get up, help me William,' Richard moaned in utter frustration. 'See there,' he nodded, 'pass me that spear from the wall to support myself.' William reached for the spear and lifted him to his feet, setting the spear shaft to his hand. Richard hobbled to the door calling for Margaret, who on entering realised the predicament at a glance.

'Watch my Lady for a moment, comfort her and pray to the blessed Saint Ann.' She gestured to the painted stone effigy on the mantelshelf, 'I will tend to the rest,' with that, she ran off. Esther groaned every few minutes much to the disquiet of Richard and William. Fortunately, Margaret quickly returned with the midwife and other servants, and the two men were unceremoniously ushered from the room into the passage and the door was firmly closed. William took Richard's arm and helped him to a nearby room. It was not long before Sir John joined them.

'Here, sit Lord, you have come with too much haste.'

'I'm well, and Esther!'

'She sounded in great pain, she was screaming fit to rupture the tendons in her throat, but more than that I fear my knowledge of such mysteries is severely limited.'

No more than an hour had passed when there was a knocking at the door, 'Come,' shouted Richard. 'Yes, yes, what is it Margaret?'

'You have a son, Lord.'
'My wife is well, and my son!'
'Both are well, Lord. He is small but hearty.'
'Thanks be to God,' Richard had half risen from his chair his pains forgotten, and slumped down upon it once more as he was abruptly reminded.

The young Lord Maillorie was to be named Jacob after Esther's grandfather. Esther did eventually have some moments alone with Richard. He'd recovered rapidly from his encounter with the outlaws on the day of William's arrival, but not as rapidly as Esther, the whole experience of bearing their son seemed as naught to her. All her fears and doubts were forgotten, now she held her son in her arms.

Esther's mind was set for home; it would be difficult to leave Tattershall and Sir John, they had been there for nearly a year. It was going to be a torturous thing for Sir John to have to say goodbye to them, not least to his grandson, William. He was toddling now and Sir John barely left his side, but he was resigned that William must go with his father.

When it was time to leave, Sir John had quietly asked Richard if he would tell his grandson of him so that he would be remembered. Richard had embraced Sir John, 'you are a father to me John, fear not I will tell him everything; he has the right to know. Some may say it was a sin and they may be right, but I know he was born of love and he will forever be loved.'

Richard knew that ultimately, he would have to run these three estates, his own, Sir John's and what was Sir Guy's estate. He was a very wealthy man now, Sir Guy had never been heard of since he took flight, and his name was never mentioned.

Sir William Marshal returned to France and the tutorship of the Young King Henry. His life was not easy; he seemed to be forever in conflict with the Young King, who was now twenty-two. King Henry complained remorselessly to Richard about the bad influence William Marshal was on his son. Richard had to exert all his willpower to prevent him asking why, when he was so dissatisfied with the Marshal's tutorship that he did not recall him and send someone he considered more fitted to the work. Richard suspected that in his heart, Henry knew that he and Queen Eleanor were the root cause of young Henry's failings and not the Marshal, but he would never own that possibility.

It would be Christmas 1182 before Richard again saw William Marshal.

Chapter 7

Louis VII of France 1137-79

'Esther, Esther!' Richard ran into their apartment, Esther immediately rose from her chair and stared at him with some anxiety.

'Richard, is there some menace which has befallen us?'

'A letter from the King has this moment arrived by rider,' he waved the parchment before her.

'And whatever on earth could a missive contain to cause you such breathlessness?'

'The King of France has landed at Dover...' he said gasping as if to confirm her observation.

'WHAT, he's invaded! Dear Mother of Christ,' she exclaimed, and fell back in her chair, her face ashen.

'No, no, he's not invading. He has come with an entourage of priests, servants and *some* men-at-arms, to visit Becket's tomb,' he said yet waving the document.

'He is *visiting* England; I have never heard of such a thing!'

'Neither have I, this must be the first time a King from another country has come to these shores without the intention of conquering the land.'

'What does the King require of you?' She remained seated, staring at him and shaking her head in disbelief.

'Rouse yourself woman, help me dress and I will tell what I know.' Richard reached to some pegs, and hurriedly took down his gambeson and passed it to her at the same time loosening his sword belt from his waist. 'The King will be here from Winchester within the hour, and I am to be ready on the road with a troop of men waiting for him.' He turned to Walter, who was now at the door, 'summon Tristram, go man, and make haste, run man, run.'

Richard was still in the process of dressing when Tristram skidded into the room and drew to a stop by grabbing hold of the doorframe as he entered.

'Whatever is it Richard, Walter talks of the King arriving any minute?' While Richard was sitting on a chair, Esther was fastening the leather laces on his gambeson at the same time as he pulled on his boots.

Before Richard could respond to Tristram's question Esther interrupted, 'Will you sit still Richard how can I tie these laces when you are putting on your stockings and boots at the same time?' With that, she tugged at the neck of his gambeson and dragged him upright with such force he gasped. He now sat still, with his boot half on.

'Speak to me Richard!' called Tristram.

'I'm trying, but I have at this moment been near garrotted.'

'There, I've done, now you can pull on your boots.'

'Thank you,' he said running his finger round the neck of his gambeson, which felt exceedingly tight. 'Get twenty men turned out, the King will be here any minute, if the letter is to be believed and if I know Henry it will be so. I have not time to explain, I will be with you directly, go.' Tristram turned and ran from the room.

'Ah Walter, quick help me with my hauberk, it might be less painful if *you* help.' For which remark he received a sharp jab in the ribs from Esther. 'Ouch… now I will have to suffer a broken rib for the journey.' Richard bent forward and Walter slipped the mail over his head. 'Now, where are my coif and my helm?'

'Here, Lord, perhaps you might want your sword first.' and Walter passed him his sword which he buckled to his waist and then he reached for his coif and flat-topped helm.

'Come, I'll carry the helm for the moment, I'll only wear my coif for the time being.' He stepped to Esther and kissed her cheek, 'kiss the boys for me I have not time.'

'I will, God keep you safe.'

'Amen, I don't know when I will return, I will send word,' with that he dashed from the room.

'Richard, Richard,' Esther called after him. He stopped abruptly and looked back. 'Your gauntlets,' he saw her walking briskly to him with his gauntlets in her hand. 'How on earth you manage to even walk in all your armour defeats me, these gauntlets all but weigh me down.'

'In truth I feel naked without it, bless you,' and he kissed her once more, but on the lips this time and held her tightly. 'I love you,' he said, his haste, Henry, the world, forgotten for that brief second of intimacy, then he turned on his heel and continued down the stone staircase into the courtyard. The men were already mounted and waiting, there was a moment of pride when he saw them, pride that these men were so well trained that they could be assembled and made ready at such speed. He knew that speed and organisation won battles.

'Well done, you two are the finest comrades,' he said patting Raymond's shoulder, 'how could I manage without you.'

Both Sir Raymond and Sir Tristram nodded their appreciation of the kind words.

Tristram smiled as he mounted his horse, 'You are kind, but in truth we quake with fear for our lord is a severe master,'

Richard threw back his head and laughed. Ares suddenly tugged at his bridle startled by the laughter; Raymond who held him stroked his soft pink nose to settle him. Ares was getting old now, but he was yet a fine animal. He had never been the easiest of horses, but he had become even more edgy as he'd grown older.

Richard swung himself into the saddle; he had no time for the use of leisurely mounting blocks this day.

'We must make for the main thoroughfare to Dover and await the King, lead the men Tristram. Take care Raymond, Esther will tell you all, go to her.'

Raymond reached up his hand to Richard, and bade him farewell, 'Aye and you take care too, Richard.'

It was no more than half a league to the junction with the Dover road, they drew to a standstill, and Tristram ordered the men to dismount. Richard told him the contents of the letter whilst they waited, all the while watching in the direction from where they expected the King. They had not long to wait; they saw the dust of mounted men travelling at haste towards them.

'This will be him,' Richard said.

'Mount,' Tristram ordered, 'and keep to the side to let the King through, we will follow at the rear.'

The King never even broke speed when he reached them, and Richard drew alongside him at a steady canter. The King smiled and reached over to him offering his hand as they rode.

'I knew you would not hold me up, on time as ever. We must not keep our dearest Louis standing in the sea at Dover,' the King laughed, shouting above the noise of the pounding hooves.

Richard smiled too for he knew fine well that there was no *dearest* affection between Louis and Henry. They had a complex relationship, like two caged cats, they circled each other, hissing and spitting, ever watching for a weakness when they might pounce.

Louis VII was the son of "Fat" Louis, as he was known, and Henry eternally referred to him as such. Louis married Eleanor at Bordeaux when she was fourteen. She was the heiress of Aquitaine. Richard could easily understand how their relationship with the one woman in itself would forever be a complex barb between them, all other problems aside.

Louis' accession was marked with some troubles. A short time after he was crowned, he came into violent conflict with the Pope. The archbishopric of Bourges became vacant, and the King supported as candidate his chancellor, against the Pope's nominee. Swearing upon holy relics, Louis made known that so long as he lived, he would never allow such an appointment. This brought a papal interdict upon the King's lands.

Richard smiled at his thoughts, for this was the same problem as Henry had with Becket, and an ongoing problem faced by every other monarch, the question of who had ultimate power in a kingdom.

At his court, King Louis declared his intention of going on a crusade. Louis set out from Metz on the overland route to Syria. The expedition was disastrous, and he returned to France two years later, overcome by humiliation and failure.

For the rest of his reign, he showed much feebleness and poor judgement. He committed a *grave* political blunder by having his marriage to Eleanor of Aquitaine annulled, under the pretext that he'd now discovered that she was kin to him, citing her own declaration. The truth was that is was owing to violent quarrels between them during the crusade.

It was no secret, and Richard knew well the tale. Eleanor's uncle, Raymond, decided that the best strategic objective of the Crusade would be to recapture Edessa, thus protecting the Western presence in the Holy Land. Eleanor sided with his view. Louis, however, was fixated on reaching Jerusalem. Louis demanded that Eleanor follow him to Jerusalem. Eleanor, furious, announced to one and all that their marriage was not valid in the eyes of God, for they were related through some family connections, which were to an extent prohibited by the Church. To add further insult, Eleanor mocked him saying, "I'm married to a monk not a man".

Wounded by her protestation, Louis nonetheless forced Eleanor to honour her marriage vows and ride with him. The expedition failed, and a defeated Eleanor and Louis returned to France in separate ships.

Once her marriage was annulled, Eleanor, now thirty-one, quickly married King Henry, ten years her junior, a love match it was said. She had been the French Queen for fifteen years.

Chapter 8

Henry and Eleanor

Eleanor was a great beauty, clever too and she brought to the marriage the duchy of Aquitaine.

In 1154, Louis married Constance, daughter of the King of Castile; they had a daughter Marguerite whom he betrothed *imprudently* to young Henry, eldest son of King Henry, promising land as a dowry.

Richard remembered William Marshal telling him about Marguerite and how fond he was of her. When Constance, Marguerite's mother, died, Louis married Adèle of Champagne.

King Henry was furious at the threat the marriage brought to his kingdom, and acted quickly to counterbalance the advantage the union would give the King of France.

King Henry needed Marguerite's holdings on the French-Norman border. Henry saw that a papal dispensation was granted to the two infants to permit the nuptials even though she was only nine.

He had both manipulated the Church *and* King Louis who had given his only daughter into the safe keeping of Henry's court. King Louis had assumed, rather naively, there would be many years of betrothal between his daughter and young Henry, but they were married almost immediately.

In the troubles between Becket and King Henry, Louis reluctantly received Thomas Becket when he fled from England *and,* out of character, tried to reconcile him with King Henry. Louis regularly supported any acts of rebellion against Henry, but acted slowly and without firm resolve, never giving adequate support to make any significant difference to the outcome.

Finally, the Pope intervened to bring the two kings to terms. Adèle, the new wife of Louis had given him an heir, Philip Augustus. Louis had him crowned at Reims, but the boy was stricken with paralysis and was now dangerously ill. His distraught father took the unprecedented decision to go to Canterbury, and seek succour from the Saint, Thomas Becket.

Louis' decision had caught Henry on the wrong foot. Richard could not help but smile as they rode. Henry was not the sort of person who was normally caught on the hop and certainly not by the King of France.

They rode through the night without a stop in order to be able to greet Louis on Dover beach.

As they rode down the steep slope at Dover and onto the beach, the morning glow was just touching the fading night sky. They slowed their exhausted mounts to a walk, and made their way steadily down to the water's edge. The light was now such that they could clearly see Louis' flagship off shore. Once dismounted, to a man, they bent and stretched to relieve their aching muscles.

'Remove your saddles, we have time and rub down our horses then walk them in the surf, they will be as weary as we.' It had been a fine night thankfully.

As they watched, they saw boats being lowered and rowed towards the shore.

'I can't pick out Louis' pendant, can you Richard?'

'No, not on either of the two boats coming towards us, I think they will be merely a forward guard to ensure that we are friendly, Lord.'

'Aye, most likely,' Henry turned to him and smiled, 'now there's a thought, never a better chance to rid myself of a tiresome King,' and his smile turned into hearty laughter so much so he had to remove his gauntlet, to wipe the tears from his eyes with the back of his hand.

When the boats touched ground, sailors leapt into the surf and took the painter ropes to the higher ground. A nobleman by the look of his dress, thought Richard, jumped from the second boat, came up to the King, and knelt.

'Lord, I am Count Philip Debussy, a humble servant of the high and most noble King of France, your friend King Louis. He requests that by your most gracious permission he may come ashore.'

Henry gestured with his hand for him to rise.

'Signal to him, my dear friend King Louis is forever welcome to my kingdom.'

Richard smiled at the sincerity of Henry's endearment. Henry had once said to him, "The real skill of governing is about being totally honest with your people, and being able to make that lie convincing".

One of the sailors then proceeded to wave a flag, and within a short time, Richard saw someone in a sling being lowered into a waiting boat. He assumed that it was the King.

Henry never spoke – or moved – standing perfectly still. Any display of emotion was limited to a steady tapping of his foot on the wet sand. He simply stared out to sea as King Louis' launch drew nearer. Once it had touched ground several sailors jumped into the water, some made the vessel secure whilst others, yet onboard, manoeuvred the chair Louis sat upon over the side and into the waiting hands. It was tricky employment, there was an intake of breath by all watching, as those struggling with the seated king stumbled and nearly tipped Louis into the sea. Richard could see Henry biting his lip endeavouring not to laugh; Richard was compelled to turn away and mask his merriment with a coughing fit.

Louis was positioned before King Henry; all the while, his chair was sinking into the soft sand. Fortunately, he rose from the chair, not without some difficulty, before he ended up sitting on the wet sand. They embraced and touched cheeks offering words of greeting. A fine mount was brought forward and offered to Louis, he was helped into the saddle and they rode up the long incline to Dover Castle where the party was to spend the night.

They had sent word to the castle as they'd passed on the way to the beach that they were to ready themselves to receive the two kings and their men. Richard imagined that the poor sentinel of the castle would be frantic with the impossible task of making the necessary preparations to receive them, having no more than three or four hours notice.

However, to his credit there was a meal of some note set before them, it may not have been the delicate fayre

Louis was accustomed to, but Richard knew it would suit Henry well enough. There were even musicians for their entertainment. Richard wondered if either of the kings would give the slightest thought to the work they had brought about. He supposed that it was their normal understanding of life, what they ordered was done and he imagined they never thought beyond that.

Henry asked after the health of Louis' son, and was told how ill he was, Richard thought that Henry showed genuine concern, after all, he knew what it was to lose a child. His first son William had died when he was but an infant.

On the next day, Henry escorted Louis' train to Canterbury, where Louis prayed, even wept at Becket's tomb, and on leaving, gave generous offerings, including a great ruby.

All the while, Louis and his priests were in the cathedral intent on their supplications to the saint, Henry waited in Canterbury Castle, a stone's throw from the cathedral. When their devotions were completed, Henry escorted Louis back to Dover Castle, where the two kings spent another night.

Strange, thought Richard, Eleanor only bore Louis two daughters, Marie and Alix, in the sixteen or so years, they were married, but she has born Henry five sons and three daughters.

Just one month after Louis' pilgrimage, Henry began to spend coin on Dover Castle, in fact to Richard's certain knowledge, more coin than he had spent on any other English castle. It was easy for Richard to connect the sudden expenditure with this extraordinary visit of King Louis and conclude that the prospect of more foreign rulers making the pilgrimage was the stimulus that had triggered the King's decision to build something truly spectacular at Dover. Henry built a great tower – in particular the fore building, with its three flights of steps leading up to the upper floor – which was clearly designed as a setting for ceremonial entrances and exits.

Richard knew when Henry had visited Paris, and stayed in the royal palace, he had been impressed. Henry wasn't a man who indulged in a lavish lifestyle, he was a warrior, but that palace had unsettled him and made him think. What palatial residence could *he,* the most significant ruler in Europe, offer important guests coming from abroad to visit the Holy Shrine? Of course, he had fine palaces, but none en route to Canterbury. No doubt, it would have been possible to improve the castle at Canterbury, but unfortunately, Canterbury would always be the city of the archbishop and monks of Christ Church and he wanted a statement about who *he* was, Henry the Second, ruler of the largest empire in Europe. It became clear to Henry that Dover was obviously the place for a great building, which could not only accommodate foreign princes, but their courtiers. Louis had come with Dukes, Counts and many Barons in his train and Henry wanted a symbol of his royal prowess visible from afar, which would overwhelm visitors even before they set foot on English soil. Evidently, Dover Castle as it was, did not satisfy Henry's need to demonstrate his vision of superior power. He was determined to create a dynastical display of Plantagenet wealth, supremacy, and taste, which would be the envy of all.

Henry was at the height of his power. He had become the arbiter of Europe. His sons and daughters were all provided for. His wife, Eleanor of Aquitaine, was safely locked up and he had settled his mind to that.

Ironically Henry, was now even to find reconciliation with his once friend turned enemy, the now "Saint" Thomas Becket. Becket, as one of the foremost saints in Christendom, had managed to give in death what he was unable to give in life, his unerring support to Henry, enabling him to dominate his world.

Chapter 9

Caen, Normandy (1182)

The last five years had seen some peace in the empire; there was even a willingness to forgive and move on, to some "Measure", between Henry and his family, how deep below the surface the wounds were healed Richard was yet to be convinced. He struggled to see any lasting restitution as long as the matriarch of the family, Eleanor of Aquitaine, was a prisoner of her husband King Henry. She was at this moment, in Haughmond Abbey near Shrewsbury in England.

Richard and Esther had made good use of the time of peace. They were perpetually busy running their large estates and on top of this work, King Henry made constant demands on Richard's time. He enjoyed Richard's company and respected his counsel, even as far as asking his advice on the work being carried out on his palace at Clarendon, of which he was immensely fond. The project had been a joint venture with Queen Eleanor, but because of their conflict, Henry now needed someone else with whom he could share his passion, and Richard was often the one chosen. Richard didn't mind Henry's company, if Henry took to someone, he was a good friend, he trusted Richard and that set him at ease.

All the while Richard's two sons were growing, William now five and Jacob, four. The two boys usually travelled with their father and mother wherever they went, but often on the trips with Henry, Esther and his sons were left behind. William was the double of Richard, but Jacob favoured Esther in nature as well as appearance.

Travel with his family was now more complex; he was compelled to journey with a retinue of servants when he visited his holdings. They lived at Aylesford, which was what they considered their home. Alwin, who had been Richard's personal servant, was now seneschal, responsible for managing the domestic running of the castle, whereas his long-time friends were the castellans. Tristram de Brûlan at Aylesford and Sir Raymond Fitz-Valerie at Frainingham, an easy day's ride to the west of Aylesford, which had been Julianne and Sir Guy Molineux's home before he'd absconded and was never heard of again. Richard only went to the castle at Frainingham, when he had no other option. For him - it would forever be haunted by ghostly dark memories from the past. He shuddered every time the castle came into view, and would leave as soon as ever possible.

The four, Richard, Esther, Tristram, and Raymond had been the best of friends for many years.

All the Maillories were wintering this Christmas-tide in France; they had been invited to a great family Christmas reunion celebration at Caen.

It was clear to Richard that Henry II had spared no expense in the name of family restoration. There had been lavish Christmas' before, but Richard knew fine well that the Young Henry could not have remembered them. His first Christmas in 1154, which he spent with his elder brother William and his parents at Bermondsey, London, just days after their magnificent coronation, he *was* there, but still residing in his mother's womb. At the next extravagant Christmas, in 1155 at Westminster, he was yet two months shy of his first birthday, thus he would have no recollection of that one either.

This gathering in Caen was the greatest assembly of Henry II's reign, thus far. Over a thousand knights and other members of the nobility had attended on the day of the nativity of the Christ.

Richard and Esther walked amongst the assembly quite overwhelmed by the lavish surroundings. The great hall was decorated with all manner of finery; silver, painted ornaments, even coloured glass baubles, and long swags of evergreens hung from every surface. All was aglow with the light from hundreds of the best beeswax candles, there had been no expense spared.

'Quite magical, a magical kingdom,' Esther commented. Richard wondered if that was how Henry saw his empire, a magical kingdom and he the new King Arthur. Such decoration had changed little since the Celtic days, be it now more lavish. The evergreens, mistletoe, ivy, and holly, were from that time past. Mistletoe, because of its pagan associations was forbidden in churches. Henry also had the floor strewn with fresh rushes. The centrepiece of the high table was the wild boar's head, the crowning of Christmas feasts. Richard had heard the anecdote many times of how, at the young Henry's coronation banquet in 1170, the boar's head was served in person by his father, which probably delighted Henry the Elder, but shocked all the others. How true the tale was Richard didn't know, but whenever a boar's head was served the tale was retold, even Esther knew of it, and this was no exception.

Esther looked at him with a puzzled expression, 'Richard call me a fool if you will, but can you explain why Henry the Second had his son crowned so that we now have two King Henrys at the same time. To my simple brain it is a recipe for disaster?'

Richard smiled, 'my dear Esther would that you had been an adviser to the King at the time of that decision. If you recall King Louis did the same with his son Philip, that said, I have never clearly understood, and Henry has never made mention of it. It is my guess that Henry took that unprecedented decision to avoid any ambiguity when he departs this world. He might have had at the back of his mind that his grandfather Henry the First had the Barons swear to accept his mother as Queen when he died. However, when he died his Barons forgot all their oaths, and Stephen took the throne. Perhaps Henry hoped to avoid civil strife on *his* demise, and be assured that the future of the Plantagenet dynasty was secure, for there will already be an anointed king in place.'

'There may be some virtue in that, from what I have heard, that was a terrible time of civil war and uncertainty.'

'Aye, as you know it cost my father dear when Henry took the throne. My father supported Stephen, driven by his honour to give fealty to him once he was the anointed King. Henry made him suffer as were all who stood against his mother, the Empress Matilda.'

She reached over and touched his hand, 'How different our lives might have been, but for your poverty you would not have gone to France and met William Marshal or me.'

'Aye, the Mother of Christ saw fit to bless this unworthy sinner and I am thankful to her,' and he leant to her and kissed her.

This time of year, was also a deeply religious time, which meant praying and attending mass. The mass was central to the celebration of the Nativity. Richard and Esther were expected, along with all the nobles, including the Young King, to attend three masses on Christmas Day. The first at midnight, so called the Angel's Mass, the second at dawn, this was the Shepherd's Mass and the third, the Mass of the Divine Word, during the day.

There were also other religious feasts during the Twelve Days of Christmas. On the 26th of December the feast of St. Stephen, the first Christian martyr, and on the 28th, the feast of the Holy Innocents to commemorate King Herod's slaughter of thousands of children in the attempt to kill the baby Jesus.

Each night they would roll into bed exhausted, they didn't even have time for their sons. There were nurses aplenty to entertain the children who were excluded from the adult festivities. Esther was not happy about such an arrangement, but Richard could see that the association with these children of royalty and nobles was an important playing ground for his sons, who would need to grow with an understanding of the world in which he now lived.

Despite the religious character of Christmas, this was primarily the occasion for socializing and easing the monotony of winter nights.

The revelries and entertainment varied, and the King took pleasure in every aspect, even more so when the he'd been young and vigorous so Richard had heard – and young Henry, his son, was certainly no different – with his head full of mischief and frolic.

Young Henry enjoyed immensely all the frivolity of this Christmas gathering, *in addition to the "Farter", whom he thought quite incomparable; there were also minstrels, prostitutes, dice-players, flatterers, hucksters, nubulatores, actors, barbers, buffoons, story-tellers and harpers.*

The Young King, was given pride of place along with his brothers, Richard and Geoffrey, his sons, and Henry, Duke of Saxony, and his wife, with *their* sons and daughters, and a large retinue, together with Richard, Archbishop of Canterbury, and John Cumin, Archbishop of Dublin. Now there was a family with a chequered past, who understood the twists and turns of survival in high places, Richard thought as he glanced at the Archbishop. There was in fact a host of bishops, earls, and Barons.

The Caen celebrations were intended to be a true family reunion, with only one notable absentee, Queen Eleanor. Also missing, Richard was told, were two of Henry and Eleanor's daughters, Eleanor married to Alfonso VIII of Castile and Joanna married to William II of Sicily.

As they enjoyed the revelry Richard's eye caught King Henry the elder several times – when he thought no one looking, pressing his fist to his belly, appearing to be in some discomfort. When he noticed someone looking, he would smile and pretend all was well. Kings must not be ill, they must be strong, their health was indicative of the nation's health; a weak sickly king suggested a weak sickly kingdom. Richard thought if the opportunity arose, he would mention Bernard, Sir John's chirurgien, to Henry in passing conversation, if anyone could help Henry, it was Bernard.

Chapter 10

William Marshal's shield

Confrontation

Richard was distracted from his concern for Henry, uneasy with the absence of his friend William Marshal. He was reluctant to ask where William was, but thought it strange that he was not amongst the honoured guests. William was after all a leading member of the Young King's retinue. He should have been present.

The guests gleefully watched the much-demanded encore of Roland, who was able to leap, whistle and fart all at the same time, even Esther had laughed, but Richard seemed distracted and was not amused. She touched his arm, 'Are you – troubled? Richard!' She touched him again.

'Sorry Esther, did you speak?'

'I asked if you were troubled.'

'Mmm, do you not find it strange that William is absent from the festivities?'

'You refer to William Marshal I take it?' Richard gave her a look as much to say; of whom else would I be speaking. 'I did wonder; perhaps he has business somewhere else in the empire and was unable to attend.'

'Perhaps, but I have never even heard his name mentioned, not once.'

No sooner had Richard aired his concerns than a hush spread across the assembly, the door was now standing wide open and all eyes turned to William Marshal with his cousin William de Tancarville. Once again, Richard was struck by how William appeared to actually grow in stature on such occasions, as if to demonstrate that he was in every way – larger than life. The multitude parted before him and he strode unhurriedly towards the high table and the King. Even King Henry seemed transfixed by his presence; William's face was as carved granite.

He bowed before the King, 'It is our delight to see you, Marshal, you honour us with your presence,' said King Henry, clearly, he too was unsettled by this unexpected appearance. 'Will you not join us, Sir?' King Henry asked warmly. The Young King offered no such greeting, but stared down at the table before him, sliding his forefinger and thumb uneasily up – and – down the stem of a silver goblet.

'My Liege Lord, you commissioned me with work, which, so help me God, I have endeavoured to undertake to the best of my ability. Even though I have been maligned, insulted and now, that which I hold most dear, my honour, has been questioned.'

'This is grievous indeed, Sir William. By whom have you been insulted thus?'

'Chief of all my accusers is *your* son, the Young King.' There was a ripple of muttering around the hall; Henry twisted his head slightly to face his son, glared at him, then turned once more to William Marshal.

William's fellow knights in the Young King's *mesnie* had become jealous and began to spread rumours that William was guilty both of showing contempt for the Young King's majesty and, more seriously, had engaged in an adulterous affair with his Lord's wife, the French princess Marguerite, daughter of King Louis. They also accused William of promoting his reputation as a tournament knight at the expense of his master's own considerable prowess.

The Young King feared the shame of being "Proved" a cuckold. Queen Marguerite sat silently with her head bowed in unwarranted shame, her hands clasped tightly before her. Esther felt sickened for the poor girl's embarrassment at being openly named as such before all the assembled nobles of the land. She could only be a little over twenty years old. Neither she, nor William Marshal, so much as glanced at each other. For William's part in her public shame Esther thought it unforgivable of him, in any event she didn't believe a word of the scurrilous accusations. She was furious; this was typical of all she detested about court life, the idle whispers without the slightest concern for the hurt, which was inflicted. It was all a fine distraction unless you were the one subjected to the gossip.

William's confrontation was bordering on impudence, Henry could have taken it as a challenge to him and might have done, but for his utter surprise.

William continued, 'By the measure of your *own* law of combat, I demand a trial by such a yardstick of God's righteousness and challenge the Young King that I may rightly prove my innocence.' Henry did not usually take well to people making demands of him, but in this instance, he was only able to stare. William Marshal was asking for justice and citing the law that *he*, Henry the Second, had upheld.

The Young King suddenly stood and shouted at William, 'I will *not* fight you Marshal.'

William Marshal calmly offered to fight any three of his accusers on three successive days. If any one of them defeated him, then the Young King could hang him. Still the young Henry refused. William went even further, by offering to allow them to chop off a finger on his right hand as an added handicap. Young Henry was at a loss for words, but was yet unmoved.

Esther gasped, King Henry never flinched, but he'd heard her and cast his eyes in her direction.

William Marshal then turned his attention once more to King Henry II and demanded, if he was to be treated thus, that he be given safe conduct out of the King's realms so that he could depart for places where he would be treated with greater honour and justice.

The King responded with a nod of his head, 'You may go Marshal… your honour is untarnished, you will not be hindered or harmed by any, on pain of death, *my* word on it.'

William bowed, turned, and left with supreme dignity.

A family reunion it might have been, but it was also an occasion of wealth, power, and generosity aimed at enhancing the reputation of its royal host. Unfortunately, it all ended up in a public quarrel, Young King Henry accused his father of failing to support him and thus humiliating him as always. Young Henry suddenly stood and stormed from the feast, roughly dragging his young Queen with him, upending chairs and table settings as he went.

King Henry was *incandescent* with rage. He grabbed at a bowl of fruit, and threw it violently in the direction of his son and his poor wife as they sped from the room.

'I should have let the Marshal slice up your liver you ill begotten son of rebellion, you are your dam's likeness; not any spawn of mine,' Henry shrieked at the top of his voice. His face was pulsating red, so much so Esther feared he was about to have a seizure and she grabbed Richard's arm. Those in the way were compelled to duck and dive for fear of being hit by the flying contents, or indeed the wooden vessel itself. Such was the force with which the bowl struck a tabletop it scattered the food and drink set upon it in every direction.

In a single moment the ever-present rift within the family was renewed and revitalised with even greater Plantagenet passion and would lead to a war, between the Young King and his brother Geoffrey on the one side, and Richard, Duke of Aquitaine and Henry II on the other.

Any laughter and amusement was now only a distant memory, all such merriment had ended abruptly, and the guests silently made their exit as soon as possible, Richard amongst them.

'Go to our rooms and wait for me there,' he instructed Esther. 'I will make my way quickly down to the stables to see if I can find William, and learn from him what is his intention. There might be something I can do to support him and bring some painless solution to this conflict.' Esther nodded and he hurriedly left.

He ran to the stables only to discover that William, some men-at-arms and his cousin William de Tancarville had already gone, and no one could tell him to where, or in which direction they had ridden. Richard thumped a rail on the stall in frustration. Once again, the two friends were driven by honour in differing directions. He discovered that the Young King and his retinue had left too, only moments after William Marshal.

'By Christ's beard I pray they do not come across each other on the road and one or the other is killed,' he said as he stared to the palace gates from the stable door.

Chapter 11

Betrayal

Richard hesitated and rested his forehead against the stout oak door to his apartment, then wearily turned the worn wrought-iron handle to enter, before he had set foot over the threshold Esther greeted him with, 'The King wants you to go to him without delay.'

'Ah... William has left the palace and so has the Young King,' He shrugged his shoulders in despair, merely kissed the distressed face of his wife and went to find King Henry.

When Richard found Henry, he was pacing back and forth in his stateroom. Other leading nobles were already assembled including his son the Count of Aquitaine. There was a clear mood of despondency and gloom hanging over the assembly and a reluctance to be the first to offer advice.

To a man, they turned to Richard as he entered, and there was suddenly a distinct air of expectancy on their faces, as if he might be bringing some news of hope, perhaps he knew of a change of heart by the protagonists.

'Richard, come in, come in, what news!' asked Henry.

'I have this moment come from the stables,'

'Yes, and?' the King asked impatiently.

'As much as I know Lord... your two sons and the Marshal have left the palace within a short space of time between them.' Chins dropped to chests once more, any vain optimism dashed.

'Henry will be making for his father-in-law's if I know him, and Louis will be only too pleased to hear of our troubles. So... Geoffrey has gone with him, damn their eyes. Is it too much for a father to expect some loyalty from his sons, am I not a generous lord?' He shouted thumping the table with his fist and spilling a cup of red wine, which dripped over the edge, forming a shimmering pool on the stone floor. Henry cast his eyes in its direction; Richard wondered if he saw not wine at his feet but Plantagenet blood seeping away between the flagstones of his empire.

'Indeed, you are my Liege, all here bear testimony to your generosity.' There were murmurs of agreement. Henry glanced at the faces before him; it was true that Henry was generous to those loyal to him. 'It's good to see your son the Count here Lord, he has not deserted us,' the prince bowed graciously to Richard. He was a strikingly handsome fellow Richard thought as he returned the acknowledgement.

Henry looked briefly towards his son, then back to *Sir* Richard and smiled. 'Aye, and I have always my son John's support, young as he is, he never lets me down.' Not *yet*, thought Richard, but – as sure, as eggs are eggs, he will. Richard didn't like John when he was a child and his opinion had never changed. 'Richard, I want you to make some plans to subdue this rebellion before it escalates into open war.'

'Very well my Liege,'

'Strike quickly and decisively, that's your method, and I like that fine, then we will speak again. Choose from these loyal knights before you, anyone you feel can help, these are all good fellows.' Henry now addressed those present. 'We will meet again once we have decided on a course of action, thank you gentlemen.' They acknowledged Henry with a bow as he left. Richard then bowed to the men before him, spoke to those he had fought with before, and the others left to await orders.

'Let us be seated gentlemen. Sir Godfrey, would you instruct a servant to fetch writing materials.' The group sat around the table, and Richard addressed them, after he'd offered his initial thoughts, he gestured with an open hand for the others to make their offerings. Richard had confidence in the men before him and *they* respected him, having been under his command when they defeated the Scots and the Earl of Leicester. Richard delegated each with specific duties, while a scrivener, with ink stained fingers and the smell of fusty parchment about him, made notes, he clearly spent his life riffling through piles of old documents. Sir Godfrey had gone one better than merely bringing writing materials. It was their collective opinion that young Henry would have problems with funding his venture. Henry's massive debts were common knowledge and the leaders were confident that even his supporters would be reluctant to advance him further funds. They were certain the Barons would have grave doubts that Young Henry would prevail in yet another conflict against his father, who had a proven machine of war, with any greater success than he had previously.

Over the next month it was clear that young Henry and his brother Geoffrey were intent on making war, but how he would do it was not clear.

There were some skirmishes, but young Henry was struggling to raise funds as Richard had anticipated. He was compelled to employ mercenaries; he had no national resource of manpower to draw upon. Therefore, to raise an army of any credibility, which was able to make a serious challenge to his father, was proving difficult. Whilst his father-in-law, the King of France, was happy to stir up dissension within the King of England's family, he knew he had to tread carefully so that he did not overreach himself, thus provoking King Henry to turn the might of his empire against *him*. Louis provided some funds and men, but young Henry needed more. He took the unprecedented decision to fund his rebellion, by raiding churches and stealing whatever of value he could remove.

Neither Richard nor Henry believed it when they were told that William Marshal was fighting with the Young King Henry, and that the relationship had now been restored.

Richard was yet mulling over in his mind his despondency and disbelief when he met with Esther, before she could open her mouth in greeting, he beset her with his despair.

'I cannot comprehend William's involvement in such as this Esther. His name is now linked to the pillaging of sacred places like a mere brigand, and all after that embarrassing tableau on the night of the great feast at Christmas, which was a considerable factor in creating the conflict in which we are now engaged.'

Esther frowned with equal sadness; she too was experiencing the painful disappointment and hurt, Richard was feeling. His suffering, she knew, was all the worse because it was delivered by someone he held as a model of honour and right living.

'Now there is all manner of outrage dispensed, *and* as if naught had ever been said or done, *all* is forgiven and they are master and servant once more. What of honour now, I ask you *William Marshal!* Young Henry is making a monumental mistake if he likens what he is now engaged in, as simply another tourney, *and* – if I dare say this, so is William Marshal.' Richard slumped down into a chair and threw his gauntlets so violently at the wall in frustration and disgust a chunk of lime plaster was dislodged, revealing fibres of the horsehair binding.

'Perhaps you have been misinformed Richard!' Esther said, going nervously to him.

'Dear God, I prayed so, whatever is William thinking of? When I first heard of such a thing, I discounted it as utter nonsense, but I fear from the reports it is the truth, I am quite at a loss.'

'What of the King?'

'He – is – *furious*, threatening to remove the Marshal's head if he ever gets his hands on him. He has convinced himself that the whole scene at the feast was preplanned by the Marshal to further his own ends.'

'Do you think that possible?' Esther asked in disbelief.

'I cannot believe such a thing of William; *no,* I will not accept such a thought.'

They both sat quietly, though the air was charged with energy. Eventually, Richard struck the arm of his chair so violently with his fist that Esther jumped.

'I can't sit here; I will have to go out again, the men are at this moment readying themselves for such work. I have reports that young Henry has been raiding churches near Limousin. We are scouring the countryside looking for him and his bands of mercenary thieves. As we speak, the King himself is employed at such work.'

'No, surely it is too dangerous for the King to traverse the countryside searching for bands of armed men. He must be constantly open to ambush or being overcome by unexpected numbers.'

'I am afraid it is so, but I for one – am not going to tell him of what he is already aware, he's not in any mood for hearing the obvious stated. Esther, I am sick to my stomach to think *he* whom I hold in such esteem is even mentioned in the same breath as this shame.'

Esther reached to the floor for his gauntlets and passed them to him, and kissed him.

'Take care Richard, you have not eaten or drunk.'

'I have no stomach for such, Walter will have seen to it that I have supplies in my saddle bags, I will be right enough.'

'Do not let your troubled heart distract you, if you meet with the enemy.'

'What if I meet with William, what then will honour demand, will I kill him, or let him kill me?' he sighed, glanced once more at her, spun on his heels and left; he didn't even take time to close the door. Esther was distraught and confused, what a wicked predicament.

'Fear not my Lady, our Lord be a great warrior,' Margaret said trying to offer a crumb of comfort to Esther.

Richard and fifty men-at-arms and knights were riding at some pace towards Limousin. He had sent scouts ahead.

Lifting his arm, he signalled his troop to come to a standstill. He tried to make sense of the dust ahead of them. The horses milled around eager to be on their way.

'Horses coming, can you see them Sir Hugh?'

'Aye, it's only a small number, it may be our scouts,' he said standing in his stirrups and lifting his hand to shade his eyes from the sun.

Richard shouted to his men to be ready, 'Present your arms!' Sir Hugh was right; it was two of their scouts hurtling at speed towards them. They galloped up to Richard and drew their horses sharply to a standstill by his side.

'What news for us?' demanded Richard, the energized mounts of the two scouts danced excitedly, turning around and round. 'Hell's teeth – bring those animals under control. I can't hear a word you say, concentrate on what you're doing,' Richard said greatly agitated.

'Forgive me Lord, grim news,' Sir Roland gasped, out of breath, he tugged harshly on his reins once more; he had ridden with such haste his mount could not settle.

'Tell me the worst of it then, before I dispatch that damned horse you are sat upon!'

'The Young King is *dead,* Lord.'

'What nonsense is this you present me with?'

'It be the truth Lord, he died in the arms of the Marshal by all accounts.' Richard was dumfounded.

'Died, died of what?'

'While pillaging some local monasteries, Henry contracted dysentery, so we were told. He was taken to Martel near Limoges. They were certain he was dying. A priest was fetched, once he'd confessed and received the last rites, as a token of his penitence for his rebellion against his father, he prostrated himself naked on the floor before a crucifix. He made a testament, and since he had taken a crusader's vow, he gave his cloak with its red cross stitched upon it, to his mentor, the Marshal. Begging him to fulfil his vow to go on crusade and lay the garment upon the tomb of the Saviour.'

'And do you know the Marshal's response?'

'It is said he vowed to do as the Young King begged, so that he might go to his Maker in peace.'

'Ahhh, William, William… How in God's name will we tell the King of this?' Richard said to no one in particular.

'We were given to understand that the King *already* knows, Lord. A message was sent to him as soon as it was understood that the Young King was dying. On his deathbed, it was reported that he asked to be reconciled with his father but, King Henry, fearing a trap, refused to go to him. The Young King died this morning, a date to remember – or forget.

'What day is it?' asked Richard, 'I barely know what year it is my head is so addled at this moment.'

'The 11th of June, Lord,' answered the scout.

'Aye – of course, Saint Barnabas' day, the one we invoke as a peacemaker, I pray he fulfils his calling this day. I will light a candle to that end when we return.'

'The Young King died, we were told, clasping his father's ring. On refusing to go himself the King had sent his ring as a sign of his forgiveness.'

'Where is the King now, do you know?'

'He's with his court in Caen, in a pitiful state by all accounts.'

'Dear Mother of Christ, I imagine he is. Have you heard this news?' Richard shouted to his men, 'the

Young King is dead, God rest his soul.' There was a sudden hush amongst the men followed by murmurs of disbelief. 'What of his men?' Richard then asked his scout.

'They have all dispersed and are on the rampage; no doubt hoping to make some gain, for they are without any reward.'

'Aye, getting coin from Henry was ever a challenge when he lived; it will be the Devil's own work getting it from him now he is dead. Come, we must make our way home. Be watchful for trouble as we ride.'

Chapter 12

Forgiven

Richard and his troop rode into the palace at Caen wondering with what he would be faced. He slowly dismounted; his warm saddle creaked as he transferred his weight on to one stirrup then down onto the ground.

'See to the horses and men, Sir Hugh, and then go to the hall where there will be mete and drink. I will leave you and go to find my Lady and my sons.'

'Very good, Lord,' he said and bowed his head.

Richard went to his room, but Esther wasn't there, Walter told him that Lady Esther had gone to the orchard with her sons. 'Help me disrobe from my hauberk Walter.'

'Do you want to bathe Lord?'

'Not now, I want to see my wife, later perhaps. Have you heard about the Young King?'

'Yes, the King is in the chapel, in prayer, so I have heard. He went straight there when the hellish news broke two hours passed.'

'How was he do you know?'

'I didn't see him, but I heard he was very quiet, he spoke to no one.'

'Does Lady Esther know?'

'Yes Lord, as soon as she was told she collected your sons from the nurse and they went to pick some cherries. She'd heard they were abundant and ripe. I think that she wanted some time alone with the two Lords.'

'Thank you, Walter, I will be there if I am needed.'

Esther looked up when she saw Richard come through the gate and smiled. He lifted his hand in greeting and his two boys ran to him.

'Papa,' shouted William and leaped into his arms followed by Jacob who stumbled before reaching Richard and lay on his tummy holding his muddy hands before him. Richard stepped to him and swept him into his arms kissing them both and tightening his hold on them.

'Esther.'

'Richard, I'm glad you are home. I wanted some time alone with our boys, suddenly the pain of losing our William haunted me and I needed to be with our children. I imagine parents all have a mixture of feelings, sorrow for another who is suffering the loss and fearful for their own. Most families lose children but I don't think the pain is one a mother will ever get used to.'

'Nor a father, I am hurting for Henry. By all that is rational, Henry should be rejoicing at this moment that a rebellious wilful son has his just reward. However, love is a contrary master, contrary to all logic and parents are subject to its powers above all else. As children, we do not understand, but we get our turn, God willing. I remember Sir John saying to me that perhaps our wilfulness as children helps us to be more understanding as parents.'

'Will you go to Henry he will need a friend? Queen Eleanor should be with him at this time, he must wonder what it is all about as he waits before God.' Richard lowered his two boys to the ground and sat on the grass against a fence with his sons on his lap. Esther sat next to him and wrapped his arm around her.

'Aye, I will go and see Henry, though I don't know what cheer *I* can bring him.'

Richard found Henry on his knees in his private chapel, and knelt quietly some distance from him. He knew Henry was aware of his presence, but Henry continued with his devotions. From where Richard knelt, he could see the rosary beads passing rhythmically through Henry's fingers. Eventually Henry crossed himself and wearily rose to his feet, genuflected, and came to Richard, who stood and bowed.

'Thank you, Richard, for coming, this is devilish,' Henry said gripping Richard's shoulder.

'Aye, Lord, devilish indeed.'

'He wants to be laid to rest at Rouen – so I have been told. It is my wish for you to go to him, and ensure he is treated with all respect; will you do that for me? It will be dangerous I know that fine well, he has caused much uproar, his mercenaries will be in no mood for the concerns of a grieving father, they have hungry purses to feed. However, he is my son and an anointed King. I want his entrails buried at the Abbey of Charroux and the rest of his body to be laid in Rouen as was his wish.'

'Of course, as you desire, I will go on the first light. Too dark for travel now.'

Chapter 13

Young King Henry

Restoration

Richard set off with a dozen men before first light as he'd promised. He was uneasy, he didn't know with what they would be faced, and was not looking forward to meeting William Marshal. He knew that it would be awkward, it could mean the end of a special friendship, and that was pitiful to him. The small troop rode in silence through the French countryside, the jingling of their harnesses, the creak of leather and the rhythmic pounding of hooves on grassy lanes was all that could be heard. Villages were slowly coming to life in the burgeoning new day. The fragrances of differing blossom floated on the air, released from the dew by the warmth of the early morning sun. There was the odd stirring of roosters bringing the farmyards of outlying villages to life as they galloped through, but no more, it was early yet.

It took three days hard riding to get to Martel where the Young King's body was reported to be. The place was in disarray when they arrived. Henry's mercenaries had ransacked his residence for anything of value. There was furniture, clothing, and household belongings strewn all over, and the bodies of murdered townspeople lay in the streets. Places of trade had been looted too. It was clear that those who lived there were afraid to venture far from their own doorsteps.

Richard slowed his troop to a walk, they were fully armoured, with their shields raised and swords drawn. Eyes were everywhere, but they saw no one, *until* Richard glimpsed from the corner of his eye the feet of a small figure lying in the shadow of a stone horse trough. He pretended not to notice as he rode past, and then suddenly leapt from Ares and grabbed the boy, who wriggled and kicked for all he was worth. Richard held him fast. He was but nine or ten and with no more flesh on him than an arrow shaft.

'Calm yourself, I will not hurt you, I only want to know where the dead King lies, here, a silver coin for your help.' Richard held him fast with one arm, reached into his purse, and produced a shiny silver Angevin penny with the head of King Henry the Second upon it. The boy ceased his struggles and stared for a moment at the coin, he had never seen one before, never mind owned one. He dragged one of his arms free from Richard's hold, and pointed to a church.

'He be in there Master; I will show you. I have seen him.' He suddenly drew his neck into his shoulders thinking he'd said too much and would get a swipe for the impertinence of such as him daring to look upon the dead king.

On the contrary, the knight praised him. 'You're a bright young fellow, would you walk with me and tell me what has been going on here.' The boy narrowed his eyes and stared at Richard then held out his free hand, Richard smiled and pressed the silver coin into the grubby upturned palm. The boy took it, bit it, and then smiled.

Richard set him to the ground and crouched down onto his hunkers, placing his arm kindly around the boy's shoulders. 'A trusting ragamuffin aren't you! Do I look like the sort of fellow who would cheat a fine young man such as yourself?' the boy smiled. 'Come walk with me,' Richard said standing.

Richard passed the rein of his horse to a soldier and strolled along the street with the boy, who now chatted freely with this new friend. He told Richard of the terror in the town.

'Have you seen a tall knight much like me?' Richard asked.

The boy thought for a while, 'they was all big to me Lord, but there was one a giant of a man, aye like you, he's in church, with the King, I's seen him.'

'What's your name?'

The boy hesitated, 'Pierre, Lord.'

'Well Pierre, if you have any more threats or fears, seek me out, I will be here for a day or two with my men. Speak to any wearing this livery,' Richard pointed to his chest, 'they will tell me and I will see that you are safe. Where are your mother and father?'

'I only have a father, Lord; me mother died the year just gone. Me father was beaten for no reason three days past, by some soldiers who were drunk. He's laid up, but getting better.' Richard reached into his purse once more and drew out another three pennies, took the boys hand

and gave them to him. The boy was astonished… 'You's not a soldier, you's a Saint, Lord.'

'Not quite,' Richard laughed. The boy bowed and ran off yet staring at his hand.

'Wait here, keep a keen eye on what's about you, I will go into the church on my own,' Richard said to his mounted knights, and went up the steps into the church, dipping his fingers in the holy water at the door, crossing himself, and then genuflecting. He immediately saw William Marshal standing by the body with three other knights, obviously watching over the dead King. William turned to the sound of the church door; saw Richard, nodded to him as if he'd been waiting for him, and Richard went to his side.

With a movement of his head, William indicated that they take a seat nearby, which they did. Richard noted that William now wore a white surcoat with its red cross stitched upon it, signifying he was a soldier of the cross, a crusader. William noticed Richard glance at the emblem, but neither made any comment.

William did not speak for some time; Richard sensed that he was assembling his thoughts to say something, which was of great importance to him, and Richard was of a mind to wait.

'We are once more on opposing sides, Richard.'

'It seems so. I cannot pretend that I am not confused and cheerless after all that happened on the feast of our Saviour's nativity.'

'I left the feast wounded and dishonoured. I had not been long gone when I heard horses galloping after me. We of our small group turned to face whatever pursued us, expecting that we were to be overwhelmed and slain. I cared little at that moment what became of me, for I felt so low in spirit. As the riders neared, I saw it was the Young

King, my *sworn* Lord and I still bound by honour. He'd chosen not to fight me at that feast in the great hall when I demanded what was my right, then by law we would have been equals before God. Though we were both shamed, he remained my Lord. Having come upon us, he drew near, stopping fifty paces from us and shouted, asking if I yet did honour him as my sworn Lord. I said I was honour bound to him, he nodded then apologised for any slur he had brought upon my name and honour and begged that I stand by my fealty to him. I told him I could do no other. Never have those words been more difficult to spit from my lips, for I detested the man and all for which he stood. I knew he was not sincere in his forgiveness; the words were but words of convenience that dripped as easily as honey from his tongue, and they sickened me. Then there were other words from the Eternal Liar, which slipped into my mind with the cunning of a snake. "You need not hold fast to your honour to this man he is not worthy of you, you will be named amongst the dishonourable like he", and by the grace of Him who resisted such temptation in his own wilderness where such whisperings ever dwell, I too stood firm to my honour.' William hung his head; Richard could see that even the recollection of the moment clearly brought him great anguish; it was some time before he could continue. All the while Richard was seated in silence until William had settled himself and carried on. 'Henry was merely in need of my experience; I knew such and yet I was bound to him. If he thought he had me for some country fool, he was sorely mistaken. He polluted and tarnished all I hold dear and at that moment, I had a choice to be like him and reject the demands of honour, which I had made to him on the request of his father, or stand by it. I was driven by my honour, which I will live by and by the grace of God, die by.'

Richard now stared at the crucifix on the wooden screen above him. Hanging before him was a man in agony, with nail-pierced hands and feet; He was tortured, rejected, beaten judged less worthy than a common criminal because He placed submission and service before His own well-being and it had cost Him His life. Richard looked down now and felt ashamed that he had doubted his friend and what's more, he'd judged him harshly. All he knew of him he'd discounted, and had rejected him.

'You *shame* me William, for I have failed the bond of *friendship*. I judged you when I should have unconditionally supported you.'

'Aye, well let me not be guilty of judging *you*. I will do all honour demands and take the King to Rouen and will be glad of your support if you feel able to give it. There are a few mercenary knights yet with us, some of whom you see standing here,' he gestured with his hand to the three knights, 'but we are without coin we will be beggars as we go.'

'I will be honoured to ride with you, if you will have me, William. Do you know ought of Prince Geoffrey?'

'He has disappeared, gone with his friend Prince Philip of France; the pair are as thick as thieves, they have an unhealthy friendship in my eyes, what a family Henry has brought into the light of day.'

Young Henry's body was taken to Le Mans. The knights accompanying his corpse were so penniless; they had to be fed by the charity of the monastery at Vigeois. Richard had used what coin he had, but it was insufficient for their number.

There were large and emotional gatherings wherever the Young King's body rested.

At Le Mans, the local Bishop halted the procession and ordered the body buried in his cathedral, perhaps to help defuse the civil unrest Henry's death had caused. The Dean of Rouen recovered the body from the chapter of Le Mans a month later by lawsuit, so the Young Henry could be buried in Normandy, as he had desired in his testament.

Richard presented William Marshal to King Henry who was hostile to him at first, until Richard told William's story.

King Henry listened out of his respect for Richard, understood, and was touched, appreciating the loyalty that William had demonstrated to his son. Richard knew how highly Henry respected those around him who set honour above personal advantage. He not only agreed to permit William to go on crusade, but also offered him a place in his household on his return. He took two of William's warhorses as a pledge for his return, and gave him one hundred pounds of Angevin coin to cover his travel expenses.

Chapter 14

Parting of Friends

William Marshal was faithful to his promise, that *he* would honour the vow which – Young King Henry – *had made,* before he became ill, to go on crusade.

Richard had tried to dissuade William from going, arguing that a vow made by Henry could in no way be fulfil by someone else, but William had given his word and that was all there was to it.

'You are a fool William, but a fool I love and this world might be a better place with more fools such as you,' William laughed and slapped Richard's back.

'I hear the pot calling the kettle black my friend.'

'You are *both* beyond hope,' Esther added.

They embraced; William kissed Esther, mounted his eager horse signalling to his men to do likewise and set off with a final wave. Richard stood with Esther and watched him, until all that was to be seen was a small cloud of dust in the distance.

'We will pray for him Richard, he is a man who forever carries the weight of greatness upon his shoulders, he will return, of that I am certain.'

Richard lost contact with William whilst he was in the Holy Land he simply disappeared from sight. He'd heard boasts that the Marshal had done more in two years than most had done in seven. There was the odd passing conversation over the months, which perhaps had their beginnings in tales from returning knights. All made it known how William had demonstrated to both enemy and fellow knight that he was worthy of his reputation. It seemed with whatever he was faced; his honour, dignity, wisdom, and generosity never wavered.

Though Richard held William in the highest regard, he listened to the tales of his achievements with a pinch of salt. People would always need a hero like the Marshal who was all they aspired to be, a brilliant light in which lesser mortals would hope to bathe. Richard knew that great deeds would begat even greater deeds as the tales were told and retold, but it was all hearsay, he'd had no correspondence; sent to him or the King, as far as he knew. There was even a rumour that William had joined the Templars a very strict religious order of holy knights. Richard could see how that would fit with William's understanding of the way of life, but he also knew William was ambitious for position and rank. He was left nothing by his father, if that rankled, he never complained, and poverty, once tasted; left a sour tang in the mouth. He had a keen eye for advancement, but honour first, always honour first. He was no monk either; aye Richard knew that fine well, and gave a wry smile, the tourney was no place for monks.

Richard did pray for him, as Esther had said, many died following the cause of the cross and mostly from disease not deeds of heroism. *What* was it all for he asked himself, was this really the way of Christ whose unerring message was to *love* and more than that – love one's enemies, a quality which seemed most noticeable for its absence in all the crusades of which he'd heard tell.

He missed his friend, but for now – he and his family were allowed to return to their estates in England, that was his future and he needed to set his mind to the work ahead.

Richard was at *last* leaving behind all the politics, intrigue and half-truths, which was the court of King Henry and sailing home. He was at this minute standing with Esther on the deck of the Saint Nicholas; clearly, this ship owner was taking all precautions with his ship's well-being, by naming it after the patron saint of sailors. Richard's thoughts were full of what was ahead, both what needed to be done and what he wanted to be done. He was ambitious too; he had risen from poverty, in much the same way as his friend William Marshal, and like his friend, he wanted more for his family than merely the scrapings left behind by others. He had worked hard and Henry had rewarded him, it was for him to make the most of whatever God *and* Henry sent his way.

Since the crossing with King Henry from Wales to Ireland on that stormy night in autumn, when they went to stamp Henry's rule on the rebel Normans, Strongbow de Clare and the like, neither Richard, nor Esther were ever eager to step from dry land unless under duress. However, this short Channel crossing was endeavouring to rekindle their love of the sea, it was warm and the sea was calm.

The weather this day was much the same as it had been when Richard journeyed on his way home from the world of tourneys those many years past.

Both he and Esther leaned on their elbows against the gunwale and stared out to sea. They laughed and talked, thrilled to be going home, their two boys played hide and seek between the barrels, coiled ropes and stores, which were stacked on the deck.

Richard casually turned from watching the silent blue water pass by, and now leaned with his *back* against the gunwale, looked up narrowed his eyes and stared through the rigging into the blue sky above, much as he had that day long ago. Then he lowered his eyes and gazed to the far side of the ship. He was suddenly caught unawares, the past unexpectedly flashed into his eyes, and the smile fell from his face, Esther looked at him out of the side of her eye as she turned to face the same way as he.

'You are serious now, my Lord!' He only gave a slight flick of his head in acknowledgement of having heard her.

Richard was in another time, the summer of 1170, sixteen years past. Much water had travelled under the bridge since that day, but he felt the pain as keenly as ever as he gazed across the deck to the gunwale on the other side. His throat closed, his heart pounded against his chest and he could barely breathe. This was more-or-less, the same position in which he had been standing that day, be it on another ship. He could see her as plain as if she was there before his eyes. There were no sounds; all was quiet, as if in reverence for his precious memory. Her eyes caught his and smiled at him – he would never forget that glance – as long as he lived. He shook his head, that's not how it had been that day, she had been furious that he had seen her looking at him and then she exploded at her brother for losing her precious emerald. Slowly, he realised… it was not Julianne's eyes he now saw, but that of her son, their son, William, but he could only see her eyes smiling at him. He had to blink several times before he could bring himself back from that day, it was as if the past had gripped him and held him fast for those brief few moments, in those perfect eyes. "Dear Mother of God" he thought, "How can the pain be so keen after all these years!"

Esther touched the tear on his cheek and it soaked into her kid glove. She wrapped her arm around his and drew close laying her head against his shoulder.

'Are you all right Richard?'

'Aye… yes, fine, the sun is bright in my eyes, no more.'

'Mmm…' she accepted his answer at face value. 'Do you think that it's safe for the boys playing like that amongst the cargo on deck?'

'I suspect not, though Margaret is with them, but we will be in Dover soon so I will round them up.'

'What will our new baby be, do you think?' Esther was again with child.

'A boy most like, but I would choose a girl if the choice was mine. Fathers need daughters to love them when they grow old and warrior sons to protect them.' He looked at her and smiled into her eyes.

'Will your wife not love you when you get old?'

'Ah… yes, *my* wife… perhaps by then she will see what a poor bargain she has made and wish for another.'

'Yes, that is true…' she laughed and he twisted towards her, lifting her from her feet and kissing her, she eagerly pressed her lips to his, there was never a moment when she did not wish to be in his arms. He felt a tugging at the knee of his breeches.

'Put Mama down Papa, you might hurt her,' Jacob shouted up at him and Richard smiled and set her once more to the deck. He quickly grabbed Jacob and threw him high into the air, he giggled and twisted as he fell into Richard's arms. 'Again Papa, again.'

'*NO!*' Esther shouted.

Richard pulled a sad face at Jacob, pressed his nose to his, and whispered in a fearful voice, 'your mama has spoken, Jacob, and we all must obey her.'

'But it is you who are Lord Papa!'

'No, your Mama only lets me believe I'm the Lord, Richard said smiling at Esther.'

'Ha, don't you believe him my son.' Jacob now looked utterly confused.

'Where's your brother William?' Richard asked smiling.

'He's hiding and I'm "It" and have to find him, but I'm tired.'

'Come we will find him together, for we will soon be in Dover and you must both stay by my side, do *you* promise?'

'Yes, Papa.'

'Good boy, now let's find William.'

Chapter 15

Geoffrey Plantagenet

That night they stayed in Dover Castle. They knew Richard; he was one of Henry's counsellors and generals and as such, was treated with great deference. He had servants, knights, and men-at-arms with him, so the Castle suited him well. They would continue on to Aylesford on the morrow's first light and, God willing should be there before nightfall.

It was a great relief to step down onto their own courtyard, and be welcomed by Tristram and Alwin. Alwin only bowed, but Tristram hugged Richard and kissed Esther.

'Welcome home, are you all well?' Tristram asked now holding the two boys one on each arm. Of course, they loved Tristram, all did, he was an easy man to love.

Esther was distracted for a second as Tristram set down the boys and reached up to lift Margaret from her horse, there was a moment of eye contact that intrigued her.

'Indeed, we are happy to be home there have been many difficult days. No doubt you heard of the Young King's death?' Richard asked.

'Indeed, we have, there is talk of him being canonized no less,' said Tristram, Richard drew back his head and narrowed his eyes in disbelief. 'It is reported many were healed at the sight of his funeral cortège.' All the while Tristram talked, he stood with his arm on the shoulder of Margaret, the boys having run off on hearing there was a new litter of puppies in the stable. Richard never appeared to pay the slightest heed to this.

'If there were miracles, I never saw any and I was part of that rite of passage. I saw a few angry French merchants and Flemish mercenaries clamouring to be paid for the debts he'd accrued, and some monks demanding retribution for the theft from their abbeys. It was indeed miraculous that we were not murdered on his behalf, but *no* such miracles the like of which you speak,' they both smiled.

'No… are you sure we are talking of the same sinless man, surely not? By what I hear, the man is a saint, I'm sure that our beloved King will be seeking your confirmation of the miraculous wonders as a reliable witness. That exchange will be worth the seeing, when a man of high honour is faced with the dilemma as such an inquiry may present.'

'Thank you, I am so pleased to see you Tristram, you forever place a fellow at his ease…' and they all laughed.

The estate was in fine order; Richard and Esther could see that as they rode around the villages.

'It is essential that we make ourselves known to our people Esther, but this is the last time you will ride until you are delivered, you would not be doing this now if it were not of the utmost importance.'

'I'm fine, we are making a gentle pace and will soon be home.' Once home, Richard lowered Esther from her saddle and smiled, 'go now I will attend to the horses.' Esther left him and Richard spent a moment with the two boys who'd rushed from the stables.

Richard crouched down and talked to the boys, he laughed with them for a while then stood, ruffled the hair of one of the boys, and bade them see to the horses. Glancing up he saw Esther waiting, nodded and followed her to their rooms.

Over the following two years whilst William Marshal was on crusade, life assumed what could be called a sedentary pace for Richard and Esther. Even the birth of their new son, Marshal, whom they named in honour of their absent friend, was an uneventful occasion. It was a rare time to have with his two sons. He enjoyed them more than ever now that they were able to do things with him.

Richard stepped from the keep in good spirits; he was on his way to the blacksmith's shop when he saw Alwin making for him with some haste.

'Good news by the look on your face Alwin.'

'This came for you from The Marshal, the rider told me the news,' Alwin passed him the parchment.

'The Marshal you say, he must be home, he's not hurt, is he?'

'Not to my knowledge, Lord.'

Richard broke the seal, unfolded the parchment, and quickly cast his eye down the page. 'Ah… by Christ's beard, do you know the contents of this, Alwin?'

'Just what the rider told me, Lord.'

'Well, you know that Prince Geoffrey's dead!'

'Aye, I know that much.'

'He died in Paris; there seems some doubt about his death. Come let us go inside and make this known to Tristram and Esther.' They walked in silence back to the keep bumping into Tristram on the way. 'Come with us Tristram, do you know the news?'

'Aye, I was there when the rider came, I have been looking for you, Alwin found you first I see.'

Esther was in deep conversation with Margaret when they entered. 'My… Margaret, we are to be honoured by the presence of three handsome gentlemen.'

'I fear this is no honour we bring but ill news.' Richard seated himself at the table unfolded and straightened the parchment with the heel of his hand. 'The good news is that clearly my friend William Marshal has returned, by the very presence of this letter, and I pray in good health,' He then returned his attention to the document and they all listened in silence.

Dear Friend,

'It is with regret that I am the bearer of such ill tidings; Prince Geoffrey is dead.

Firstly, there is evidence to suggest that Prince Geoffrey was planning another rebellion with Philip's help during his final period in Paris, in the summer.

As a participant in so many rebellions against his father, Geoffrey has acquired a reputation for treachery…'

Richard knew what was said of Geoffrey. "He had more aloes than honey in him; his tongue was smoother than oil; his sweet and persuasive eloquence has enabled him to dissolve the firmest alliances and by his powers of language able to corrupt two kingdoms; of tireless endeavour, a hypocrite in everything, a deceiver and a dissembler."

'... Geoffrey died on the 19th of August this year of 1186, at the age of twenty-seven, in Paris. There is also evidence that supports a death date of the 21st of August. We are presented with two alternative accounts of his death. The more common first version holds that he was trampled to death in a jousting tournament.

At his funeral, a grief-stricken Philip was said to have attempted jumping into the coffin...'

Richard paused and glanced at the faces before him, but said naught, they all knew of the talk of his relationship with Philip.

Richard read on.

'... In the second version of Geoffrey's death, it was said he died of sudden acute chest pain, which reportedly struck immediately after his speech to Philip, boasting of his intention to lay Normandy to waste. Possibly, this version was an invention of its chronicler, sudden illness being God's judgement of an ungrateful son plotting rebellion against his father, and for such wickedness as he perpetrated against our Mother Church. Alternatively, the tournament story may be an invention of Philip's to prevent Henry II's discovery of a plot; inventing a social reason, a tournament, for Geoffrey's being in Paris, Philip attempting to obscure their meeting's true purpose.

Whatever the truth of it and as you can see there are many "Truths", the young Prince is now dead. You will comprehend from this that I have now returned from my crusade and hope that we will meet again soon for I have much more news to impart, which due to the tenor of this missive it is not appropriate for me to convey on this occasion.

May He who is able to do far more than we think or ask bless and keep you all.

William Marshal.'

'I hope William was careful with his choice of scriviner for he says things here that would be better not recorded.'

'But such as this he would have surely written himself,' responded Esther.

'Dear Esther, William has been a warrior since a boy, he can neither read nor write, his skills are for a greater purpose than merely daubing inky marks on parchment. One can always find someone without a brain to call their own, who can read and write, and God bless them for their menial ability, but the skills William Marshal has, are not so easily found.'

'What now, Richard?' asked Tristram.

'Who knows, Henry will send for me if I'm needed. Poor fellow, he will be distraught if he believes that Geoffrey was planning to betray him once more. His sons die one by one, God spare us if we are left with the runt of the litter. Then we will know what Hell has to serve for a daily offering, a person with fewer scruples and totally without honour I have never known. He is as slippery as an eel, and as deadly as a viper, one that dwells in the darker places of this world, a true revenant of the night. God in his mercy spare us from that outcome.' There was an uneasy silence in the room.

'There is a postscript, William writes of his concern for the King's health. He begs that we remember him in our prayers. I am sure that we will all do this, and in addition I will fund the monks at the monastery next to us, to say daily prayers for him with greater vigour.'

Chapter 16

Leaving

Richard and William Marshal sat on the riverbank of the Medway, idly throwing pebbles into the slow flowing water.

'A fine water course you have here Richard.'

'Aye, it keeps us supplied with fresh fish.'

'Spring, my favourite season Richard, a time of new life, fresh pastures and hope, yes hope. I always feel hopeful at this time of the year.'

'You have much to be hopeful about my friend; you are now a man of property. The King has been generous giving you the ward-ship of John of Earley.'

'Aye, there are some fine lands in Somerset and Berkshire.'

'How old is he?'

'Fourteen and a decent lad by all account, same age as your boy William.'

'And the custody of Helois of Lancaster, a royal ward and heiress to the Barony of Kendal in Lancashire and Westmoreland.' William threw a stick into the water and watched it drift off, his hound Bari leapt from the bank to retrieve it, there was such a splash as he hit the water it drenched both Richard and William.

'Saints preserve us, where did you get that donkey, in fact I've seen smaller donkeys, he's feral, more wolf than dog?' William laughed, 'you can laugh, by the amount of food he consumes, that he is your dog can be in no doubt, old "Guzzle guts",' Richard pushed William and he rolled over laughing even more.

William lay back on the sward yet laughing, 'I was naught but a growing lad when I was given that nom de plume, I needed lots of food and sleep.'

'Aye, so I heard,' Richard laughed and threw his coif at him.

'Anyway, on my way home from my crusade Bari – befriended me. We landed in Bari in Italy, hence his name, we'd sailed from northern Greece, and he was sat on the quay as if he was waiting for me. We unloaded our horses, I did no more than pat his head, mounted my horse, set off and he ran alongside me and has done ever since.' Bari had retrieved the stick and set it at William's feet, and was now sitting panting, eager for more attention from his master, his alert eyes fixed on William's every teasing twitch. Richard and William were distracted from Bari, with the employment of continually flicking the midges from their faces; the cloud of torment was growing denser by the second.

'The little beasts are out early this year, it must be the warm day, come let us ride home, we can ride slowly and talk as we go,' suggested Richard.

Their horses were contentedly eating the new shoots of grass and seemed reluctant to move off.

'Tell me of your travels, William,' Richard asked once they were on the move.

'It's a hellhole; you complained of the flies at the water, believe me that was nothing like the monsters out there. Sometimes we had to bind the eyes of our mounts to give the poor beasts a little relief from the torment. The heat is relentless, the wells were often poisoned, and we were continually thirsty. My head felt like a coney in a cooking pot when I had my helm on. Some fine horses though, a touch light for our needs, but nimble and fast, and the women were much the same.' They both laughed.

'But no wife yet?' Richard turned to him; William continued to look straight ahead.

'No – not yet and the years keep slipping away, I'm forty-ish now, where's the time gone Richard? You are a lucky fellow to have a wife like Esther.'

'Aye, and I know it. What were all the rumours, I heard tales of you joining the Templars?' William looked surprised.

'You heard about that!' William ducked his head under a branch and the sound startled his horse, he steadied it without thought.

'There was some talk,' Richard answered, tightening his own rein as his horse reacted to William's sudden movement.

William hesitated before he went on, 'they are noble men of honour; you would like them. I bought two lengths of silk from a source they recommended in which to be buried.'

Richard looked surprised and drew his horse to a sudden standstill. William rode on, realising Richard had stopped he turned back to him. 'Forgive me William, but I have never even thought of such a thing, that was very forward thinking of you.'

'You should think on it, in our line of work death is a constant companion, but that aside I swore to join them before I died.'

'But are they not celibate? That might limit your value on the marriage market…'

'Well… I'll cross that bridge when I come to it,' he smiled at Richard and they both laughed, and rode a little way in quiet.

'What of the King, William?'

'Ah, the King,' he squeezed his eyes together, pulled a face and rocked his head from side to side, unsure how to paint the picture. 'You would hardly recognise him; I was shocked when I saw him. In the two years I've been gone he has become a shadow of his former self.' Richard frowned. 'He was always full of energy, famed for it. I have heard, but don't repeat it, he is often physically sick, passing blood and suffers much pain, here,' William pressed his fist to his middle just below his ribcage. 'His temper was never the most sanguine, but it is far worse now. If you gave him King Philip's head on a plate, he'd probably bite yours off, and he often seems slow of thought. What can I say, he lives under constant pressure and most of it comes from his own brood.'

'So, it's no better, with his family, now it's smaller?'

'No, worse, Richard is spending much of his time with Philip and Henry fears that will result in trouble, and I can't blame him, they all want him gone. Which is one of the reasons I'm here,' he once more stared into the distance; he had been avoiding the moment. 'Yes, to visit my new lands and see you, but he wants you with him and with men. He expects us to return together, with an army of sorts. I may be wrong, but I detected an unwillingness to prop up an ailing king against his son who will soon be the next king, and whom may not take kindly to those who supported his father against him.'

Richard looked thoughtful, 'Ahhh, and so history repeats itself, as you know, my father supported King Stephen, and was made to suffer for it by King Henry. Now I may well be honour bound to support the losing side and reap the same reward. Esther's not going to be pleased with such news, she won't be able to come, it could be dangerous and *Marshal* is too small to travel all that way.'

'That was kind of you to name your new progeny after me, I am flattered,' William said hoping to distract Richard from his despondent thoughts.

'Aye... I will take William with me, he's fourteen now. A favour of you!' William looked at Richard wondering what he was about to ask. 'Would you take him under your wing as your squire?'

'Glad to; I am honoured that you would ask me. He will be good company for young John Earley.' Richard was struggling for conversation now and relieved that his castle was in sight. William could see his furrowed brow and was content to be quiet; he knew that leaving Esther and his sons would not be received well.

William was correct in his assumption; he never made any mention of the underlying reason for his visit throughout the rest of the afternoon or during the evening's meal, but he could see Esther was suspicious.

Whenever Richard had something important on his mind, he had the unerring sense that Esther already knew. It was as if she could see into his thoughts, it was most disturbing.

That night in bed he twisted from side to side, the more he reached for sleep the harder it was to grasp hold of it.

Eventually he raised himself on his pillow, Esther never moved, though he knew fine well she was not asleep.

'William has brought news from the King,' Esther still never moved, but now even her breathing stilled.

'And!' He could feel her stiffen.

'He wants me to go to Le Mans with an army.'

'Can William not do this?'

'He wants William there too.'

'Will you be gone long?'

'I can't rightly say, Prince Richard and the now *King* Philip, or his son Louis, probably all of them, are intent on destroying King Henry. Come here my little mouse,' he said and he turned Esther and took her in his arms. 'I will leave Tristram with you, he will take good care of you all.'

'You will be a stranger to Marshal!'

'I pray that I'll not be gone for too long,' he tried to smile.

'I fancy this will be for longer than we have ever been apart before,' Esther said despondently. He kissed her and she responded eagerly, to the brief moments release from her fears.

It took a month or more before Richard and William Marshal had assembled their troops, stores, arms, and the shipping required to transport them. They had sent riders to Henry's fleet at Portsmouth with letters, instructing that there be suitable ships sent to take three thousand men, two hundred horses and supplies to France, and that they were to be met at Dover on May the 29th. They knew that the numbers were not enough, but it was the best they could do under such constraints of time.

Assembling the army took longer than Richard wanted, but the time passed all too quickly for Esther. The preparation was sufficiently protracted for her to be sure that she was with child. It was a tense moment when she made it known to him, he was delighted of course, but was ever conscious that he would most likely not be here when the child was born, and it would have to be faced by Esther alone. She was stalwart as she would be, but he knew her fears, he doubted she would ever forget their first child, who was stillborn, hellish days they were too, he thought.

The morning of their parting had been a tortuous affair. They clung to each other, neither trusting themselves to speak, for fear of burdening the other and making their parting more difficult than it already was. They released each other; Richard now held her at arm's length and smiled.

'Do not fret yourself for my safety dear Lady for I now have this fine young man to protect me, thanks be to God,' and he playfully punched his son's arm.

'Come, Father, let us be on our way,' William was impatient to begin his adventure.

'Less haste, often brings with it greater speed, my son. Your backside will not be so eager to be on that saddle in a day or two, when it is beset with aches and pains. Lean down and kiss your mama once more then we will leave.'

'You take good care of your papa and do all that your new master, Sir William, tells you. You are very privileged to be the squire of the most famous knight in Christendom, next to your papa that is.'

'Ha,' Richard laughed, but his son William visibly swelled with pride. Jacob stood next to his mother, looking none too pleased that he was being left behind.

'Wish your brother well, Jacob,' Esther instructed.

'Take care Will, but I still don't see why I couldn't come too, *and* you have a new horse. I'm as strong as you.'

'No, you're not!' William came back quickly.

'That – will – do…' Esther said, firmly emphasising each word.

'*You* are staying to protect your mama and your brother Marshal as I have bidden you,' Richard said, Jacob didn't look convinced. 'One of the first disciplines of a knight is to be able to obey orders.'

Richard mounted and poked Jacob in the chest with his toe, 'Surely you have one smile for your papa, Jacob.' Jacob stepped forward and hugged his father's leg.

'I love you Papa and I will miss you, you too, Will.'

'Next time we will ride together Jacob, be sure to take care of my hound Raq.'

'I will.'

Richard nodded once more to Esther and Tristram and rode off. He didn't look back, that would have been more than his heart could bear.

Chapter 17

Young William goes to war

Richard, his son, William Marshal and their men rode for three days, travelling at speed from Le Havre to Le Mans.

Richard was forced to smile when he looked at the face of his son as they galloped through the French countryside. It was clear that he was in great pain, and Richard was filled with pride at the way he bore his suffering, never complaining once. He was a good horseman, Richard knew that fine well, but he had never been in the saddle for this length of time or distance. Perhaps that was some of Julianne's determination, that he was now witness to, never to give in and show she was beaten, 'Aye, she was stubborn and it cost her dear, God rest her soul,' he said to himself.

They gleaned on the journey, from an innkeeper, of the widespread rumours. He had told them it was common knowledge that Count Richard, as he was known to him, had rebelled against his father and was at this moment assembling an army in France with support from King Philip and his son, Louis.

'This may be a different kettle of fish this time, William,' Richard said as they sat on the wall of the well at another resting place.

'Aye, I too fear for the outcome. I have already told you; that you will be shocked when you see Henry. His health will be a deciding factor on this campaign and from what I've heard, King Philip is more formidable than his father. We will give a good account of ourselves, but I am not hopeful of a favourable outcome. Sick kings do not garner support.'

Richard was distracted for a moment as he glanced past William to the nearby stream not fifty paces from where they were seated, and smiled. William noticed him looking at something and twisted his head to see what had caught his eye, and he smiled too. Young William was seated in the cool water; Richard guessed that he was seeking some relief his lower regions.

'He's a good lad, Richard, you must be proud of him,' William once more looked to Richard, 'I give him tasks, no favours, and he does them without a single objection.'

'Aye, I'm proud, but that very joy is ever tinged with pain, how I wish his mother could have seen him.'

'Nevertheless, his grandfather will be proud of him.'

'He is, he's the light of his eye, it blesses me to see them together. Alas, Sir John is not well, dropsy; I pray that we can get home to him before he passes on. He's seventy-two now, and has always been like a father to me.'

'Will must have cooled off his aches and pains, he's coming to us, be it with a rather ungainly gait. Say naught Richard, and save his blushes,' they endeavoured not to smile as Will neared them.

'Fine night for a swim, son,' William kicked Richard's leg.'

'Aye,' was as much as Will responded as he walked past.

When they eventually stepped into the king's hall at Le Mans they were not welcomed with shouts of acclamation, but with mutterings of clear disdain; Henry showed not the slightest gratitude for their endeavours and made his displeasure known to them.

'Where in the name of Hell have you been, it's weeks since I sent for you. Have you walked here; nay crawled?'

'We came with all speed, Sire, it took time to assemble the force and supplies, there were ships to organise, and they are ever subject to the vagaries of the wind.'

Henry only gave a low muttering grumble. 'Are you telling me how to suck eggs! You think I do not understand the moving of armies. Let me tell you I was about such work when I was no more than a fresh-faced youth and you no more than a glint in you sire's eye. In my day… ah what the hell. The whore's spawn are taking what they like from me, and – *he* – that is no son of mine aids them, aye even leads them. I'll geld him when I get my hands on him, and he'll see what that French manikin Philip, thinks of him then.'

Richard was indeed shocked, more than he'd imagined he would be. Not so much at the King's tone, he knew Henry's temper well enough by now, but at seeing how ill Henry clearly was. His skin was translucent, pale as pale could be. He was gaunt, so gaunt his eyes appeared to be bulging from their sockets. His hair was thin, dishevelled, and ragged, he'd always worn his hair short for convenience, but now it was dirty and unkempt. Richard was sorry to say, he *even* smelt; poor Henry he thought, how the mighty are fallen.

He was irritable and the affronts he was now faced with were not helping his demeanour. His leaders were all there, Sir Geoffrey de Brûlon and his brother with him, Sir Peter Fitz-Guy, and Sir Robert de Souville, who preferred town business to fighting business and they were all mightily cowed, by the look on their faces.

Henry continued, 'As for these, these courtiers, who posture with their polished regalia for the court ladies to swoon over,' he flicked his hand contemptuously in their direction, 'Not one of them are worth the price of a pile of fresh horse dung, not one of them,' he mumbled. Suddenly Richard and William were elevated, when Henry addressed his counsellors directly. 'The two men afore you,' he now stabbed his bony finger towards Richard and William, 'are real warriors, they know how to win *battles*, and it's not by giving my land and castles away, either. This fellow standing here beat the Scots *and* captured their King… aye – *and* with one arm tied behind his back. He had barely one tenth of the men of that Scottish ne'er-do-well. You would do well to take heed and learn how real men make war. What say you to that? Ahhh… what the *hell*, I'm going to my bed, I'm weary to my heart, these charlatans, Richard, are naught but dried up old camp followers, good for naught the lot of them. Better for me if they joined the rebels, *aye*, ship them of to that garlic eating so-called King in Paris; his breath near pole-axed me when last we met, that's the way ahead, they'd suit him well enough, for they sap the very life from out of me.'

The King sat quietly for some moments, drumming his fingers agitatedly on the arm of his chair. His tirade if nothing else, had brought a surfeit of colour to his cheeks. He coughed once more and held his gut, as a convulsion racked him yet again with pulsating pain. He fell back in his chair, closed his eyes, and gasped for breath, his chest rising and falling as he attempted to gain control of the spasm. Eventually he half raised his head and gasped from between his purple lips. He bade them rise on the morrow and make haste to find the French army, make sense of what they're about and return quickly.

'Yes Sire, it will be done as you instruct,' Richard assured and bowed.

All the while, the King abused his loyal counsellors; William Marshal's two new squires pressed themselves to a shadowed wall, hoping they were invisible, fearing that they would be next to feel the lash of the King's tongue.

Henry pushed himself from his chair and shuffled from the room, using his sword as a walking stick, they all bowed respectfully as he passed; Henry never acknowledged any of them. Once Henry left there was an air both of despondency *and* relief, despondency at the unenviable predicament in which they now found themselves but relief, from the unrelenting abuse to which they were constantly subjected.

Richard went first to speak to Sir Peter Fitz-Guy, 'Sir Peter,' Richard bowed, 'Difficult times, sad to see the great man in such a poor state of health.'

'Aye, that's how we all felt at first, now I would like to *strangle* him.'

'You speak treachery, Sir Peter,' Richard smiled.

'*Aye* fluently,' and Sir Peter smiled too. 'The poor fellow is ill, and it is my guess, in constant pain, death is ever hanging on his shoulder I would say. In fairness, I might not be in the best disposition either, if I felt as he does. He must be unimaginably frustrated, he has always been at the forefront of his battles, but now he is compelled to rely on others and that does not rest easy with him, it's contrary to all that makes him the man he is.'

'Yes indeed, and we will have to make the best of it, mindful of that. We need to quickly decide what can be done with regard to the French threat.' Richard turned to the gathering, 'Gentlemen might we be seated and seek out what is to be salvaged, before this king's – ship sinks without trace.'

William and Richard did no more than listen to the men's accounts of the actions to date. When each had said his piece, it was agreed to assemble a small scouting party in the courtyard on the morrow's first light, as the King had ordered. Richard appointed each of the leaders to various responsibilities, some to organise the scouting party, and others to ready themselves for the subsequent action, and they left to make such preparations. Richard and William were now alone at the table.

'Not so many loyal Barons here, William.'

'So much for oaths my friend, it looks like the rats are jumping from the ship you mentioned. You know as well as I this has only one outcome, we have already spoken on it.'

'I fear so, William, but we will make the best fist we can of it, ever driven by our honour.'

Chapter 18

Henry flees Le Mans

They armed themselves in the early morning light and were all in surprisingly good spirits, full of easy good-natured, mindless talk and laughter. They set off just after dawn and crossed the nearby river Huisne.

There was a very dense low-lying fog that morning; it would be an easy matter to ride right into the enemy if they hadn't their wits about them. William bade them all to keep their ears open and their mouths closed, as he cuffed away a drip, which formed on the end of his nose.

'And no idle chatter, do you hear,' he commanded. Informing them that God knew what He was about when he gave them twice the capacity for listening as for talking. They would keep their pace slow for now, they were all wet, 'This damned mist is wetter than rain,' William griped, but he was sure as the morning went on the mist would burn off and then they could make up for lost ground.

They rode for perhaps an hour before their scouts returned; they were upon them before they could see them.

'Hell's teeth William, I had not the faintest idea from which direction these fellows were coming. They could have been falling from heaven for as much as I could make out. Thank God, they were not the French,' Richard said gratefully. William bade the men dismount, until he'd heard what the scouts had to say.

'We're sorry to have been so long, Lord, we found the enemy right enough but couldn't find you when we returned.' The scouts didn't paint a favourable picture of what lay ahead. After some debate, they again mounted their horses, took up their shields and lances, and set off slowly towards the direction of the enemy sighting; drawing on the information, they'd just been given.

Robert de Souville said to the Marshal, 'In Christ's name, my Lord, I suggest that I go to the King and tell him at what great speed the King of France is riding to attack him.'

'My Lord, to distress the King with such miserable news would serve little or no purpose. Until at least, we are as sure as we can be, what the French are about, we are unable to give him any worthwhile information. I have no inclination to upset him unnecessarily. No, we must do the best we can and cause him the least torment possible,' said the Marshal. 'With such in mind Richard, I think we should take a closer look, to see what manner of men those riders are of which our scouts made report. Perhaps we can make sense of what they intend and outwit them.'

'I will come too – if I may,' Sir Geoffrey de Brûlon suggested with enthusiasm.

'Aye, as you wish,' William said turning to him and hesitating. 'At least we will be better informed once we see with our own eyes, William. If we have actually seen their position, it may give us some idea of their intention. *Any* information might give us some advantage.' They clambered up a small grassy bank. When they neared the top, they crawled the last few yards and carefully peered over the brow of the hill. They were shocked to see the number of French.

'Hell's teeth Will, this is far worse that I ever imagined. Keep low; I could hit their scouts with a crossbow bolt from here. Let's get clear of this place before we are spotted and there's hell to pay.'

'Aye, we'd better get back to the King as quickly as we can and tell him what we think,' Richard agreed.

Once more, Robert de Souville said: 'Marshal, do you wish me to ride and now make this known to the King?'

'My dear Lord,' William said wearily, 'I've told you already, it will serve no good purpose, by God's lance how many times must you be told, you have seen the way it is with him. If we send a messenger tearing back to him merely on a sighting, he will be confused and unsure. We will return as one and I will deliver the news as a proper balanced assessment of what we have deduced, with as much hope as I can dredge up.'

Then Geoffrey said, 'Well perhaps, since the scouts are coming so close, and are not aware of our presence, we should ride to attack them. Before anyone could come to their aid, we could, at the very least gain some spare mounts of which we are sorely in need.'

The Marshal responded rather tersely, 'and the French army will sit by and cheer us on no doubt. Do you really think, that the possibility of gaining, at the most, perhaps, twenty to thirty hacks, would be worth the risks? I understand your frustration and appreciate your eagerness to make a mark, but in this we will do as I say,' and Sir Geoffrey bowed his head at the obvious rebuke.

Richard offered no more comfort to the disconsolate knight, 'Leave us Sir Geoffrey and see to your men and horses, be ready to act quickly on command, there's a good fellow.'

Geoffrey stood, 'Keep your head down for *pity's* sake, or you bring them down on us. Your neck might be worth little but mine is,' William said grasping his sleeve. Sir Geoffrey then knelt and crawled hurriedly away dejected.

'Ah... we were hard on him, he is young and wants to make a show, for sure, it is a hellish prospect with which we are faced and our options are few,' Richard said to William, as he watched Geoffrey now clear of the brow of the hill, stand and walk off.

'He needs to wake up or he'll forever be young, you're too generous by far Richard.'

Richard smiled, 'we were all young once William.'

'We were never young,' William said returning his gaze once more to the French army. 'It looks like the King of France, without pausing for rest, is riding straight for Le Mans, by the rake of those forward riders, Richard.'

'Aye, that looks to be the truth of it, we had better make haste now we know the way of things and get back to Le Mans before we are isolated and cut off.'

Richard and William crawled clear of the ridge then speaking quietly instructed the men to make haste for Le Mans. He told them to make best use of the topography, keep to the low terrain and in the shade of woodland wherever possible, and pray that they were not seen, or worse captured.

'Keep your eyes peeled, there are yet pockets of mist in the low areas take care, they will give cover right enough, but they might also bring confusion.'

They mounted and galloped hell for leather towards the city, foam flying from the flanks of their animals. The poor beasts were panting fit to burst as they endeavoured to fill their lungs with enough air to fuel their burning muscles. The pounding hooves thundered into the town, through the gates of King Henry's palace, and drew to a dusty steaming standstill in the courtyard.

William and Richard endeavoured to make known to the King the predicament as succinctly and "Hopefully" as they could. They advised *him* to withdraw with some of his counsellors for safety's sake; he would need support if perchance it did not go well with them who remained at Le Mans. Henry thought for a while staring from William to Richard.

'Sire, we will do better if we are not concerned for your well-being, but for the grace of God the numbers will soon overwhelm us, though it pains me to make this known to you, nevertheless it is the truth.'

'When have you ever bothered about upsetting me, Lord Maillorie, you have never been a sycophant, I should have removed your head years ago for your liberty,' Henry *almost* managed a smile, then coughed and held his middle. 'Dear Mother of Christ, what have I done to deserve this torment, is this your revenge Thomas *Becket*?' He said casting his eyes heavenward. 'Well, enjoy your moment for I'm coming soon and I'll kick your backside until your nose is bloody, you ill-begotten son of a Cheapside clerk.' Servants went to him but he pushed them roughly away, 'Leave me be or you'll feel my toe up your arse before that miserable saint, Becket does.'

'What will you do, Sire?' asked William, determined to keep Henry's mind on the work at hand.

'I will heed your wretched advice, but know this, I hoped for better from you both. Now, where are you, you idle lackwits?' he called to his servants. Two nervous attendants rushed to his aid and he begrudgingly allowed them to support him from the room, grumbling and cursing as he went. Richard and William waited until the door closed.

'Right Richard, let's do what we can, which is not much, the odds are a-gin us.'

'We must try to slow down their advance; we need to find some time to see a bigger picture. First, we'll cut down the bridge over the Huisne, and block the fords with sharpened stakes, so that it will at least make for a difficult crossing, be it on foot or horseback, it's little enough, but we can only do what we can in the time we've been given.'

'Aye, that's a start, it may hold them for a while and give the King time to get clear. He's not long for this world, what will happen then, God only knows.'

'It does not bode well for either of us, if Richard becomes King and that's the likelihood. It's an ever-changing flow of fortune in the world we live in William. Perhaps we should desert Henry.'

'Ha, Aye, perhaps Esther's right and we are fools to be ever driven by honour.'

'We can dig a few ditches, to afford us some cushion from what might befall us,' Richard smiled as he offered his ambiguous suggestion. 'The physical ditches first, I'll organise that, anything to slow them. One of my problems is that I have little real knowledge of the geography of the area. What Henry neglected to say as he eulogised my past history, was that, when I defeated the Scots, *we* were the attackers and that is a position I forever favour, for the attacker drives the engagement.'

'Aye, true, but we as attackers had little advantage at the Holy City when I was there, alas here we are defending the indefensible Richard, that's the top and bottom of it.'

As they set about their work, they looked at the other side and saw beyond the river, the King of France riding with the whole might of his army. His intention, it appeared, was to make camp for the night. The French began to erect tents pitched at the edge of Le Parc wood, an arrow's distance from where Richard and William were standing.

'Do they know something we do not, Richard? They are approaching this engagement with a very casual attitude.'

'Who knows what's in their minds, I would have pressed on and finished this. Perhaps they are not as sure of our numbers as we think. Once they have overcome what we have laid before them, we must burn everything outside the walls, anything, which may give them some advantage over us. I want them to be faced with open ground before they can engage us, that will give our archers something to aim at.'

At first light, Henry's men celebrated mass and received the priest's blessing.

The Marshal lost no time in arming himself. The King, quite unarmed, left on horseback; he went via the gate at the southeast of the town and headed for Maison Dieu. William had ridden with him as far as the gate and a short way beyond to be sure he left, said his farewells and promised that they would hold the French long enough for them to get clear.

William returned to Richard's side looking disturbed, 'the strangest thing Richard, the King said to me, "Go on, take that armour off, Marshal. Why are you armed?" At first, I was lost for words, and then managed to reply in a fashion. I said if it pleases you, Sire, I am very happy to be armed and my arms do not impede me in the slightest. It is my will to protect my King and I will do better to fulfil that service if I am armed. When I'm sure of your safety, I will be glad to remove this weight from my back. An unarmed man cannot last out for long in a crisis or a grave situation such as we face this day. The King then said, "Upon my faith! You won't be coming with me then." After this exchange, the King made his son, Count John, disarm, as he did Lord Gerard Talbot, Sir Robert de Tresgoz, and Geoffrey de Brûlon. Indeed, all those who left the town with him, disarmed themselves first, and headed off in the direction of Maison Dieu. Talbot said it was a days ride west of Le Mans, from there they are to travel to La Fresnay. I could only sit in the saddle and watch them go; it was the oddest thing in the middle of this impending disaster for men to be casting aside their arms.'

Richard looked as bemused as William, 'This is bizarre, the poor fellow must be addled with his pain, we need keep our wits about us if we are to make anything of this catastrophe, or we might end up skewered without a friend in the world.'

Chapter 19

Battle of Le Mans

'Listen Richard, I must ride out once more to satisfy my conscience that the King is clear of the town. I should never have let him go defenceless as he was. He will soon be out of the safety of our defences, such as they are, they will not hold the enemy for long.' William mounted and rode off in the direction in which he had last seen the King riding.

As William made his way towards the King, he saw ten French knights making to intercept him, he shouted to distract them, they stopped and turned their mounts to face him. On seeing the loan rider, one of their numbers lowered his lance, raised his shield, and rode at William. The knight clearly did not know whom he was charging towards or he may have reconsidered. William, with consummate skill honed over years on the tourney circuit, merely steadied his mount, and adjusted the position of his lance settling his fist comfortably to the vamplate. Putting spur to flank he unleashed his horse like a taut bowstring. His lance was the arrow and it delivered the knight such a blow on his shield that it shattered, splinters of dry ash flying in every direction. The French knight was flung over the back of his galloping horse and was ignominiously deposited in a thicket of gorse bushes. By this time, Sir Richard Fitz-Herbert had seen the threat to the King and called for other knights to assist. He himself then galloped at full tilt towards another of the French knights and unhorsed him as skilfully as William Marshal had done.

'Much like the old tourney days, Fitz-Herbert,' William called to him.

'Aye, indeed Marshal, they have seen enough by the look of it, they are leaving the field.'

'Praise be, we will make our way back to the town; the King is safe for now, but I am sorely unhappy that they are unarmed.'

'The King's unarmed, what do you mean?'

'That's a tale for later, I have not time or inclination to tell of the folly at this moment,' and he put spur to flank leaving a confused Richard Fitz-Herbert staring after him.

William Marshal rode back to where he'd not long since left Richard. He drew his mount alongside him and reached out his hand, Richard slapped his hand in friendly greeting.

'Thank God you've returned my friend, you are in good time, they are yet deciding what to do by the look of it. Did the King get clear of the town?'

'Aye, the King's clear of the town thank God. It's by God's grace I went to him or he would have been taken. Now we can set our minds to the work before us, without fearing for him.'

'I'm thankful, mightily thankful, that you've returned, William. Though I fear that it may have been wiser to go with the King.'

'Ha, I prefer the company here,' William laughed.

Richard was no longer listening; his eyes were now firmly affixed on the French. He was resolutely positioned to defend the main gate into the town. His horse pawed at the ground anxious for the work, he could see the French horses coming towards him, in a moment they would be upon them. Richard was anxious too, as was William. The adrenalin pumped through his muscles and at this moment he was fearless.

'You two boys keep well behind us, do you hear, John of Earley and William of Aylesford!' William bethought himself to shout over his shoulder a moment before the impact of lances on shields.

'Yes, Lord,' two nervous voices responded.

The French rode up towards them and launched a fierce attack. Suddenly all Hell was unleashed, in a thunderous cacophony of sound, but William and Richard defended their position so well that the French made no gains. Those standing on the wall above the gate on the parapet were yelling abuse at the top of their voices.

'Over here, God is with the Marshal' Baldwin de Bethune heard the shouting. Baldwin had known both Richard and William for many years, not that Richard particularly liked him. He was loud and vulgar, but that apart he was a brave warrior. It was an established fact that he was a friend of the Marshal's company, and that he loved William as he had proved many times before.

Sir Hugh de Malannoy also came to their side. Sir Reginald de Dammartin spurred his horse to give his support. Richard saw Hugh de Hamelincourt running to help. Sir Eustace de Neuville came galloping down through the town and, finally, Ralph Plomquet and Sir Peter Mauvoisin came out of the gate. The result was a good and fierce encounter, not embarked on with a spirit of jest. All of a sudden there was Sir Andrew de Chauvigny, a knight from the company of the Count of Poitiers and renowned for his deeds of great valour, riding in the direction of Richard and William's position. Lances shattering one after another and much clashing of steel swords on helmets.

There was no word spoken there by way of threat, there were none of the usual gibes, for there was much else to occupy them. Richard was tiring, they all were.

Fight as they might, they were yet being driven back. The numbers set against them were simply too great. Sir Hugh de Malannoy, who had distinguished himself in the combat, was knocked into the moat, both he and his horse together. William Marshal, in the company of Baldwin and Reginald de Dammartin, launched a vigorous attack on the French, driving forward once more and they recovered some ground. The air was rife with the smell of blood, sweat, and leather. The French were driven back as far as the flight of an arrow from the gate so that Richard's men recovered some of the ground, but such was only for a breath in time.

The battle changed from moment to moment. It was no longer two armies facing each other they were in a melee now, groups fighting everywhere, total mayhem. The Marshal stretched out his hand and took a French knight's horse by the bridle. Someone on the parapet above threw down a huge stone, which struck the knight on the arm. His arm snapped in two, and he cried out in sheer agony, someone else threw down another large stone, which hit his horse's head and blood poured from the wound. The horse reared up, and the Marshal was left with the bridle in his hands. He threw the bridle through the gate in frustration and returned to the fray, which was still not at an end, these were hardened warriors, and none wanted to withdraw.

The damage was on a huge scale, broken lances with their heads lay everywhere. One struck the leg of Richard's horse, with the result that it stumbled and he was nearly thrown. His mouth was parched, as dry as dust; he would have given a king's ransom at this second for a cup of cool fresh spring water. His costrel of small ale had been torn from his saddle and lost, God to be free of this and a chance to find a drink, was the cry in his head.

Men were being hacked to death for no gain, and Richard was soaked in the stench of combat. It was decided that they had given all that honour demanded and the better part of valour would be now to make haste to the King's side.

'Find a mount, if you are without, or share a saddle if you must, we have done all that can be done here,' William shouted. They did as they were ordered, grabbing whatever horse or hand that was offered. Once mounted they made one *final* brutal surge into the thick of the enemy, so vicious was their intent that the attackers were compelled to withdraw from the ferocious slashing, scything, blows of sword, and mace, to regroup.

Richard struck a final blow with his war hammer as they turned. He drove the four-inch square spike with such force into the shoulder of a French knight, it was lodged to its full depth, and he had to let go of it for fear of being unhorsed himself. The miserable fellow slumped forward onto the neck of his horse as it sped away from the action, only to tumble from its back under the hooves of others making their escape.

In that moment of bloody calm Richard, William, and their men set off at a pace away from the dusty action in the direction the King had taken to Fresnay.

As they galloped through the burning smoke-filled streets, Richard was distracted, constantly worrying for the safety of his son.

'For mercy's sake keep tight to us, Will, whatever you do.' Richard shouted over his shoulder.

'Yes, Father,' young William yelled back. Richard noticed his nervous twitching out of the corner of his eye. He'd been on the wrong end of a battle now, and survived, Richard knew he'd never forget this first time.

There were crowds of people with bundles of precious belongings, some loaded on handcarts, some on horseback others simple carrying as much as they were able on their backs. Crying and panicked screaming voices completed the vision of Armageddon; they fled the town through every known gate, door or hole, like spouts of water squeezed from a holed leather costrel.

Their group of knights were now hotly pursued by the French, William was furious when he saw that Prince Richard was one of the pursuers. William forgot his escape, spun his mount and charged directly at the Prince.

Richard tugged so sharply on the rein his horse stumbled as he turned to face the oncoming threat. He saw the Prince and yelled, '*NO, WILLIAM!*' It was enough to bring him to his senses; at the last second, he lowered the point of his lance and drove it into the chest of the horse instead of the Prince. The animal's forelegs buckled, and it tumbled headfirst into a ditch, squealing and writhing with half the broken lance protruding from the bloody wound to its body. Prince Richard lay on the road dazed and defenceless. The knights with the Prince drew their mounts to a sliding standstill. William leapt from his horse before they could get to him and stood over Prince Richard, possibly England's future king, with his sword at his throat. There was a moment of great tension and Richard rode to support his friend positioning his horse between William and the Prince's men, *and* he prayed God – William would stay his hand.

'God's legs Marshal! Do not kill me,' the prince yelled, 'that would be a wicked thing to do, since you find me here before you completely unarmed by that unhorsing.'

The Marshal replied savagely, 'I would not taint the honour of my sword on you who are traitor to your own father and country. You deserve to have the mantle of shame nailed to your hide. I'll let the friend of traitors, Beelzebub have your life for I want it not, to Hell with you and the likes of you.' With that, the Marshal sheathed his sword, mounted, glared at the knights around Prince Richard, tugged on the rein, and galloped off in the direction of Fresnay.

The knights and soldiers with the Prince were intent on pursuing William and Richard.

Prince Richard jumped up and shouted, 'Cease this chase, for if you continue, you will have lost all; we are behaving in a foolish, reckless and dishonourable manner. The Marshal shames us, he is an example to us all, which we would do well to heed.' There was some discord amongst the French knights with him, but they did as the Prince bade them and returned to the city.

Chapter 20

Death of Henry II

They rode at a steady pace in the direction they knew the King had taken. They were leaving behind them the burning city and the people of Le Mans, it was a battle they were never going to win, but they had bloodied the French King's nose and slowed down their advance. The French may well have won the day, but they had paid a heavy price. The knights and men-at-arms rode in silence, apart from the creaking of leather, the jingle of harness, the panting of horses and the rhythmic drumming of hooves on the French lanes.

This was mindless work for Richard, riding like this no longer required conscious thought, all his movement and balance was done without thinking. As the countryside, villages, and small hamlets flashed by the riders, he tried to assemble his thoughts and make sense of the recent failed conflict.

He knew that it was not the Henry of old to be simply reacting to events. Henry always drove history, history didn't drive him, and yet *he* was the defender, the man with his back to the wall in this débâcle.

The relationship between Henry and his son Count Richard had finally dissolved into violence shortly after the Young King Henry's death. Richard knew King Henry couldn't really in all conscience; lay all his troubles at the door of his son, Count Richard, or King Philip's son, Louis.

They had held a peace conference in November the year past, making a public offer of a generous long-term peace settlement with Henry, conceding to his various territorial demands. The conditions all hinged on the promise that King Henry would finally consent to the marriage of Richard and Alice, Countess of Vexin, the fourth daughter of King Louis, and announce Richard as his recognised heir.

Henry refused the proposal, whereupon Count Richard himself spoke up, *demanding* to be recognised as Henry's successor. Richard strongly suspected that Henry favoured his youngest son as his heir. Richard knew that such an outcome was never going to be and never understood why Henry pursued it against all hope. The Prince, Count Richard, was the next in line, he was popular, and he was everything that John was not. Perhaps Count Richard's claim was not helped by the fact that Queen Eleanor favoured him above John. Richard smiled as they thundered along; he knew that Henry would do the opposite to anything Eleanor said on a matter of principle. Richard was aware that Count Richard's relationship with Prince Philip of France had blossomed since Count Geoffrey's death and that disgusted Henry. However, Henry remained silent much to the frustration of those gathered. Suddenly Count Richard, to the surprise of all, publicly changed sides at the conference and gave formal homage to Philip of France in front of the assembled nobles and thus the meeting broke down in bitter acrimony.

The Papacy intervened once again to try to produce some last-minute accord. The Pontiff's efforts resulted in a fresh conference at La Ferté-Bernard. Richard had been in England at the time of these negotiations and William was on crusade. He was sure if either of them had been there, they may have been able to steer Henry towards a course of pragmatism, and not intransigence, but alas, that was not to be.

By now, Henry was suffering from some internal ailment, which had been troubling him off and on for a few years. The discussions achieved little, although Henry is alleged to have made the concession to Philip that John could marry Alice instead of Richard, reinforcing the rumours circulating over the summer that Henry was considering openly disinheriting Richard and naming John as his heir. The conference broke up with war appearing more likely.

Even though war seemed probable with Philip and Richard, Henry was caught off guard when they launched a surprise attack immediately after their discussions, during what was conventionally a period of truce in the interim after such talks.

William Marshal glanced over at Richard as they rode. Richard had been deep in contemplation for some time, never giving thought to where they were, but now that he thought on it, they should have caught up with the King's party by this time. When he glanced at the other faces, he detected that there was a clear uneasiness amongst the riders.

Eventually William Marshal put action to their concerns and drew their travel to a halt.

'What do you think, Richard? There is no sign of Henry,' he called as they drew to a standstill, their horses twisting and turning yet excited by their pace.

'Surely he has not met French soldiers and been taken prisoner!'

'I think not, we have never seen any troops whatsoever. It is my guess that he has changed his mind and gone elsewhere. Where else would he go?'

'You don't think they are yet in Maison Dieu!'

'Surely not it would be folly to settle so near the action at Le Mans, no they were certain to travel further south, but where, that's the question!'

'Yes, I think he would have pressed on into the heartlands of Anjou where he is most likely to find support.' They both stared into the distance of the surrounding countryside.

'If one is to get lost, this is a fine place for such a failing. I think we should make camp here for the night and hear the views of us all, then we will decide the morrow's direction.'

They dismounted and their squires unsaddled the horses and rubbed them down with handfuls of cut hay from the field next to where they'd settled.

'Father,' said young William as he came to his side after completing the work the Marshal had set him.

'Yes, my son, what is it?' Richard said placing his arm around his son's shoulder. 'Is all well with you?'

'I was wondering if Prince Richard and the French would pursue us this far south, Lord.'

'They may well. I don't think Philip or Louis would do so on their own, but with Prince Richard determined to have his hands on the crown of England, it's likely he will force their hand.'

'Is not the fortress of Chinon somewhere near here?'

'Ha… out of the mouths of babes and children. It's not a great fortress; imagine yourself in a dusty stone place, which looks to be from Biblical times. It's cold, dirty, and uncomfortable, set next to our home at Aylesford. The poor live in caves in the soft limestone cliffs surrounding the stone fortress, barely able to communicate with each other, they are but savages. Not a place I like, but it could be where Henry has gone. Chinon is on the banks of the Vienne River, a beautiful location for sure. I will mention it to the others.' Richard hugged him, but he shrugged himself free, it was unseemly for such before his fellow squires. Richard stepped from him, nodded, and told him to be about his work or he would feel to sharp end of his boot, and winked at him.

Richard walked to where the leaders were in conversation.

'Have you come to any conclusions?' Richard asked.

'It is the consensus that he will have gone to Chinon or Saumure but we will go to Chinon first, Henry must have turned off *somewhere*. Blois is another option, the truth of it is, we have no idea.'

On the morrow, they rode back the way they had come and turned towards Chinon. It wasn't too long before they had their decision confirmed by villagers who told them of the King's train passing by. They said that the King was riding in a litter.

When they reached Chinon and reported to the King, he was quiet, none of the vitriolic abuse they had been subjected to at Le Mans. It was as if he was resigned to his fate.

It was not more than a day after Richard and William Marshal arrived, that a rider brought documents from Count Richard demanding a meeting with his father on July the 1st at Ballan-Mire, a day's ride to the northeast.

All the counsellors were grievously concerned that it would be too much for Henry in his state of health, but he was determined to go. They would transport him by litter then at the last he would mount his horse and meet the rebels as a King.

Henry, only just able to remain seated on his horse, agreed to a complete surrender: he would do homage to Philip. He would give up Alice to a guardian and she could marry Richard at the end of the forthcoming crusade, if that was their wish. He would recognise Richard as his heir; he would pay Philip compensation, and key castles would be given to Philip as a guarantee.

A solemn band of his loyal knights rode beside Henry on the way back to Chinon after the humiliating encounter with his son. He lay in silence on the litter, supported by cushions; his horse was tied to it and trotted contentedly alongside its master.

The red silk saddle drape with its golden lions fluttered in the breeze under a now empty saddle where the invincible King of England, ruler of a vast empire had once been seated. Richard wondered who would next sit upon it; he doubted that they would ever fill it as Henry had.

Henry was carried with reverence to his bed in the keep, yet in pain, he sat with pillows packed around him. His son Geoffrey was the only family member with him as he lay dying, and *he* was illegitimate.

Henry asked to see the surrender document he'd signed, perhaps hoping it was all a mistake. He read it at arms length, most likely for the first time. Richard watched him drag his skeletal finger to the list of signatures, he gasped, his finger frozen to the page and stared in tortured disbelief. Richard knew he had seen Prince John's signature, even his most beloved son had betrayed him, and the document fell from his hand as he sunk back into his pillow. He twisted his head with some difficulty, his scrawny fingers grasped at Geoffrey's hand.

'Son… you are the only one who is *not* a bastard,' these were his last words before he died. It was June the 6th 1189 and Henry was fifty-six.

The King had wished to be interred at Grandmont Abbey in the Limousin, but the hot weather made transporting his body impractical, and he was instead buried at the nearby Fontevraud Abbey.

After the funeral, the now *King* Richard forgave Sir William and Lord Richard for standing against him, saying that he was humbled, that even at the last when all was against them, they had been driven by their honour and remained faithful to their oath to his father.

Prince John was there seated next to his brother the new king. Richard and William knelt before King Richard and swore fealty. As they were kneeling, Richard saw John's eyes narrow mockingly, relishing no doubt, what he would see as their humbling.

'You are too generous, my King, I pray that your goodness is not abused by these two fellows.' Richard ignored him. 'Perhaps I will have to teach them about loyalty, when I as your regent have to govern England in your absence while on your noble quest to take the Holy Land from the infidels.

William felt the muscles in Richard's arm flex, and he touched his shoulder as they rose.

William said as he made to bowed, looking straight at Prince John, 'is it possible that the castle vermin would be foolish enough, to lick from the bowl of cream belonging to the castle cat? A precarious occupation I think,' both he and Richard bowed once more and walked from the room.

Chapter 21

Return to England

Richard and William made their way to Ouoistreham. Richard was bound for Aylesford and his home and William Marshal was to go to one of his new holdings. He was ambitious, Richard had always known that, and he'd secured promises from King Henry, which the now *King* Richard had confirmed. He had been given lands in France and William's very first landed fief, Cartmel, a large royal estate in Lancashire. William had finally become a landed Baron. To round off his patronage, Henry II had given William the custody of Helois of Lancaster, a royal ward and heiress to the Barony of Kendal in Lancashire and Westmoreland. Apparently, Henry II intended to settle William in northern England. If he married Helois, William would achieve an equivalent status to his father and his older brother, John.

William, however, was apparently dissatisfied with the fief of Cartmel and the hand of Helois of Lancaster. When he returned from the crusade William complained to Henry that he felt that his rewards were not worthy of the service that he given over the years. In response, Henry II promised to give him the great castle of Chateauroux in the county east of Poitou and all of its holdings. At that time, the castle had been in Henry's possession, but now it was firmly in King Philip's hands and for William to make gain from the gift at this present time he would have to offer fealty to Philip.

William was the consummate politician and Richard knew that fine well, he was astute, and had an elegance with words. Yes, he would watch with interest how he managed the serving of two masters, a difficult task for a man driven by honour.

They were sat discussing their differing futures while they broke their night's fast and washed down the fine pie, which had been set before them, with small ale. William glanced continually out of the window towards the harbour and the ships.

'You look as if you are excited at the prospect of your voyage, my friend.'

'Ho, ho, ho, you missed fine employment at the court as a jester,' and he dipped his fingers in his tankard and flicked Richard with droplets of ale. Richard laughed as he wiped his face. 'You know that I hate sea travel, and it's a long way to Portsmouth from here across raging tempestuous oceans, eager to devour those foolish enough to venture upon them.'

'My dear friend, can it be possible that you have not seen from that window, even though your eye has never turned from it since we sat here more than an hour past? The sea is like unto a mill pond, or a village duck pond.'

William didn't seem convinced; 'It's difficult to be sure at this distance!' he said seriously, narrowing his eyes and straining his neck to look once more in the direction of the beach.

Richard threw back his head and laughed, 'Dear oh dear, William, is this the bravest knight in Christendom I hear? Aye, well you have another day to think on it,' Richard said wiping his eyes. 'Unlike me, I leave within the hour. In truth, I am no great sailor myself, but I will suffer aught to be home and see my dearest wife and family.'

'I pray all is well,' William responded, distracted for a second, 'and that your new daughter and her mother prosper, *Isabelle* you say.'

'Yes, I like the name fine. What about you, now you are a Baron and a man of property, surely a wife is now required. I suspect that it will be a goodly while yet before the grave sets its eye upon you, and you are called to fulfil your promise to the Templars of chastity.'

'Mmm, would that I was as fortunate as you. I yet have that raging sea to endure. It would be like the thing to be cast into the foaming ocean to a salty death, and the silk burial garments, which cost me considerable coin, to lie wanting for all eternity. In such a likely event I bequeath them to you.'

'Ah… William, I do love you, it's worth a bag of gold marks to behold your face at the mere mention of a boat trip.' William was not amused. 'Forgetting the sea for a moment, it is kind of you to allow William to come home with me, we will go to Tattershall as soon as we can, we needs must see his grandfather, Sir John.'

'I will send letters to you so you will know where I am, then when the time is right you can send William back to me, he is proving to be a fine squire,' promised the Marshal.

'Come walk with us to the ship, William. I must board with my men; young Will is already there. Who knows what our futures will be, at last you have been rewarded for your many years of service and now have new responsibilities.'

They embraced and were slow to release each other. 'I will miss you my friend, I fancy it will be sometime before we meet again,' said William Marshal.

'Aye, it will be strange, God bless and keep you my friend,' their hands slid slowly apart. Richard walked up the gangplank, once on the ship he put his arm around the shoulder of his son and lifted his hand and waved one last time to his friend.

Richard and young William leant on the gunwale and watched the figure that was William Marshal as it disappeared into the early morning heat.

All reserve and decorum was thrown to the wind when Richard rode through the barbican into the courtyard at Aylesford. Esther ran to him and leapt into his arms. He set her down and she hugged William too. He was not quite at ease with this show of affection, he was a man now home from war and having one's mother hugging him in front of others, he found unbefitting. The image of a boy being hugged by his mother was not the picture he wanted to create. He felt that he now deserved some respect from the other boys, after all he now knew the heat of battle, which none of them had experienced. Thankfully, Jacob was out riding, he would meet him in private, he was desperate to see him he'd, missed him.

'Come meet your daughter, Isabelle and Marshal, he is learning to talk now and can say many words, Papa, Mama, I have been teaching him.' Both Marshal and Isabelle were asleep, but Richard was delighted to see them nevertheless. No sooner had they entered their apartment than in ran Jacob straight into his father's arms, and then he hugged William.

'Take Jacob to your room, Will, and show him what you have brought for him.'

'A gift for me, will I like it?'

'Of course, you will, would I bring you anything that was not the best? Come on and I'll show you.'

'This is wonderful to have you home; I can't tell you how happy I am…' There was a knock at the door. Margaret went to it, turned the latch, and Tristram pushed it open and kissed her, she wriggled away from him, turned, and blushed. Richard was distracted and didn't immediately respond to Tristram's greeting. 'Richard it's wonderful to see you safe home,' he said stepping to him and hugging him. He stepped once more to Margaret and wrapped his arm around her. 'Aren't you going to congratulate us?'

'I'm sorry Tristram, but you have me at a disadvantage!' Richard said turning to Esther.

'Tristram and Margaret are married, Richard.'

'Married!' Richard said more than surprised, Tristram a knight, should by all normal expectation have had his eyes set higher than a servant, even a senior servant, be it even a beautiful, intelligent servant. She could have been a mistress, but no… such would *never* be Tristram's way. Yes, of course he would marry Margaret. William Marshal was a man of honour that would never be in doubt, but he always had an eye to advancement, much like Richard, not Tristram, he seemed ever to be content, a man at peace with himself, always having time to just "Be". It was no wonder people liked, and even sought out his company.

'Yes, *married* my dear friend *and*… what's more I am to be a father.'

'Well to say I am at a loss is an *understatement*, but please accept my sincerest congratulations, to you both, and may God protect you, Margaret,' he added smiling. Richard now took Tristram in his arms then kissed Margaret who was not at ease with the situation, but managed to smile.

'This makes my news of new kings and battles against the French of little interest.' Richard noticed Margaret's unease, 'Margaret, Tristram is my dearest friend, *but* don't tell him, and that makes you our dearest friend and you will call me Richard from now on, in private anyway.'

'I don't think I can, Lord,' she blushed bright red.

'Yes, you can, try now.'

She hesitated looking at Esther, and then Tristram, he nodded to her. 'Thank you… Richard.'

'There, that wasn't so difficult. You have always been more than a servant to us, from the first day we came here, do you remember, those wicked days with that thief Faulks?'

'Aye, I remember fine well, Lor… Richard,' they all laughed at Margaret's struggles.

There was a knock at the door, 'Enter,' Richard said twisting towards the sound.

Jacob was first in with his *new* sword, 'Look what Will has brought me, Mama; he took it from a French knight he'd slain.' Richard glanced at William and lifted his eyebrows, but said naught, William turned from him. 'William was in the thick of the battle Mama.'

'That is the truth, he did his duty and I could ask no more of him,' Richard said proudly. 'We will all feast together tonight; I am the happiest man on God's earth to be home with you all.'

'I will speak to Jane, my Lady,' offered Margaret.

'Thank you, Margaret, Jane is my new maid, Richard. Margaret has kindly offered to train her; I have given

Margaret a maid now she is with child and has Tristram to care for.'

'Excellent Esther, as it should, be for the wife of the castellan, a position of great importance. Now Tristram and *Lady* Margaret are going about their business, you leave us boys, I wish to talk to your Mama.'

'May I ask of Grandfather, Mama?'

'He is very sick William; he asks constantly for you.'

'Papa, may I go to him?' He asked softly.

'Yes, indeed Son, we must go without delay, not on the morrow, but the next day, I give you my word.'

'Thank you, Papa,' William said and put his arms round his father, Richard held him and pressed his lips to the crown of his head. 'We do not wish your grandfather to suffer, do we?'

'No Papa, but I do so want to see him, I always feel better just being with him.'

Once they left, Richard seated himself thoughtfully by the fire steepling his fingers under his chin, Esther watched him for a moment then touched his shoulder and seated herself on his knee. He wrapped his arm around her waist, kissed her neck and a tremor ran through her, right down to her toes.

'William and I will have to travel alone, by the tone of your voice John is only hanging to life by his finger tips.'

'Yes, is seems so, Bernard has written to us begging that you do not linger, once you return.'

'I know that you would wish to see him, but to organise such an entourage would take too much time. If we discover that not all is as urgent as it seems, we will send for you. I will take the Ulfberht with me; I think John should pass that precious sword onto his grandson it is his heritage, a warrior's inheritance. I know that it will mean a great deal to John to be the one to present it to William.'

'Fear not, I have seen John, Tristram took Jacob and me, and we said our goodbyes to him. It was very sad to see him, he is the kindest man, and I have loved him dearly. He thanked me for loving William and being a mother to him, he was very upset.'

'Aye, forgiveness is an honourable thing Esther, which seems ever part of your nature, you have made all that we have a blessing, and for such I shall forever be thankful.'

'Do you not know why? Because I love *you*, and love always forgives, it can do no other. Have I not told you that I love you, my dearest knight?'

Richard smiled, 'no, but there is time enough before this night's mete, to make right such neglect,' and she laughed, slipped from his lap and raised him from his chair.

Chapter 22

Remembered

Richard was finding the conversation with his son difficult as they rode north to Tattershall. He thought that perhaps William was so distressed with concern for his grandfather he was unable to, or did not wish to enter into conversation. Richard persevered hoping to distract him and lift his mood. He chatted about their time in France, the weather, anything. He asked William how he felt about their visit to see his grandfather. Richard even told him that his grandfather had a very special gift for him, but nothing would change the downcast face he presented.

Richard could see clear enough that William was disturbed and he wondered if there was anything else troubling him apart from his worries for his grandfather. Was it something connected with the fight he'd witnessed in the tiltyard the day they'd arrived home from France? He knew William was conscious of becoming a man and didn't like to be spoken to, or seen as a boy and that ever rankled with him.

There were a couple of moments when Richard felt as if William was about to speak, but then he'd appeared to think better of it, his shoulders slumped once more and the moment past. The morning dragged on and yet he never spoke. Whatever was gnawing at him, he was struggling to flesh it out into words.

Richard remembered how such struggles had come between him and *his* father, and he had eternal regrets for that.

He knew now that he'd never taken into account how *his* father might be feeling. No consideration of how much he'd missed his wife or the pressures brought about by the unrelenting demand on his ever-diminishing purse, and his guilt, warranted or not, at failing the people who looked to him as their Lord. Richard was now ashamed that when he was a young man, it was all about *him* and his wants, as it was with most young people he guessed. How he wished that he could have that time over again. He often prayed that he could turn his failings into understanding, but he was struggling with Will this day.

'So, tell me, Will,' Richard tried once more. William looked guardedly out of the corner of his eye in his father's direction, 'what was the cause of that unrest in the tiltyard yesterday? I was witness to some unseemly behaviour as I glanced from my window and saw my two sons in the midst of a brawl with the other squires. You know how I deplore that sort of activity amongst young men preparing for knighthood. You and Jacob are in a privileged position as the Lord's sons, thus I expect you to forever set an example to the others, as the Marshal will expect of you when you return to his mesnie.'

William lowered his head and stared at his hands before him resting on the up-stand of his saddle. He raised his eyes slowly and gazed thoughtfully into the distance, Richard waited patiently for his response.

'It was naught of significance, Lord.'

'At this moment you are taking to your "Father", not your Lord, and this father cares deeply, about everything to do with your life, even the insignificant things in your day, don't ever forget that.'

'Aye, I know that Father, and I'm am thankful.'

'So, if this thing is of such little significance, as you say, it will be of no matter to make it known to me.' Richard watched William's eye fall once more to his hand and noticed his fingers tighten on the rein he held, much to his horse's disquiet, the poor beast shook its head agitatedly, trying to loosen William's hold.

'*Will,* give your horse some rein, I don't think it is over pleased at having its neck so bent.'

'Sorry Father,' he did as his father said and at the same time reached forward and patted his horse's neck. Still he did not speak, but settled again to staring at his hands. Richard was biting his tongue now, he was growing angry, he could not abide sullenness, and he was about to pursue an altogether different tack when William spoke.

'Jacob took exception to one of the other boy's taunts.'

'Oh… and what taunt could be the excuse for such behaviour, might I ask?' Once more William was quiet as the horses continued to walk on at their lazy pace, and Richard saw him cuff quickly at his eye with the back of his gloved hand. Richard furrowed his brow… He was deeply concerned, none of this was in character; William was a straightforward boy.

'The boy said…' William continued.

'Yes.'

'…That *you* betrayed Mother and that I… was a – bastard.' Richard was *stunned,* he suddenly felt sick to his stomach, whatever could he say, it was true, but it told not *the* truth.

'Jacob leapt at the boy, I was too shocked to do aught at first, then once I'd collected my thoughts, I dragged Jacob from him. All the while Jacob was shouting "liar, liar" and threatening the boy with a flogging.'

Now it was Richard who stared into the distance, what to say – he just didn't know? How could he ever hope to make William understand, something so emotionally complex. It had been spoken out in black and white shards of soul piercing reality, a dozen or so words to sum up all the pain and suffering, from years of heartache. He could lie, and spare William some of the pain, not for his own pride, he didn't care for himself – he'd long since found an inner peace, but he did care for his son's anguish at this moment. *Julianne,* he said to himself.

Who sets such rules that cause us so much pain, could it really be a loving God? Richard remembered that he'd once told Esther that love was simply God's means of tormenting man, and that it was merely a way of delivering pain, ultimately it always brought unbearable suffering. William would soon find out when his grandfather died – what pain love brought.

Richard, knew he must say something, but what? He should have prepared for this; he'd always known, eventually this moment would have to be faced.

'It's midday, we should rest the horses,' he said as casually as he was able. 'Let's rest over there where there is a small stream of sorts.' He signalled to his men and shouted over his shoulder that they would rest a while. The men dismounted and talked amiably amongst themselves.

Richard and William sat some distance from them, Richard took a leather costrel of small ale from his saddle and offered it to William, but William shook his head avoiding his father's eyes.

They seated themselves on the grass with their backs resting against a fallen tree trunk.

'First of all, I must say this, *Esther*, your mother, would be very hurt indeed if you considered her any less than your mother, for she loves you and has cared for you as such since you were a baby. She adopted you as her own – and that means that instead of growing in her tummy *you* grew in her heart.'

William rested his arms on his raised knees, hung his head, and stared at the ground between his legs. There was a long pause; Richard didn't know how to progress his story. He wanted to tell the absolute truth to his son. Didn't the scripture exhort us to speak the truth in love? He thought as he pondered how to – or where to – begin his tale. He'd heard many speak "The truth" with *malicious* voices, relishing the hurt; their *truth* would bring to others. If *God* was love and truth – then it seemed to him that truth could only be a reality when spoken in love. Facts in themselves surely did not amount to *truth*, and it was the truth that set one free, was it not? Richard took a deep breath.

'Your mother was called *Julianne*, your grandfather's daughter, and I had loved her from the first moment I set eyes upon her. Has your grandfather ever mentioned her?'

'Yes, he has spoken often of her, I always felt that he wanted to tell me something, but he always stopped short.'

'I wondered if he had said anything, but anyway she was committed to, and did, marry another man whom she did not love. He was not really a bad man but he was weak and foolish. He ran away, deserting her, having stolen coin from the King, and has never been seen again. However – I did hear a rumour that he was now working in the French

King's court, but I know not the truth of that. I married Esther, whom you know as your Mother, I feared that she might be in danger because she had a Jewish background, there were threats against the Jewish community at that time and I wanted to protect her. I loved her deeply, she was my dearest friend, but I was not – *in love* – with her, might I say that I am now? Moreover, I fancy on refection, I always was but didn't realise it, because I only had eyes for your mother. Esther is a truly special human being, but you know that without any need for my affirmation. That aside I was seriously wounded at the battle of Leicester with a severe head wound, and had been carried unconscious to Tattershall. Your grandfather and Julianne cared for me. Your mother – Julianne – sat with me day and night for several weeks. I recovered slowly, before I was fully well, I had to leave Tattershall to lead the King's army at Fornham, it was tortuous for us both. In a moment of time, two human beings loved each other and you were conceived, be it wrong and a wicked sin, I have no regrets. Now *you* must judge me as you see fit, but I have tried to tell you the truth, as clearly and simply as possible, the whole story would fill a book. You might find it difficult to understand, but I pray to God that you can and I pray also that *you* never discover *yourself* in such a pitiful dilemma. You might learn to forgive me when you fall in love and experience its power. If you wish, you could ask your grandfather, *he* has no regrets for what happened, because he has you, and you have helped him through the torment of loneliness, after his only son murdered his only daughter. Your grandmother was also murdered, can you imagine for one moment how special you are to him. Life is often complex or we make it so. Although, on one level your poor grandfather has no regrets, as I have said, he also blames himself for everything. He believes if he'd been stronger, he would have forbidden Julianne to marry when he knew she was not in love. Aye… we can all heap blame for our failings upon our own heads, but to what end, we do as we do and must learn to live with the consequences, and move on.'

William had never moved or showed any reaction as Richard told his story. Then suddenly he turned to his father, and fell into his arms and wept.

'Do you love me as much as Jacob, Papa?' he sobbed.

'I am not going to answer that, for you already know that I do, and I am prouder of you than you could ever imagine. Might – *I* – ask for *your* forgiveness, for the hurt you now feel!'

'Father, there is naught to forgive. I would not change anything about you.'

'You humble me, William. Let me say this that you are never to feel ashamed, for you were conceived in love. If you want to see your mother, go and look in yonder water,' and Richard pointed in the direction of the gentle slow flowing stream in which the horses were standing. 'Look at the face before you from – the eyes *she* bequeathed you, and you will see *her* eyes. Let some time pass and when all this has had time to settle in your mind, if you want to ask anything about your mother, Julianne, you can ask, either your mama, or me and we will gladly answer your questions, if we can. Come now, my Son,' Richard smiled at him, and squeezed him once more, 'your dearest grandfather is waiting for you, he will want to hear of the men you've slain in France, of which you made known to Jacob,' and he nudged him, winked and smiled.

Chapter 23

Tattershall

A servant answered the door and bowed, Richard gazed with apprehension beyond him, and Bernard, Sir John's chirurgien, looked up at the sound of the familiar voice and smiled. He was sitting by Sir John's bed; he rose and came to greet Richard and William.

'My Lord,' Bernard bowed, and spoke quietly, 'I am relieved to see you both, Sir John continually asks if you have yet come. He is not long for this world, I'm sad to say.'

'Is grandfather sleeping?' Asked William nervously, fearing the answer as he looked at the still grey face of the old man laid before him.

'He drifts to and fro,' as Bernard spoke, they heard Sir John stirring, he opened his eyes and looked towards them. He clearly recognised them for a faint smile touched his face.

'William – my dear boy,' he said in the softest voice.

'Yes, Grandfather,' William answered, his eyes filling with tears, 'Papa is here too.'

Sir John lifted his fingers and gently patted the bed by his side, motioning to William to come and sit by him.

William went to the chair where Bernard had been seated and glanced back to his father and Richard nodded for him to sit. William leant forward before he sat down, and kissed his grandfather.

'How do you feel, Grandfather? I'm sorry I could not come before this, perhaps you know we have been in France fighting for the King, Henry.'

'Aye, your Mama told me of your adventure. As for me, I'm a little better, I think,' he cast his eyes towards Bernard who smiled at him.

'It's a tonic to see your grandson and Lord Richard is it not?' Bernard asked.

'Aye... give me a day or two and I'll be up and out of bed. I feel better than I have for a while to see you both here before me.'

Richard came to Sir John's side and laid a long package wrapped in cloth next to him.

'Richard, my son,' Sir John cast his eye to Richard, 'he's the finest young man, is he not?' Sir John looked once more to his grandson, as ill as he was the pride in his grandson radiated from his eyes. 'What's this, you have set by my side?' Sir John said touching the bundle with his fingers.

'It's something you must give to your grandson, it is your gift to him, do you remember? And it will mean all the more for you to personally give it.'

Sir John, looked puzzled for a second, then smiled as he understood, 'Ahhh, but I gave this to you, it is yours to give.'

'It was never rightfully mine, but it is William's.'

Sir John was silent for some moments touched by Richard's thoughtfulness. 'This would always have been yours one day dear boy, it has been handed down through our family from generation to generation, open it!'

William stared at the package wrapped in cloth, which had been carefully bound with a leather cord. He loosened the cord and unrolled the waxy covering to reveal an old sword; he'd never seen one quite like it. He ran his finger along its length then picked it up and held it in his hand, clearly feeling the weight. Standing, he made several slashes with it through the air. Richard smiled for he could see from William's stance and movement someone who was naturally balanced with a sword in his hand. William felt the edge with his thumbnail, it was nicked it had obviously been used; yet it was razor sharp, this was not merely a decoration.

'I have never felt a sword like it, Grandfather, what's this written into the blade.' He read the word, 'Ulf – berht,' is that right?'

'Indeed, it is son; it is the sword of swords. No one knows who made such swords or what the name means, some say it comes from the Viking spirit world.'

'It's as if the sword has a life of its own, I'm drawn forward into action, it floats, an extension of my arm. What can I say Grandfather this is the most wondrous of gifts. I will tell of this moment when I pass it to my son,' he lowered the sword and kissed his grandfather once more. 'There are no words fitting for this moment, to say thank you, sounds so inadequate, Grandfather.'

'All I have is yours, William.'

'Let's not talk of such things, Grandfather, I want to fight with you in the tiltyard using my new sword.'

'Aye, perhaps… but let me say these things to you, first, I fear not death my son, so do not be anxious for me. It is the last battle and it has been already won by our Saviour, and secondly, this moment, with you here, makes my life the better for having lived.'

'Sorry Grandfather, tell me whatever you wish.'

Sir John looked pensive, 'Richard will you tell him some day?'

'He knows John, we talked on the way here.'

'Ahhh… well, all is complete, your mother loved your father and he loved her. I always knew that and *I* love them both, be proud of who you are son. You will be Lord here one day, listen to your father and you will not go far wrong, he is the finest knight. Kiss me once more then I will sleep a while.' William kissed the wrinkled cheek and laid his head gently on his grandfather's chest and the old man tenderly patted his cheek.

William sat by his grandfather that night; Richard suggested William take some rest and he would sit with his Sir John, but William would not leave the old man's side. Over the next few days, William and his grandfather talked whenever he awoke, but as the hours passed, the times for talk grew shorter.

Richard was asleep on a chair and awoke suddenly; the light from the new day was only just cutting through the shutters. He saw William holding his grandfather's hand and he realised that the old man had died. Richard rubbed his eyes and went to William's side.

'He's at peace now, son.'

'Aye…'

Sir John was laid to rest next to his wife and his daughter, Julianne; there was no marker to be seen for his son, if he was there, there was naught to show of it. William wore his new sword and saluted his grandfather by kissing the cross guard as his coffin was placed in the family vault.

Whilst they ate their evening meal William asked, 'what shall we do Father? I need to return to Sir William's mesnie until he sees fit to knight me.'

'Fear not Will, I know this place and the people well, I will leave Sir Gerard in charge, he is the best of men, and you and I will come regularly until you finally return as their Lord.'

Richard set in place all that was needed and they left that chapter of life behind them.

The instant they dismounted at home, Tristram made known to Richard the activity in London.

'Much has happened since you left Richard, you have had letters from the King, Esther opened them fearing that they may need your immediate attention.' Once dismounted a servant brought refreshment, they took a moment to slake their thirst and talked with Tristram. He told Richard what he knew, and Richard listened intently.

William begged to be excused, he would go to his mother and find Jacob, and Richard nodded his consent.

Tristram paused for a moment while Richard spoke to William; then he carried on as they walked slowly towards the keep. 'King Richard is raising vast funds any way he can; he has even released the Scottish King from his oath of subservience at a cost of ten thousand marks. Richard is yet in France as far as is known.'

'What of William Marshal, is there any news of him?'

'Yes, you have been ordered to go to the palace of Clarendon, immediately. You are to meet with him and train men for the crusade. The King feels the place is ideal for the purpose being near the great plain at Salisbury. He is to build many ships for the work of transporting an army and all its needs for war. Richard has appointed as regents

Hugh, Bishop of Durham, and William de Mandeville, of course all will be overseen by his mother, Queen Eleanor.'

Richard drew his head back in surprise. 'God's teeth, John will not be pleased with that decision.'

Tristram smiled, 'apparently John is *furious*; he assumed that *he* would be regent and no doubt fill his coffers on the back of it if I know John. I fancy Eleanor advised the King against making John his regent, and he will always do whatever she says.' Richard smiled at Tristram as he held the door of the keep open for him. 'The worry is, I don't think King Richard gives a holy fig for England, except as a source of revenue to fund his adventure. There is a jest going around that he is supposed to have said that he would sell London at the right price.' Richard gave a derisive snort. When they reached Richard's apartment, Richard asked Tristram if he would give him some time with Esther and his family, he would send for him once he spoken to them. Tristram bowed and left, Richard smiled once more as Tristram walked away; he could see all the activity in the country was consuming Tristram's thoughts, but at this instant, the death of Sir John and seeing Esther were foremost in his mind.

'Esther,' he smiled as he opened the door, she came to him, and they embraced.

'I saw you arrive and Tristram pounce on you, so I decided to wait for you here.'

'Are you all well?' he asked, his son Marshal clung to her dress uncertain of him. 'No hug for your Papa, Marshal,' but he merely turned his face into Esther's skirt.

Esther lifted Marshal into her arms, Richard touched him with his finger and he pressed closer to his mother, Richard laughed, 'and Isabelle, how is she?'

'She is a sleep, but she is well. Come sit, we have much to share, you have had letters and it seems that you must leave us once more.'

'How so?'

'You are to go to Clarendon; you are becoming a stranger to us.'

'You could not go to France because you had quickened with Isabelle, *all* my family will go to Clarendon, I would have it no other way.'

Esther's downcast face slowly brightened into a broad smile, 'Thank you, Richard, I hoped for such.'

Richard told Esther about his conversation with William and that he'd spoken to him about Julianne, Esther listened, but said nothing, listening was all that was required for now.

Richard sat quietly for some moments as if at a loss to know what else to say, and then abruptly changed the subject, 'I will send for Tristram, for I will want him to come with us *and* of course his new *wife*, "Lady Margaret".' While he waited for Tristram, he read his correspondence. His face lit up; there was even one from William Marshal. 'You've seen this Esther!' Esther nodded, 'Well I never, William is to marry Isabelle de Clare, Strongbow's daughter, our old enemy from Ireland, that will make William *de facto* Earl of Pembroke in South-Wales. They met at the Tower in London apparently and are to go to Ireland…' Richard paused, 'Prince John is Lord of Ireland and William will have to give him fealty. I would not have the moon, if I had to give such to John, the once Lackland as his father called him, now has much land. I pray that William does not rue that gift. He has moved up in the world, but he may have to pay a fearful cost. He has now offered fealty to the French King for his French holdings, John for his Irish and

Richard for his English estates. I can see problems with that complex arrangement, that may even be too much for the great skills of William's political tongue.'

'Do you know how old this Isabelle is, Richard?'

'Mmm… eighteen perhaps, and beautiful from what I've heard, and as you know William is over forty. King Richard must dearly want William's support with the giving of such a gift, everything carries a price.'

While they travelled to Clarendon, they learned that William de Mandeville, one of the King's regents had died and was to be replaced by Richard's chancellor, William Longchamp, which further infuriated Prince John, because he hated Longchamp. The chancellor held the purse strings and John was never satisfied. He had great estates now, but that was not enough, he ever wanted more and saw Longchamp as his nemesis. 'William may be content to place his head on the lion's plate, but I intend to remain on the outside of the cage, if possible.'

Little did Richard know that he was about to step into the cage; Prince John was at Clarendon with William Marshal and John wanted men where he could see them, for he trusted no one.

Chapter 24

Prince John hunting

Clarendon

Once Richard and Esther had settled the work in their minds, they actually looked forward to going to Clarendon Palace, meeting William Marshal's new wife and renewing their friendship with him. They knew that they would also see their son William who had gone ahead of them to take up once more his duties of a squire to the Marshal.

Clarendon Palace, was a few miles east of Salisbury, it was large and a favourite of King Henry and Queen Eleanor. Henry had spent considerable coin developing the site to his liking and had taken Richard there many times.

The location had been occupied since the days of the Saxons, probably for the hunting in the forest of Clarendon. Within its boundaries, the park was laid out with lawns, coppices, meadows and wooded pasture.

Queen Eleanor had a compact suite of apartments, comprising of a hall, a chapel, three chambers, and a wardrobe. They were situated on two floors. The rooms were spacious, two of them extending to a length of perhaps, forty feet, and the amenities of her chambers had been greatly improved by the recent adjacent construction of a two-storey building providing access to a privy chamber, well vaulted on both floors.

The focal point of the Queen's hall was an imposing new fireplace with double marble columns on each side and an over-mantel carved with representations of the twelve months of the year. The windows of her rooms were glazed, mainly in plain glass, but some were delicate silver-grey *grisaille* patterns, also with some figured glass, which was coloured. The windows of her hall overlooked a garden.

The chapel, on the upper floor, had a marble altar, flanked by two windows, which could be opened and closed, and above the altar was a crucifix, with the figures of Mary and John. Religious imagery was not confined to the chapel; in the window of one of the Queen's chambers there was a representation of the Virgin and Child with the kneeling figure of an earthly queen, presumably Queen Eleanor herself, with an *Ave Maria* scroll. The walls of the chapel were painted with scenes from the life of St. Katharine. One of the distinctive features of these rooms, were the tiled floors. The tiles were figured, glowing in muted shades of gold, grey, and warm pink. Their power to induce admiration was incomparable; all who saw them agreed they were quite astonishing.

William Marshal said that he would take a troop of young knights out on horseback to complete some exercises on Salisbury plain. King Henry had forbidden tourneys anywhere he ruled, fearing that large bands of armed men not under his control were potentially a threat. Therefore, such practice, as William was about to conduct, was not familiar to most English knights. Whilst, William worked with the men in the field, Richard worked in the tiltyard with Sir Tristram, training other young knights at the quintain and the pell. They would take turns at the different work, one day Richard would be in the tiltyard, the next he would be in the field and so the young knights would experience the differing approaches of the two experienced knights. Richard was pleased to have his long-time friend with him, he'd missed him and they were enjoying working together, it was like old times.

It was hot dusty work in the tiltyard and both Richard and Tristram had stripped down to their shirts, discarding their hauberks. Their young – would-be knights – were not so fortunate, he had insisted that they were fully armoured and was content to suffer their complaints.

Whilst Richard was working, Esther and the now Lady Isabelle *Marshal*, Countess of Pembroke, would pass their time enjoying the magnificent palace and its grounds.

'This place we now find ourselves in, is lavish indeed Isabelle,' Esther laughed.

'To be sure my Lady, but I prefer my home in Ireland where my mother lives. I do not feel at ease here. I have always preferred the simple life; even the great tower in London where I have been all but a prisoner for years, is shaded by the opulence here. Albeit I was born in Pembrokeshire, I prefer my grandfather's home in Striguil; this is too grand for the likes of me. I know *all* at home, there are many strangers here.'

'But you are at great heiress, a Countess no less!'

'So, they tell me,' she laughed.

'Are you happy with William now you are married? William told us honestly that the marriage was forced upon you.'

'*More* than happy, I love him. At first, I was simply relieved to be free of my imprisonment and I gave the marriage little thought. I'd only briefly met William once before, but now I see God's merciful grace was at work.' Esther thought she even glowed as she spoke his name, and she affectionately squeezed Isabelle's hand.

'I lived on a small farm in France when I was a child?'

'Really my Lady, I thought you had always been a great Lady.'

Esther smiled, 'ha, I am no great Lady, you only think so because I'm older than you, in truth, I always feel uncomfortable at court just as you do. There are forever furtive eyes assessing and judging whilst lips smile and heads bow most congenially.'

Esther and Isabelle paused their conversation for a moment, to look at the gardens from a window in the hall. They were about to continue when they saw Prince John and three other men walking towards them. Esther and Isabelle bowed as the group neared and John's party stopped.

John turned to his companions and bade them leave him, 'I will pass the time with these fair ladies,' he said and they laughed and went on. 'Walk with me, good lady,' he said to Esther.

Esther glanced nervously at Isabelle and took the arm John offered. 'A fine day, my Lady.'

'Yes, my Lord.'

'I trust you are entertained, let me show you the rare view from in here,' and he opened the door and guided her into a large bedroom. Isabelle was about to follow, but John closed the door on her and slipped on the bolt.

'My *Lady Marshal,* Lord!'

'She will not be needed; Esther is it not?'

'I think that perhaps I should join her, Lord.'

'Nonsense.' John drew closer to Esther and put his arm around her waist.

'My Lord!'

'Come, come, my Lady, time for a little sport I think.' John took hold of her gown and ripped the front, Esther screamed and pushed him away.

Isabelle heard Esther's scream and ran as quickly as her legs would carry her in the direction of the tiltyard, she knew very well John's reputation as a rapist. She was running at such a pace she nearly collided with Richard who was making his way from the yard towards his rooms.

'My Lady, whatever is it child? Still yourself.'

'Oh Lord, thank God it's you,' she panted, 'my Lady, has been taken by Prince John and I heard her screaming.'

'WHAT, show me!' Isabelle turned and they both ran bowling those who would impede them to one side.

'She's in there, Lord…' Isabelle pointed gasping for breath and bent forward resting her hands on her knees, not that Richard needed to be told where Esther was, her screams were loud enough to bring the walls down. Richard tried the door and realised it was secured; he took one step back and burst the door open with a single kick from his boot. John was grappling with Esther on the bed. The crash distracted John and he twisted his head towards the door, before he could defend himself Richard lunged for him, grabbing hold of the collar of his doublet, nearly choking him, such was the force Richard had exerted to pull him from Esther. John was now frantically clawing at his collar with his fingers trying to get breath. Richard threw John against the wall and grabbed him by the throat, drawing his dagger and pushing the point into John's extended neck.

John was only a little over five foot six, Richard was over six-foot, and build to match, his presence consumed John, but he lowered himself so close to John's face his nose was pressed against his. 'You *miserable,* pox ridden, guttersnipe, I have a good mind to slit your miserable throat. *Get* from this place, Esther!' He shouted over his shoulder. Esther did as he said and ran to Isabelle who was now standing at the door.

'She enticed me, she is known for it,' John whimpered, reaching for Richard's arm. Richard merely slapped his hand to the side, pulled him forward, and then brutally lashed his head back against the wall; with such force, he clearly stunned John.

At that second, three guards ran in to the room having heard the furore and dragged Richard from John. Richard struggled, but they held his arms securely. John pushed himself from the wall, blinked, touched his head, and saw his hand was covered with blood. He stepped to Richard and spat in his face, Richard writhed yet again trying to shake free of his captors, a guard struck his head with the pommel of his sword, and Richard slumped to the ground.

'You will hang for this, you dog,' John yelled, trembling with a mixture of fear and rage, 'take him away and lock him up.' As the guards lifted Richard from the floor, John kicked him viciously in the face whipping his head back.

Once in her room, Esther collapsed on her bed shaking uncontrollably.

'Take this my Lady,' her maid Jane knelt by her and offered her a goblet of wine. She took it, and drank it without thought. Suddenly there was a thunderous hammering at the door, they both jumped.

'It's me, Tristram, open the door.'

'Quickly Isabelle, let him in.'

Tristram burst into the room, sword in hand. 'Esther, what in God's name has happened? Richard has been arrested, he is to be hanged, he looked to be unconscious so he is spared for the moment.'

'God in heaven, quick get me fresh clothes Jane and help me dress!'

'What are you going to do?' asked Tristram.

'Is Sir William here, does he know of this?'

'No, he is out with men on the plain. I know not when he will return.'

'Leave us, wait outside whilst I change from this dress.' Tristram hesitated then went to the door, closing it behind him.

'Let us make haste Jane.' Esther hurriedly changed, washed her face, and brushed her hair. 'Come.' Isabelle looked mystified, Jane opened the door, and Tristram appeared equally bemused.

'Where are you going, Esther, it's not safe for you, stay in your room, I'll see what I can do, Richard has many friends here,' Tristram said anxiously.

'*Not – safe*, can you be serious! My husband is about to hang. Go to the gates and wait for Sir William then make known to him what has happened, pray God that he comes before it is too late.'

'What about you, Esther!'

'Do as you are bidden; I'm going to plead with John for my husband's life.'

'You *fool* Esther, he won't listen, I must come with you if you are bent on such madness.'

'Tristram is right, Esther,' Margaret, Tristram's wife who had now joined them said, equally worried.

'He *will* listen; don't argue with me, I must do this alone. Now go, you have your work for this minute.' Tristram hesitated, '*Go,* I tell you.' He reluctantly went as he'd been told. Esther and Margaret made their way to Prince John's apartments. All she passed looked and turned awkwardly away from her, clearly, the news has flashed through the palace. When she reached John's apartment, she saw two guards at the door.

Chapter 25

Revenge

'Tell the Prince, Lady Maillorie, wishes to speak with him.'

The two looked fearfully at each other then one bowed and went inside. When he returned, he opened the door wide and motioned her to enter. John was lying on his bed.

He smirked, and beckoned her forward, she bowed, 'And to what do I owe this honour, dear Lady?'

'I come to *beg* for my husband's life.'

'Ah… beg, you say, is he still in the land of the living? How remiss of my guards, I ordered that he be hanged.' Esther face was as stone. 'Mmm, perhaps he *is* yet with us. I flatter myself that I am a good judge of character. I was expecting you. Why should I spare that treacherous dog of a husband?' Esther held herself rigid she would not be provoked.

'I come to you willingly, I offer myself for my husband's life.' John studied the corner of his shirt, stroking it between his thumb and forefinger, smiling. 'You see I always get what I want in the end.'

He rose, brushed by her, caressing her face as he passed. He opened the door and spoke quietly to the guard, the guard nodded. John smiled, came to her, gently pressing his lips to her neck. 'I have spoken to the guard and *if* you please me this night the guard has orders to release your ill begotten husband in the morning, he will have to be flogged you understand, but he will yet have his life. A fine bargain is it not? Come dear lady let us not linger, let me be witness to what you offer in this trade, is that garment you wear really necessary between friends?'

Esther tried to loosen her dress, 'Let me help you,' John again kissed her neck. She almost vomited, the bile came into her mouth and she was compelled to swallow it down, but she would do this for Richard.

Suddenly – the door swung open and the shadow of William Marshal seemed to flood the whole room. 'My Lord, my Lady.'

'How *dare* you enter my private rooms, Marshal, without my instruction, *get* out!' William graciously bowed but never moved.

'I must beg your forgiveness my Prince, I have seen to your orders and I assumed that you would want immediate confirmation that your commands were carried out.'

'What are you talking about, you clod?' William showed not the slightest reaction to the offensiveness, but replied in the calmest voice.

'I was informed that you wanted Lord Richard Maillorie released and I have attended to such.'

'What, you blithering fool! Marshal, I ordered him hanged not released.'

'I'm most sorry Lord, I have been misinformed, mere confusion in the heat of the moment no doubt.'

Esther shook free of John, 'You *vile* treacherous animal, you never intended to free my husband.' John actually recoiled at the venom of her rebuke.

'May I have a word alone my Prince?' William spoke in an ice-cold tone that made it clear he was not asking, but demanding. 'Leave us my Lady, I see that your maid awaits you,' William instructed Esther. His eyes never left John's, there was no doubt, *he* was the master here, John's boldness had vanished into his feeble malicious nature, and he was now visibly trembling, clearly terrified by this man's overpowering presence. Esther stood unyielding for a moment in this highly charged atmosphere; she stared at John her eyes were on fire with undiluted revulsion.

'You disgust me – you evil – slimy creature,' she spat out the words at him through her teeth and then abruptly turned on her heels and stormed from the room.

Lady Margaret, Tristram's wife, embraced Esther when she found her.

'Thank God you are safe, I was sent to find you,'

'Fear not I am well enough.'

'Sir William said we are to make haste and go to the courtyard, there are horses saddled and waiting for us, my Lady. Lord Aylesford, and your children are there including your eldest son, Sir William has bidden him ride with us for safety's sake.'

'Oh… we must first go to our room it's on the way to the yard, I will gather some essentials we will be but a moment.'

They carried their bundles into the yard, and rushed towards Richard and her son William, who ran to them taking her and Margaret's packs. Richard wrapped his arm around Esther, asking if she was hurt.

'Richard, am I hurt! Dear Mother of Christ, your face!' She looked at him in horror, his jaw was so swollen that he could hardly speak and one of his eyes was all but closed.

'I am well enough, only bruised; it perhaps looks worse than it is,' he mumbled, 'let us make haste.'

'Where is Tristram?'

'He is with William's men who released me, come he will catch up with us soon enough. William has it under control, he has instructed us to wait at a small hamlet called Stockbridge east of here; it is no more than a crossing over the river Test, on the drover's road from Wales. We should be there well before nightfall.' Esther and Margaret were helped onto their mounts and they set off immediately riding out of the palace compound at some pace and onto the road heading east.

They were hot and weary by the time they rode over the brow of the hill and caught sight of the small hamlet in the valley bottom. It was no more than a few houses set either side of the track crossing a wooden bridge. The horses were tired; they'd been ridden hard; they were glad to come to a standstill where there was a stream of cool water.

'Don't let them drink too much,' Richard called. There was an inn of sorts and food for the travellers, but no beds, this was a place of much activity, men, women, children and animals all vying for attention.

'We will sleep under the stars this night and be thankful for God's mercy, Richard.'

There was a dozen in their small band, knights and men-at-arms, who had come with Richard from Aylesford. Food was brought to them, it was simple country fare, but it was good and plentiful. Esther and Richard sat apart from the rest; Richard wanted to know all that had happened.

When she told him, he was beside himself with rage, as much with her as with John, for endangering herself. So much so, Esther was unable to calm him, he threw his helm with such force to the ground a rivet holding the chinstrap sprung loose. He kicked it some distance from him, swearing without restraint, and clearly injuring his foot. 'I swear by all that is sacred, that turd of Beelzebub will pay for this day's outrage, and I will *laugh* as I watch him squirm, so help me God.'

'Richard, was it not you who said if a man seeks revenge, he'd better dig two graves.'

'Aye, and it would be worth it.' They were distracted by the sound of a horse galloping towards them. 'Thank God, Tristram.' As the horseman drew nearer, they could see that it was *not* Tristram. The man rode into the camp and called for Lord Aylesford.

'I'm here man, what is it?'

'A letter from Sir William Marshal, Lord.'

'Give it here,' the man reached into a wallet at his waist and passed the letter to Richard, who tore it open, and read it eagerly to Esther.

My Dear Richard, God forgive me for I have failed your friend…

'What nonsense is this, Richard?' Esther demanded, he stopped reading aloud, stared at the document and then let it slip slowly from his hand, it floated down onto the grass at his feet, he turned and set his head against a tree next to him, gripping two branches with outstretched arms so tightly his knuckles turned white. Esther bent down, picked up the missive and read – with horror – what was written.

...Prince John, that evil spawn of darkness, gave orders that Sir Tristram be brutally beaten and then hanged immediately, without redress. It was done unknown to me, by some of John's cronies, in a wooded area outside the castle. They must have taken him when he left us to join you. No doubt, they were intent on demonstrating their loyalty.

I fear it was no more than a vindictive act of the most heinous kind, solely to punish you. They left him hanging; I have tended to him with all the respect due to a brave knight.

I am truly ashamed, that a knight and a Prince of the realm could act with such dishonour, in this place of law making, the place where the Assize of Clarendon and the law of Compurgation was drawn up by the Prince's father, King Henry, to put an end to such wanton evil.

May God, have mercy on me for my shameful neglect, Ever your humble servant,

William Marshal.

Esther fell to her knees yet clutching the document, and cried out, 'Dear God in heaven, my – dearest – kindest, Tristram. Oh, help me please Mother of Christ, whatever will we tell Margaret?' but it was too late Margaret had heard and she collapsed at Esther's feet.

Chapter 26

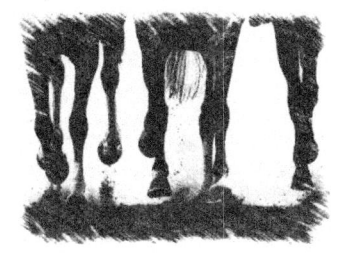

Sorrow

The journey home had been a sombre affair for Richard's party. There was little interaction between any of the travellers and Richard never spoke to a soul.

They had set off for home in a cloud of thunder and lightening after an unprecedented confrontation between Esther and Richard, the worst they had ever had in their lives. They had argued because Esther had categorically forbidden Richard to return to Clarendon.

In the end, Richard, without the slightest hint of grace, had been dissuaded against returning to satisfy his need for vengeance. It was not even that she'd had stood up to him in front of his men, that had angered him so, but that she was standing in the way of him pouring the balm of revenge upon his anguish. After he had succumbed to Esther's unrelenting barrage, he had as of yet refused, or been unable to, speak to her, or anyone else. His face was as ice, frozen, unreadable, frightening, Esther kept glancing at him she was fearful of what was going through his head she had to cling to her saddle for fear of falling from her horse such was her agitation.

Deep down Richard knew she'd been right – but that didn't assuage his pain and utter frustration that such as John could escape any sort of retribution, for the murdering of an innocent man. Tristram was not *just*, an innocent man; he was someone who had stood against tyranny of any sort, a man of compassion and honour. That John, whom Richard despised, a creature wholly without any vestige of honour, could take the life of his dearest friend without any redress – heartily sickened him. It would have been foolish to return, he could concede to that, now his initial heat had cooled. He would have been outnumbered, men would have taken sides it would have been a bloodbath, many would have died and in the end, King Richard would probably have hanged them all as rebels, it would have achieved nothing other than to exacerbate the situation. He knew that he needed to learn to play John at his own game. A game that was not driven by honour or right, a game played out on the darker side of life and he feared that he was not equal to it. Perhaps that's what was driving him to this despair. For John to win against all right and decency could surely not be possible in a country purporting to be a Godly nation.

Richard would have gladly given his life to be rid of John, but it would not just have been his life. The fury and indignity he felt at the total disregard for any sense of right and honour was more than he could stomach.

On their arrival at Aylesford, Richard did not help Esther from her horse; he instead went to Tristram's pregnant wife Margaret and lowered her from her mount. He embraced her, he didn't know if it was for his comfort, or hers, but she never responded, she only stood rigid, showing no reaction whatsoever, clearly unable to assimilate the torment she was now experiencing.

Alwin aided Esther from her saddle and once dismounted she stood silently and watched Richard. Alwin made no comment, but it was clear to all who saw them, some great tragedy had befallen them.

There were tears in Richard's eyes when he released Margaret and turned to go. Esther looked at him; her face was the picture of understanding and the deepest sympathy. Richard ignored her, striding past her and Alwin, and their two sons, making his way to his rooms.

It was sometime before Esther joined him in their room. Richard could not still his anger. He was in his hauberk and yet armed, sitting at the fireplace when she entered their room. She glanced at him, hesitated, and then sat opposite him.

'Richard…'

He lifted his hand to still her, 'I do not wish to talk to you. You had no right to speak to me as you did in front of my men, that was unforgivable.'

'You gave me no choice, you would have ridden back to Clarendon, and innocent people would have died because of *your* passion.'

Richard rose from his chair and glared at her, 'PASSION,' he shouted stabbing his finger at her, 'you have no idea how hurt and angry I was and continue to be, *no* idea whatsoever.'

Esther stood, now *she* was furious with *him,* her glare was scorching, 'I – have – no idea! How *dare* you say such a cruel thing, I loved Tristram too, he has always been there for me… and *he* has *never* betrayed me as *you* have…' The words hung in the air suspended by their innate energy. They both merely stared at each other, those words had never been given voice before, and what had just been said, could not now be unsaid.

Richard slumped down into his chair, and stared at her as if he'd been unexpectedly struck with a blunt instrument, which in a sense he had. Her words had humbled the righteous inferno of indignation, which had been burning within.

'*No*…' he said softly, he could do no more than shake his head; he had judged; now he had *been* judged. 'Tristram never betrayed anyone, and never once did he upbraid me for failing him *or* you,' Richard said quietly.

Esther's teeth were chattering, she felt sick, she'd never meant to inflict such hurt she had even shocked herself. 'F-Forgive me, Richard, I did not mean to say that.'

'No doubt… but it's the truth – you spoke only the truth. Do not reproach yourself; it is I who must apologise, I lost all sense this day and but for your courage, I would have caused untold suffering. I behaved like an irresponsible fool. It took that blow to my pride you have just delivered to bring me to my senses.'

Esther was yet shaking as she stood before him, 'we are both wounded, this day has seen Hell visited upon us and there will be more to follow – of that I am certain. John will not forget this.'

'I don't know how to make this right, Esther. I thought that all your pain was in the past, but clearly it is yet there just below the surface.'

'You are mistaken; I could not live if I had harboured such. You hurt me, discounting my pain at the loss of Tristram and I wanted to hurt you… I am ashamed, but he who knows how to hurt is ever nearby to prompt us. This is what the John's of this world do, they give life to hate, then water and feed it, and like lambs to the slaughter we succumb to his evil.'

'We have never fallen out like this before. I cannot still the pain I feel at the loss of Tristram, as I said, he never once reproached me for the way I betrayed you, or failed him, and he had the right. Aye he was a better man than me I was not worthy to tie the laces on his boots. I could tear John limb from limb, so help me God – he will pay for that day's evil. What about Margaret, where is she now?'

'She is with her sister, that's where she wanted to go and I took her. She was very quiet, struggling to walk. I will go and see her later. I fear for the child she is carrying.'

Richard stood; 'Might I touch you?'

'Do you really need to ask?' He took Esther's hand and drew her into his arms.

'Forgive me Esther, it is a shameful thing to see one's *real* self. I love you more than life. I should have killed that spawn of the Devil when I had the chance, you see a man filled with revulsion, how could I forgive someone like John? I will never be able to do such, never.'

'I know not the answers to your questions, I do know that God forgives me, that is our belief and hope, is it not?'

'You do not compare yourself to that thing, I cannot even say man,' he looked at her in astonishment.

'Are you then saying that some are beyond redemption, is that correct?'

'Yes, and John is such, you are the best of people, your goodness is known to all, it is right that His forgiving hand would be stretched out to you.'

'I though only God was good!'

'Enough, I will not think on such, it is foolish to imagine a righteous God could forgive his wickedness, he should and will, burn in Hell. I do know we must ever be watchful, one thing I am certain of, as you have so rightly said, John does not forget. As long as he prowls this earth we will be in danger.'

He was holding her so tightly she could feel the tension rippling through his muscles as he spoke.

Chapter 27

Prince John

They heard little of John directly over the subsequent weeks. They knew what was happening in his world because William Marshal kept them informed. It seemed that King Richard was determined to indulge his brother John, no doubt hoping to assure John's support and loyalty whilst he, Richard, was away on crusade.

John was made Count of Mortain and he married the wealthy Isabel of Gloucester. He was also given other valuable lands in England and France to add to his Lordship of Ireland.

Richard struggled with William's relationship with John and it caused a division between them, he had not seen William for some time even their once frequent correspondence had ceased. Richard remembered how harshly he had judged William when he submitted to the Young King Henry in France. He had said then that he would not judge him again after he'd witnessed his torment because of his honour. However, Richard would not see him whilst he gave support to John.

In John's wranglings with Longchamp, William had inexplicably championed John's cause even though it was clear to Richard that Longchamp had the right of it. Richard suspected that William had even encouraged Queen Eleanor to favour John's claims. Richard knew only too well the close relationship William had with Eleanor; he'd openly spoken of his devotion to her.

Richard's son, William had never returned to William Marshal's mesnie, which had been a great disappointment to him. He knew that was not possible, because of his connections with John, and William remembered vividly John's attack on his mother and murder of Tristram. William had instead, gone to finish his training under Robert de Vere, from Hedingham in Essex, an ally of his father's. His new tutor whom he liked had now knighted him, but he was no William Marshal. Whilst he was there his betrothal was arranged with Grâce, the fourteen-year-old daughter of Baron Robert de Vere and she now lived with Richard and Esther. Richard liked de Vere; he was one of the growing numbers of Barons who despised John. He wanted his Earlship ratified by the crown and John had spoken against his request, because Baron Robert refused to curry John's support with a gift of coin. Unlike his brother Richard, John would never sell parts of his kingdom for a cause, even the cause of avarice, which was a cause most dear to his heart. John knew once the fruit was sold one could no longer extract its juice and he was ever thirsty for more juice.

Esther liked Grâce, she was pretty, and though she was now amongst strangers, she tried to make the best of it always smiling and never complaining. She was infatuated with William, he was taller than most his age, startlingly handsome and stood out in a crowd. He had the most sparkling azure blue eyes just like his mother's, and Grâce lit up in his presence. Although William clearly liked Grâce, he appeared to only see her as he did his sister, but he was always kind to her. Esther hoped that as she grew older and developed into a woman, he would see her in a quite different light, not only to want her, but also to love her.

Richard rarely mentioned Prince John, but Esther knew he followed his every move it was an obsession and she continually feared where it would lead. Lady Margaret, Tristram's widow, had become Esther's constant companion she was like a sister to Esther. She had given birth to a boy whom she called after his father, Tristram. Richard could not say the name; he always called him little fellow or young man, but *never* Tristram.

They heard that the King had married while in Cyprus, which had surprised Richard; for he knew that the King was not the marrying kind, his preference was of a very different order.

'Perhaps you are mistaken about the King, Richard,' suggested Esther.

'Well, we will see, but John will not be pleased of that I am certain, it's interesting, I have heard that Richard has named his nephew Arthur as his successor,' and he laughed.

Esther did not even smile for she was disturbed by Richard's laughter; it was not the laughter of joy and amusement, but of callous satisfaction. She knew he was taking delight from what he assumed would bring John misery.

However, Richard's mood of merriment changed shortly afterward when John's hand once more reached into his life. He received a correspondence from John; he didn't open it for some time, but held it in one hand and tapped it against the knuckle of his other hand.

'Come Richard open it and be done with it!'

'Mmm,' was his reply as he reached for his dagger, broke the seal free of the parchment and unfolded the missive. He stood suddenly. 'He wants Jacob to be his squire as assurance of my loyalty to him!'

Now Esther rose just as abruptly as Richard, 'he wants Jacob as a hostage because you refused to give fealty to him. I knew he would not let that snub pass.'

'He shall not have Jacob.'

'Oh – thank you Richard, thank you,' and she all but collapsed into her chair with her face in her hands.

'Did you think for one moment I would let Jacob go into the nest of that viper?'

'I don't know what I thought; he means to destroy you Richard. Can he take our home?'

'He can try; it will not be likely while he is subject to King Richard. I must write to Will at Tattershall and Raymond at Framingham, they must be on their guard too. Though John has never turned his attention to Will, we cannot take anything for granted.'

Richard's son William, now newly knighted had ridden to Tattershall to begin the Lordship of his inheritance. He had always gone there over the years whenever he was free, and had taken every opportunity to learn from Sir Gerard who had lived and worked for his grandfather for most of his life. William knew that he had to tread carefully; Sir Gerard was a gruff dour sort of Scotsman, but as straight as a spear shaft he could remember his grandfather saying.

William had new ideas, things he wanted to change and was sure Sir Gerard would struggle if he simply trampled over him. He liked Sir Gerard and knew he needed him they would work together. His father exhorted the value of having someone that could be trusted and able, whom he could leave in charge. He knew fine well that his father had often been called away upon the old King's business, and Tristram had stayed behind and managed his estate, well for now he had Sir Gerard. He smiled cynically to himself for he could never see himself having such a relationship with the King; his best hope was that the King forgot he existed. He'd met King Richard briefly when he was a squire for William Marshal at Le Mans and his view was tainted, because at that time Richard was the enemy. He remembered when they were escaping how the Marshal had nearly killed him.

William's other consideration was *Grâce,* he thought increasingly of her, but was nervous about all the responsibility that he was suddenly facing. She would be coming here soon enough, and that would involve change for everyone.

Chapter 28

Taken Prisoner

The political turmoil continued. John began to explore an alliance with the French king, who was freshly returned from the crusade.

John hoped to acquire Normandy, Anjou and the other lands in France held by Richard in exchange for allying himself with Philip. John was at first persuaded not to pursue such an alliance by his mother. Longchamp, who had left England, after Walter of Coutances, the Archbishop of Rouen intervened, now returned, and argued that he had been wrongly removed as justiciar. John interfered, suppressing Longchamp's claims hoping to curry favour with the Barons in return for promises of support from the royal administration, including a reaffirmation of his position as heir to the throne.

When Richard did not return from the crusade, John began to assert that his brother was dead or otherwise permanently lost. Richard had in fact been captured en route to England by the Duke of Austria and was handed over to Emperor Henry the VI, who held him for a ransom of 100,000 marks, which amounted to twice the annual revenue raised in England.

John, ignoring his mother's counsel, decided to seize the opportunity of his brother's absence to go to Paris, where he formed an alliance with Philip. He agreed to set aside his wife, Isabella of Gloucester, and marry Philip's sister, Isabella of Angoulême, in exchange for Philip's support.

Richard heard that the girl was very young, they said twelve, but he'd heard she was possibly only nine.

Even in this, John had managed to make powerful enemies in his desperation for *more*. Isabella, or Helen as some called her, was a wealthy countess in her own right and already betrothed to Hugh le Brun, Count of Lusignan who was understandably furious at being robbed of such a prize. It seemed that the brightness of coin, "*Now*", forever blinded John to the long-term cost of his actions.

Richard and other disgruntled Barons saw this as an opportunity to hinder John's ambitions in the name of loyalty to the King. Not that they had any great love of their absent King, but they loved Prince John less. There were skirmishes with John's loyal followers of which William Marshal was said to be one, though Richard never encountered him.

Richard met regularly with several Barons, Henry de Bohun, and his friends John de Lacy and Robert de Vere to decide how best to limit John's aspirations.

The four were sat around one of the campfires of their combined forces, trying to decide their next move and be prepared for what they might have to face in the future. They had been harrying John's supporters for some weeks now. The Barons having been crippled by the taxes, which John had imposed, allegedly, to raise the staggering sum being demanded to pay Richard's ransom, saw the unpopular treaties with Philip as an opportunity to claw back ground. Each had been ordered to pay three times the usual tax, once for their normal tax and twice more for Richard's ransom.

There was poverty and suffering everywhere they looked, some Lords were being robbed of everything and could not even afford the coin to buy the next years seed for their fields.

Their deliberations were suddenly interrupted when a guard called out that there was a small troop of armed men riding in their direction. The four leaders glanced at each other then quickly armed. Lord Robert kicked soil over the fire and ordered that the others did likewise, and then they ran to their horses, squires were already saddling them. They positioned some men in the wooded area where they were camped for the night and waited. They would close the trap, once the riders were in the midst of them. Richard narrowed his eyes *desperately* trying to see the oncoming men. He could just make out that there was a young man leading the group and he was riding at some pace straight into their ambush, but he was unable to make sense of the device on his surcoat.

The command was given, and they encircled the strangers who made not the slightest attempt to defend themselves. Their leader lifted his hands in surrender, and quickly called out for fear of being struck down.

'I come in peace, my Lords,' he said in a clear voice. Lord Robert was first to confront the man.

'And what are you called by, Sir Knight?'

'These are dangerous times to be riding in the dark with armed men and no forward scouts. You are either an innocent or a fool, which is it?' asked John de Lacy before the knight could give his name.

'I have had forward scouts and knew of your presence, number and allegiance, my Lord. I am not such a fool, or innocent, that you imagine.'

'If that be the case, I should mind your tongue, when you address me!'

'Forgive me Lord, I meant no impertinence. I heard that Lord Maillorie was fighting in this area and hoped to offer my sword to him.' Richard now pressed *his* horse forward to face the fellow; he was unsettled by the man's features.

'I'm Lord Maillorie,' Richard said calmly, 'and yet *you* have not given your name, though you have been asked.'

The young man bowed, 'I am honoured to meet you, I have been brought up with *your* name ringing in my ears.'

'Mmmm, is that so, and your name is?'

'I am known by the name of *William* Marshal.' An uncanny silence swept over the listeners and they fidgeted uneasily in their saddles.

'We hear William Marshal is a friend of Prince John…' Richard said softly, his gaze never leaving the bright hazel eyes before him. This was a young man with disturbingly cool nerves. Richard could see there were things below the surface, which drove this man, perhaps *beyond* wisdom.

'Not this – *William Marshal* – that is where my association with the man you refer to ends. I denounce my family for they have betrayed me.' Richard drew back his head in astonishment, for the words "Betrayal and William Marshal" were words that were not easy bedfellows. 'I will never give fealty to that murdering manifestation of the Antichrist, John, he is no lord of mine nor ever will be.' Richard leant forward on his saddle once more and stared at the young man.

'Would you have us believe that you are related to my long-time friend, William Marshal and you now stand *against* him?' Richard pushed his horse even closer to the young man to better see his face.

'It is so, he is my father, and as long as he is with John, he is my enemy.' The Barons listening to Richard and the young man glanced uneasily to each other.

'What has John done to a young man such as you, to engender such hatred?'

'I have been his hostage since a boy and I know well what sort of depravity he is surrounded by and engages in. He has caused me grievous injury, of which I wish not to speak. For the iniquity is raw in my heart and forever will be, as long as this son of darkness lives.'

'Aye… we here are all witnesses to John's failings. You have the look of your sire to be sure, but you come to us too late for fighting. It is our intention to separate on the morrow for we have heard that the King is in England and John has fled to France. We wish not to be judged as rebels against our King for our grievances are not against him *directly*.' The young man looked unsure about this information.

'But there is yet fighting, I have seen it!'

'Aye, I dare say there will be groups who have not yet heard the news, yourself for example. Get from your horses, and we will talk more, have you eaten?'

'Not for two days.'

'We have rabbit stew in a pot going cold, thanks to you, plenty for you and your men. Come join us and tell us what you know, then we'll decide if we are to hang you or not,' Richard smiled.

They talked, ate, slept, and at first light made their farewells. Richard liked the young knight and asked him if he would return to Aylesford with him, and he said he would be glad to for he was without home or employment at this time. Richard embraced his friends and bade them farewell promising to keep in close contact.

'John has made known over these months, if we were ever in doubt, that he intends to have the throne by any means. This time together is only the start my friends; we are all agreed on that? He will have to be brought to heel eventually, and so it has been from the very beginning.' Each with concerned faces murmured their agreement, this was not the end of the conflict with John, and they knew it.

On approaching his home, Richard became aware that there had been fighting, they came across several dead soldiers and burned out campfires.

'What do you make of this, Sir Hugh?' asked Richard drawing his horse to a standstill.

'There is no sign of a battle in the immediate vicinity. The dead who lie here have either been brought here or made it here by themselves, died and were left unburied, which means that their comrades were in a hurry to get clear of the place.'

'Let us make haste to Aylesford, that may have been their target, pray God that they failed.'

The troop now galloped for Aylesford and as the castle came into view, they could see that the drawbridge was up and they noticed that there was suddenly a great deal of activity on the battlements.

They must have been recognised for the drawbridge started to lower and they galloped over it and into the courtyard. Richard's sons William and Jacob greeted them, and Richard dismounted.

'Is your mother safe?'

'Aye, Father, fear not, we have had some trouble but they were of no threat, no more than fifty is my guess. They attacked the village, but we saw them off, we raised the drawbridge for safety's sake.'

'Thank God, it's good to see you son, what brings you here from Tattershall?'

'I needed to know what was happening and that you were safe, I came via Framingham to see how Raymond faired, but he'd seen nought of the troubles.' William's voice trailed off as he caught sight of the young man standing behind his father, Richard turned to the young Marshal.

'Ah…' said Richard, 'let me introduce the son of William Marshal, to make things simple he is also known as William Marshal.' Richard's son bowed and offered his hand to the young man. 'Come let us make our way to my rooms where you can meet my wife. I will call you Young William, if you don't mind, to help us know who's who, for it appears we are beset with a plethora of Williams.' They all laughed.

The King had finally returned to England, and John's remaining forces surrendered. John retreated to Normandy, where King Richard finally found him later that year. Richard declared that his younger brother – despite being twenty-seven years old – was merely, "A child who has had evil counsellors" and forgave him. However, Richard was not completely blinded by brotherly love, for he confiscated John's lands with the exception of Ireland.

Chapter 29

King at last

Esther was delighted to have William home, as was Grâce, his betrothed. He was ever more inclined to seek out her company, which he had not been in the past and on this visit, they often went out riding on their own. Esther was increasingly convinced that they should be wed sooner rather than later they were both young and were *very* affectionate.

Young William Marshal fitted into the household with ease and was enjoying the attention of Isabelle Esther's youngest, but Esther thought it no more than friendship, for sure on William's part; William and her were much of an age. The three young men practiced together in the tiltyard and laughed a great deal in each other's company. This was a good time, and Esther glowed in satisfaction.

Richard never made mention of the grief young William Marshal had referred to on the night of their first meeting, but he suspected that he now knew of the cause.

He had been told that William had been married to Alice de Bethune for no more than nine months; whilst he was away fighting, she was murdered *inside* his Father's castle. She'd been pregnant and in the care of his mother and father at the time, no one had been apprehended for the crime, but William was convinced that Prince John had been behind it. He was furious with his father because he'd defended John for lack of evidence. William had accused his father of being in league with Prince John and had not spoken to him since that day.

Richard had written to William and Isabelle to reassure them that their son would be cared for and that he was safe. The Marshal had written back with his usual pragmatic outlook, saying that it was forever wise to have a foot in each camp. Richard shook his head and smiled as he read the letter to Esther.

'Even such a sadness as this enmity with his son and heir does not dampen his ever-positive outlook.'

'What does he mean, "A foot in both camps", Richard?'

'He means that whoever prevails in the end, be it John or Richard, the Earl of Pembroke will be on the winning side. I would hate to think that William made capital of Alice de Bethune's death by falling out with his son, merely to secure his position, but I would not put it past him.'

'Well, I think that disgraceful!'

'Esther, our hold on what we have is tenuous, and reliant on favour; William knows such and will make some advantage of whatever befalls him. He has risen from a simple stipendiary hearth knight to one of the highest positions in the land and yet never failed his honour. I was made painfully aware of that when he supported the Young King Henry and I unfairly judged him for it. Such adhesion to honour is not the condition of most I know, therefore I will not pass judgement on him a second time.'

'Ha, you stick together, but I detest the manipulation of what I see as right, under this guise of honour.'

Richard smiled at her, 'Ah… we must be a rare trial to you, my beautiful mouse.'

'You are,' she answered, and she raised her head from her embroidery and smiled coyly into his eyes.

Suddenly, there was a furious banging at their door fit to awaken the dead, they were both startled, and Richard instinctively reached to his waist for his dagger.

'God's teeth, Jane, see to that hammering whilst we have yet a door to hammer upon.' As soon as she lifted the latch, Sir Hugh tumbled into the room. 'Sir Hugh, what in the name of the Blessed Mother of Christ warrants such as this?'

Sir Hugh made an offering of respect with a token bow, 'Lord, grave news has this moment come to my ear from monks who have travelled from France, making for the Abbey next to us… The King is dead.'

Esther stood and raised her hand to her lips, 'Dead!' She stared at Sir Hugh in horror. She was no lover of Richard, after all, he started his reign by persecuting Jews and they were still her people, but he was yet the King and his sudden unexpected death shocked her.

'Yes… dead.'

Richard was too stunned to move, he sat frozen, trying to absorb what he had this moment heard and the implications.

'When, where?' asked Esther.

'Some castle of little significance, at a place called Châlus-Chabrol, a few miles south west of Limoges. He was not slain in some mighty conflict against the forces of darkness, but by a stray crossbow bolt, fired, not even by a soldier, but a *cook* who'd picked up the bow and fired for the sport of it. It struck the King in the neck, the wound was minor, but it had turned putrid, and he died a day or two later.'

Still Richard never moved. Esther looked to him then back to Sir Hugh. Richard slowly shook his head from side to side in disbelief *and* concern for what it might now mean for his family.

'And who is to replace him, need I ask?' He enquired wearily closing his eyes and pushing his head back against the chair.

Sir Hugh calmed at the question, looked to the floor, and coughed awkwardly. 'The monk said that Prince John is now King…' he hesitated.

'Yes – go on man!' Richard raised his head and was now staring at Sir Hugh.

'…And, William Marshal has proclaimed him as such on their journey home from France. For his support John has elevated the Marshal to Earl of Pembrokeshire in his own right, not simply because he is wed to the Countess, Isabelle de Clare.'

Richard now stood, *very* slowly and deliberately leant forward and set the horn beaker he held onto the table by his chair and walked from the room.

Sir Hugh turned to Esther, she shook her head and touched his arm saying, 'Leave him, Sir Hugh, he will need to find a place of peace in the midst of such news. Be about your work, no doubt we will speak again later.' Sir Hugh bowed and left, Esther turned her attention to her maid, 'Jean, send for Lady Margaret, ask her if she would join me, I wish to see her, fetch us wine.'

It was almost dark when Esther heard a horse riding over the drawbridge. The sound of its hooves echoed against the barbican walls as it galloped into the courtyard immediately below her room. She quickly went to the window and looked down to see whom the rider was. It was Richard; the horse appeared to be lame. Richard was at that moment bent down feeling its leg, and she heard him speak with some concern to the boy who came to attend to his mount. The boy crouched down on his hunkers and he too ran his hand over the leg. Esther could just hear him say, 'it feels hot Lord,' then he stood and led it away to the stables.

She nervously watched for a moment fearing what she was about to face. By the time she had returned to her chair, Richard was at the door of her room. He came to her and embraced her; he seemed reluctant to release her. When he lowered his arms, her eye caught sight of a sealed document in his hand.

'What is this?' Esther asked pointing to the letter.

'Alwin has this moment placed it in my hand as I dismounted. I don't even need to open it; it's from our new King, I recognised his seal immediately. We must have been first on his mind; he can only have been in London for a day or two.' Esther lowered herself slowly down into her chair.

'Please open it!'

Richard tore at it; he didn't bother to break the seal with any respect to the King's office. He scanned down the text, 'ha, he demands that I go to London to give fealty to him as my Lord and King or give up the royal privilege I have enjoyed as part of my fealty to his father, the manor of Aylesford. The ill begotten slimy toad has personally signed it, "*J Reg.*".'

'Dear God in His heaven what does that mean as if I cannot guess?'

'I must give fealty to him or he will take Aylesford from us as simple as that.'

'What will you do?'

'I will wait. He will be occupied with regaining and retaining his holdings in France. That will cost him time *and* coin and the Barons will not be rushing to fund such. Therefore, we have time to think. I will not be the only one on his list, I will find out whom he has unleashed his stored-up vengeance upon and we will meet, those of us in the same boat will sink or float together. There will be plenty enough of us Barons who had stood against him, of that I am certain. John needs be careful he does not bite off more revenge than he can swallow, he may yet choke. The country was left beggared by King Richard, the coffers are empty, we Barons will not and indeed some *cannot* readily pay yet more.'

'Do you think it will mean civil war?'

'Perhaps, I would give a years rent to speak with William Marshal, what is he up to? I rode off on hearing his involvement, hurt, disappointed, let down, confused, call it what you will, but it gave me time to think. Why would William support John? Yes, John is his feudal lord in Ireland and William will have already given fealty to him for his lands there and William will always honour an oath no matter how it offends him. I suspect that William imagines he can do more for England if he stays by John's side and manages to retain his confidence.' Richard narrowed his eyes and absentmindedly tapped the parchment against his lip. 'This game has many moves yet before checkmate is finally pronounced, believe me.' Richard seemed far from beaten, even though on the face of it the future appeared woeful; on the contrary, he was now energised by the challenge ahead. 'I have letters to write, I will find out who else he has threatened and we will plan a course of action together.'

'What about William's marriage to Grâce?'

'We will organise that directly, send for them, young Marshal too and we will talk of our future over this night's mete. I must make known to them of my intentions, they will probably already know about our new king.'

'Yes, they have all been here whilst you were out, desperate to see you and know your thoughts.'

He clapped his hands, 'Very well, if it's a fight he wants, I'm his man, and I fancy it will be to the death.' These words were not the sort of talk Esther wanted to hear, but she trusted Richard that he would do what was right and best for them all.

Chapter 30

The Wedding Feast

Esther was seated on the lead-covered ramparts at the top of the keep. Richard had instructed the carpenter to make a seat for him and Esther, so that they could sit and survey their manor on an evening. It was a place, she hoped, where the two of them might be alone, for such was a rare treat, there were forever people clamouring for their attention.

It was the most glorious view from the top, they could see for miles in all directions and it was away from the hustle and bustle of castle life.

'Ahhh, so peaceful' she whispered to herself as she slipped from her new shoes and stretched out her legs, in this, their sacred place. Richard didn't sit there often, he never sat anywhere for any length of time, there was ever work he could think of that needed his immediate attention, but Esther loved this place and had made it her own. Whenever she needed to be alone with her thoughts, this was her hideaway and *this* was such a moment. She knew she would be required somewhere and that servants would be looking for her, but she didn't care at this minute, she needed to be alone, to think.

She could not deny that she was fearful for what they might have to face now that John was their King. For her this wedding, any wedding, voiced only the future, and the future was always ahead, new horizons, new life and adventures. Perhaps that was how it should be, a moment of hope, a new start, putting behind all one's mistakes.

She yet remembered *her* special day. It had been all consuming, she smiled and a lump restricted her throat as she recalled that moment when she'd seen Richard standing by the priest. He spun round on hearing her and Sir John's footsteps, he'd beamed, and she'd all but floated towards him on the waves radiating from his smile. She'd felt like a princess and he, her prince. She never imagined there would be times of sadness ahead and wondered if *everyone* saw nought but sunshine at that moment, she supposed they did.

'Dear Mother of Christ, you who understand the anguish of a mother, I pray for William and Grâce this day, may they know the love I know, keep them in the love of your Son, our Saviour.' She was distracted from her meditation by someone calling her name; it was Richard. She knew fine well that this moment's escape from the world and its bitter winds would only be brief. She smiled as she heard Richard's plaintive call once more. Whilst pushing on her arms to raise herself from her seat and go to him, she glimpsed a skylark soaring and diving, sweeping through the beams of sunlight. It hovered and floated effortlessly, and for that moment – she was mesmerised afresh by the beauty of God's world. It was not defiled or soiled – it was perfect. She recalled as she watched the skylark, how God had looked down at His work, and saw *everything* that He had made, and behold, it was very good. This was such a moment; she could see goodness even in the midst of the unrest, jealousy, greed, and hatred. This ought to be a day to remember, she thought, one that William and Grâce would ever commit to memory with fondness. She contemplated how God had also given His children the best of beginnings and they had cast His gift aside, it was all too much for man's simple brain, hers for sure. Life is an enigma wrapped up in a mystery she thought, but at this moment, she had perhaps an inkling of God's sorrow.

'*Esther*…' Richard's voice came from the stairway yet nearer and she turned to see his head pop through the door opening. 'Ahhh, Esther, we have been looking all over for you, I have shouted and shouted.'

'*Really*, how strange that I never heard you,' she said biting her lip, trying to keep her face straight and yet project the correct amount of surprise. He narrowed his eyes suspiciously, and she returned his look with one of complete innocence.

'Come, woman, make haste, the Baron's wife, Isabel, is with her daughter and I have been told that they needs speak with you. I have not time for this employment, I wish to eat with the men; there is much of importance hinging on this day, more than simply the joining of families. I pray for greater ties to be forged before we say our farewells.'

'Go ahead, I'm coming,' Esther rose and followed Richard clambering down the steps onto the landing, straightened her dress, then made her way to the rooms which had been allotted to Grâce and her parents. As she passed the door of the hall, she saw that Richard was at that moment, taking his seat at the table amongst his fellow Barons. Henry de Bohun saw her, smiled, and gestured to her with the wave of his hand and she offered a token bow in response.

'Forgive me, gentlemen,' Richard said to those seated, 'I pray that my sons have been caring for you. Your mother was on the roof, I ought to have known she would be there,' Richard whispered leaning to William who was seated next to him. 'Are you prepared for this day my son; Grâce is a fine young lady?'

'Aye… she is Father.'

On overhearing their remarks, that both *father* and son were pleased with the contract, Lord Robert, Grâce's father, felt suitably contented. He was very fond of his only daughter and hoped that she might be happy.

'I pray I am never a disappoint to you, Father.'

'William my Son, will you forever doubt my approval? Neither of us are perfect, you *will* disappoint me, aye – and I you, as will many others in your life, often unintentionally. What is more important is that *you* do not disappoint yourself, for there is naught more difficult to live with than one's own failings, I have learned as much the hard way. For one example, I will forever regret misjudging William's father when he supported the Young King Henry.' Richard nodded in the direction of young William Marshal who was sat opposite him, he looked to Richard and Richard held his gaze for a several seconds until the young man cast his eye once more to his mete. Lord Robert gave Will Marshal a friendly, but unexpected slap on the back.

'And how was it to live in the shadow of the great man, young Will?' He asked jovially.

The young Marshal was silent for a while as if he was not inclined to respond to Lord Robert's question; Richard was about to save him from his obvious malady when he spoke.

'I knew of little approval from my father he ever preferred my brother, Richard. I understand he was named after you, my Lord,' William cast an eye to Richard.

'Is that so? Clearly, your father returned the kindness, never a man to be in anyone's debt, Marshal, my youngest, was named after him. Where *is* that rascal! Now that his name has come to mind, have *you* seen hide or hair of him Jacob?'

'If I may be excused from answering in any detail, Lord, let me just say he was engaged in some occupation with a young lady when I last saw him.'

'Mmmm, he'll get engaged in some occupation with a young lady, if his mother catches him. I'm sorry to have interrupted you, Will.'

Young Marshal glanced for a second at Richard then returned his gaze to his platter, and spoke once more, 'my brother, Richard, is more like my father; he can hold his peace, and reveals not his heart. I cannot do such, I tend to say what is on my mind, and I was forever more ready to stand my ground against him, my father that is. He would put up with no end of abuse from the then *Prince* John, I've seen it, John would make him the fool and he would not so much as flinch, I would be furious at his attitude of pathetic acceptance.' They were all a little awkward at the frank confession of the young Marshal.

'This is very serious talk for such a happy day; sing to us a song Jacob, one with some merriment.' Jacob smiled, leapt onto the table and began to sing a bawdy tavern rhyme, all the time stamping his foot on the table to keep the rhythm. The song told of a lusty maid from Pontu who'd only one bosom for all that he knew. Richard's eyes widened as the ballad entered into the particularly descriptive chorus, he was more than a little shocked, and relieved that Esther was not with them. In a very short space of time, all who were gathered had caught on to the refrain, and were now raucously singing and clapping.

Richard saw the young Marshal quietly rise, and leave the room. After a moment, he rose too and made to follow him. Once outside Richard spotted him leaning in the shadow of a stone buttress. Richard hesitated for a moment and then ambled over to him. William acknowledged him with a nod.

'Do you need to talk, or do you wish for your own company? Let me afford you either.'

William replied in a soft voice, 'this is difficult for me, I mean to be here on this day of rejoicing... I was married once, did you know?'

'Aye – I knew.'

'You never made any mention of it, Lord.'

'That was your place to speak of it, if you wished and my place to wait on your time.'

William chewed at his lip trying to strengthen himself. 'I blamed my father for her death.'

'And is that yet your opinion?' asked Richard. William stared at his foot as he tapped his toe repetitively against the stone of the buttress.

'I know not what to think on that now, the pain is yet keen.'

Richard gently touched William's arm then lay back against the sloping stonework of the buttress, folded his arms and rested his chin on his chest, 'Mmm,' he sighed, thoughtfully.

They were both pensive for some time. After several minutes Richard spoke... 'When I was a young man much like yourself, perhaps a little younger, I fell out with *my* father. I thought him weak and felt shamed by him. He supported King Stephen against the Empress Matilda and when King Henry came to power, after Stephen's death, he made those who stood against his mother suffer. I hated the way my father allowed himself to be treated and we parted that day in bad faith. I knew I'd hurt him, I wanted to, I thought him weak.' William now looked at Richard, his brow furrowed as he listened to the tale. 'I went to France to seek fame and fortune on the tourney circuit, that's where I met your father… I wanted to prove that I was a better man than *my* father was – I never saw him again – he'd died while I was away.' Richard wiped his face with his hand and sighed. 'No matter how much I wish for it, and by the God who is able to do all things – I have wished for it, believe me, and *yet* do. I can never have that moment when I left, back again; that day and all that was said is as clear and forever will be as if it was spoken this day.' Richard squinted and looked up into the sunlight, blinked and cupped his hand over his eyes to give some shade from the bright light.

William watched him for some time, waiting in case Richard wanted to say more; satisfied that he had finished William then spoke. 'That is a sad tale for sure Lord, and I'm saddened by your pain, we have more in common than I thought. It's strange how we see others – it's ever difficult to look below the surface of another's life. Perchance we need pay greater attention to those who smile most, and give less time to those who grieve, for perhaps those who grieve have learned how to find some succour for wounds.'

Richard smiled and laid his arm on Will's shoulder, 'I came to comfort you and it is you who have given to me. Come – let us return to my surprisingly bawdy son and his tavern songs, I'd best silence him afore his mother hears him and faints with shame.' William smiled and the two walked back to the hall.

Richard had invited as many Barons as were willing or able to come to the wedding, they had talked much about the new King and his obsession ever for more, at *their* expense. Richard listened and studied what was said, making careful appraisal of who would resist John and who was prepared to wait and see. None were prepared to suffer indefinitely if John continued in his past vein. Richard knew they were all decent men and he respected them, but nothing would be decided either way, this was too soon. It was clear that they had been pushed to the edge of their tolerance and several like Richard were withholding their fealty to John. John would find out in time of this assembly of Barons, perhaps this show of unity of like-minded people might cause him to think again about his alienation of such powerful men.

Richard knew that such a gathering would be brought to John's attention, he would even know in time what was said and by whom, secrets were ever clamouring to be free from their hiding place, and subtly making known of their intention was Richard's wish.

The day was a great success, the weather had blessed them; the bride before them had become a woman overnight. Richard could not believe how she had been transformed from a mere slip of a girl to this woman before their very eyes. She wore a bright red damask silk wedding gown; she even exhibited the figure of a woman. By the look on his son's face, he was equally surprised. There was one moment which flashed with *crippling* pain through Richard's heart, for Grâce wore Julianne's emerald, and it rested on the breast of her red dress as it had on the strikingly similar dress worn by Julianne on her wedding day. In fact, Richard had to blink several times to clear the image of Julianne from his eyes as Grâce walked past him. William must have given the jewel to her for a wedding gift, unbeknown to Richard, which was right and proper, what more could Richard say, it was his to give to whomever he wished.

Chapter 31

Eleanor of Aquitaine

'Over eighty years old, can you imagine such a thing, Esther? She was born when Henry the first was yet King.'

Richard, Esther, and the whole family, which now included their first grandchild, Alys, were walking to Aylesford Abbey.

Richard had paid the Abbot for a mass to be said on behalf of the old queen's soul and he prayed that her time in purgatory would be lessened by such an offering. It was a solemn procession, for those who'd known the Queen it was an introspective time. All who were able, from the castle and villages on his estate were ordered to attend.

Richard looked at his son William, the new father, and he was proud of him. After William's initial disappointment on hearing that he had a daughter, he now seemed totally enamoured with his child. He had always been utterly convinced that his wife, Grâce, would bear him a son.

Following a resolute scolding from his mother, who made it known to him, "In no uncertain terms" how she felt about his attitude, his disappointment turned slowly into a smile. She told him that she would be *furious* if he showed any of his disenchantment to his exhausted young wife, Grâce.

'This is no smiling matter, William!'

'But Mama, you are *already* furious,' William pointed out, once he had gained his equilibrium after the initial shock of Esther's onslaught.

'*What!*' Esther faltered for a second. '*Well* – I will be *even more* furious!' on the conclusion of her tirade, she was compelled to smile at herself. William stepped forward, took her in his arms and embraced her. '*Gently* boy, you're crushing me, I'm your mother not Will Marshal you are squeezing the life from.' As she cast her eyes into the face above her, she remembered that innocent little baby. Yes – he was *her* son.

It had been so very difficult in the beginning when she realised what had happened between Richard and Julianne. Even now, she could yet remember that precise moment of unbelievable – confusion, yes confusion; that was the word when she first understood, what a trusting fool. The sickness, the fear, the feeling of failure all pack into one word, "William". At the very same moment that *her* William, who was conceived in the holy state of wedlock, was dying, *Julianne's* William, was conceived in sin, and lived. Where was the right judgement of a righteous God in such as that? She had not hurt or betrayed anyone and yet it was *she* who had suffered, even to this day. Nice, kind, ever forgiving Esther, she tried to hide her feelings even though she at first wanted Richard to burn too with her unquenchable fire of pain, but hating was simply not her nature. Perhaps she *was* a fool, others would say so, but she loved Richard and God had blessed her for it. He gave her Jacob in the *very midst* of her anguish when she was thought to be without hope of quickening. Her life was filled with overwhelming joy at that moment, not only with the news of Jacob, but also because Richard had been set free from the grasping bony fingers of the hand of death – such was her bliss, all hate was taken from her.

William was thriving on parenthood. Richard had forever felt to be deficient as a father, never more so than when he watched his son with *his* daughter. He didn't really enjoy the time with small children; he decided that he was too selfish by far. He'd always thought that he must work hard to establish a position and security for his family. Perhaps he ever felt insecure after his own childhood and didn't want that for *his* children. He had more time now, at least slightly more, and he had to concede that little Alys was adorable. He liked nothing better than to have her on his knee and it was always *he,* whom she reached to, knowing she would be picked up no matter how busy he was.

Esther saw his smile and was curious; she interrupted his contemplation as if she had been reading his thoughts. 'You were never so contented to be with your own children when they were small, Richard.' She had noticed him smile and pull a face at Alys who lay in her father's arms. She had responded by chuckling and lifting her head to see more of him and he tantalisingly hid from her view behind William's shoulder.

He looked surprised at Esther's observation in the light of what he had been thinking. 'Is that how you saw it? I can't honestly recall, but to be sure, I have this minute past been trying to think on it. I was away a great deal on King Henry's business or it seemed so, that *is* true.'

He walked on in silence now, his brow furrowed, thinking about his role as the father figure, perhaps he *had* neglected them when they were small. Sir John had said that he'd learned – *too* late – that the most expensive gift a parent could give was their time. He knew many lords who rarely saw their children. Their offspring were suckled and cared for by servants until they were of an age to secure their position through propitious marriages.

He was not *so* detached from their lives; it wasn't because of any lack of love, that he failed to be there. "Mmm, perhaps I would do it differently if I had my time again. Aye, and make different mistakes too, no doubt", he thought.

Richard was distracted from *his* own failings as a parent thinking of Queen Eleanor and wondering if she had reflected on her family and its troubles as she lay dying. As the foremost family in the land, they had been a miserable example of unity. Yet *she* was an exceptional person by any measure, almost to the end she'd rode around her son John's kingdom, on his behest trying to secure his position, even to the extent of standing against her grandson Arthur's claims to the English throne.

Richard despised John, but from what he'd heard Arthur was every bit as bad, if not worse. It was said he was a petty-minded spoiled brat, who was driven by aught *but* honour. Who would know what the truth of it was, it would be in John's interest to spread such a disparaging description, Richard had only seen him once, perhaps fifteen or so years past, and he was only a babe in arms at the time. Arthur was John's prisoner at this moment, but there were ugly rumours circulating. Richard heard that Arthur had been held at the Chateau de Falaise in Normandy, guarded by Hubert de Burgh. It was said that John had ordered two of his henchmen to gouge out Arthur's eyes; de Burgh had refused to let them, but then – there were *forever* dark rumours surrounding the dealings of John. From there, it was alleged, that Arthur was taken to Rouen and placed in the charge of William de Barose, a faithful supporter of John's. In any event, the latest talk to reach Richard's ears was that Arthur had disappeared. Apparently, no one had seen hide or hair of him since leaving the Chateau de Falaise.

Of course, the high and mighty moral standard bearer, Philip of France was enraged and demanded to see the young prince. It was common talk that John himself had *murdered* Arthur in a drunken rage. Philip made what advantage he could of the rumours taking the moral high ground, citing John's part in Arthur's disappearance as a justifiable reason for taking his lands and castles. Richard had heard that John was now fleeing from France fearing capture by Philip's forces, and was compelled to leave what castles and land he still owned to the mercy of Philip.

The mass for Queen Eleanor had been simple and quiet, as she would have liked, she was never the spendthrift; *that* much she had in common with King Henry. The time in church had been more a time of reflection, certainly for Richard, who'd known and liked the Queen.

She had been unquestionably beautiful, *perpulchra* – more than beautiful – she'd been described as when she was young, forever an inveterate flirt. Richard remembered the attention she'd given him as a young knight new to court life and how flattered he'd been, but it was never more than that. She was courageous, ruthless even, literate, more than that – *a* scholar, truly an exceptional woman in every respect and Richard hoped that history would remember her as such. Right until the end it was said she'd been captivating and a joy to be with. It was impossible to understand how this woman could have produced such disappointing, low achieving progeny, and out of the whole wretched brood, the one who was left, John, was the least promising of all.

She'd died at her favourite religious house, the abbey of Fontevrault, where she had often retreated to find peace during various troubled moments of her life, of which there were many. Eventually she had been laid to rest there next to her husband Henry the Second. Richard prayed that the pair would at last find rest from their endless disputes and lie together reconciled until the day of the glorious resurrection.

On the return walk to the castle after the mass, Esther told Richard that she'd prayed that he would not take any unnecessary risks when King John arrived in England.

'I have always taken risks Esther; I believe life in its fullness is spelt R-I-S-K. Failure to me is – *not* – stepping out, because of the *fear* of failing. Failing in itself worries me not. *I* fear the *hold*, which the – *fear* – of failing can have on one's life. I'm convinced there will be risks to be taken when that tyrant returns, and I for one will not sit back while he destroys all for which we have worked. He will pay dearly for what he takes from me. One day I will have my revenge for his crimes against my family.'

Such talk frightened Esther; for she knew that Richard could not, and would not, forgive John. 'What about William Marshal?' Esther asked nervously.

'He will be watching John and no doubt John will be watching him – *and* – I will be watching them both.'

'I will pray that you might all be content with just watching.'

Chapter 32

Siege

No sooner had John returned to England from laying his mother to rest at the abbey of Fontevrault, than the increases in taxation began, he was determined to make good his great financial losses in France.

All that his father had worked and fought for, throughout his entire life, John had now lost in but a handful of years.

John needed a *vast* amount of money if he had any hope whatsoever of funding an army to regain his lost lands in France, and if there was one thing John could do, with unerring skill – it was extorting coin. The tax revenues were now pouring into his exchequer.

The Barons were furious with the escalating levels of taxation; John was beggaring them. The dissention was worse in the north, because the northern Barons had little interest in France. They resented the expense they were facing to secure or regain properties John and his French vassals had lost. In no small part, he had been vanquished from his estates in France because of his own shortsighted greed, which forever overrode sound judgement. Next to John's skill at raising coin, he had an equally proficient talent for losing it.

Richard's son William, who now lived at Tattershall, was a northern Baron and he was no exception to the other Barons who railed against the greater and greater levels of taxation.

Richard had no interests in France either, so John's losses mattered not to him, and he like the rest begrudged the increases, in his case to the point of refusing to pay. To compound the animosity, he had still not given fealty to King John, and knew that sooner or later he was going to be faced with John's wrath, unlike "The Marshal", who *had* given his fealty to King John, and that was a continual thorn in the side of Richard. However, even the Marshal's life was not one without its difficulties, for apart from his holdings in England and Ireland he *also* had considerable interests in France, some of which were his wife's, and had given fealty to the King of France for those holdings. Richard knew that such commitment to the French King would rankle with John. Eventually it would cause problems for William Marshal, "As sure as eggs are eggs", Richard had said to Esther, but for the present John seemed to be tolerating the arrangement, which could only mean one thing – he *needed* William Marshal at this time. Richard had heard that William wanted to go to his wife's home of Leinster in Ireland where her grandfather had once been the King, but John had expressly forbidden him to go. None were safe from John's wrath, no matter how one had supported him in the past.

All knew of the appalling tale of William de Braose and his family. Even John's most ardent supporters were sickened by these new depths of evil to which he was prepared to stoop, it seemed his depravity knew no limits.

De Braose his most loyal supporter had fallen out of favour with John. The precise reasons remained obscure. King John cited overdue monies that de Braose owed the Crown from his estates, but the King's actions went far beyond what would be necessary to recover the debt. He seized the de Braose domains in Sussex and Devon. Beyond that, he sought de Braose's wife, who had made no secret of her belief that King John had murdered Arthur of Brittany. She'd been there when Arthur had disappeared whilst in her husband's charge. Richard knew her for the most stupid of women and could not abide her, but he was sickened at her treatment.

De Braose fled to Ireland, and then to France where he died shortly after arriving. His wife and eldest son were captured. They were imprisoned at Windsor and allegedly; they were murdered on John's orders, by starving them to death.

Jacob and young William Marshal were resolutely behind Richard's stance against John's total disregard for the law whatsoever. Richard knew very well, John's *father*, King Henry, was a great advocate of a society ordered by laws.

Esther trusted Richard's judgement but was fearful for her family; she could see clearly that Richard was playing a dangerous game for the highest stakes.

Richard, William, Jacob and Sir Hugh gazed into the hazy distance. Sir Hugh had, to some degree, filled the void left in Richard's life by Tristram's murder, they were of a similar age, but that pain of losing Tristram was ever close to Richard's heart and it didn't take much for it to rise up and make itself known.

Esther knew his thoughts were of revenge for Tristram, he blamed himself for his murder. She could see it in his eyes and etched into the ice-cold expression on his face, even when he said nought. A dark cloud would envelop him; his knuckles would turn white as he flexed his fists, staring straight through any who were before him. There had been times in the middle of the night, when she'd had felt for him at her side and the bed was cold. She'd gone to the window and seen him in the moonlight, pacing back and forth along the battlements. Any greeting from the night-watch was ignored; she suspected he'd never even heard them speak. It was truly frightening.

The four men knew King John was coming, they'd had it made known to them, and they had been preparing for such as they now faced. At last, the reality was upon them, or very shortly would be. Riders had arrived hours since with news of an army coming with siege engines, wagonloads of timber and ladders, all heading towards Aylesford. Everything that was needed to take a well-defended position, John was bringing with him. God help them all if Richard's plans failed, Esther thought, but she was determined as she buckled a dagger to her waist, John would never take her.

As they waited Jacob asked without taking his eyes from the view before him, 'Can we prevail against this force with which we are to be faced, Father?'

Richard narrowed his eyes, pursed his lips, and looked thoughtfully down to the toe of his boot, which he tapped gently against the foot of the battlements.

'Mmmm, you take me for a soothsayer, Jacob?' Suddenly Richard turned to him and his mood lightened, he struck the top of the castellation before him with the flat of his hand then slapped Jacob's back. 'Fear not, Son, we are prepared and will give a good account of ourselves. This day will be ours.'

'I am not afraid, Father, it is simply that I could not tolerate being humbled before *that* man; I carry the same pain as you, do *not* forget I was at Clarendon too. Tristram was also my friend and I will *never* forget Mother's screams as long as I live.'

'Aye... I remember right enough,' Richard replied and the smile instantly fell from his face.

'We will know soon what we are to face, Lord,' said young William Marshal pointing to the movement in the distance. Richard stared once more into the low morning mist before him and could just make out the bright colours of the standards, in particular the large red standard, which he knew even without being able to make out the device upon it – that it was John's.

'He is here then, at last... and never was I more delighted to see that spawn of darkness. Have the men make ready William, we have some time yet, let it not be wasted.'

There was a surge of activity now, men rushing back and forth. Bowmen ran to their positions and lined up along the battlements with their sheaves of arrows standing in boxes of sand, which had been dug from the nearby River Medway, so they could be easily drawn and fired.

'Look Father, there are three riders coming towards us!' shouted Jacob as he leaned over the battlements to better his view.

Richard rested his weight on his forearms, drumming his fingers on the top of the stonework and watched with curiosity as the riders came close enough for their faces to be recognised. Richard gave a sardonic smile.

'John,' he whispered to himself as the horses were drawn to a standstill short of an arrow's distance.

'MAILLORIE,' John shouted. 'Do you raise your defences against your King?'

'Do *you* come to parley with siege machines and men armoured for war?'

'Open these gates and face me and bring that that whore of a wife for some sport.' Jacob thumped the castellation with the side of his fist; Richard laid his hand on his arm.

'Be still, Son.'

'I will have your fealty, or by God I will destroy this nest of traitors and malcontents and gut the lot of your brood.'

Richard calmed his fury before he responded. 'You can try. Neither I, nor this country, will ever submit to someone who is a tyrant such as the likes of you, who is without the slightest notion of honour or decency. You've lost France, it will be England next, mark my words and I will be there to hear you squeal like the stuck pig you are, you ill begotten cretin.'

'Do you presume to threaten me?' John screamed at the top of his voice.

'Ha… *nay*, I wish not to threaten you; I'll leave that to your dear cousin Philip. My intention was to *insult* you, but you lack the wit, *and* land, come to think of it, to grasp clear speaking,' Richard laughed.

John's face turned puce, he was beside himself with fury, he eased himself from his saddle and stood in the stirrups as if he intended to leap over the castle walls and grab Richard by the throat and to hell with his army. He was further enraged because all who were on the walls above him laughed and mocked him shouting, "Lackland, Lackland, Lackland". He gave Richard a scorching glare and tugged so violently on the rein, his horse reared and John was all but thrown, which only served to re-energize the fading laughter. The frantic horse turned awkwardly, stumbled and set off at a pace back to their lines. Soldiers in his path had to leap to the side for fear of being trampled as he rode through them.

'I think you upset our beloved King, Lord,' said Sir Hugh, yet laughing.

'Surely not,' Richard replied smiling.

Late into the night, Richard walked back and forth on the battlements; he turned his head to see Jacob running up the steps to where he was standing.

'Father, I have this moment come from Mother's side and she is concerned for you. Would you not go to her and rest? If not for your sake for hers, we will call you if there is any change, I beg of you.'

'It would be wise, Lord,' agreed William Marshal standing not five paces from Richard.

'Aye, indeed, I will do as you advise.' Richard removed his helm and coif and scratched his head; 'Call me if there is any movement.'

Jane opened the door and Esther rose as Richard entered.

'Richard, thank God you have come, did Jacob send you?'

'Aye, he pestered me.'

'You must be tired Richard, come drink some wine and take some rest.' She poured Richard a chalice of wine and passed it to him.

'Thank you, Esther,' he said as he slumped into his chair.

'Will we be able to stand against John?'

'You're as bad as Jacob; it depends on the resolve of our good King. I have made all preparation these past months; he will not have us, fear not,' and he smiled knowingly with satisfaction at her as he set the goblet carefully onto the table. 'Yes... this will be our victory, supposing we lose this place,' he gestured with a sweep of his hand to the room.

'I pray that it be so, let me help you with your footwear and you can lie on our bed,' she suggested.

'Aye, perhaps,' and he set his foot on the stool before him.

She knelt and with some struggle tugged off his boots.

'Thank you, Esther I can't manage the task with my gambeson and hauberk on. I can put them on, but can't bend to pull them off.' Richard reached forward and touched her shoulder saying tenderly, 'Bless you for such kindness,' she smiled up at him.

'No matter, there is little enough I can do to support you, just do as you are bidden and rest. Time to let the younger ones do the work.'

'Esther, woman, have I ever told you how much I love you? You have been my strength for the better part of our lives.' she tugged his boots free, stood and took his hand raising him from his chair, hugged him and he clambered onto the bed and lay back against the pillow with his hands behind his head.

She looked lovingly down at the man whom she had loved from the first day she'd seen him. 'We are one flesh, is that not what the scripture tells us, does not my head belong as part of your chest? From whence woman came, is that not so? Now let me lie beside you and we will rest and be all the better to face what is before us.'

It was sunrise when Jacob ran into his father's room. 'Father, father they are coming.'

Richard only took a moment to waken and rise. Esther was in her nightwear and leapt from the bed to aid Richard with his boots, but he was too quick for her and stamped his foot into the tight-fitting boot before she could get to him. He kissed her and nodded.

Chapter 33

Escape

'Be ready with all you need to travel at a moments notice, only that which is essential, you know what we have planned.'

'I understand, it will be done as you have ordered.' Richard turned and ran with haste behind Jacob. He paused for a second as he stepped from the keep and looked up to the leaden grey sky and took a deep breath of the fresh morning air, 'and so it begins,' he said to himself.

Jacob glance back, 'Are you well, Father?'

'Never better. Go to your men, and God keep you Son, we must hold them this day.' Jacob did no more than smile then ran off.

Richard stood next to the young Marshal; 'They have pushed their trebuchets into place, Lord.'

'Aye, no doubt they will pound us for a while, I can't stand the man, but I will say he is no timid warrior, he's brave enough, but no leader.'

'FIND COVER!' shouted William, as a missile was hurled from a trebuchet, but it fell well short of their walls.

'They will find our range soon enough,' Richard said to himself, as much as to William Marshal. The second missile struck half way up the wall, large and small fragments of stone flying in every direction, the third flew over the wall and decimated the roof of the bakery, but none were hurt.

'No fresh bread this day, Lord,' William smiled, and Richard laughed. They were subjected to the bombardment for much of the morning, destroying many of the wooden structures within the castle, *and* their unfortunate rooster, who had disappeared in a cloud of brightly coloured feathers after spending the morning running back and forth with indignation at the disturbance to his domain. However, the barrage had little effect on the castle walls. Richard assumed that they had exhausted their supply of stone shot for they withdrew the machines.

Men were now racing towards the walls with long split pole ladders. William ordered the archers to fire at will. The men carrying the ladders were taking a beating, even though comrades ran alongside them trying to give some protection with their large kite shields. Ladders were raised against the walls and men began to climb. They were being murdered. Sheer weight of numbers enabled some to clamber over the walls and now there was hand to hand fighting. One assailant came at Richard, clearly weakened by his climb he was unable to find the strength to parry Richard's blow, stepped back, lost his footing on the ramparts and tumbled headfirst onto the yard below. Richard did no more than glance as he struck the floor in a cloud of dust and his head disappeared inside his chest cavity. More clambered over the walls, but were quickly dispatched, Richard's men were hurling all manner of objects at the attackers even the severed head of one who had made it over the wall only as far as the edge of Jacob's sword.

They were withdrawing now this attack had been repulsed. Richard spied the crowned helm of King John glittering in the sunlight, he was mounted on his white charger cursing and waving his arms as the terrified animal skittered back and forth, he even sliced at one of his own soldiers who was running back to their lines. The wretched fellow lifted his arm in self-defence then tumbled to the ground at the feet of John's horse as the blow struck him.

'Throw their dead over the wall, have we lost many, do you know, Jacob?' asked William.

'None, but a few cuts as much as I can see, Will.'

'Well done men,' Richard walked amongst the men, patting backs and giving praise to keep their spirits up. He knew that men drew confidence from their leaders and he made sure *whatever* he felt; they saw him with his head up.

'They must have lost a hundred by the look of the number laid below,' Jacob said making a rough count.

'Aye, but that will only serve to strengthen John's resolve, men's lives mean nothing to him, but seeing us as victors will drive him on. Organise our men to be fed and watered in turn, they'll fight all the better if their insides are not grumbling for lack of mete and drink,' Richard said to William Marshal. William, momentarily wavered at Richard's command and asked with the sound of concern is his voice…

'Do you think my – father – is against us this day?'

Richard hesitated and touched his shoulder, 'No – I think not Son; he would have ridden with John when he came to challenge us at first light. Your father would not have rushed into conflict without more talk. I fancy he will have found good reason to not be here.'

'Ah, perhaps you have the right of it.'

'I will return once more to Esther, she will be worried, see to your own needs too, Will.'

Before dawn of the second day was upon them, the enemy were once more coming with ladders, no missiles this time and they were repulsed as they had been on the previous day. By the forenoon, they had withdrawn, but there was now a new activity. They were carrying wooden covered shelters, fit to shield ten or so men.

'What's this?' Sir Hugh asked trying to make sense of the activity.

'These are to protect the miners, that's my guess. A method of taking a castle that the French favour, John has learned something from his time on his campaigns across the narrow sea.'

'What are they about?'

'They intend to dig under our foundations and undermine us to cause a collapse of our walls. Once they have a breach in the walls, they will attempt to overwhelm us, but we will have a surprise. You keep an eye on them Hugh, I'm going to see my wife, time to make our move.' Richard left Sir Hugh, called to Jacob and William, as he made his way down from the battlements, and the three ran quickly across the courtyard, into the keep and up to where Esther was anxiously waiting.

'Be seated, I have not much time to talk, but this is it, it must be tonight, and you two young fellows will lead the escape as we have planned.'

'What of *you*, Richard?' asked Esther.

'Fear not, I will join you on the morrow's night; I need to be seen by John or he will be suspicious. Twenty men will stay here with Sir Hugh and me. We will harry their efforts they will not waste any more men on ladders. John will hold back until there is a breach in the wall, and that will not be completed in one day, then he will intend to have a major assault, so fear not I will be safe.' Esther did not seem sure about such risk, but said nothing. 'We have planned this for months; you will escape through the tunnel into the cover of the wood and make haste to the manor at Laybourne Lakes. The old derelict manor is perfectly situated for such a purpose, being secluded in the wetland and not on any thoroughfare. There is food and horses; all things we have of value have already been taken there. You will unite with the men there and then make for Frainingham; Sir Raymond will be ready and waiting for you. As soon as I knew of John's forces, I sent riders to Raymond with instructions to ready himself to leave.' Richard paused and glanced at the faces. 'As soon as we can, we will go north to William at Tattershall it will be safe there for the time being. John will not venture north yet, he has little support so far north, are you all clear what we are about?'

'Aye, we know what to do,' said Jacob and William nodded his head.

'Very well, Esther do not waver you have brave men around you and I will join you soon enough, but if I am held up you will go without me. Now leave us and I will bade farewell to your mother,' he said to the men. 'Go with your brother Marshal and you too Isabelle,' Richard hugged them and Jacob guided them from the room and closed the door.

Richard took her in his arms, 'So this is it, a sad moment Esther, to leave all we have worked for, but nothing meant anything as long as I had you by my side.'

'Richard,' she wrapped her arms around him and pressed her lips to his. She tried to still her shaking but he could yet feel it. 'You're not going to come with us, are you? You are going to stay and face John and you will be killed, I can't leave you.'

'You tempt me my little mouse, but I am no fool and will not have John gloating over my corpse in my own home, no, this is not my time. I will join you soon enough, trust me.'

'Do you promise me?'

'I promise.'

'I will pray.'

'Aye, we must all pray.'

The tunnel was wet and dark, but for the rush lights. However, they all made it, just as had been planned.

They were closer to the action than they'd expected when Jacob and William pushed their heads from the bushes covering the entrance. They scrambled out and knelt either side of the opening, and helped the dirty and wet into the fresh air, once out they ran crouched into the darkness of the forest. Jacob clambered down into the tunnel once more to make sure all were clear, and then he and William re-covered the entrance and joined the others. When William and Jacob came to them, they saw Esther busily counting the group, all were accounted for, sixty-two in total. Richard had already sent most of his men and servants to Frainingham.

'Come let us get clear, Mother we must go,' Esther was distracted for a moment as she cast her eye to her home one last time and offered a quick prayer for Richard's safety.

They made their way to the manor at Laybourne, William ran ahead with some men-at-arms to be sure that all was well and he was greeted warmly when he arrived.

'We's 'ad men out and them see'd the battle, but none has come near us, Lord.'

'Fine fellow, Matthew,' said William squeezing his shoulder. 'Let us saddle the horses and load the pack animals.'

'I's seen to that already, Lord Richard learned us always to think ahead and be ready.'

'Good fellow, well he *learned* you well,' William smiled. 'The rest will be here directly and we will be on our way to Frainingham, and friends.'

They didn't have long to wait and they mounted the excited horses. Esther made sure that horses they were leaving were saddled and readied for Richard, she knew the poor beasts would be uncomfortable for they might be saddled for all the next day, but it had to be. She knew Richard would be under even greater constraints of time when he arrived.

Chapter 34

Northwards

They made their way northward avoiding any major settlement. If they were seen by any who favoured John's cause, they were never challenged. Either they were never seen or their numbers made any potential attackers decide against a confrontation.

Richard and the men left the castle the night before, after they had harassed the attackers any way they could for the better part of that day, tipping burning embers upon the wooden structures that had been erected for the miners, and hurling down large rocks upon them. They had managed to set one of the wooden shelters on fire causing untold panic; it burned for more than two hours.

After dark, they had made their escape. Nothing of value was left behind, not even a single loaf of bread. What with the damage John's trebuchets had inflicted and the lack of any sort of life about the castle it looked more like a derelict ruin than the place that had been their home for many years.

Richard had left a message for John nailed to a post supporting the roof of the castle well; addressing it to John

Lackland, saying that he hoped his gain was worth the coin. Richard knew John would be furious. He would have dearly loved to be there, when John discovered that after all his trouble and expense, the cupboard was bare. Heaven help anyone near to him when he reads my note he thought and smiled.

Esther ran to him when he entered the castle with Sir Hugh and his men and he lifted her onto his horse.

'Thank God, thank God,' she said kissing him. He drew his horse to a standstill.

'All we have suffered was worth it for such a greeting,' he said lowering Esther into Jacob's arms and jumping from the saddle. Raymond welcome him, taking his hand and embracing him, it had been sometime since they'd seen each other. Richard cast his eye around the place, for him it was forever haunted by Julianne's ghost, he hated the place, John could have it, and welcome to it, he thought.

'Are you well and ready Raymond?'

'As ready as can be Richard, what we cannot take has been destroyed or given to the serfs, they are well provided for. Coin has been given to old Walter the headman and I have made ready to fire the place when we leave as you ordered.'

'Good, I will leave only desolation behind me.'

'I hope that whomever comes here they will be good lords Richard, for I like these people.'

'I hope so too, but these are devilish unsettled days, no man can be sure of his future. I will light a candle for these people when we get to Tattershall.'

There is mete to eat now, simple but good, and we have ample for our journey too,' said Raymond pointing to the tables erected in the courtyard. Richard placed his arm once more around Esther's shoulder.

'Are you ready?'

'Oui.'

The new day was just breaking; Richard had not slept for two days and was tired. He wanted not to linger and the excited energy was driving him on. John would no doubt guess where he had headed, but it would take the best part of this day before they realised that something was amiss, first he would have to force a way into the castle to be sure that they had indeed flown the coop and that their missing faces on the battlements was not some clever ploy.

They would have as much as two days start on John if he dared to follow them. Richard was sure John would follow with care for fear of ambush; he would not want to risk his life if there was some chance of being caught by Richard Maillorie, all these considerations would slow him down.

Whilst they rode, Raymond asked if Richard had heard the news that John had been excommunicated.

'Excommunicated!' Richard shook his head, wondering what Raymond was saying. 'Is this a jest?'

'I think not? All Hell will be let loose, when he finds out they have surely sent riders from London. When he's told, he may even be too preoccupied to pursue us. It's all a matter of priority and John has plenty of them to deal with.'

'Why, what has he done to so annoy the Holy Father to such an extent as he would doom him to Hell? Though in truth it be a right judgement as far as I'm concerned,' Richard smiled.

'It's the old recurring problem, the appointment of church leaders. John wanted John de Grey as the next

Archbishop of Canterbury, but the Pope wanted Stephen Langton, John refused Innocent's request that he consent to Langton's appointment, but the Pope consecrated Langton anyway. John was incensed about what he perceived as an abrogation of his customary right as monarch to influence the election. He'd complained both about the choice of Langton as an individual, for John felt he was overly influenced by the Capetian court in Paris, and about the process as a whole where a leader was appointed against his wishes. He barred Langton from entering England and gave orders to seize the lands of the archbishopric and other papal possessions. Innocent has apparently made every effort to convince John to change his mind, but to no avail. Innocent has now by all accounts placed an interdict on England, prohibiting clergy from conducting religious services, with the exception of baptisms for the young, and confessions and absolutions for the dying, so it's going to be difficult for those about to marry.'

Richard listened and was more that a little disturbed. 'That damned fool, he is determined to set the whole world against himself. It would be difficult to comprehend a more incompetent king who was so eager to set his foot upon the path for total destruction. Who knows what this new blunder will lead to Raymond, never was there such a fool. Any news of William Marshal?'

'No, as far as I know he's yet in London. Aye, I fear that sooner or later we will slide into civil war, there is already talk that *King* Philip the Second of France has been offered the crown of England for his son Louis, and it is said that he is actually preparing to invade.'

'Dear oh dear, what an unmitigated mess, King Henry will be turning in his grave, thank God his mother Queen

Eleanor has at last passed on,' said Richard wearily shaking his head in disbelief.

'And there is more.'

'Some good news surely Raymond!'

'Well, you tell me, how true it is I no not, but it is rumoured that John threatened the Pope that if he did not let him have the Archbishop of his choice that he would turn this country in to a Muslim state.'

'What… has he taken complete leave of his senses?'

'He has written to a London cleric Ai-Nâsir with his proposal.'

'This cannot be true.'

On nearing Tattershall they were met with riders coming towards them, Richard was relieved to see one of them was William. He rode in a sweep round his father and mother then came alongside his mother and reached his hand to her.

'Thank God, I'm relieved to see you. When riders reported to me that they'd seen you I couldn't wait to ride out.'

'We are happy to be here Son,' said Esther.

'Are you all safe?'

'Aye, how are Alys and Grâce?' Richard asked.

'All well, and she knows her grandfather is coming never fear,' Esther laughed. 'I have much to tell you, Father, but it will keep until you are rested and fed.'

When the entered the castle at Tattershall, they immediately saw Grâce holding Alys.

Chapter 35

Meeting of Barons

Richard knew that the shambles into which the country was now slipping, must be faced up to for the good of all. There had been an uprising in Wales. Several of the Welsh princes had taken the opportunity of John's troubles to revolt, orchestrated by Llywelyn ap Iorwerth. It seemed, though they'd been defeated, they had ended up with even more independence. John had taken their sons as hostages, fourteen in total, God preserve them Richard prayed, for no one could predict the actions of this madman.

William Marshal was now in Leinster in Ireland, he had tricked John into gaining his permission to go and John was livid.

The northern Barons organised a meeting of the like-minded to decide on their response to the country's unrest. They were to parley at Bolsover castle near Sheffield. Richard knew that there would be many such meetings before there was any final agreement. He was sure that most of these Barons would have already sworn fealty to John and that was no small thing. They would need to be convinced that they must rebel against their anointed king, for no matter how wicked he was, he had been anointed by God and such a rebellion would place their immortal souls in jeopardy. The fact that there were to be clergy amongst them may salve their consciences to some extent, nevertheless they were stepping onto a perilous path.

It was the end of October 1214 and a cold day; an icy wind blew sleet from the land of the frozen north, straight into the faces of the wet miserable riders.

'Are you well Father?' Jacob called to him raising his voice above the wind, his father was not a young man now, and yet he never ceased his work. Jacob was frozen, his fingertips were numb, he could barely feel the reins in his hands because of the cold, but his father never complained, he only gave him a smile and wiped the drip from his nose.

'We'll soon be at the castle now, and find warmth, thanks be to God, you are made of sterner stuff than I, Lord,' young William Marshal shouted.

'Don't talk Will that loses heat from your body, grip your knees to your mount and gain what heat you can from it. Every little helps.' With that, they rode on in silence. It was no more than half of the hour before Bolsover castle came into view, not a big fortress, but for all that, it looked imposing set on the cliff top as it was. The castle belonged to the Earl of Derby, it was chosen as the meeting place for this first assembly of the northern Barons, because of its central location.

Richard and the two young men rode up the twisty track to the castle gates and into the courtyard. Jacob leapt from his horse intending to aid his father and stumbled, for his legs were numb with the cold, he rubbed them trying to restore the circulation. His father dismounted with more care, transferred his weight onto one iron, his saddle creaked, and he stepped to the ground, and offered Jacob his hand.

'Steady lad, fear not for me – there is life in the old dog yet,' he smiled and patted Jacob's back. 'Come boys, can you make it inside on your own legs, or shall I give you a pick pack?'

William laughed, 'I think we might just make it, Lord, with the help of your hand.'

Richard smiled, 'These good fellows will tend to our weary mounts and we will melt the ice from our veins by this good Lord's hearth.'

Their clothes quickly began to steam as they walked into the warmth of the hall.

'Richard – a warm welcome this stormy day, to you and to these fine young fellows, unseasonable weather is it not?' the Earl said offering his hand in greeting.

'Bitter, my friend, bitter,' Richard replied as he tugged his glove free and grasped the offered hand firmly. 'Aye, bitter days, and not only for reason of the weather,' Richard added sardonically.

'Indeed, indeed – warm yourselves and I will have you shown to your rooms where you can change from those wet clothes.'

Richard, William, and Jacob did as the Earl had suggested. As they stood by the fire, they were greeted by the others present. They were all men Richard was familiar with, to whom he introduced his two companions. It seemed to him that many of the great and good of the land had assembled. Richard nodded to Rodger and Hugh Bigod and they warmly acknowledged him, they were his old enemies from Framlingham whom he'd defeated at the battle of Fornham, near Saint Edmunds in 1175.

'Aye, alliances change with the seasons,' Richard said quietly into William's ear. He knew men of power rarely held grudges, it seemed all understood it was merely the way of things; all fought for their homes and knew that was how life was ordered, if you were to survive, you'd better learn to bend with the wind. Richard had seen a few over the years who'd been unable to bend, they merely fallen from view and life had simply moved on without them. William de Mowbray was there from Yorkshire, William de Huntingfield, John de Lacy Constable of Chester and many more. There must have been fifteen or so of the most influential Barons in the north.

Much discussion was made at the night's feast but they would meet on the morrow and begin in earnest making plans for the future.

They knew John was at this moment in France with a mercenary army, endeavouring to regain his lost lands, from what was said, he was making heavy weather of it and the war was not going his way. If he failed and spent all the coin from the taxes he'd raised, all Hell would be unleashed on the Barons when he returned home to England.

Richard slept badly that night his back ached from yesterday's ride. Eventually he gave up, rose, and washed. He opened the shutters, it was yet dark, but he could see that the snow had ceased falling. He closed them, dressed, and went down to the hall. A few were already assembled, sipping on warmed wine, they greeted him, and he was offered a goblet.

After they'd broken the night's fast, the tables were cleared and they were seated ready to begin. The Earl of Derby stood and suggested that Lord Maillorie be asked if he would lead the meeting. He was known and respected for a man driven by honour; some had even fought under him. There was a rumble of agreement and slapping of hands on the table before them. Richard stood and bowed.

'I am humbled and honoured my Lords, it is a fine thing to have lived to my age and still have friends who are yet content to hear your voice,' they laughed. 'I will gladly watch over this gathering; we have fought alongside each other before *and*… even *against* each other.'

Hugh Bigod laughed, 'Aye, and I lost the battle, you were lucky that day.'

Richard smiled, 'Aye, ever lucky, though I bear no grudges here, I know you to be all men of honour. History may judge us traitors for be in no doubt that's what we are, or proposing to be, and will you be satisfied that what we are preparing to undertake is worth that legacy affixed to your name for all time?' There was a muttering of disagreement, for some did not see what they were proposing as treacherous, or had not until this point thought of it so. 'Forgive me if the words sound painful to your ears, but to stand against our anointed king denotes us as such however righteous you feel our cause to be. I know that you good fellows do not do this thing lightly; some have even sworn fealty to John and all that means to a knight…' Richard paused. 'I judge you not, for it is a grievous thing to which we have been driven, but I believe what drives me is the highest state of honour, that of right and justice. We have tolerated that which perhaps we should have not tolerated, and ignored that which we should not have ignored. I am as guilty as you are, for John has offended my family and me, greatly over the years. Our wives and daughters have been molested, aye, and from amongst us here, without redress,' Richard cast his eye to Eustace de Vesci; he was Lord of Alnwick in Northumberland as well as Cottingham in Yorkshire, in fact he was an extensive landowner in the whole of northern England and Richard knew that John had pursued his wife. Richard went on, 'John's offences against any measure of decency known to me are legion. We all know of the twenty-two captive French knights who were taken to Corfe Castle in Dorset and starved to death, as was Maud de Braose, and her eldest son, to name but two of the many acts of shame perpetrated by he who is known as our King. I can't pretend that she was an easy woman, but to treat her and her son so was wicked. I feel that I must bear some of the guilt because I did little enough to make amends. Whatever are your feelings towards The Marshal, I know that he did try to protect the family and incurred John's displeasure for his pains. This may be the beginning of a reckoning for this King. If he does not prevail in France he will be in a desperate state of finance when he returns and will come to us once more. This time by the grace of God we will be prepared as one voice with a clear charter of conditions to lay before this tyrant, so let us be about such work. We will listen to all,' Richard's voice was now rising in tone with the passion of the moment, 'all will have a voice, and all will decide, and all will set their honour against what is agreed. This time will give us the chance honour demands, to set at peace this land of ours.' Richard seated himself once more and one by one, those gathered applauded his speech.

Over the next few days, the Barons and clergy came to an agreement over the basic demands of the charter to be presented to King John. Richard knew that the meeting had been far from perfect but he also knew that what they were about could fundamentally change how the country was governed. How he wished his friend William Marshal had been with them. He knew John might be compelled to agree with their demands at this time, but he'd cast them to the wind when it suited him. For them to have William Marshal on their side could have made all the difference. It was decided that all there would go their separate ways and give more thought to what had been decided then another meeting would be organised to finalize their demands.

Chapter 36

Christmas 1214

Richard had changed from his travelling clothes, bathed and was now dressed in a warm woollen robe and seated by the fire, meditating over his cup of wine. He gazed into the red liquid as if he was trying to see the future. He hadn't spoken much since he'd arrived home earlier this day from Bolsover and his meeting with the Barons. Esther didn't question him even though she was anxious to know what had been said, she'd asked young William Marshal and Jacob but neither of them had been able to satisfy her.

She now sat opposite her very stern-faced husband and busied herself on her embroidery. She hated it at the best of times, and she was finding it ever difficult to see the work unless the light was good, which it was not, where she was seated at the present moment, by the fire.

Richard after some time of staring into his cup, lifted it to his lips and sipped the wine, smacked his lips together and sighed.

'Has all been well here whilst I have been gone, Esther?'

'Yes, Alys has constantly asked for Ganfarer, Ganfarer, where Ganfarer, where Ganfarer.' That brought a smile to Richard's face, as Esther knew it would.

'I bought her a wooden doll from a beggar.'

'What, you have been plotting to overthrow the King of England and you had time to think of Alys!' Esther sat wide mouthed.

'It is only a small doll,' Richard replied in his defence.

'Oh, only a small doll!' she smiled, 'I see, I may have a passing interest in the meeting you have been to…'

The glow of the firelight touched the creases on his face as he smiled despondently, 'ahhh, the meeting,' he sighed deeply. 'Yes, the meeting, there were fifteen or so there, good fellows to a man and clergy, both groups saw things differently. The clergy seemed more concerned that the King should acknowledge the authority of the church than with the Barons concern of crippling taxation and the total disregard to any rule of law.'

'What will happen now?'

'Ahhh, I was asked to lead the meeting and sent them away to contemplate on what had been said. Some wanted immediate action, but I was resolutely against that, what we are about is too serious to act upon without *much* thought. Some even went as far as to suggest that we invite Philip of France to invade and overthrow John.' Richard smiled at Esther, 'why do you ask me these things for I know my wife well after all these years and she will have wrung all the information from Will Marshal and Jacob.'

Esther laughed, 'they were no more informative than you,' and Richard laughed too, rose from his chair took her embroidery from her and sat her on his knee.

'I'm weary of all this, Esther.'

Esther kissed his cheek, 'Why not let the younger Barons take the lead?'

'Aye, that would be a fine thing, but differing ages bring differing gifts and that has to be acknowledged. What does the scripture say? "Your old men will dream dreams; your young men will see visions". It is as it should be that the young have visions; they hunger and want to press on. Dreams draw life from what is past and if we forget, we are in danger of repeating the mistakes of the past. I've learned that wanting is not enough and that our actions ever have consequences so we need tread carefully. This path we presume to step onto will have a fundamental effect on the future and there will be no turning back.'

Esther nestled her head into his chest. 'You have always thought of the future on a grander scale than I have. I worry about the here and now, you and knowing your love, but I have always had unerring trust in your wisdom. Time has proven again and again that you have been right and you will have my support whatever you decide.'

Richard twisted his head awkwardly to look at her and smiled, 'Do you mean for example, when I wanted to ride back to Clarendon to avenge Tristram, that sort of wisdom?'

'That was an exception,' she said sadly.

'Aye, it was that,' he responded to that memory by kissing her brow.

Richard corresponded with the Barons he'd met with at Bolsover and it was decided that they would try to arrange a meeting with the King in early January. He'd received their thoughts and then decided to write to William Marshal, who apparently was back in favour with John, having been forgiven for disobeying him and going to

Ireland. In this one thing, John had shown some wisdom, and that was that he appeared to recognise the value of having William Marshal on his side.

In due course Richard received a reply from William and a meeting with John was arranged for the following January in the Templar's church in London. It would suit the purpose well enough; it was a round building down by the river, built to resemble the church of the Holy Sepulchre in Jerusalem.

Richard was sure that ice would, at this moment, be forming in Hell if John had had a Damascus road experience. To *prove* his sincerity, he would sign a charter and henceforth be subject to the law, determined to repent of a life of wickedness.

'No, never,' Richard smiled contemptuously, he was certain the truth was altogether earthier; John was bankrupt after his ignominious defeat in France at the Battle of Bouvines, and was now desperate for coin.

Richard could only see two possibilities for the future, once John had gained some financial ground, he would tear up the charter and the Barons would either crumble, or there would be civil war. Both options were not ones that lightened Richard's heart. There were other considerations now that John had repaired his relationship with Pope Innocent. He had now become in affect the Pope's vassal, surrendering his kingdom to having "The Pope" as overlord. Richard wondered how the Baron's proposed actions would be viewed by the Holy Father.

Esther managed to find some solace in the troubles, which beset Richard. She could see that the time he spent talking to his two sons and Will Marshal was a time for Richard to lead them into manhood, the world of Lordship and its greater responsibilities. Esther laughed as she heard Richard telling them that working with the Barons and the

King was like banging two heads together with one hand tied behind his back.

Alys was the one to bring relief to Richard's woes, she loved his attention and he loved hers. She could do anything she liked in his presence, if any dared to challenge her Richard would say, "She'll be yoked to life soon enough leave her be for this short time." Richard had even brought her a pony though she could barely walk, a servant would lead it, and Richard would hold her in the saddle. It seemed that whatever she demanded of him was not a trouble to him. Grâce was not so pleased for Alys would toddle to Richard before even her.

Christmas passed by at Tattershall with the normal festivities and ample food, they'd had goose and woodcock covered in saffron which gave it a golden colour. However, it was in the main a time of devotion to the Holy Babe. Carols had been forbidden by the church because villagers took the word literally, singing and dancing in circles causing disruption to services and the solemnity of the occasion. Such revelry was now banned to the streets. William as the new Lord had continued as his grandfather had and ensured that the poor and needy were allowed to have the deer's "Umbles" the heart, liver, tongue, feet, ears and brains, mixed with whatever else was leftover, all such were made into a pie known as "Umble Pie".

After the festivities, Richard became more distant; Esther knew he was becoming anxious about the January meeting, he always feared that he would not be measured when it came to dealing with King John. To give him any voice and hear his treacherous scheming lies was something that instantly fired Richard's temper and then reason was a distant memory to him. Esther wondered if it was because John thought Richard a fool, and that he was blind to his lies and he bettered him, which galled Richard so.

Chapter 37

Second Charter

Richard was thankful for the mild January weather as they rode south. They rode in number having joined forces with other northern Barons en route. The largest force by far was that of Robert Fitz-Walter. By his own account, King John had attempted to seduce his eldest daughter; he had been outlawed and escaped to France but returned under a special amnesty after John's reconciliation with the Pope.

Richard had some reservations, but Fitz-Walter seemed to want to take control of the intended meeting and Richard, if not happy, was to some extent relieved, because he feared his own temper could do more damage than good.

Once again William, Richard's son did not ride with them and Richard was content with such, for he thought some distance between the meeting with John and the Barons may be no bad thing for the time being. What the outcome would be was an uncertain length of twine as far a he could see. For any king, never mind a king of John's arrogance, to cordially give up his power, would be a hard thing to imagine. Yet the same old distrust was ever near to Richard's heart, he was sure that John would make any promise to get what he wanted, because he was without honour his oath was worthless. They could leave the Temple with every demand met, and it would not be worth the parchment, on which it was written. Civil war was inevitable as far as he could see and worse, there was yet a faction, which was for inviting King Philip Augustus and his son Prince Louis to replace John.

'Aye, I'm happy for Fitz-Walter to speak, and I will watch from the shadows. He despises John every bit as much as I do, and will say what must be said without any fear of John,' Richard said speaking out his thoughts as they rode.

Richard had reached the ripe old age of sixty-five two days before they set off. Esther and Grâce had surprised him with a large spiced pudding made with all the leftover vegetables, eggs, apples, and French spirit. There was a small one especially from Alys, which John declared was the finest he'd ever tasted, much to Alys' delight. He laughed for he'd never given his birthday even a passing thought. He was fortunate not many reached his ripe age, perhaps God had allowed him, even wanted him to be part of this, both him and his old friend the Marshal and he was even older. It saddened him that he and his dear friend, who were both driven by honour, were somehow driven to opposing sides. As his thoughts wove paths round, and round his mind, he cast an eye to young Will Marshal; he'd growing to love the lad. He was different to his sire, sure enough, a little hotter headed not so pragmatic, one always knew what he was thinking. Richard smiled, for his son Jacob who rode alongside Will was not like him either, more like his mother, ever kind and gentle always seeing the best in folk.

'Aye, fine lads,' he said. Richard hoped that this meeting would go well for Will. His father almost certainly would be there; their separation was a sad thing to Richard.

It was mid-morning when they arrived at the Temple, by the number of horses it appeared that John was there before them. That surprised Richard, for John was renowned for his tardiness, if he turned up at all. The leaders dismounted and strode into the holy place, Richard was not so eager and held back reckoning to adjust his saddle straps.

'Is all well, Father?' Jacob asked

'Aye – hold a moment,' Richard replied, Jacob and Will did as they were bidden.

'Come Father, you can attend to that after we have presented our charter to the King,' Jacob said, anxious not to miss anything of the confrontation, Will was not quite so eager to go in, for fear of the inevitable meeting with his father.

John was seated in an elaborately carved chair at the far end of the chancel; Richard was told it was made from olive wood brought all the way from the Holy City, the garden of Gethsemane to be precise. Apparently, the tree had blood stained marks upon it, from the blood the Saviour had sweated in His hour of tormented prayer. More likely, a camel or some such mysterious beast had lifted his leg against it thought Richard cynically, and he quickly crossed himself in case he was wrong. He waited for a moment for the bolt from heaven, and then shrugged his shoulders, just as I thought – a camel.

John sprawled *contemptuously*, his elbow rested on the arm of the chair supporting his chin between his thumb and forefinger. He clearly wanted to give the impression that the whole event was a tedious irrelevance to him, but Richard knew it was not or he'd never have troubled himself to attend. There was a table before him and as Fitz-Walter made to draw the charter from his pouch John raised his hand as if to instruct him to bide his time.

'Do you approach your King without a bowed head, is this the level of disrespect I am to be faced with by he who was until recently an outlaw, but for my generosity and grace.' Fitz-Walter stared, his face as stone, and then dipped his head. Richard could see the smirk on John's face as Fitz-Walter placed the charter of demands on the table before him. William Marshal stood behind John, his face was expressionless, William had mastered the art of giving nothing away on his face, but Richard knew William had seen him and *his* son, young Will.

'What is this you lay before me?'

'These are the right conditions that – *your* Barons have agreed upon and demand…'

'DEMAND!'

'Aye, demand you adhere to, no more than your grandfather, the most noble Lord King Henry the First, set in place and now you sorely abuse,' Fitz-Walter said without wavering.

'*Barons*, you say, and whom are these – stood with me, but even more noble Barons of my kingdom, you speak as if you are the voice of all? Have *they* sanctioned this, this outrage before me?' John flicked his hand contemptuously at the document. Fitz-Walter eyed the Barons who had come with John and they shuffled uneasily, for they might be standing with him because of their sworn fealty, but not because they had any liking for the man.

John suddenly rose to his feet and hissed through his teeth, 'I will not deal with men who have such disrespect for our beloved Church,' Richard shook his head at the theatre, 'that they enter this holy place armed for rebellion. Are these the men, who set themselves to judge me? I shame myself, and my God, that I even listen to their blasphemous tongues,' and he turned to go. William Marshal touched his shoulder and whispered in his ear; John paused then half turned back to face Fitz-Walter. 'I will take this treasonous scrap and study it for I can read unlike the majority of you illiterate ne're-do-wells, who come armed to threaten a peace loving man of God, such as your King,' and he nodded to William Marshal, he picked up the charter and they left followed by his supporters. The northern Barons stood frozen to the spot for some moments, stunned by John's audacity.

'And I thought to worry about a bolt from on high,' said Richard to himself.

One by one, the Barons left the building to where their horses yet stood. Richard's eye caught sight of William Marshal across the courtyard, beckoning him from the shadows.

'Will, tell Fitz-Walter to wait, stay his hand if he is mad enough to do something foolish, I will return directly.' Richard strolled casually in the direction of where he'd spotted William, glanced back over his shoulder, and then slipped into the shadows beside his friend. They faced each other for a second then embraced warmly.

'You've aged, Richard!'

'Aye and you, but you are yet older than me.'

'Ha… good to see you, listen, let me speak quickly, I will do what I can to see that he does not disregard this charter, make for home and wait. The threat of these armed men might work against you. He needs their support so he will read it, but let it rest for now. I must hasten, take care,' and William turned and quickly disappeared out of sight.

Richard walked back to the Barons yet standing by their mounts; Fitz-Walter was clearly not pleased at being confronted by the son of an enemy.

Richard told them what the Marshal had said and reluctantly they decided to be advised by him.

Chapter 38

War

'Dear, oh dear, Esther...' Richard said wearily scratching his head as he stared at William Marshal's letter. Esther looked on nervously, fearful of the news contained within the missive. 'John has rejected the demands of the Barons. His one concession is to give more powers to the Church, though that is some small crumb for that has even served to annoy me, because apparently, the clergy had already met with him in secret in November and agreed such. Divide and conquer, John never ceases his scheming. I would truly be surprised if he has ever had a single straightforward dealing in his whole life. If he told me it would be dark tonight, I would not believe him,' Richard said, once more giving a long drawn out sigh.

'What will this mean now? As if I didn't know,' asked Esther fearfully.

'Civil war – as simple as that, nothing short of a miracle will prevent such an outcome now. I will have to send copies of this letter to the other northern Barons. I fear John has played right into the hands of Robert Fitz-Walter. This is exactly what he wanted, and perhaps he is right – he never wanted peace, not on any terms of John's that's for sure. He wants John humiliated, he has scores to settle, but I seem to have spent a lifetime at such activity and I'm weary of it. Don't misunderstand me, I too want John humbled and brought to book for his wickedness, but God forgive me, I want others to fight my battles.'

'And rightly so, you have done your share, your life has been one of fighting to see law and order established,' Esther said supportively. 'But with regard to this missive, what will you tell young Will Marshal and our sons?' Esther asked dreading to hear where such information might drive them.

'Mmm… I will tell them naught, I'll read this letter to them, and they must decide for themselves. They are men and as such have the right to do as they see fit. It is their future and their children's future that is at stake. Thank God *my* future has a limited horizon.'

'Don't say such a thing Richard, you are well and yet strong.'

'Aye… you think it so, do you? It's not how I feel at this moment believe me.'

Esther showed him her hands, 'what about me, your hands are not old like these *lumpy* old woman's hands and you have not eyes that can no longer see to sew.'

Richard laughed at her, 'I must say in truth, I have had no more trouble with my sewing of late than I ever had,' he laughed once more and rose from his chair, took her in his arms and kissed her.

'Ahh… I will go and find our young men.' With that, he released Esther from his arms kissed her once more, tried to smile, and then turned to go. Esther's maid Jane bowed and opened the door for him, he nodded to her as he left the room.

Richard caught sight of Jacob through the open door of the blacksmith's forge, rhythmically pumping the leather bellows for the smith, as he held with his tongs a piece of glowing red-hot iron in the furnace. Jacob was stripped to the waist and as sweaty and dirty, if not more so than the smith was.

'You've a new apprentice, I see Robert!' Richard called over the noise of the bellows and roaring forge.

'Aye, fine and willing he is too Lord; I could find him a place. The young Lord's as keen as mustard,' the smith joked.

'*Jacob*, whatever in the Blessed Virgin's name are you about, Son?' Richard asked him, compelled to smile at the two startling white eyes peering from the black sweaty face.

'It's my new sword, I told you about it Father, don't you remember?'

'Ahhh, so you did, but I didn't think you were forging it yourself.'

'Not quite by myself, but I am an ingredient of the work, I want it to be part of me. After you told me of the Ulfberht's history, the sword Grandfather gave to William; I liked the idea of putting oneself into a sword. I wanted my own sword to have *my* life woven into it, and when I pass it onto my son, he will know it's part of me he is inheriting.'

Richard nodded, 'A fine thought, son. Have you seen Will Marshal or your brother?'

'Aye, they are both in the tiltyard working with Will's new courser, have you seen it yet?'

'So, it's arrived has it, he told me this morning he was expecting it.'

'I have seen it, it's a fine beast, he was very coy about the price he'd paid,' Richard smiled. 'I would have been with them now, but I'm busy as you see.'

'Can you leave your employment? I wish you to come with me and hear my news. We will go to the tiltyard and I'll share it with you all, for it concerns each of us,' Richard waved the letter in his hand.

'One moment, Father, I'll wash off some of this sweat and don my shirt,' and Jacob sluiced his face in a bucket of water and dried it.

'Will it be all right if I leave you for a while Robert?' Jacob asked as he laid the dirty towel over a rail.

'Aye, fine enough Lord; I've a young lad here eager for the exercise. He's growing idle whilst you do his work, isn't that right Mattie?' The boy's smile was less than convincing; it was hard toil pumping the bellows for hours on end.

Young William Marshal saw Richard and Jacob coming, and signalled to Richard's son as he rode this way and that, enjoying the work of putting his new acquisition through its paces. He guided the horse to where Will was standing, and jumped from the saddle, patted his horse's soft pink nose, and passed the rein to a squire.

'Be sure to rub him down Mark, there's a good lad,' the squire bowed and led the horse off to the stable. 'You look very serious Father,' his son said, narrowing his eyes. 'I take it you're not here to admire my new horse.'

'Your horse – aye, a fine beast, Spanish by the look of him, has he a name yet?'

'I have this minute been discussing such with Will…'

'And!'

'We thought to consult you; Ares is ever the horse in my mind from boyhood. The name of your much beloved horse.'

'Now there *was* a fine horse, I've never seen the like since, long gone now. Perhaps you should think on it a while longer. Your Grandfather William's horse was called Hecuba, at least the one I recall.'

'Perhaps, I quite like that, *Hecuba*, mmm,' he pondered the name looking to the sky as if the answer might be there. 'I'll think on it. Now your news!' William nodded to the letter in his father's hand.

'I have heard from the Barons we met with at Bolsover. As you know Will, I sent copies of your father's letter to them, here is their response,' he lifted the letter in his hand. You need to hear their intention as a result of all that your father wrote.'

'I can guess what they have written in response, Lord,' said young Will Marshal.

'No doubt, but I will read it to you nevertheless.'

The young men leant against the fence. Richard unfolded the document and began to read. On completion, his arm yet holding the letter fell wearily to his side reflecting his despair.

'What are your thoughts, Will, is it as you expected?'

Young Will Marshal laid his gloves on the rail behind him before he answered. 'Aye, I am afraid so. I will fight if it comes to it. I have always been prepared for this outcome. John is incapable of any act of honour. To be sure, Lord this pleases me, if I can hurt that man in any way I rejoice.'

'Aye, and I too,' Jacob said unequivocally.

'And what about you, William?' Richard asked, turning directly to face his eldest son.

William stroked his chin thoughtfully avoiding his father's eyes. Taking his time to assemble his words before he spoke, he then lifted his head. 'I'm thinking on things you have said to me before Father, and the tale of your own father, my grandfather and name sake. How he lost all, or near enough all, in the civil war between King Stephen and the old Empress, John's grandmother. It goes against everything I feel in my heart – for I could strangle the ill begotten spawn with my bare hands. I will not fight against John, at *this* time, unless my hand is forced. It is wise that we have family in both camps, not that we are in any disagreement, for we are not, but for the safety and future of our family. Whoever is left standing, after there has been enough killing to satisfy our lust for death, will take care of the other, if needs be, as my Grandfather John's brother took care of him in that last civil war, to which I have this moment alluded. I'm sorry if I disappoint any of you,' William glanced to the others, 'but I have greater considerations than that of salving my own wrath at this time.'

Richard nodded his approval, 'It's a sign of a true Lord that you don't allow your heart in isolation to make a judgment. Let your heart and your head work in harmony when you make decisions. Your father, Will,' Richard turned his attention briefly to young William Marshal, 'once said to me, when we have a difficult decision to make, strip away all the words surrounding the problem, and when you have done that, all that will remain is a simple choice – is it right – or is it wrong to do this?' Richard said squeezing his son's shoulder. '*I* will ride with you two fellows,' he smiled, 'to look after you, someone must do it,' they all laughed apart from Jacob.

'Father, I don't want you to come, and neither will Mother.'

'Oh… and why might I ask?'

'Father you know as well as I, you are not as young as you were and it will be hard employment.'

Richard smiled, 'Fear not Son, though I am touched by your concern, I will leave all the fighting to you fellows. I'll only watch the fun – from a safe distance, and help you off and on your horse as I did at Bolsover,' he poked Jacob with his finger and wrapped his arm around him.

However, Jacob was right about one thing Esther was furious when Richard told her he would be going, but he would not be moved.

'Esther, my dearest, I must be there. There will be high passion aplenty as there is in all battles, as I know very well and there will be a need for old heads. That will be my part, when the dust has settled and time has drunk her fill of blood.'

Esther knew he spoke the truth; the passions of youth could well escalate any conflict unnecessarily. Yet she could only think that most, if they lived even near his age were in their dotage, not roaming around the county armoured for battle. He would have to do this she could see that, but what would she do if aught happened to him, he was everything to her. Why Mother of Christ, must I always have to be the one to give up my husband, she prayed.

In due course, he received directions from the northern Barons; they were to meet, ready for war at Stamford in Lincolnshire. The following days were spent in preparation, such time passed always too quickly for Esther, as it did now for Grâce, William's young wife. Esther would be strong for her, for she knew very well the feelings of a young mother like Grâce, remembering the times Richard had ridden off to battle.

Richard took Esther in his arms having hugged and kissed Alys, Grâce and his son, William. All tried to be brave and cheerful, which in some way made the parting more difficult rather than easier.

'My dearest Esther,' he whispered into her ear, 'I wish there was another word to convey how much you mean to me. The word *love*, falls easily from the tongue, but it seems inadequate to express the completeness of my feelings for you.'

She kissed his lips and whispered, 'Not when "I", is set before it. To hear you say "*I*" love you is all my heart has ever needed.' He now held her at arms length and smiled into her tear-filled eyes.

'Fear not woman, I will be home and I'll bring these two young men with me.' He set his foot in the stirrup and mounted.

Chapter 39

Ronimed

The Barons assembled an army at the Stamford tournament field near Peterborough during Easter week the 19th to the 26th of April. Five Earls and forty Barons arrived with horses and arms, and they brought with them a countless host most of who were northerners.

Richard estimated they were comprised of about two thousand knights, plus other horsemen, sergeants-at-arms, and foot soldiers.

From Stamford, they marched to Northampton. On finding John's army had moved to Brackley, twenty or so miles to the southwest they followed, intent on forcing his hand.

John, obviously fearing the worst, sent William Marshal and Steven Langton, the Archbishop, to speak with them to discover exactly what they wanted of him.

They met with the Barons on 27th of April, and the Barons presented to the envoys their schedule, which consisted for the most part of ancient laws and customs of the realm. The Barons made it known that if King John did not at once adhere to these time-honoured laws, and confirm them with his seal, they would compel him to do so by force, and that was their certain resolve.

Langton and the Marshal returned to the King, now in Wiltshire, with the list of demands. One by one, the articles were read out to John by the Archbishop.

According to Roger of Wendover, after he had heard them John said, *"Why do these Barons not ask for my kingdom at once... their demands are idle dreams, without a shadow of reason",* then he burst into a fit of rage kicking a nearby dog. He swore that he would never grant to them such liberties, which would make *him* a slave to the demands of *his* subjects.

He sent the two back to the Barons and instructed them to repeat his words *verbatim*. On hearing this, the Barons immediately renounced their fealty to the King and chose Robert Fitz-Walter as their leader, to whom they gave the grandiose title of "Marshal of the army of God and Holy Church". They marched back to Northampton, occupied the town, and laid siege to the castle. However, they had not brought any siege equipment and after two weeks were forced to give up, but not before many had been killed including Fitz-Walter's standard-bearer.

Richard listened agitatedly to the commanders; he could tell though they were resolved to make John submit to their just demands they were unsure of their tactics. He wondered if deep down – they had doubts. Eventually he could stand their prevaricating no longer and was compelled to intercede and told them if they wanted to inflict *one* decisive blow, they must take London, and soon. They looked to one another and hesitantly... one by one, they acknowledged that Richard had spoken the truth.

The Barons moved on to Bedford where William de Beauchamp readily gave up his castle. Next, they advanced on to London itself, which they reached on the 27th of May and took control of the city. They had covered much ground over the last days and Richard was forced to admit, if only to himself, that he was as Jacob had said, too old for all this riding.

Whilst the main rebel force was in the south, the townsfolk of Northampton rose against the garrison of the castle, killing several of them. In retaliation, the garrison soldiers charged into the town, killing a number of townsfolk and setting houses on fire.

With London under Baronial control, John knew he was beaten. He had been waiting for letters from the Pope hoping that they would strengthen his position, but by the time they arrived, it was too late.

At the beginning of June, he sent William Marshal once more with a message to the Barons saying, "...*that for the sake of peace and for the welfare and honour of his realm, he would freely concede to them the laws and liberties which they asked. That they might appoint a place and day for him and them to meet, for the settlement of all these things.*"

Such a meeting was duly arranged where John would *hopefully,* at last agree to the Barons demands. The assembly was set for the 15th of June, and the place, a meadow between Stanes and Windsor called Ronimed.

Richard drew his horse to a standstill in a wooded area a few hundred or so yards south of the two tents where he assumed that John would eventually show face. Richard had ridden from Stanes where he and the other leading Barons had stayed that night.

He had risen early after a nervous night's sleep and did not feel rested. The location for the gathering had been chosen because it was a traditional site of signing agreements, so Richard had been told. He had talked to one old man who'd said the Saxon council, the Witenagemot, had met there from King Alfred's day; in fact, he said the name was Saxon for "Meeting Meadow". It was on neutral ground between the royal fortress of Windsor, were John was, and the Baron's campsite at Stanes.

The location gave neither faction any military advantage. Ronimed, as it was known, was situated on grassland, which was subject to occasional flooding by the River Thames that bordered the site one hundred yards to the east, but this June day it was dry and sunny, a fine day for such employment Richard thought as he glance up to the clear blue sky. There was not a cloud to be seen and he prayed that such was the future of this land from this day on. However, he knew fine well, that clouds had the most vexing habit of appearing from nowhere "Out of the blue", as it were.

The meeting today was the second meeting of the two opposing forces. The Barons had met with envoys from John ten days previously and they had presented them with their articles.

Stephen Langton's pragmatic efforts at mediation over the next ten days turned these incomplete, disordered demands into a charter, capturing the essence of the proposed peace agreement. Richard was sure that William Marshal would have had a large say in the wording of the document, for he of all men was best placed to accurately predict what would be acceptable to both John *and* the Barons. He would know that there must be compromises if there was to be any hope of agreement. Assembling of the words so that both parties appeared to have their considerations adhered to – was no easy task.

Richard had sent Will Marshal and his son Jacob on ahead and he had stopped at the Priory of Saint Mary's to pray for the day's work and light a candle, that his prayer might be remembered by the saints. He knew that this day's gathering would need all the help heaven and all its saints could muster.

He now stood watching from the small coppice, he saw the King arrive with William Marshal and a group of maybe a dozen knights. They dismounted and he made his way to the larger of the two tents, William had walked past his son and as he lifted the tent flap for the King to enter, he paused for a second and glanced at him. Richard couldn't tell from where he was standing if he'd spoken to Will or not.

They were in the tent for no more than half of an hour before they emerged, John looked sour faced, and Richard smiled at his obvious discomfort. He mounted his horse and rode back in the direction of Windsor from whence he had come.

Richard looked intently at the riders as they left, but could not see William Marshal amongst them.

There was one knight holding the reins of a horse, which he assumed was William Marshal's mount. After a moments study Richard recognised the young fellow as John Earley who'd once been the Marshal's ward. He was no more that fresh-faced boy when he'd last seen him at Le Mans, now he was a man. Richard watched for a moment longer and then saw William emerge lifting the tent flap with a sweep of his arm, straightening himself and tug on his riding gauntlets. He hesitated, looked up to where Richard stood, mounted, and rode towards him.

Richard pushed himself from the tree he was leaning against and walked a few steps to meet him, he lifted his hand in welcome, and William reached down from his horse and took the proffered hand.

'Are you jumping down then, William?'

William Marshal laughed, '*jumping*, I think not, but I will dismount, and we can walk a while if you wish.'

'Shall we stroll by the river? Do you know, I think the last time we had together was by a river, do you recall?'

'Ha... so I do, it was at your home at Aylesford, it must be – Hell's teeth, that was when I'd just returned from the Holy City in eighty-four, that's... over thirty years ago.'

'Hell's teeth indeed, but no, I'm wrong there, we fought together at Le Mans after that,' Richard corrected himself.

'*Aye*, so we did, how could I forget that débâcle... your memory is better than mine, but to be fair to us, we have more to remember than most, anyway it's been too long. You're looking well, my friend, a little more hair than me I think,' William smiled and patted Richard's shoulder.

Richard smiled too, 'as I said to you at the Temple a few months past, I'm much younger than you are. Perhaps you might take some comfort in the fact that grass seldom grows on a busy road.'

'Ha, if that be the case, it's a wonder I have any hair at all. As for my age, each morning I have a new ache to remind me, without your need for making such known. There are not many of us left now from the old days,' William said tying his horse to a branch and then embracing Richard. He left his arm around Richard's shoulder as they ambled leisurely towards the riverbank.

'Is Isabelle in good health?' Richard asked.

'Aye, fitter than me, but then she's less than half my age. What about Esther, pray God she is well too.'

'Well enough, but growing older, she'll be worrying until I get home. I pray for good times after all this trouble.'

'You think it over now, Richard?' William paused and looked him in the eye.

'The truth, I'm afraid not, I take it he agreed at this moment to all the demands?'

'Aye, John agreed right enough, but I noticed that there was no seal of Lord Richard Maillorie upon the charter!'

'Ha... no, John's hand was forced, and I will stake my life on it that he's had no sudden and lasting change of heart. I will not put my seal next to any mark that fellow has made. For to my certain knowledge of our good King John, he will hold that document in utter contempt and put a flame to it as soon as he can.'

'You think so?' William smiled.

'And, what of the great William Marshal, is his seal upon it?'

'Aye... William Marshal's name is upon it, for better or worse, I will say no more than that.'

'Mmm, but there is one Marshal who is prepared to hope for better things,' Richard said, as he pointed to a place on the riverbank where they might sit.

'Well, perhaps he's not so cynical as me, God bless him.'

'Did you speak to the lad?' Richard asked as he eased himself down onto the grassy edge of the bank.

'I tried – I said that he was always welcome at his home, and that his mother missed him, which she does. I could see he wanted to speak, but he couldn't find the words. John has had both my sons as his *squires*. Richard, your names sake, was summoned after I upset John by going to Ireland, he was determined to keep me in check.'

'Mmm, he demanded my son too, but I refused, which one of us did the right thing only time will tell. You heard about the hanging of the Welsh hostages at Nottingham?'

'Aye, a shameful thing, the oldest was but fourteen, it was done without my knowledge.'

'A sad thing and no mistake, you can't punish yourself for all that paltonier's crimes. However, with regard to your son, the time passes and the pain deadens, but finding one's way out of the dark hole gets more difficult as we let the years rumble on.'

'You speak the truth, and I know it… but I am at a loss, there are things yet tormenting his heart and *he* needs more time it seems.'

'Yes, he told me.'

'I pray that God in His mercy will one day give him peace. What about us my old friend, honour has driven us both over the years. I have thought about you many times and I decided that at the bottom of it, we both want the same thing. A decent place to live where there is justice and people who respect and care for each other, *gently* guided and *supported* by a rule of law.'

'Aye, we are dreamers that's our trouble, William. Come, I must make tracks for home and Esther, before John reneges on his part of the day's employment and all this is for naught.'

'To my mind Richard, I have little enough faith in either party, your side is as likely as John to have second thoughts once they take their ease this day. There is too much scepticism by far, and too many scores to settle for a scrap of parchment and sealing wax to heal the wounds, the trust was just not there, but who knows.'

'We must move before my joints seize up and the King thinks *you* have joined the rebels.'

William laughed, 'he's always thought I was one of the rebels,' Richard laughed too and slapped William's back.

They both pushed themselves to their feet; the spring of youth had left them now, and they strolled back to where they'd left their horses. They embraced once more and William mounted and rode off.

'God keep you, my friend,' Richard whispered under his breath as he watched William ride towards his protégé, John Earley, who was now engaged it conversation with Jacob, Richard could see them laughing, no doubt Jacob had told him he was William's brother. Jacob would have heard tell of John from his brother, for William and John had been friends at Le Mans. John grasped Jacob's hand, patted his back, and leapt onto his horse as the Marshal drew near.

Richard led his horse towards his son and young Will Marshal knowing he would be riding home without them.

'You made yourself known to John Earley, Jacob!'

'Indeed, he was very friendly, a fine fellow. He asked after William and I told him he was a married man now, with a daughter. He'd been fighting in Ireland he said, alongside Will's mother. Apparently, the King had encouraged an uprising when the Marshal was away. Because John Earley had stayed to help Will's mother, he had been stripped of all his lands in England.'

'That sounds like the King we know and love, and yet – there they are both supporting that unworthy turd. What do you make of that for honour, young Will?' Richard pointedly asked the young Marshal.

'It vexes me sorely to see my father treated in such a shameful way and to watch him make not the slightest effort to stand up for himself, it is truly sickening.'

'What if you felt honour bound to stand by someone Will, are you only bound when you approve of them…?

Do we not all support those who think like us even without the bond of honour? Should I only love Jacob when he does what pleases me, or are there some commitments, which are absolute? You see your father lives his life by a standard that only the strongest men can adhere to, and that sets him above most you will ever meet. Think on that Will, before you judge him too harshly.'

'All I know Lord is how it pains me to see, that parasite sucking his blood and spitting it out in the dirt as if it was worthless.'

'You are a good lad Will, give him a chance, I love him as you clearly do.' Richard said no more for he could see he had touched the young man. 'This is farewell for now; I can see that much in your eyes, no need to say the words. Take care, remember you have homes and people who care more than life for you, may God keep you both,' said Richard by way of a blessing.

'Give my dearest love to Mother,' Jacob asked.

'I will do that, never fear.'

He said his farewells to young William Marshal and *reluctantly* to Jacob, whom he'd wanted to return with him, but he knew Jacob was determined to remain with the army to ensure the enforcing of the charter.

Chapter 40

First Baron's War

Esther was in the courtyard with Alys by her side when Richard rode in, she stared past him looking for Jacob and was clearly troubled to hear from Richard that he'd stayed with the army.

'He's a man now Esther, he must make his own way and we best let him go,' she thought on his words for a moment and sadly nodded her head.

'I am so pleased to have you home,' she said, as Richard bent down to pick Alys up, she was clearly delighted to see her grandfather.

'Where is our Will?'

'He's out with his steward and Grâce is in her chamber, she is with child once more,' Esther said smiling.

'Well, God be praised, when is it due?'

'Oh, not until January,' she smiled, 'perhaps on your birthday. Come, I will take you to her.'

'Alwin my friend, how are you?' Richard asked as he spotted him sitting on the keep steps.

'Not as well as you Lord, I struggle to walk but a few steps these days, however I tried to get out to welcome you as of old.' Richard offered his hand to him. Richard knew fine well time had not been kind to his old steward; he was bent over now with swollen joints. Richard raised him gently to his feet and embraced him.

'I will go to my daughter-in-law after which I will return to you and we will drink some wine together and talk of better days, when the sun forever shone.' Alwin smiled.

'Father, Father,' Isabelle called and almost knocked Richard over as she leapt into his arms. She was followed by Marshal who was a little more restrained; he only patted his father's back.

'Can we marry now, Papa or are we yet excommunicated?' Isabelle asked.

'Ha, what's this talk of marriage I thought you would stay with me and care for me in my old age. No doubt, your long-suffering betrothed Lord Thomas is as eager as you. You must pray that the Pope is forgiving to us rebels. Perhaps we might find a willing dairymaid to take you on Marshal,' his son reddened.

'*Richard!*' Esther said sharply.

'For now, let us go to Grâce and I will tell you all'

Over the next weeks, neither King John nor the rebel Barons seriously attempted to implement the peace accord. The rebel Barons suspected that the proposed Baronial Council would be unacceptable to John and that he would challenge the legality of the charter.

They packed the Baronial Council with their own hardliners and refused to demobilise their forces or surrender London as had been agreed at Ronimed. Despite his promises to the contrary, John appealed to Pope Innocent for help, making it known that the charter compromised the Pope's rights under the 1213 agreement that had appointed him John's feudal Lord. Innocent obliged; he declared the charter "Not only shameful and demeaning, but illegal and unjust" and furthermore he once again excommunicated the rebel Barons and all connected to them. The failure of the agreement led rapidly to the First Barons' War.

The Barons offered the throne to Prince Louis of France. Louis accepted and landed unopposed on the Isle of Thanet; he was proclaimed "King of England" in Saint Paul's in London, on the 2nd of June 1216, with great pomp and celebration. However, though he was not crowned, many nobles, even King Alexander of Scotland, attended the prestigious event.

Richard's honour was truly confused for the first time in his life. He hated John who true to form, had seen to the annulment of the charter, which was no surprise, but neither could he ever support Louis or Philip, they had too many unsettled scores. He knew Jacob and young William were fighting for the Barons which, in effect, amounted to them fighting for Prince Louis, even if they preferred not to think of their actions as such.

Richard and Esther were out leisurely riding when they spotted Jacob and a dozen or so knights heading towards Tattershall.

Esther stood in her stirrups and shouted for all she was worth; Jacob saw her, broke from the group and galloped to them.

'Mother, Father!' he shouted as he neared, on reaching them he leapt from his horse, reached up to her and lowered her down from the saddle. He lifted her off her feet and she covered his face with kisses. After setting her down, he reached up his hand to his father.

'Good to see you home and well Son, is Will Marshal not with you? I pray God he is safe.' Suddenly the smile fell from Esther's face.

'Fear not, he's right enough, or was when I last saw him.'

'Where is he now, Son?' asked Richard.

'Come, dismount Father, we will walk for a while and I will tell all. God knows my backside needs to be free of that saddle after these past months,' Richard dismounted and he too embraced his son. Esther linked arms with Jacob as they walked and Richard passed the reins to the servants who had ridden with them.

'Shall we wait here, Lord?' The servant asked.

'No, follow us,' Richard ordered then turned and laid his arm on his son's shoulder. 'So, tell us Jacob!'

'Well, we have seen some hard fighting, but we now have the better of John. You asked of Will, he and I were camped at Worchester Castle. We with Prince Louis forces had captured it; Will and I knew we were not strong enough to hold it, that night we had a visitor who walked as bold as could be into our tent. We both leapt for our arms and were about to challenge the fellow. He lifted his arms and bade us put up our weapons, at the same time he threw off the hood he was wearing. Guess who it was.'

'Prince Louis, King John, the ghost of Richard the Lionheart, I have no idea?' Esther said smiling.

'It was… William Marshal, we were dumfounded. He told us that he was going to attack us on the morrow and begged us to escape for our lives. We said we could not desert our comrades.

We knew what the Marshal told us was the truth; we eventually convinced Ranulph De Blondeville that our position was hopeless and we would be better to save ourselves and live to fight another day. It was futile to sacrifice our lives for naught, and we all escaped that night, thanks to the Marshal… *except*, Will.'

'You talk in riddles, Jacob,' Esther said never one for listening over-patiently.

'Will – went to fight *with* his father.'

Both Richard and Esther were stunned. 'Well, praise God. They are *united* once more, you have brought the finest news, Son, and it warms my heart, as I know it will do for my dearest William.'

'William proved himself to be his father's son and Prince Louis named him Marshal of his army, no less, but they fell out. William wanted Lordship of his family estates at Marlbourgh in Wiltshire and Louis refused, more fool him. William was seriously chagrined, I have discovered that he is every bit as ambitious as his sire, *but* as you say, it's an ill wind, which blows no good. The unexpected meeting, broke down many barriers, perhaps the timing was just right and now they are together.'

'Aye and I praise God again. So, what news of Louis?' Richard asked with genuine concern.

'Alas, Louis grows stronger by the day and John is being pushed north.'

'Mmm, so John comes to me… interesting,' pondered Richard.

'Forget John, for now Jacob is home, and we will be thankful, let us ride, you have a family who will be overjoyed to see you Son,' smiled Esther. With that, they mounted and made for home.

Chapter 41

Esther

The breath was driven from Esther as she tumbled over the cliff. She desperately tried to grasp hold of branches or rocks, anything, to stop her falling into what seemed like a raging fire below. She was in agony from the searing pain in her heart; touching it with her hand, she was horrified to see her fingers turn deep crimson red. This must be what it is to die, she thought. The flesh was being ripped from her body as she fell through the hellish burning brush.

'Dear Mother of Christ, save me,' she cried out. The faces of her children flashed before her eyes, Marshal, Isabelle, William and… Jacob, where was Jacob? She panicked, but then her eye caught sight of him below, his empty eyes stared up at her as she plummeted downward, downward ever downward towards him. When they drew closer, she realised that it was not so much she who was falling towards him, but rather, it was he, who was coming towards her.

In an instant, his tortured face was transformed into that of an angel. Suddenly she was distracted, there was another man, of whom – until this moment – she had been completely unaware, and *He* was now carrying Jacob on His back. She was transfixed as her eyes stared in disbelief at the sight before her; the wounds on Jacob's body were being transferred onto the body of the Man carrying him. Blood streamed down the face of the Man from vicious black thorns sticking in His brow.

He said nought as they passed, He did no more than glance into her eyes, it was the briefest glance, but it reached into the deepest recesses of her soul and touched every doubt and fear she ever had. In that moment her falling ceased, her eyes flickered – and she awoke.

Her body was bathed in sweat, but she felt strangely calm and in a place of peace. She lay for some time – never moving – apart from her eyes, which scanned the room, *her* room, she was alone, she wanted to be in Richard's arms. Drawing back the bedcovers, she slid her legs carefully over the edge of the bed, slipped on her soft bejewelled shoes, and went to find him.

Richard and Grâce stared impatiently over the battlements; he'd sent men out to look for William and Jacob, they should have been home hours since.

William had wanted to spend some time alone with his brother, to catch up and Jacob had said, "what better way is there to be on our own than to go for a gentle hack together!" They had taken two or three servants with them, no one was quite sure of the exact details, but they had armoured themselves, be it no more than with their light hauberks, these were troubled days and some precaution was ever wise.

William had promised Grâce that they would not ride too far from the castle, but she knew once they were away, they would be distracted and forget all they'd promised and drew some comfort from that thought.

It was almost dark now and Richard was very concerned, but trying not to show it for Grâce's sake. He had wanted to go with the men when they'd set off to search for his sons, but felt compelled to stay and support Grâce and Esther.

He'd tried to reassure Esther, but she was no fool, she was actually more anxious than Grâce. She was asleep in her room at this moment; Father Aidan had given her a tisane.

Richard thumped the top of the stone castellation and was about to make his way down into the courtyard when he heard a guard call out.

'RIDER APPROACHING!' Grâce nearly jumped from her skin.

Richard stepped once more up to the wall, narrowing his eyes, trying to see who it was. Even at this distance, he could tell the rider was hurt by his awkward position in the saddle. The unsteady gait of his mount, favouring its left foreleg, showed that it was also injured. Slowly – the face of the horseman came into focus... it was William.

He stared for a moment longer, his eyes searching beyond William, hoping to see Jacob. 'Hell's teeth,' Richard swore and they both ran down the stone steps to the main gate. William's horse stumbled as it stepped onto the slippery wet wooden drawbridge and William was almost unhorsed, the guard at the gate quickly reached up to steady him.

William's arm was obviously broken and lay supported, in a fashion, across his saddle. How he'd made it home Richard couldn't imagine. The horse stood wearily as Richard took its bridle.

'Leave him be Grâce, let the servants deal with him,' and Grâce stepped clear to make room for the men. They lowered William carefully to the ground, he groaned and squeezed his eyelids together gasping in agony.

'F – Father,' he panted.

'Save your strength, Son, there's time enough for talk. Carry him to his room,' Richard ordered the servants. There were suddenly plenty of helpers, soldiers and servants alike, all eager to do what they could to assist. 'Andrew, run and fetch Father Aidan, tell him Lord William has a broken arm and other wounds, which need immediate attention.'

Richard and Grâce followed anxiously behind those carrying his son. As they walked, he glanced at William's mail entrapping his damaged arm, and instructed another servant to get the blacksmith. The servant bowed and ran off.

'Tell him to bring his mail cutters with him,' He shouted after the servant, who instantly paused and turned to Richard, 'Lord William's hauberk will need to be cut from his arm.' The servant bowed once more and did as he was bidden.

Chapter 42

Captured

They laid William on his bed, and Grâce sat anxiously by him, fearing even to touch him concerned that she might exacerbate his suffering. Richard could see he was unconscious; obviously, the struggle to carry him to his room had been more than he could bear. At that second, Father Aidan rushed in followed by the blacksmith.

'Stand back, make some room for the smith,' Richard said to the servants who'd carried William, Grâce jumped up so as not to impede the smith in any way. 'Cut the mail free from his broken arm Robert, as quick as you can, so that the Father can set it whilst Lord William is unconscious.'

The smith set to work snipping through the links and the mail sleeve was quickly removed. Now the arm was free, Father Aidan went about *his* business. He straightened William's twisted arm and bound the wooden splints to it with strips of linen.

'Now turn him over,' Father Aidan commanded, 'and loosen the straps of his hauberk and gambeson then gently remove them so that I can dress the wound to his side.'

Once they'd done as he instructed, Father Aidan slit along the seams of William's undershirt with a knife and removed that too. William's torso was now naked and the blow to his side could be clearly seen. The slash was not deep, but there was a large red swelling to the side of his chest. Grâce placed her hand over her mouth and gasped as she saw the wound.

'It's not too serious, my Lady,' Father Aidan said, touching it lightly with the tips of his fingers. 'It looks like a blow from a mace. His hauberk and gambeson have taken the worst of it, but I fear that the blow has broken at least one, perhaps two ribs. I will bind his chest; it will give some support whilst his ribs knit together. I can do no more, they will take time to heal, that is in God's hands, but by the grace of Him who is able to keep us, Lord William will live.'

They turned to the sound of the door, as it swung open; it was Esther. The candlelight from the room illuminated her face and touched the jewels on her gown. Set against the dark background of the door opening, it gave her almost a ghostly presence. Richard went to her, but she lifted her open palm, bidding him not to touch her.

'It's *William*, he's hurt but alive, and he'll recover, God willing,' said Richard.

'But – *no* – Jacob!' She said calmly, slowly shaking her head from side to side.

'No…' Richard hung his head.

'He's never coming home again,' Esther responded.

'We don't *know* that!' Richard looked up anxiously, on hearing his own fears given flesh.

'I do – he's safe forever in our Saviour's arms. He has left the land of the dying for the land of the living.' she said and then gave herself into Richard's embrace; he pressed his lips to the top of her head and they clung to each other as if to merge their two souls into one.

At that moment, William groaned and panted, plainly trying to still the pain that racked his body. Richard released Esther and they went to him. She sat on a chair by the bed taking his hand in hers, gently lifting it to her lips.

'Drink this my Lord,' Father Aidan said, offering to his lips a silver embellished horn cup, containing a willow bark infusion, 'it will help with the pain,' and William obediently swallowed the brew. He grimaced at the foul taste and lay back onto his pillow for a moment, before he spoke.

'Grâce, fear not, I'm well enough,' and he touched her hand, she was unable to respond such was her trembling, and he once more took his mother's hand. Then he looked to Esther. 'Mother – I tried to save Jacob,' tears filled William's eyes. 'A dozen or so men, wearing the King's leopards on their surcoats, rode from the darkness of the forest and caught us by surprise. They were upon us before we realised. It was as if they'd been waiting for us. They struck down our servants almost immediately; alas they were unarmed but for daggers, thus unable to offer any serious defence.' William took several breaths before he could compose himself and carry on.

'It's alright, take your time,' Esther pressed her lips once more to his fingers, which she yet held.

'I killed one of them, Mama,' his eyes were almost pleading for forgiveness for being here when his brother was not. 'I struck at another but he resisted my blow with his shield and it was deflected into his unprotected knee, all but severing his leg. I saw Jacob stab one of his assailants through the eye slit in his helm, and the man tumbled from his horse, Jacob fought bravely, Mother. Father – we did try to defend ourselves as you have shown us, by keeping close together, but there were too many of them and they forced us apart.'

'I'm sure you did all that could be asked of a brave knight my Son,' Richard touched his cheek with the back of his hand and felt the coarse bristles. He was no longer that small boy who would leap into his arms when he returned from time away on the old King's business, and badger him to tell tales of the dragons he'd slain.

'I tried to close the gap between us and called to Jacob, but I was charged from the side, and my horse and I were tumbled over an embankment and tumbled down into a stream. They must have thought me dead. When I came round, my horse was standing next to me and I was alone. At first, I could not make sense of my predicament, but the pain in my arm quickly brought me to my right mind. I crawled up the bank and saw our dead servants and the men we'd killed, but there was no sign of Jacob.' William agitatedly lifted his head in distress as he relived that moment of horror and fear for his brother.

'Rest son, be still,' Richard touched his cheek once more.

'No, no, I must tell you, it seemed that they had come for Jacob; I don't know why I thought that. I slipped and fell once more down the bank to where my horse was yet standing, the poor beast was injured too; he stood quietly, clearly in pain. Don't *destroy* him Father, he gave everything to bring me home.'

'He is a brave animal, fear not, Jack will do all he can for him, you know how good he is with horses. I'll see to it.'

'Thank you, Father,' William breathed out and relaxed once more into his pillow. 'I must have passed out again, when I came round, I hoisted myself into the saddle and my horse brought me home. *Father,* you must find Jacob! He may be in danger.'

There was a knock on the door, both Richard and Esther were startled and turned to the sound. 'Enter,' Richard called and Sir Raymond came in, his boots covered in mud, he was still in his mail and wearing his helm, which he now removed and held under his arm.

He bowed, 'Forgive me Lord, for my unsightly appearance, I have only this moment returned with the men and came straight to you, may I speak with you?'

'Aye, speak up man.'

'Not here, Lord,' he said reticently, glancing at Esther and Grâce.

'You stay with William, Esther, I will go with Sir Raymond.' Sir Raymond stepped to the side to let Richard go before him. They walked in silence down the stair to the courtyard. As they stepped from the keep Richard saw the men yet standing by their horses.

'So, tell me Sir Raymond, by the look of these tired horses and faces, the news is not that which I wish to hear,' Richard said acknowledging his men with a dip of his head.

Sir Raymond hesitated, 'we came across a place where there had been a skirmish and recognised Lord William's dead servants, there were dead soldiers too wearing the King's coat of arms. There was no sign of either Lords. We followed the tracks of the horses and they led us to a small village, near Swineshead Abbey south of here. We inquired of Lord Jacob and were told that he'd been hanged at King John's behest.' He paused and wiped his eyes with his gloved knuckle, Richard could see he was upset. 'It appears King John's men came across the young Lords, they thought Lord William had been killed in the ensuing engagement, that's what I was told, praise be that I have seen he is alive. King John is rushing north to Lincoln, the rebels hold London and most of the southern counties, and they are pressing northward as I speak.' Sir Raymond looked down at his feet and twisted his toe in the dust.

'Come on man, let's have it all!'

Sir Raymond sighed and cleared his throat… but continued to stare at his foot as he spoke. 'I found Lord Jacob's precious sword at the scene Lord.' Sir Raymond reached to his horse, which was yet stood where he'd left it. 'They were clearly in a hurry, and had no time to retrieve it,' and he passed the weapon, which Jacob had made, to Richard, who took it reverently from his hand. His throat was so restricted he could hardly get breath. Still Sir Raymond struggled, eventually the words fell like lumps of rotten clay from his lips, '…they cut off his hands and feet and emasculated him before they hanged him, Lord. The King had yelled like a madman it was said, he shouted that Lord Jacob, in so many words, was to be an example for all families who stood against him, their anointed and rightful Lord and King.'

Richard's jaw muscles flexed, but that was his only visible reaction, he stood – statuesque for some moments. Calmly, in an ice-cold voice, he told Sir Raymond to assemble one hundred knights and men-at-arms. 'I will finish this once-and-for-all – so help me God. This tyrant's contempt and disdain for his people and all that is honourable and right – has this day gone beyond charters.'

Chapter 43

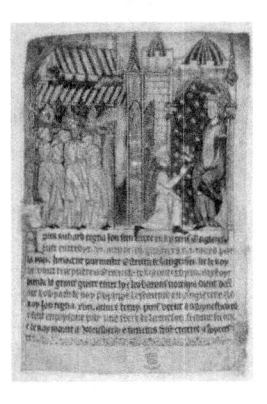

King John's final cup

Esther peace was uncanny; her calmness disturbed Richard as he bid her farewell. He left her, turned once more before he closed the door, stared at her and she smiled.

'We will ride west; the travel is easier, to Spalding then come up behind John's entourage. There will be many travelling with him, we need to keep out of sight and wait our moment to strike we might only get one chance. Are we all ready, Sir Raymond, Sir Hugh?' Richard glanced at both men.

'We are ready Lord and one with you.' Sir Hugh assured him, not that Richard had the slightest doubt of their loyalty.

'There is not a single person in the castle who has not been enraged by this crime. Lord Jacob was the sort of person that drew people to him, he was liked by all,' Sir

Raymond added. The news of Jacob's murder had spread like wildfire around the castle.

'Thank you, Raymond,' Richard gave a quick nod of his head in appreciation. 'We must carry all we need on horseback, no pack animals or carts, is this attended to?'

'Aye, all is as it should be, Lord,' Sir Hugh once more assured him.

Richard slipped his foot into the stirrup about to mount his horse and hesitated pressing his forehead against the skirt of the saddle, 'I must see Esther again before we set off, I am worried about her. Raymond will you ask Lady Margaret to go to her?'

Raymond sympathetically squeezed Richard's shoulder, 'I have already done that Richard she is making for your rooms as we speak.'

'Thanks be, I will be but a moment, then we will make haste.' Richard was yet ill at easy with Esther's strange calmness and knew he must see her again before he left, if not for her, for his own peace of mind. He glanced up to the swirling clouds and narrowed his eyes. The first light was heralding the new day as he turned and strode briskly towards the keep.

He walked into their apartment and the servants scuttled out. He did no more than stand until they had left the room and closed the door. It was a cold October morning and Esther was standing in front of the fire, Lady Margaret was by her side. She looked tired her face was strained; she had not slept the night past. Momentarily she was distracted and glanced to the shuttered window as it rattled on its fastening. The cold north wind whistled threateningly – in – and – out of the nooks and crannies of the castle walls as if it was part of a conspiracy to steal any hope of warmth from their lives. She returned her eyes once more to his, all the while, she calmly smiled at him her peace was beyond his understanding, and he stepped towards her. It seemed like the first time she'd ever noticed how grey he now was, but she thought him yet – the most handsome man, she'd ever known and a shiver ran through her at the love she felt for him.

'I have given my kiss of blessing to William, and now – I bless and thank you, my dearest Esther, wife and most faithful friend.' He took her in his arms and they kissed tenderly, he held her tightly to him, pressing his face against her head, her hair was warm and soft against his cheek.

'Richard!' he now looked into her eyes and set his finger across her lips.

'Say naught my love, if God is with me, no one can stand against me. If *He* is not, then I will fail, either way I wish His righteous judgement upon this man who has followed the path of evil his whole life. A life which is awash with the tears of the innocent.'

She kissed him once more, he nodded to Lady Margaret, turned on his heels and left, and a lifetime of memories sneaked from her eye and trickled down her cheek.

It was midday before they spotted John's surprisingly small entourage. The scouts reported that there had been some catastrophe; the entire royal regalia had been lost. For some unknown reason, John had attempted to cross the fens near Wisbech, before the tide was at its lowest, and his baggage train had sunk into the mud and was lost.

'It is rumoured Lord, that the King has been poisoned by the monks at Swineshead Abbey. The tale is that they trapped a toad in a goblet and pricked it with needles until it released its poison then they filled the goblet up with wine and gave it to the King,' the scout shrugged his shoulders with indifference. 'Whatever the truth of it, he is now very ill, they say dying, and he is being carried on a litter, as we speak, to the castle at Newark.'

For the whole time that the tale was being told Richard leant forward both hands resting on the up-stand of his saddle, he never even blinked, only stared into the distance.

'What are your wishes, Lord?' Sir Raymond asked nervously.

'What armed men has he around him?' Richard asked the scout; still he stared into some remote far off place.

'Barely a handful, Lord, he has sent all his Welsh mercenaries south, three hundred we were told, to aid Savaric de Mauloen, his Poitevin general.'

'Making for Newark you say?'

'Aye Lord, that's what we have been told.'

'That castle belongs to the Bishop of Lincoln. Well that settles it we must go and see to it that our King finds his way to his maker, *whomever* that is, quickly and without any earthly hindrance.'

'Shall I send the scouts ahead of us to Newark, Lord.'

'Aye, let's not be over cocky. Have some men at our rear too.'

It was almost dark by the time the River Trent came into view, the autumn moon was admiring its beauty in the still surface of the water and kissed the sharp edges of the castle before them with its glow. Richard drew his men to a standstill some distance from the castle. The horses were tired and sweat rose from them in clouds of warm pungent steam. Richard glanced to Sir Raymond.

'Pick out a small band of men and we will slip in under the cover of darkness and see what we can see.'

They dismounted from their warm saddles, which creaked and groaned as they transferred their weight onto one stirrup and stepped onto the ground. Richard stretched and bent his knees. He knew that the years were no longer in his favour, but he had this work to complete and complete it he would.

'We'll lead our horses, don't walk to closely together and we'll merge into the night's traffic.'

The guards on the gates were talking when they reached the castle and paid little heed to them. There was an unsettling casualness about the place that belied the fact that there was a dying king in their midst.

Once inside, Richard looked around to be sure he knew where his men were, they nodded in turn to acknowledge his glance. He casually walked up to a soldier who was warming himself by a brazier.

'A cold night ahead of us,' Richard said in a friendly tone.

'Aye, you with the King's party?'

'Aye, he left us behind when his baggage train was lost, bad affair, much of the King's personal possessions have sunk and been lost in the mud. We have only now caught up.'

'Aye, I heard tell of such a thing, but from what I hear he's beyond caring.' The man wheezed, hawked up some phlegm, and spat it onto the fire. The glutinous tubercular green substance sizzled as it touched the hot embers, and spat back at him.

Richard had to take a deep breath and look away before he was sick, gathering his wits he said, 'I suppose we should report to him and see what he wants of us. Where is he?' The man pointed to a shuttered window in the keep, Richard mentally noted to where he pointed.

'He's in there, so I'm told, but you have little or no chance of seeing him, anyway try if you must, he's through that door yonder,' the soldier said, flicking his hand with little interest towards an iron studded oak door, which was just below the window he'd pointed to previously.

'We better show face, I wouldn't like to get my backside kicked at this late stage.'

'I hopes for your sake you's been paid or you can whistle goodbye to ought *he* owes you. He's expecting the Abbot of Croxton, the good Abbot's been summoned to hear our beloved King's last confession, that will be no five-minute job,' the soldier said sarcastically, laughing at his jest and spitting once more into the fire. Richard smiled and walked off towards Sir Raymond.

He leant his head to him, 'This is it, send for some more men then discreetly seal off the castle, give some tale about it being for the King's safety, if you're asked. When the Abbot of Croxton arrives, make sure that we see him safely to the King's side, brook no arguments. I have made it known that we are part of the King's personal guard. When we are out of sight, *I* intend to be the Abbot, who hears the sinner's confession, and you will keep him out of sight until you see me again. Go now we have not a moment to waste.'

Raymond did as he was bidden, and then came near enough to Richard to signal that all was as he had commanded.

Chapter 44

King John's effigy

Driven by Honour

They had no longer than an hour to wait before a small group of monks came into the courtyard. The Abbott rode rather appropriately on a donkey, and four others followed on foot behind him.

Richard walked towards him and noticed a courtier coming quickly to greet the Abbot; the courtier bowed and kissed the proffered hand.

'Take me to your master,' the Abbot commanded. He then turned to the monks who were with him, and bade then go to the chapel and pray. Richard followed at a discreet distance and his knights walked a few paces behind him, drawing ever closer to the Abbot and the courtier.

'Leave us now fellow, I will take the Abbot to the King.' The courtier looked startled, but the knight was clearly a man of note, so he merely shrugged his shoulders and walked off glad to be out of it. Raymond and two of Richard's other knights then passed them, opening doors and checking rooms as they went. They needed to be sure of a room that suited their purpose. Sir Raymond turned and nodded; Sir Hugh, one of Richard's men took hold of the Abbot placing his hand over his mouth. The room was empty, they manhandled the Abbot in and closed the door, the two remaining knights, Sir James and Sir Andrew, stood outside as guards.

'We must apologise for such unseemly behaviour, but your orders have been changed, my dear Abbot,' Richard nodded and Sir Hugh released him and pushed him firmly onto a chair. 'Sir Raymond and Sir Hugh will stay with you. Now I need your tunic, cowl and skullcap.'

'This is outrageous, have you any idea why I'm here?'

'We know *exactly* why you are here, now do what our Lord has asked, and quickly, or I will slit your holy throat,' Sir Raymond answered drawing his dagger and pressing its sharp point to the Abbot's neck.

The Abbot stood and undressed, without further challenge, and Richard, having removed his hauberk donned the Abbot's mantle.

'You will be *excommunicated* for this wicked act.'

'But my dear Abbot, how harsh you are. I detect a certain ingratitude, for we are about the Lord's work and have concern for *your* eternal soul, fearing that you may be likened to an adherent of this King who is destined for the torments of Hell and thus doom yourself to the same fate.'

Sir Raymond set his hand to the now near naked Abbot and pressed him down into the chair.

'One final piece of advice, when we release you, I should not make it known that I failed the King in his hour of need, if I was you. If you say naught you can rest assured neither will we, and all will be happy, but you do as you wish. No one would believe such a fanciful tale anyway.'

Richard left the Abbot in the care of his men and went to The King's room. He asked the guard at the door if this was where the King lay.

'I must not be disturbed on *any* account whatsoever; by another living soul… do you understand? On pain of eternal damnation.' The poor fellow's face drained of blood and he visibly trembled quickly opening and closing the door on Abbot *Richard*. There were two servants in the room and Richard bade them leave and not return. The room was heavy with the stench of faeces. John lay moaning, curled up in agony. He was almost naked so that he could be cleaned more easily. Richard watched the two relieved servants go, closing the door quietly behind them. Richard followed them to the door and drew across it the heavy wrought iron bolt.

'By the guardians of Hell, we need some fresh air in here it smells like old Beelzebub's backside,' and he opened the shutters wide, a gust of freezing night air blew in straight from the frozen north. 'Ahhh… that's better,' Richard made an exaggerated show of breathing deeply.

'You fool, I'm freezing, John manage to mumble.' Richard went to him and threw back the Abbot's cowl. He could tell that John was not able to grab hold of the information his eyes beheld. His yellow bloodshot eyes simply stared, and Richard sneered.

'Yes – it's me… here to listen to your confession and then – toss it into the sewer where it belongs.'

'Maillorie...' he whispered in disbelief, 'have mercy, I'm dying.'

'My Dear John, do I hear you asking, nay – *begging* for mercy? Those are pleas you must be well acquainted with. Now tell me from your vast experience of such requests, what is the correct response from the one able to deliver such a gift of grace? For I only have your example, and as we both know, even the pleas from the *wholly* innocent were refused, am I not correct? Is it not, the measure we give, that we are to receive? Now my dear King, not even by *your* own perverted yardstick of justice, could you be counted amongst the innocent. So, on what grounds do *you* offer your plea for clemency, that *I* – your judge – may consider worthy of such a generous gift as mercy?'

John groaned again and expelled more faeccs and blood adding to the excrement in which he was already laid.

Richard casually picked up a leather bag that was beside John's bed and opened it.

'Not that,' John whispered, 'It's my cap of unction I'm to be buried in it, it was soaked in Holy oil at my coronation.'

'Ha – was it now?' Richard laughed and removed the Abbott's cloth coif, which *he* was wearing and held it next to John's cap of unction, they were almost identical. A smile lit up Richard's face, as the most gratifying notion came upon him. 'You must watch this dear King.' John was so weak he could only turn his eyes. Richard took John's cap of unction and gently laid it on the red embers of the log fire, it smouldered for a moment then twisted as the flames took hold. The sound that left John's lips was the pitiful, plaintive cry of a tortured animal, and it slowly died to a tormented whimper. Richard now took the cowl, which he'd taken from the Abbot of Croxton, lowered his breeches, loosened his braies and in front of John's eyes, emptied his bladder into the cap.

'Know this, you wretched evil creature, that you will be wearing the blessing of Lord Richard Maillorie upon your head for all eternity – in Hell, and my beautiful son whom you butchered will be forever in the arms of his Saviour.'

Richard now sat some distance from John on a bench under the open window, for the stench was indeed hellish. You confuse me John, you are a scholar who reads vociferously, a collector of books, but you appear to have learned nothing. Richard began the catalogue of John's life of debauchery, the women of his nobles whom he'd defiled, his avarice, theft, lies, and unrelenting wickedness, the hanging of the boys who were Welsh hostages. They had been taken from their play – some screaming, others pleading in vain for mercy – and they were hanged on the Castle walls at Nottingham in front of John. The eldest was only fourteen, all of which Richard spoke John knew to be true. There were the murders too, of his nephew Arthur and the starving to death of Maud de Braose, and her eldest son, William, whilst held captive. He reminded John of the dubious honour he held of being the first English king, as far as he knew, to have been personally accused of murder.

'And not least – wilfully and wickedly, for no other reason than he was my friend, you murdered Sir Tristram de Brûlan and finally you butchered my son who was everything that you are not, but he has had what you will never have, and that – is tears shed at his passing. It is no wonder John, that you fear this certain meeting with He whom is the judge of all. Did you *never once* consider this moment when you prayed, "Forgive my trespasses as "I" forgive others"? You may at last grasp the unerring repercussion of such a contract, which you made freely with your Maker, and yet treated with utter contempt. You will soon have an eternity to consider your scorn for such a binding covenant.'

Richard asked him to make a defence of his many transgressions against his fellow man. John was unable to respond, even if he'd the inclination, for he was again tormented by the spasms from Hell, expelling the rotting, repulsive, filth from his person.

Inexplicably – Richard stopped his discourse in mid-flow, rose and walked slowly to John's side. John stared up at him with wide pathetic, terrified eyes. Richard could see that his lips were dry and cracked, moistened only by the blood oozing from the fissures, and Richard was suddenly filled with compassion for this man who had caused him so much suffering; Richard's eyes filled with tears. He had never *cried* or had any feeling since he was told of Jacob's death. Now the tears ran down his cheeks and dripped onto John, and he felt sorry for the pathetic man lying before him. He bent down, gently lifted John's head, and poured some wine over his lips.

'John, you have hurt me and so many other people, more than you could ever imagine, without so much as a flicker of remorse *and* for a moment – I have been no more – than all I hated in you. Let me now ask for *your* forgiveness and give to you what peace is *mine* to give, know – that I *forgive* you and pray that our blessed Saviour has mercy on your soul, amen.'

Richard could hear the words he was speaking and couldn't believe what he was hearing, what was happening to him? His mind was unhinged; he was unable to stop the tears. He *actually* felt sorry for the wicked, evil man before him. He had to sit down and clear his head. He sat for some time with his head in his hands; something had happened to him, he genuinely felt sorrow for John's suffering; the self-destructive oppressive cloud of hate which had cast a dark shadow over his life for years, had finally left him…

For the last few hours of John's life, Richard did what he could to ease his suffering. He washed him the best he was able with the water the servants had left and bathed his brow with cold water. There was never any option for him, for he was now, as he had always been…

"Driven by honour"

It was at midnight, the 19th of October 1216; John gave one last distorted gasp, and died.

Esther was standing at the castle gate at Tattershall when Richard saw her and he slowly rode to her side, dismounted, and took her in his arms.

The End

Author's notes

The Death of King John

King John's Tomb

Medieval effigies usually show the subject in the prime of life. John's tomb has been opened twice. Once in 1529, and his head was covered with a monk's cowl. It was thought that this was John's "Cap of Unction" **but *we* know the truth**.

The box part of the tomb was added to match the tombs of Prince Arthur and Griffiths ap Ryce. The tomb was opened again in 1797 when an antiquarian study of the body was made.

John was found to be 5 ft 6½ inches. (1.689m) A robe of crimson damask was originally covering the body, but by 1797, most of the embroidery had deteriorated. The remains of a sword lay down the left side of the body, and parts of the scabbard. The internal coffin was made of white stone from Worcestershire. The coffin rests on the pavement of the Quire.

At the time of burial, a silk canopy was placed over the tomb, and the body was covered in silk. The cost of candles round the tomb was paid for by the royal government giving Worchester's monks Grafton Manor, and the whole of the College Green area was finally returned to the cathedral, having been taken at the Norman invasion from the cathedral by the then Sheriff of Worcester.

Conclusion

What to say about King John – was he the worst king in history? He is forever known as "Bad King John". If one considers all his wicked deeds, they were bad indeed – by *today's* standards, but in truth was he really, any worse than many rulers of that, and subsequent ages? Henry the Eighth is one ruler famed for the disposing of his wives, friends and counsellors, his daughter is even known as "Bloody Mary". Yet, we do not refer to him as, "Bad King Henry".

It was a ruthless age, which needed strong rulers, not necessary, fair, or even good rulers, but *strong* rulers.

Maybe it is Robin Hood, who has forever tainted his image. Whatever your age, you will have a picture of Robin Hood fighting against the tyranny of Prince John, from Errol Flynn, to the cunning fox in the Disney's cartoon, or Kevin Costner in Prince of Thieves, or the noble Russell Crowe back from the crusades who single handed inspires a great charter.

Perhaps it's what memories the storytellers create that tell us what we should think of a life lived.

Our memory of John F. Kennedy is one of a handsome, charismatic young man slain is his prime, and that forgives all his flaws, but John died an ignominious death at the end of a life where *everything* went wrong for him. Every decision he made seemed to turn gold to dross in his hand.

JFK's memory, on the other hand is set in stone, cemented in our consciousness by such pictures as that of a little boy, his son, saluting his father's coffin as it passed by, no such man could ever be a villain. No matter how the media tries to tarnish his memory by tales of his unfaithfulness, and shabby treatment of his wife, he is untouchable. In stark contrast, any good Richard Nixon did, a contemporary of JFK's, counts for naught, his name cannot shake villain status.

Nothing I could say will change history's opinion of King John, that it appears is carved in granite, some have tried, not me, William Marshal is my sort of hero.

Tell me what *you* think… My email address is at the beginning of the book.

Magna Carta

Talks were organised and planned for the January of 1215, and took place at the home of the Knights Templar in London. Assembled were two major fractions, on one side were King John, and group of Barons, who were faithful to their oaths of fealty to him, but none of whom had any great affection for the King himself. Opposing the King, were those presenting him with their terms, which consisted of Stephen Langton, the Archbishop of Canterbury, plus other senior churchmen, and the rebellious Barons whom had already formed a sworn association to demand, at its most basic, that the King's power be limited by law.

From the King's point of view, such demands were outrageous. He quickly made excuse to bring the discussions to an end; on the pretext that the rebel Barons had come to the Temple carrying arms, and had not shown "Proper Respect" to the Church. However, the Church got what it wanted, a second charter, guaranteeing *its* independence, which in effect repeated the charter granted at the Temple a couple of months earlier in November 1214.

After King Philip's' victory over John and his allies in France at the Battle of Bouvines, in July 1214, John was bankrupt and it was only because of his critical financial condition that he demeaned himself to even bother to attend. Now King Philip and Prince Louis had defeated John so decisively they wanted the throne of England.

As civil war became inevitable, the rebel Barons actually offered the throne of England to Prince Louis of France *if* he would bring troops to England to assist them in the civil war.

Louis was encouraged to come and eventually, as many as seven thousand French soldiers, landed on the south coast, quite unopposed, and were warmly greeted by the rebel Barons. The City of London was later to open its gates to them. The civil war was about to escalate.

Men assemble on a field by the River Thames; known as Runnymede the charter indicates Runnymede by name as *"Ronimed. inter Windlesoram et Stanes"* (between Windsor and Stanes). They were armed and prepared to fight. The rebel Barons came with their terms written out ready for endorsement. The discussions begin on the 15th of June 1215. The deal was done by the 19th of June copies of the Charter were distributed throughout the country. We still have four of the originals, and the Lincoln copy of the Charter actually says "Linconia" on the back. The Barons who forced the King to seal Magna Carta were in effect traitors. However, the King's position had become ever weaker.

Contrary to popular belief, the King never signed the Charter. He simply sealed it. It was not called "Magna Carta" or even the "Great Charter". It was just one more charter in an age of charters. The King having been forced under duress to agree to the charter's demands, rendered it unenforceable in law, in any event, the King had not the slightest intention of abiding by it.

The Pope, in his capacity as John's feudal lord, with England as his fiefdom, immediately annulled it. It was "*Utterly repudiated*" and the King was forbidden by the Pope "To *presume* to observe it". (Amusingly at this time England was ruled from Europe…)

Not all the rebel Barons were equally committed to the rebellion and not all the supporters of the King felt the same depth of allegiance to him. Llywelyn of Wales would have been unlikely to want to compromise with the King who had ordered the execution of fourteen sons of the Welsh nobility, which he held as hostage against the good behaviour of the Welsh.

William Marshal himself, had been declared a traitor by King John in about 1205, and effectively banished from court, and he went to his holding in Ireland. Only as John's situation became increasingly hazardous, did he summon William Marshal to return and assist him.

William Marshal Earl of Pembroke is the unsung hero of the Magna Carta. Until recently, he was virtually unknown. John cynically forgave William and he returned to court from Ireland to lend his support to him. John regarded Marshal as his key envoy in the discussions and negotiations. So close was he to the centre of the discussions, that some historians suggested that he, together with Langton, was one of the joint authors of the terms of the *first* charter (notice the deliberate use of the word "First").

This gives an indication of how close to the heart of the discussions he was. As the June of 1215 Charter itself makes clear, he was the first of the "Illustrious" magnates from the Baronial class to be named. When the charter was annulled, and civil war broke out, Marshal, was acknowledged as one of the foremost campaigners of the age, and he supported the King. With the French invasion, the outcome was by no means certain in fact; John's hold on the English throne was increasingly tenuous.

The death of a medieval King without an heir old enough to succeed him would have been catastrophic for the Plantagenet line. John's heir was a boy, Henry, some nine years old. When the Marshal heard of John's death, he was at Gloucester, and immediately summoned the loyal Barons to Gloucester Abbey where the boy king was anointed and crowned. Gloucester Abbey was chosen because Westminster Abbey itself was under the control of French forces.

William Marshal was appointed as Regent and he became Protector and the Ruler of the Country.

All those in the Abbey's vast crowd must have realised that this was a dreadful way to start a reign. It was not just to the solemn nine-year-old Henry's advantage that the Marshal's attitude prevailed among a few good men in England. The future of the dynasty depended on it.

Marshal's first step was to breathe new life into John's 1215 Charter. In late 1216, he issued it under his *personal* seal, together with that of the Papal Legate. It was not identical, and included a number of revisions. Its purpose was an attempt at reconciliation with the rebels, offering in its final clause the possibility of a resolution of outstanding issues when fuller counsel would be possible to achieve what was best for the common good. It was issued from a position of great military weakness. It proved unacceptable to the Barons, and presumably to Louis of France, and so the civil war continued.

Although the French invasion persisted for a while, Prince Louis was defeated in a sea battle off Sandwich. During the negotiations, which followed, Marshal, working with the Papal Legate, accepted that the liberties demanded by the rebel Barons should be restored. In November 1217, another charter was reissued, again without being in quite the same language as the two previous charters, but understood to be part of the same sequence. The difference this time was that the charter sealed by Marshal did not reflect the military pressure which forced John to seal the 1215 charter, nor the military weakness of the royal situation, which led Marshal to issue and seal the 1216 charter. In short, the defeat of the rebel Barons would still culminate in a charter. It ended the foreign invasion, civil war, and established the "Boy King" on the throne. The magnanimity was not properly recognised by the boy when he became an adult, and Marshal was criticised for the generosity of the peace terms he accepted. His work and memory was unjustly slurred. Perhaps that is why his name was obliterated from public memory. Henry III later paid the price: and that was namely by the hands of a man called Simon de Montfort often referred to as the "Father of Parliament".

Marshal died two years later, and was given a state funeral where Stephen Langton described him as "The greatest knight that ever lived".

By 1225, the King was old enough to assume power; the charter was reissued under his own seal. The deal was very simple as far as the Barons were concerned. Unless you give us our charter, you cannot have the taxation you are seeking.

It could easily be argued that without William Marshal, what we now call Magna Carta, would have been no more than a medieval document commanding very little attention from any, but the most dedicated historian. To quote Dinah Rose QC, she said of the Magna Carta, that, "It was not important for what it meant in 1215, but for the symbol it became and the significance it acquired as part of the common law." In other words, the content of Magna Carta was less important than how the document was perceived, and that has given it lasting credibility.

If you wish to pay your respects to William Marshal and his achievement, you can visit the Temple Church, the "Mother Church" of the common law, in London and see the place where the great man was laid to rest.

William Marshal joined the Order of Knights Templar a few days before his death. One of the treasures of that church is his monumental effigy.

The Children of William Marshal

William Marshal and Isabel de Clare had ten children, and of their five sons, none lived past forty years of age and none had children. This is surprising when you consider that their father lived well past the age of seventy, despite his hard and rigorous life as a knight and crusader, and produced ten healthy children *after* the age of forty.

His eldest son William, the second Earl of Pembroke and a signatory of Magna Carta, was allegedly poisoned in 1231 by Hubert de Burgh, Justicar of England, according to the period chronicler Matthew Paris, but there is no hard evidence to support this.

Richard, William Marshal's second son, was murdered. His third son, Gilbert, was killed in a tournament; three grown men prematurely lost their lives. The information available only adds to the intrigue; producing questions that beg for answers and solutions, but they may remain a mystery perhaps never to be solved.

All five of William Marshal's sons died without issue and his estate was divided amongst his daughters and their children.

Magna Carta

For those who are interested, the following is a transcript of one of the most famous documents in the world...

Be amongst the minority of people in the world who have in fact read the revered document.

The Great Charter of Runnymede
June 15th, 1215

John, by the grace of God King of England, Lord of Ireland, Duke of Normandy and Aquitaine, and Count of Anjou, to his archbishops, bishops, abbots, earls, barons, justices, foresters, sheriffs, stewards, servants, and to all his officials and loyal subjects, greeting.

Know that before God, for the health of our soul and those of our ancestors and heirs, to the honour of God, the exaltation of the holy Church, and the better ordering of our kingdom, at the advice of our reverend fathers Stephen, archbishop of Canterbury, primate of all England, and cardinal of the holy Roman Church, Henry archbishop of Dublin, William bishop of London, Peter bishop of Winchester, Jocelin bishop of Bath and Glastonbury, Hugh bishop of Lincoln, Walter Bishop of Worcester, William bishop of Coventry,

Benedict bishop of Rochester, Master Pandulf subdeacon and member of the papal household, Brother Aymeric master of the Knights of the Temple in England, William Marshal, earl of Pembroke, William earl of Salisbury, William earl of Warren, William earl of Arundel, Alan de Galloway constable of Scotland, Warin Fitz Gerald, Peter Fitz Herbert, Hubert de Burgh seneschal of Poitou, Hugh de Neville, Matthew Fitz Herbert, Thomas Basset, Alan Basset, Philip Daubeny, Robert de Roppeley, John Marshal, John Fitz Hugh, and other loyal subjects:

1. First, that we have granted to God, and by this present charter have confirmed for us and our heirs in perpetuity, that the English Church shall be free, and shall have its rights undiminished, and its liberties unimpaired. That we wish this so to be observed, appears from the fact that of our own free will, before the outbreak of the present dispute between us and our barons, we granted and confirmed by charter the freedom of the Church's elections – a right reckoned to be of the greatest necessity and importance to it – and caused this to be confirmed by Pope Innocent III. This freedom we shall observe ourselves, and desire to be observed in good faith by our heirs in perpetuity. We have also granted to all free men of our realm, for us and our heirs forever, all the liberties written out below, to have and to keep for them and their heirs, of our heirs and us.

2. If any earl, baron, or other person that holds lands directly of the Crown, for military service, shall die, and at his death, his heir shall be of full age and owe a `relief', the heir shall have his inheritance on payment of the ancient scale of `relief'. **(Feudal relief was a one-off "fine" or form of taxation payable to an overlord)** That is to say, the heir or heirs of an earl shall pay for the entire earl's barony, the heir or heirs of a knight 100s. At most, for the entire knight's `fee', and any man that owes less shall pay less, in accordance with the ancient usage of `fees'

3. But if the heir of such a person is under age and a ward, when he comes of age, he shall have his inheritance without `relief' or fine.

4. The guardian of the land of an heir who is under age shall take from it only reasonable revenues, customary dues, and feudal

services. He shall do this without destruction or damage to men or property. If we have given the guardianship of the land to a sheriff, or to any person answerable to us for the revenues, and he commits destruction or damage, we will exact compensation from him, and the land shall be entrusted to two worthy and prudent men of the same `fee', who shall be answerable to us for the revenues, or to the person to whom we have assigned them. If we have given or sold to anyone the guardianship of such land, and he causes destruction or damage, he shall lose the guardianship of it, and it shall be handed over to two worthy and prudent men of the same `fee', who shall be similarly answerable to us.

5. For so long as a guardian has guardianship of such land, he shall maintain the houses, parks, fish preserves, ponds, mills, and everything else pertaining to it, from the revenues of the land itself. When the heir comes of age, he shall restore the whole land to him; stocked with plough teams and such implements of husbandry as the season demands and the revenues from the land can reasonably bear.

6. Heirs may be given in marriage, but not to someone of lower social standing. Before a marriage takes place, it shall be' made known to the heir's next-of-kin.

7. At her husband's death, a widow may have her marriage portion and inheritance at once and without trouble. She shall pay nothing for her dower, marriage portion, or any inheritance that she and her husband held jointly on the day of his death. She may remain in her husband's house for forty days after his death, and within this period, her dower shall be assigned to her.

8. No widow shall be compelled to marry, so long as she wishes to remain without a husband. But she must give security that she will not marry without royal consent, if she holds her lands of the Crown, or without the consent of whatever, other lord she may hold them of.

9. Neither we, nor our officials will seize any land or rent in payment of a debt, so long as the debtor has movable goods sufficient to discharge the debt. A debtor's sureties shall not be distrained upon so long as the debtor himself can discharge his debt. If, for lack of means, the debtor is unable to discharge his debt, his sureties shall be

answerable for it. If they so desire, they may have the debtor's lands and rents until they have received satisfaction for the debt that they paid for him, unless the debtor can show that he has settled his obligations to them.

10. If anyone who has borrowed a sum of money from Jews dies before the debt has been repaid, his heir shall pay no interest on the debt for so long as he remains under age, irrespective of whom he holds his lands. If such a debt falls into the hands of the Crown, it will take nothing except the principal sum specified in the bond.

11. If a man dies owing money to Jews, his wife may have her dower and pay nothing towards the debt from it. If he leaves children that are under age, their needs may also be provided for on a scale appropriate to the size of his holding of lands. The debt is to be paid out of the residue, reserving the service due to his feudal lords. Debts owed to persons other than Jews are to be dealt with similarly.

12. No `scutage' or `aid' **(money paid by a vassal to his lord in lieu of military service)** may be levied in our kingdom without its general consent, unless it is for the ransom of our person, to make our eldest son a knight, and (once) to marry our eldest daughter. For these purposes, only a reasonable `aid' may be levied. `Aids' from the city of London are to be treated similarly.

13. The city of London shall enjoy all its ancient liberties and free customs, both by land and by water. We also will and grant that all other cities, boroughs, towns, and ports shall enjoy all their liberties and free customs.

14. To obtain the general consent of the realm for the assessment of an `aid' - except in the three cases specified above - or a `scutage', we will cause the archbishops, bishops, abbots, earls, and greater barons to be summoned individually by letter. To those who hold lands directly of us we will cause a general summons to be issued, through the sheriffs and other officials, to come together on a fixed day (of which at least forty days notice shall be given) and at a fixed place. In all letters of summons, the cause of the summons will be stated. When a summons has been issued, the business appointed for the day shall go forward in accordance with the resolution of those present, even if not all those who were summoned have appeared.

15. In future, we will allow no one to levy an ˜aid' from his free men, except to ransom his person, to make his eldest son a knight, and (once) to marry his eldest daughter. For these purposes, only a reasonable ˜aid' may be levied.

16. No man shall be forced to perform more service for a knight's ˜fee', or other free holding of land, than is due from it.

17. Ordinary lawsuits shall not follow the royal court around, but shall be held in a fixed place.

18. Inquests of *novel disseisin*, (in English law, of novel *disseisin* "Recent dispossession" was an action to recover lands of which the plaintiff had been dispossessed) *mort d'ancestor*, and *darrein presentment* shall be taken only in their proper county court. We ourselves, or in our absence abroad our chief justice, will send two justices to each county four times a year, and these justices, with four knights of the county elected by the county itself, shall hold the assizes in the county court, on the day and in the place where the court meets.

19. If any assizes cannot be taken on the day of the county court, as many knights and freeholders shall afterwards remain behind, of those who have attended the court, as will suffice for the administration of justice, having regard to the volume of business to be done.

20. For a trivial offence, a free man shall be fined only in proportion to the degree of his offence, and for a serious offence correspondingly, but not so heavily as to deprive him of his livelihood. In the same way, a merchant shall be spared his merchandise, and a husbandman the implements of his husbandry, if they fall upon the mercy of a royal court. None of these fines shall be imposed except by the assessment on oath of reputable men of the neighbourhood.

21. Earls and barons shall not be amerced save through their peers, and only according to the measure of the offence.

22. No clerk shall be amerced for his lay tenement except according to the manner of the other persons aforesaid; and not according to the amount of his ecclesiastical benefice.

23. Neither a town nor a man shall be forced to make bridges over the rivers, with the exception of those who, from of old and of right ought to do it.

24. No sheriff, constable, coroners, or other bailiffs of ours shall hold the pleas of our crown.

25. All counties, hundreds, wapentakes, **(Subdivisions of a county)** and trithings--our demesne manors **(Land attached to manors)** being excepted--shall continue according to the old farms, without any increase at all.

26. If any one holding from us a lay fee shall die, and our sheriff or bailiff can show our letters patent containing our summons for the debt which the dead man owed to us, -- our sheriff or bailiff may be allowed to attach and enroll the chattels of the dead man to the value of that debt, through view of lawful men; in such way, however, that nothing shall be removed thence until the debt is paid which was plainly owed to us. And the residue shall be left to the executors that they may carry out the will of the dead man. And if nothing is owed to us by him, all the chattels shall go to the use prescribed by the deceased, saving their reasonable portions to his wife and children.

27. If any freeman shall have died in testate his chattels shall be distributed through the hands of his near relatives and friends, by view of the church; saving to any one the debts which the dead man owed him.

28. No constable or other bailiff of ours shall take the corn or other chattels of any one except he straightway give money for them, or can be allowed a respite in that regard by the will of the seller.

29. No constable shall force any knight to pay money for castleward if he be willing to perform that ward in person, or--he for a reasonable cause not being able to perform it himself--through another proper man. And if we shall have led or sent him on a military expedition, he shall be quit of ward according to the amount of time during which, through us, he shall have been in military service.

30. No sheriff or bailiff of ours, nor any one else, shall take the horses or carts of any freeman for transport, unless by the will of that freeman.

31. Neither we, nor our bailiffs shall take another's wood for castles or for other private uses, unless by the will of him to whom the wood belongs.

32. We shall not hold the lands of those convicted of felony longer than a year and a day; and then the lands shall be restored to the lords of the fiefs.

33. Henceforth all the weirs in the Thames and Medway, and throughout all England, save on the seacoast, shall be done away with entirely.

34. Henceforth, the writ, which is called Praecipe, (**a writ demanding action or an explanation of non-action**) shall not be served on any one for any holding so as to cause a free man to lose his court.

35. There shall be one measure of wine throughout our whole realm, and one measure of ale and one measure of corn--namely, the London quart; - and one width of dyed and russet and hauberk cloths--namely, two ells (***ell*** **was the measure from the elbow to the tip of the middle finger, about 18 inches**) below the selvage. And with weights, moreover, it shall be as with measures.

36. Henceforth, nothing shall be given or taken for a writ of inquest in a matter concerning life or limb; but it shall be conceded gratis, and shall not be denied.

37. If any one hold of us in fee-farm, or in socage, or in burkage, and hold land of another by military service, we shall not, by reason of that fee-farm, or socage, or burkage, have the wardship of his heir or of his land, which is held in fee from another. Nor shall we have the wardship of that fee-farm, or socage, or burkage (**Feudal tenure of land by a tenant in return for agricultural or other non-military services or for payment of rent in money**) unless that fee-farm owes military service. We shall not, by reason of some petit-serjeanty (which some one holds of us through the service of giving us knives or arrows or the like, have the wardship of his heir or of the land which he holds of another by military service. (**Serjeanty in which the tenant renders**

services of an impersonal nature to the king, as providing him annually with an implement of war, as a lance or bow)

38. No bailiff, on his own simple assertion, shall henceforth any one to his law, without producing faithful witnesses in evidence.

39. No freeman shall be taken, or imprisoned, or disseized, or outlawed, or exiled, or in any way harmed--nor will we go upon or send upon him--save by the lawful judgment of his peers or by the law of the land.

40. To none will we sell, to none deny or delay, right or justice.

41. All merchants may safely and securely go out of England, and come into England, and delay and pass through England, as well by land as by water, for the purpose of buying and selling, free from all evil taxes, subject to the ancient and right customs--save in time of war, and if they are of the land at war against us. And if such be found in our land at the beginning of the war, they shall be held, without harm to their bodies and goods, until it shall be known to us or our chief justice how the merchants of our land are to be treated who shall, at that time, be found in the land at war against us. And if ours shall be safe there, the others shall be safe in our land.

42. Henceforth any person, saving fealty to us, may go out of our realm and return to it, safely and securely, by land and by water, except perhaps for a brief period in time of war, for the common good of the realm. But prisoners and outlaws are excepted according to the law of the realm; also people of a land at war against us, and the merchants, with regard to whom shall be done as we have said.

43. If any one hold from any escheat--as from the honour of Walingford, Nottingham, Boloin, Lancaster, or the other escheats which are in our hands and are baronies--and shall die, his heir shall not give another relief, nor shall he perform for us other service than he would perform for a baron if that barony were in the hand of a baron; and we shall hold it in the same way in which the baron has held it.

44. Persons dwelling without the forest shall not henceforth come before the forest justices, through common summonses, unless they are impleaded or are the sponsors of some person or persons attached for matters concerning the forest.

45. We will not make men justices, constables, sheriffs, or bailiffs unless they are such as know the law of the realm, and are minded to observe it rightly.

46. All barons who have founded abbeys, for which they have charters of the king of England, or ancient right of tenure, shall have, as they ought to have, their custody when vacant.

47. All forests constituted as such in our time shall straightway be annulled; and the same shall be done for riverbanks made into places of defence by us in our time.

48. All evil customs concerning forests and warrens, and concerning foresters and warreners, sheriffs and their servants, river banks and their guardians, shall straightway be inquired into each county, through twelve sworn knights from that county, and shall be eradicated by them, entirely, so that they shall never be renewed, within forty days after the inquest has been made; in such manner that we shall first know about them, or our justice if we be not in England.

49. We shall straightway return all hostages and charters, which were delivered to us by Englishmen as a surety for peace or faithful service.

50. We shall entirey remove from their bailwicks the relatives of Gerard de Athyes, so that they shall henceforth have no bailwick in England: Engelard de Cygnes, Andrew Peter and Gyon de Chanceles, Gyon de Cygnes, Geoffrey de Martin and his brothers, Philip Mark and his brothers, and Geoffrey his nephew, and the whole following of them.

51. And straightway after peace is restored, we shall remove from the realm all the foreign soldiers, crossbowmen, servants, hirelings, who may have come with horses and arms to the harm of the realm.

52. If any one shall have been disseized by us, or removed, without a legal sentence of his peers, from his lands, castles, liberties or lawful right, we shall straightway restore them to him. And if a dispute shall arise concerning this matter, it shall be settled according to the judgment of the twenty-five barons who are mentioned below as sureties for the peace. But with regard to all those things of which any one was, by king Henry our father or king Richard our brother, disseized or dispossessed without legal judgment of his peers, which we have in our hand or which others hold, and for which we ought to give a guarantee: We shall have respite until the common term for crusaders. Except with regard to those concerning which a plea was moved, or an inquest made by our order, before we took the cross. But when we return from our pilgrimage, or if, by chance, we desist from our pilgrimage, we shall straightway then show full justice regarding them.

53. We shall have the same respite, moreover, and in the same manner, in the matter of showing justice with regard to forests to be annulled and forests to remain, which Henry our father or Richard our brother constituted; and in the matter of wardships of lands which belong to the fee of another--wardships of which kind we have hitherto enjoyed by reason of the fee which some one held from us in military service;--and in the matter of abbeys founded in the fee of another than ourselves--in which the lord of the fee may say that he has jurisdiction. And when we return, or if we desist from our pilgrimage, we shall straightway exhibit full justice to those complaining with regard to these matters.

54. No one shall be taken or imprisoned on account of the appeal of a woman concerning the death of another than her husband.

55. All fines imposed by us unjustly and contrary to the law of the land, and all amerciaments made unjustly and contrary to the law of the land, shall be altogether remitted, or it shall be done with regard to them according to the judgment of the twenty five barons mentioned below as sureties for the peace, or according to the judgment of the majority of them together with the aforesaid Stephen archbishop of Canterbury, if he can be present, and with others whom he may wish to associate with himself for this purpose. And if he can not be present, the affair shall nevertheless proceed without him; in such way that, if one or more of the said twenty five barons shall be concerned in a similar complaint, they shall be removed as to this particular decision, and, in their place, for this purpose alone, others shall be subtituted who shall be chosen and sworn by the remainder of those twenty five.

56. If we have disseized or dispossessed Welshmen of their lands or liberties or other things without legal judgment of their peers, in England or in Wales, – they shall straightway be restored to them. And if a dispute shall arise concerning this, then action shall be taken upon it in the March through judgment of their peers – – concerning English holdings according to the law of England, concerning Welsh holdings according to the law of Wales, concerning holdings in the March according to the law of the March. The Welsh shall do likewise with regard to our subjects and us.

57. But with regard to all those things of which any one of the Welsh by king Henry our father or king Richard our brother, disseized or dispossessed without legal judgment of his peers, which we have in our hand or which others hold, and for which we ought to give a guarantee: we shall have respite until the common term for crusaders. Except with regard to those concerning which a plea was moved, or an inquest made by our order, before we took the cross. But when we return from our pilgrimage, or if, by chance, we desist from our pilgrimage, we shall straightway then show full justice regarding them, according to the laws of Wales and the aforesaid districts.

58. We shall straightway return the son of Llewelin and all the Welsh hostages, and the charters delivered to us as surety for the peace.

59. We shall act towards Alexander king of the Scots regarding the restoration of his sisters, and his hostages, and his liberties and his lawful right, as we shall act towards our other barons of England; unless it ought to be otherwise according to the charters which we hold from William, his father, the former king of the Scots. And this shall be done through judgment of his peers in our court.

60. Moreover all the subjects of our realm, clergy as well as laity, shall, as far as pertains to them, observe, with regard to their vassals, all these aforesaid customs and liberties which we have decreed shall, as far as pertains to us, be observed in our realm with regard to our own.

61. Inasmuch as, for the sake of God, and for the bettering of our realm, and for the more ready healing of the discord which has arisen between us and our barons, we have made all these aforesaid concessions, - wishing them to enjoy for ever entire and firm stability, we make and grant to them the following security: that the baron, namely, may elect at their pleasure twenty five barons from the realm, who ought, with all their strength, to observe, maintain and cause to be observed, the peace and privileges which we have granted to them and confirmed by this our present charter. In such wise, namely, that if we, or our justice, or our bailiffs, or any one of our servants shall have transgressed against any one in any respect, or shall have broken one of the articles of peace or security, and our transgression shall have been shown to four barons of the aforesaid twenty five: those four barons shall come to us, or, if we are abroad, to our justice, showing to us our error; and they shall ask us to cause that error to be amended without delay. And if we do not amend that error, or, we being abroad, if our justice do not amend it within a term of forty days from the time when it was shown to us or, we being abroad, to our justice: the aforesaid four barons shall refer the matter to the remainder of the twenty five barons, and those twenty five barons, with the whole land in common, shall distrain and oppress us in every way in their power,--namely, by taking our castles, lands and possessions, and in every other way that they can, until amends shall have been made according to their judgement. Saving the persons of our queen, our children and "Ourselves". And when amends shall have been made, they shall be in accord with us as they had been previously. And whoever of the land wishes to do so, shall swear that in carrying out all the aforesaid measures he will obey the mandates of the aforesaid twenty five barons, and that, with them, he will oppress us to the extent of his power. And, to any one who wishes to do so, we publicly and freely give permission to swear; and we will never prevent any one from swearing. Moreover, all those in the land who shall be unwilling, themselves and of their own accord, to swear to the twenty five barons as to distraining and oppressing us with them: such ones we shall make to wear by our mandate, as has been said. And if any one of the twenty five barons shall die, or leave the country, or in any other way be prevented from carrying out the aforesaid measures,--the remainder of the aforesaid twenty five barons shall choose another in his place, according to their judgment, who shall be sworn in the same way as the others. Moreover, in all things entrusted to those twenty five barons to be carried out, if those twenty five shall be present and chance to disagree among themselves with regard to some matter, or if some of them, having been summoned, shall be unwilling or unable to be present: that which the majority of those present shall decide or decree shall be considered binding and valid, just as if all the twenty five had consented to it. And the aforesaid twenty-five shall swear that they will faithfully observe all the foregoing, and will cause them be observed to the extent of their power. And we shall obtain nothing from any one, either through ourselves or through another, by which any of those concessions and liberties may be revoked or diminished. And if any such thing shall have been obtained, it shall be vain and invalid, and we shall never make use of it either through ourselves or through another.

62. And we have fully remitted to all, and pardoned, all the ill- will, anger and rancour which have arisen between us and our subjects, clergy and laity, from the time of the struggle. Moreover have fully remitted to all, clergy and laity, and--as far as pertains to us--have pardoned fully all the transgressions committed, on the occasion of that same struggle, from Easter of the sixteenth year of our reign until the re-establishment of peace. In witness of which, more-over, we have caused to be drawn up for them letters patent of lord Stephen, archbishop of Canterbury, lord Henry, archbishop of Dubland the aforesaid bishops and master Pandulf, regarding that surety and the aforesaid concessions.

63. Wherefore we will and firmly decree that the English church shall be free, and that the subjects of our realm shall have and hold all the aforesaid liberties, rights and concessions, duly and in peace, freely and quietly, fully and entirely, for themselves and their heirs from us and our heirs, in all matters and in all places, forever, as has been said. Moreover it has been sworn, on our part as well as on the part of the barons, that all these above mentioned provisions shall observed with good faith and without evil intent.

The witnesses being the above mentioned and many others, given through our hand, in the plain called **Runnymede** between Windsor and Stanes, on the fifteenth day of June, in the seventeenth year of our reign.

Other books by this author:

Restoration (Book 1)

This is a saga; spread over two novels telling of impossible love, its path travelled, and the tension between relationships, honour, pride, privilege, resentment, hate, and forgiveness.

Acceptance (Book 2)

The series plots a family's journey through the period of history from 1900 to 1946 the fears, sadness, and uncertainties of two world wars with their lottery of life and death, the only constant is love and the product of love, hope.

Set in the North East of England.

The Man Who Lived In A Book

A murder mystery played out in the Marshall Islands. You may well solve the murder but miss the mystery.
    Detective Inspector Tyyamii has a great future, how would you like to be his assistant in the Marshall Islands?

Dream World

William the Conqueror could never have imagined the impact that gruesome October day on Senlac ridge would have. This story puts flesh on the names and breath in the lungs of the people, etched into every English person's psyche from school days.

Jarl Magnus Matthewson, from Northumbria, is faced with the moral choices conflicting with loyalty, honour, and friendship, and his concern for those who place their simple trust in him.

"Live history with him."

Swallows Leave in Autumn

Set in the North East of England with its miles of beautiful golden beaches, blue sea and historic castles.

Tom Jackson decides to step out of the "Rat race" and rent a cottage in a quiet fishing village on the north east coast of Northumbria. He'd recently resigned from his job as a schoolteacher. Work he had grown to hate.

Tom was to discover the sharp reality that "True love" can be a very painful path to tread.

Sebastian Swan invites you to walk, laugh and cry with them.

A Warrior's Inheritance

Sequel to "Dream World"; Magnus' grandchildren are subjected to violent mysteries and they are in danger of losing all there grandfather left in their care.

Printed in Great Britain
by Amazon